SOUTHERN SONS

1914, Australia: As war is declared, the idyllic world of Blue Water Station is torn apart when Oliver, the eldest grandson and heir, shares his desire to enlist in the army. His enthusiasm ignites his brother, cousins and friends to do the same, but upsets his sister, Tilly. After a tragic family incident, she is left to run the cattle station. A chance meeting with a sophisticated lieutenant opens up a friendship through letters, but it's a rogue stockman who attracts her attention — with dire consequences . . . Surviving a baptism of battle fire in Gallipoli, Oliver is sent to the Western Front. But as the terrors of war impact him, he feels the heavy guilt of encouraging the others to follow him into combat. Will he, and they, ever make it home to Blue Water?

Books by AnneMarie Brear
Published by Ulverscroft:

KITTY MCKENZIE
KITTY MCKENZIE'S LAND

ANNEMARIE BREAR

SOUTHERN SONS

Complete and Unabridged

AURORA
Leicester

First published in Great Britain in 2017

First Aurora Edition
published 2019

The moral right of the author has been asserted

A catalogue record for this book is available
from the British Library.

ISBN 978–1–78782–085–2

Published by
F. A. Thorpe (Publishing)
Anstey, Leicestershire

Set by Words & Graphics Ltd.
Anstey, Leicestershire
Printed and bound in Great Britain by
T. J. International Ltd., Padstow, Cornwall

This book is printed on acid-free paper

Dedication

For my sons, Jack & Joshua.

To all those servicemen and women who
have fought in all the wars and who gave up
their lives for our freedom, and to all those
men and women who fought and returned
home to pick up the pieces of their
lives again and carried on.
You are all true heroes.

Southern Sons

They looked like men who had been in Hell
. . . drawn and haggard and so dazed that
they appeared to be walking in a dream and
their eyes looked glassy and starey.

— E. J. Rule

1

Blue Water Station,
Northern New South Wales, Australia.
July 1914

Tilly curled her bare toes into the gritty sand at the edge of the river bed, savouring the coolness of the water as it lapped her feet and ankles. Loud male conversations further along the bank didn't allow her to nap, but she laid back on the grass and closed her eyes to block out the surprisingly warm afternoon winter sun.

'Matilda Rose Grayson!'

She jumped guiltily and sat up to scowl at her elder brother, who stood above her on the bank. 'What now?'

'Pull your skirts down,' Oliver said more gently, giving a quick look over his shoulder to the young men setting up camp behind him.

'Oh hush, Oliver, for heaven's sake. Every one of those boys have seen my legs all their lives. They've seen me climb trees, swim this very river, fall off horses and bicycles. They've seen me wrestle a calf and help a foal to be born. I'm one of you.'

He scuttled down the grassy slope to join her. 'We aren't children anymore, Til.' His soft hazel-green eyes narrowed as he looked over the slow-moving water. The Orara River was the lifeblood of their cattle station, Blue Water, which spanned thousands of acres. 'We are men now, and it's time you started acting like a lady in front of them.'

She gave him a casual look. 'I am a lady when I need to be, at home; but out here, away from everything, I can be free the same as you and Gabe and the others. Besides, the boys would laugh at me if suddenly I couldn't get my hands dirty.'

'We aren't *boys*!'

She laughed as if he'd told a joke. 'Of course you are — all of you are. You'll always be *boys* to me.'

Oliver sighed, pulling his knees up and resting his arms on them, while staring straight ahead. The sound of cattle bellowing to be let out of the makeshift pens drowned out all other noise. They would grow quiet as the sun descended, and the native bird calls would reign supreme once again.

Tilly gazed at him. He'd been out of sorts for a couple of weeks now, ever since his return from Sydney. Where once her handsome brother had been full of mocking smiles and smiling eyes, he now grew too serious and not so quick to joke with the others.

'What are you two doing? The food is nearly ready.' Gabe, their younger brother, scurried down the bank to join them. He passed Oliver a brown bottle of beer.

'Where's mine?' Tilly raised an eyebrow at him.

'You have cordial in the basket.' Gabe grinned.

Snatching the bottle from his hands, Tilly gave

him a curt look. 'I work as hard as any of you. I'll have a beer if I wish.' She took a long drink from it.

Used to being at the bottom of the family pecking order, Gabe shrugged and sat on the other side of her. As always, they were comfortable in each other's company. The three of them were close, too close possibly, since they did everything together. Growing up on Blue Water, which their Grandpapa Miles had built in the middle of nowhere, they had to rely on each other for entertainment and support.

'Are you going to tell us what's wrong?' Tilly said quietly, glancing at Oliver. 'And if you fob us off with some glib lie again, I'll push you in the river.'

'Yes, do! We know something is bothering you. Just tell us, man.' Gabe pulled a stem of dry grass and chewed on it. 'Is it a girl?'

A wry smile lit Oliver's features for a moment. 'I wish it was just a girl.'

'So it is something serious then?' Tilly sucked in a deep breath, her mind working overtime. 'Are you ill? Is that why you went to Sydney with Father? What aren't you telling us?'

Oliver took off his weathered hat and studied it as if it held the answers to their questions. 'No, I'm not ill. You know I went to Sydney to see to our businesses there, now Grandpapa doesn't like making the journey anymore. Father wants me more involved.'

'You better not be lying to us,' Tilly whispered, studying him, looking for any signs of illness. His sandy blond hair was a shade darker than

Gabe's, and lean muscles filled out his healthy tanned skin. He didn't appear sick. 'Then what is it?'

'There is a war brewing. You heard us talking about it at dinner last week.'

'War! It's all the males in this family talk about! And? I'm sure there's more. Just say it, Oliver!' Tilly snapped. Unlike her brothers, she didn't have any patience. A trait her Grandmama Kitty often took her to task about.

'And I want to join up.'

'Join up?' Gabe and Tilly gasped at the same time.

Oliver nodded once, his shrewd gaze not wavering. 'I'm going to enlist in the army.'

'Father won't let you.' Gabe knelt up, his overlong blond hair falling across his forehead. 'He's dead against this war, you know it. He throws the newspaper in the fire every time he reads anything about Europe's issues.'

'I know, but I don't need his permission to go. I'm twenty-two. I've made my decision.'

'Have you truly thought hard about this?' Tilly murmured, annoyed at herself for the tears choking her throat. She didn't understand this nonsense about countries fighting with each other. But she didn't want Oliver to leave, for him to be in danger. However, she knew him better than most, and once he'd made his mind up, he wouldn't be dissuaded. All three of them were as stubborn as mules.

'I've thought of nothing else for weeks. Sydney is agog with war fever. When I was there, I listened to the talk, I read the reports.' His voice

4

became passionate. 'We have to support Britain in this.'

'But nothing has been declared yet.' Tilly frowned, desperately trying to remember heated conversations around the dinner table, but usually she lost interest and helped her grandmama to change the subject. 'It might all be a lot of hot air,' she added hopefully.

'And what do we care about what happens in Europe?' Gabe added, throwing a stone into the water.

Oliver gave him a stern look. 'We should care. We need to care. Germany is a huge threat. If they start taking over countries, it'll affect us all. Can you imagine how this country would be if Germany invaded and controlled England? We, too, would be at their mercy, their rule. Distance would be no barrier.'

Gabe took his bottle back from Tilly. 'Father says distance *is* our barrier. It won't affect us.'

'Father is wrong. Barriers can be broken eventually.'

Gabe laughed. 'Father is never wrong!'

'He is this time.' Oliver turned his hat by the brim, a frown creasing his forehead. 'I spoke to a few people in Sydney, at Grandpapa's club, and one or two had just returned from London. They said the government is on high alert. Europe is boiling up. We should not ignore it and pretend it will go away.'

'It might do, though. This might be all talk and nothing else.' Tilly tried to lighten the tone. The three of them had never talked as seriously as they were now.

'What can we do, though?' Gabe asked, skipping another stone across the water.

'We help fight to keep Germany from invading countries, especially England.'

'But to join the army, Oliver?' Tilly clenched her hands under her skirt to hide her simmering anger. 'You know nothing about being a soldier.'

'I did cadets at school. I was good at it,' he boasted. 'I'm intelligent, I can learn.'

They were interrupted by the noisy scrambling of the others coming down the bank to join them. Tilly stiffened her shoulders and tried to smile at them, but she had a sense of pending doom that things were going to change, and she didn't know how she could stop it. Damn Oliver and his noble intentions.

Their cousins from Armidale, Patrick and Freddie Grayson, sat behind her. Big Max Spencer and his brother Drew, plus the Jessup boys, Johnny and Samuel, all flopped down on the bank around them with their bottles of beer.

'Food will be ready in a few minutes.' Johnny grinned. He and his brother Samuel lived on a farm adjoining Blue Water's boundary to the north. Originally it had been her grandmama Kitty's land, but on her marriage to Miles Grayson, she had given it to her friends Alice and Paul Jessup, and they had built up a successful farm.

'You three seem serious. I've not heard any laughing from you.' Big Max, so named because he'd towered over them all since childhood, stared at Oliver, Gabe and lastly Tilly. 'You're upset.'

Tilly smiled at him, always amazed at how he

6

said very little, but knew exactly what was going on. Max and Drew were the grandsons of Tilly's great-aunt Connie, their grandmama's dearest friend. Apparently Max's size came from his grandpapa, also called Max, and who died in York, England before Kitty and Connie had journeyed to Australia in 1866.

'I've just told them, and so I'll tell you all now . . . ' Oliver took a deep breath and let it out. 'When war is declared, I'm enlisting as a soldier.'

Stunned silence greeted the announcement.

Drew, small, quiet and studious, so unlike the other men in their little group, pushed his glasses further up his nose. 'It might never be declared. The newspaper says Germany might see sense and back down.'

Oliver shook his head. 'I think it will happen. The census in Sydney suggests so. The government is preparing soldiers to send to Britain in support.'

Studying his bottle of beer, Drew nodded. 'We should support Britain. It's our mother country. I suppose I should also mention that I'm doing the same as you, if they'll have me.'

'Really?' Oliver looked surprised. 'I never had you down as a fighter, Drew.'

'Oh, I doubt they'll have me as a fighting soldier, because of my eyesight; but I'd be interested in being a quartermaster or something along those lines. I'm very good at that sort of thing, since it's what I do here at Blue Water. I can do my bit.'

Gabe jumped to his feet. 'Well, if you two are

going, so am I. I'm not missing out!'

As usual, the others followed suit, all shouting, 'Hear! Hear!'

Annoyed, Tilly gathered her skirts and stomped up the bank, only to turn at the top and glare down at the excited young men who had been dear to her all her life. Eight young men who she loved equally like brothers.

'I forbid you all to go!' she yelled, frightened at the thought of being left behind, of being without them. 'I'm not having you all leave me to be shot at. You are needed here on the land. You have responsibilities here!'

Oliver laughed. 'Matilda Grayson, for once, you have no say in what we do.'

Gabe picked up the bottle of beer. 'You aren't our mother, Til. Stop bossing us around.'

She marched back down the slope. 'Boss you around, Gabriel Grayson? I'll do more than boss you around, brother! I'll knock the daylights out of you!' She slapped him none so gently up the side of his head, like she had done since they were little. 'You need some sense knocking into you and that's a fact. If our mother was alive, she'd do the same, too!'

'Enough, Tilly,' Oliver ordered, grabbing her arm.

She swung around to slap him too, but he pinned her arms by her side.

'I said enough!'

Kicking at him, she wrenched herself away, furious with them and herself at the tears gathering. 'This war hasn't even begun and I already hate it!'

Big Max stepped forward, the calm head amongst them. 'Tilly, we must do what we think is right.'

'Be quiet Max. None of you have a sensible thought in your heads. Go get killed if you want. I don't care.' She snatched up her stockings and boots and marched away from them.

Sighing, Oliver turned back to the river and watched a kingfisher fly low over the water. The afternoon sun dazzled off its iridescent bluey-green feathers. 'Well, boys. If war is declared, are we all in?'

As one they agreed, grinning.

'Right then, we finish the branding and mustering and then we tell our families. If over the next few weeks you change your mind, no one will think any less of you. War isn't for everyone. But I fancy myself a little adventure. What say you?' He grinned as they cheered.

As the others dispersed back to the campfire for food, Oliver stayed by the river. His eyes didn't really see the slow-moving water, but instead imagined the reaction his father and grandparents would have to his news. He was the Blue Water heir going off to war, and it seems taking his brother with him. They were not going to like it. Still, it was his decision. He'd finished his schooling, years studying with his tutor, then his final years in Sydney at Kings College. He loved Blue Water and didn't want to live anywhere else. But before he settled down to serious adult life, he wanted to see something of the world. The budding war stopped any ideas of grand touring holidays in Europe, but he could still go there as a soldier.

Movement further up the bank caught his attention. Tilly walked alone, head bowed, her chestnut copper hair spilling out from the net she wore to confine it. She never could control that hair. Oliver's heart tightened at the forlorn sight. He adored his sister — she was probably his closest friend — and he hated the thought of leaving her, of them all leaving her. She'd be lost without them, her boys, as she called them.

As the only girl in the family she had been petted and spoilt by them all, but also fiercely loved. A precious gift. Certainly, her spectacular temper was something to be reckoned with, but they still adored her. She was bossy and fiery, hot-headed, loveable and kind. His sister would be hard to leave behind. With this in mind, he ran along the bank until he reached her side.

'Do you forgive me, Til?'

She turned to him with her hands on her hips. 'Are you still going to be a soldier?'

'Yes. I have to. It's what I want to do and it won't be for very long, perhaps six months at the most. Try to understand that I need to spread my wings a little.'

'Oh, I do.' Quick as a heartbeat, she pushed him into the river. When he came up spluttering and cursing, she glared down at him. 'I understand you're a fool, Oliver Grayson.'

2

Blue Water Station, August 1914.

Oliver stood with his back straight and hands behind him, and Gabe did likewise as they faced the shocked and rigid features of their father Adam and grandparents Miles and Kitty. After weeks away at the far reaches of the station, they'd come home, reported their accounts of the cattle branding and mustering to the family, bathed, and then announced their decision to enlist. Their declaration was met with stunned silence.

'I won't have it.' His father stood by the fireplace, whose heat radiated out into the study, as rain lashed the windows. He glared at Oliver and then Gabe before resting his astonished gaze back on Oliver. 'How could you do this?'

Miles coughed, and all eyes went to him. Although in his eighties, he still was the main presence at Blue Water, the grand property he had scratched out of virgin territory sixty years ago. Sitting behind his huge mahogany desk, inlaid with green leather, he leaned back in his chair. 'Lads, have you really thought this through?'

'Of course, Grandpapa,' Oliver answered. 'I wouldn't make such a decision without serious thought.'

'And you, Gabe?'

'I have, sir.'

'Wars are not all fine uniforms and fanfare, you do realise?' his grandmama Kitty, classically dressed in emerald silk, muttered from her chair on the other side of the fireplace. 'The soldiers who returned from the Boer War will testify to that.'

'I know, Grandmama.' Oliver smiled at her, willing for her to be on his side like she always was. He knew he was her favourite, though she'd rather be tortured than admit it to a soul. He loved this old woman without reservation. He had grown up hearing the stories of her, the legend that was Kitty McKenzie. She'd left England and journeyed to Australia to be with the man she loved, only for him to die on their wedding day. She'd been gifted the land north of Blue Water and tried to make it successful, despite having little money, and bad luck with droughts and fires and death. Her courage was known throughout all the area. She was still beautiful, if in a faded way, her thick red hair dulled to mostly white now; but her spirit was still as strong as ever and glowed from her green eyes. It was the same toughness of character that Tilly had inherited.

'You are needed here,' his father injected. 'You *both* are needed *here*. After all your schooling, I was aware you might have ideas to move to Sydney and run our businesses there, but I never expected you to want to join the army!'

'The boys aren't needed here just yet, Adam,' Grandpapa spoke quietly. 'Blue Water will run just as efficiently as it always has done with me and you here.'

'Father, they need to learn the running of it,' Adam said, defensive, as the dinner gong sounded, interrupting them.

'And they know most of it now anyway. Haven't they lived and worked here all their lives?' Grandpapa walked over to Grandmama and helped up from her chair. 'The boys are wanting to see the world, and I don't blame them for it. I wish I had done more of it when I was younger, but I was too busy building this place.'

'This isn't a holiday! It's a war.' Adam glared at his father's back.

'I know exactly what it is, son, and it won't change anything. The boys will go whether we want them to or not.' Grandpapa stared keenly at Oliver. 'I suggest we purchase you both a commission. You don't want to be a private.'

'I'm not sure, Grandpapa . . . ' Oliver looked at Gabe. 'Do you want to be in a position of taking charge?'

Frowning, Gabe shuffled his feet. 'Actually, I don't think I do.'

'You lead the men here,' their father argued. 'What would be the difference?'

Gabe shrugged. 'Here, I know the men, the land, what we're doing and achieving. I know nothing of war.'

'Yet you're willing to rush to sign up and be in that war!' their father spat furiously.

'Oliver?' Grandpapa asked quietly.

'If I'm commissioned, then I'll not be with the rest of our lads. I'd like us to all be together.' He wasn't sure that was the right answer for what he really wanted. He hankered after being an

13

officer, but knew it would separate him from Gabe and the others — and how would he keep an eye on them if he was forever running around after senior officers? No, it was better he stayed a private.

'I dread to think what Connie will say about this.' His grandmama shook her head.

'Well, boys, if that's your decision ... ' Grandpapa escorted Grandmama to the door. 'Come; we shall go into the dining room, eat a fine meal, and toast to their good health.'

'I don't see how this can be something to celebrate!' Adam snapped.

Oliver wanted to talk to his father and discuss his decision, but the furious look in his father's eyes dissuaded him.

In the hall, Grandpapa stopped and grinned at Tilly, who waited by the stairs, wearing a virginal white dress. 'Earwigging, Princess?'

'Of course I was, Grandpapa,' she replied with a toss of her head, the show of innocence gone. 'I shouldn't have to if I'd been allowed in to hear the discussion.' She gave Oliver and Gabe a filthy look for excluding her.

Guilt filled Oliver, but he stared her out. Was everyone against him now?

Grandpapa offered his other arm to her and she took it. 'You already know what was being discussed. Besides, it was your brothers' moment, not yours.'

'You forbade them to join up, didn't you?' she asked hopefully.

Standing behind them, Oliver gritted his teeth. 'Tilly!'

14

'No, my princess, I did not.' Grandpapa smiled gently.

'But they're needed here. You can stop them!'

'Tilly!' Oliver could quite happily have throttled his sister.

Grandpapa's eyes were kind as he paused and gave her his full attention. 'No, I cannot. They're men. Free to do as they please.'

Tilly looked pleadingly at their grandmama. 'You don't agree with them, surely?'

'Matilda, dear, men will decide on foolish things whether we women like it or not.'

'But — '

'And you might as well get used to it.' Grandmama gave her a superior look. 'Enough. Let's dine.'

As they made their way to the dining room, the front door opened; and Connie, using her cane to help her walk, stepped into the hall, bringing with her the smell of rain. 'There you are!' She stared at Oliver.

He took a deep breath in readiness for Aunt Connie's wrath.

'Connie, dear, what are you doing out in this weather? Will you join us for dinner?' Grandmama asked, helping her to take off a large waterproof coat.

'I need Miles.' She thumped her cane on the polished wooden floor before pointing it at Oliver's chest. 'You! Did yer fill my grandsons' heads with all this war nonsense?'

Offended and feeling uncomfortable, Oliver shrugged. 'They made their own choices, Aunt Connie.'

'Fiddlesticks!' Connie glared at him before looking to his grandpapa. 'Miles, yer must come and talk some sense into Max and Drew. They're not goin' off to war!' Her Yorkshire accent had never left her, and became stronger when she was upset.

'Connie, there's nothing to be done. If the boys want to go, we must support them.' Grandpapa put his hand on her shoulder. 'Come and eat with us. We'll talk about it some more.'

A maid was sent to fetch another setting for Connie, and in a tense atmosphere they settled down at the long cedar table to receive the first course of leek and potato soup.

'I don't think I have an appetite,' Connie muttered, playing with her spoon.

'Aunt Connie, we're a part of the British Empire. We must do our bit,' Oliver spoke between mouthfuls. His stomach clenched at the tense atmosphere in the room.

'You don't have to!' his father joined in. 'Australian men don't need to rush off. Why can't you wait and see what happens? The newspapers are full of the might of the British forces, so let them have a go at it first. They might have it finished within a few weeks.' He took a sip of wine the maid had just poured. An angry white line showed around his lips. 'Why should our young men leave their jobs and homes to travel halfway around the world for a conflict that might be over by the time they get there?'

'Calm down, Adam.' Grandmama patted his hand. 'Yelling won't fix this.'

16

'Mama, I have a right to be disappointed by this news. My two sons intend to go fight in a war thousands of miles away.' Adam scowled at Oliver. 'I suppose you've enticed Patrick and Freddie to go with you. Is that why they left to go straight home to Armidale after the muster? Your uncle David will be just as livid as I am. And the Jessup lads are going too, I suspect? Who will run their farm? Their father, all by himself?'

Oliver pushed his bowl away, his hunger gone. 'Try to understand, Father. I want to go. I want to travel. I want to stop the Germans in their tracks. Why should Australian men leave it to everyone else to sort out? How would we look as a nation if we turned our backs on those who need our help? And for the last time, I didn't make anyone go. I told each of them to think for themselves!'

'All the fellows take your lead, Oliver. They have done since you were children,' his father argued. 'Are you going to encourage all the station workers too? Is Blue Water to be left with a staff of only old men and women?'

'That's not my responsibility!' Oliver jerked his chair back and stood. 'I'm not accountable for what anyone else does.'

'Sit down!' Grandpapa spoke quietly, but with the tone that was never ignored.

Oliver regained his seat, his temper barely under control. He was sick of being the scapegoat for everyone else's actions just because he was the eldest. He wasn't like his father, content to stay on Blue Water his whole life. He wanted adventure and excitement. Was that so wrong?

17

Grandpapa sipped his wine before looking at Gabe. 'What is the opinion of the station hands?'

'Those I have spoken to are undecided. Many don't think it is worth the bother, but then most haven't been following the newspapers.' Gabe wiped his mouth with a napkin. 'I think if they were told or read of the troubles, they would think as we do.'

'What do yer know about anything?' Connie snapped. 'Yer nothing but a child!'

'I'm nineteen, Aunt,' Gabe defended hotly. 'And I have a mind!'

'Yer a pup, just like the rest of them silly fools.' Connie slammed down her spoon. 'Did yer think that yer parents and grandparents went through hell to raise yer only for yer to throw yourselves in front of bullets without a care?' She suddenly clutched at her chest, her face screwed up in pain.

'Connie!' For her age, Grandmama moved surprisingly quickly to be by her side. 'Where are your pills?'

'At home,' Connie whispered. 'Get me to my cottage. Adelaide will see to me.'

'Let's lift her in the chair.' Alarmed, Oliver stood and grabbed one side of the dining chair while Gabe took the other. 'We can walk her home like this. The rain has eased.'

'I'll bring the cane.' Grandmama walked with them out of the house and across the wet lush lawns towards the pretty cottage Grandpapa had built for Connie when Adam had been just a baby.

Once settled in bed, with her daughter

18

Adelaide making her comfortable, Connie took a hand each of Oliver's and Gabe's. 'I know I'm a silly old woman. And I shout me mouth off, but yer know that already, don't yer?'

Oliver smiled, relieved to see some colour come back to her cheeks. 'We do, Aunt.'

'Then yer also know I love the very bones of yer both, don't yer?'

'Yes, Aunt.' Gabe, who'd always had soft spot for his aunt, kissed her papery cheek. 'We love you, too.'

She looked up at Oliver. 'Yer the eldest of all the boys, Oliver. Yer must watch over them.'

'Haven't I always, Aunt?' He, too, kissed her cheek. She smelt of lavender. 'Get some rest.' He left the room to go talk to Max and Drew.

Once the boys had left, Kitty sat beside the bed holding Connie's hand. 'Well, that was rather unnecessary, wasn't it? Getting yourself all worked up. What have I told you?'

Connie peeked at her from half closed eyes. 'Be quiet, lass. Go back and finish yer dinner.'

'I'm not hungry now. And I think the atmosphere isn't to my liking. I'll sit with you for a bit.'

'I'm not sorry. I meant what I said.' Connie fiddled with the sheet folded over her lap. 'The lads don't need to rush off to war. I've only got Adelaide, Max and Drew of my own blood left. I don't want my grandsons to go.'

'I do understand, of course I do.' Kitty thought briefly of Connie's husband, the big loveable Max they had buried in York before they sailed for Australia; and of Connie's son Charles,

19

Adelaide's twin, who was killed when thrown from a horse twenty years ago. His wife had gone into premature labour with Drew and not survived it. Connie and Adelaide had brought up Max and Drew.

Sighing deeply, Connie rested more comfortably against the mountain of pillows on her bed. 'We've been through a great deal, lass, haven't we?'

Kitty grinned. 'Too much for one lifetime, I would say, dearest.'

'Lord, remember the first day we met in the tenements? Dismal rain, and then me showing yer the cellar?'

'I remember it all.' Kitty often recalled those dreadful days of living in York with no money and no home.

'We've done all right though, haven't we?' Connie sniffed, her eyes teary. 'Thanks to you.'

'I couldn't have done anything without you.' Kitty gripped her friend's hand.

'Can we survive a war, lass? A war that will take our boys away?'

Kitty stared at their joined hands. 'We can survive anything. We've proved that already.'

3

Sydney, October 1914.

The fanfare was shockingly stimulating to the gathered crowd as they lined the city streets to watch rows of fine young men, resplendent in new khaki uniforms, march past. The sun shone, and it seemed the whole country was celebrating. Bunting, strung colourfully from building to building, flapped in the gentle breeze while musicians played on street corners, hoping for the odd copper coin to be thrown into their hats. Marching bands and street vendors all added to the noise of one huge party.

Cheers rang in Tilly's ears as she strained to look for Oliver and the boys. 'I can't see them, Papa. Can you?'

'With all these large hats, I can barely see you! There are so many people and such noise that I can't think straight.' Adam frowned as a woman wearing a huge feather creation on her head jostled him for a better view. 'I loathe the city. Let's go back to the hotel. We must have missed the boys.'

Tilly craned her neck, angling her head so she could see past the brim of her own hat, perched at a slant on her head. Despite being in a dirty city, she'd decided to wear a white dress with small pink blossom printed on it, and her hat was covered in white silk with artificial pink flowers. She thought the boys would be able to see her better in the crowds if she wore white.

Suddenly she saw them. 'There they are!' Tilly screeched, frantically waving her little flag. Tears welled as she beamed at Oliver, Gabe, Freddie and Patrick. Behind them marched Big Max, Drew, Johnny and Samuel. She was so proud of them that she felt she would burst. She called out their names, and Oliver's head turned to search for her, but he was gone before he found her. 'They look magnificent, don't they, Papa?'

He took her hand and nodded, his eyes bright with unshed tears.

Tilly, her heart wrenched at her father's emotion, stepped back from the crowd. Her father had tried to dissuade the boys from enlisting right up until the last moment. He was taking it hard that soon they would be gone. She squeezed his hand, distraught that today was the last day they'd all be together for some time. 'We must believe that they will come home to us, Papa; that the war will be over in mere months.'

'I feel I've betrayed your mother, letting them go. She would be heartbroken today.'

'But also proud.' She smiled wistfully, thinking of her long-dead mother. 'They're doing what they believe is to be the right thing: fighting against an enemy that wishes to destroy other countries. Mama would not want her sons to be cowards.'

'No . . . ' He looked over her head at the marching soldiers. 'I miss her more today than I have for a very long time.'

There was nothing Tilly could say to that. Their father had never remarried, and had thrown himself into making Blue Water and the other Sydney based Grayson businesses great successes. He always said no one could replace her mother, so why would he try again?

Someone blew a horn close by, making Tilly jump. The gaiety of the morning was waning. 'Let's go back to the hotel and wait for the boys to join us.'

With her hand tucked through her father's arm, she walked sedately through the streets, no longer excited, no longer chatting happily to her father or strangers. A marked difference to the journey only a few hours before, when that morning they had left the hotel and eagerly joined the people streaming towards the parade area to see off their brave men to war. Now it seemed more real. They would be gone today.

Entering the grand hotel, they walked into the salon where the family had gathered. Tilly smiled at her Grandpapa and sat down on the sofa next to her grandmama and Aunt Connie.

'Did you enjoy it then, dearest?' her grandmama asked, sitting on a pale green sofa by the large bay window so she could watch the passers-by.

'It was extremely busy, Grandmama. So many people.'

Aunt Connie patted down the lilac lace at her throat, her silk gown the finest she owned in honour of the day. 'Did you manage to see them?'

'Yes, briefly.' Tilly accepted a glass of cool

lemon water from her father. 'Is Adelaide feeling better?'

'Yes, her headache has all but gone. She'll join us for the meal.' Aunt Connie glanced out the window. 'Are the boys coming straight here, Adam?'

'I don't know, Aunt Connie. I believe so. They have only a few hours before they have to report to the ship. We'll take them in the cars.'

Grandpapa took a sip of his coffee. 'I've hired three more cars beside our own to take us to the dock. David has brought his own.'

Everyone was quiet at that. Tilly glanced at her family's solemn faces. The realisation that the boys would be leaving today weighed heavy on their hearts. Home wouldn't be the same without them.

Tilly sipped her water, her mind a whirl of confused thoughts. How would she cope without them? How boring would home be now? The days would be endless without the boys. Who would she tease now, who would race with her on horseback, who would swim with her in the river, or fish with her? Who would play cards with her after dinner, or dance, or read, or play the piano with her? It was depressing, and maddening that she couldn't join them on their adventure.

She looked out of the window, where many people dressed in their best clothes walked past, smiling and talking, enjoying the atmosphere. A small group of women strolled by, all wearing nurses' uniforms of a pale blue dress and scarlet cape. As they passed, a couple of soldiers doffed their slouched hats and bowed gallantly. The nurses giggled. It seemed everyone was involved but her. She hated it.

Commotion at the door heralded the boys' arrival, and for a moment the room was full of khaki and male voices. Tilly stood, savouring the moment of Oliver and Gabe laughing and talking. To her, there was no man equal to any of the men in her family. Her grandpapa, her father, cousins and her brothers were tall, handsome, strong men, and her chest swelled with love and pride.

'Uncle David!' Tilly saw her uncle and aunt in the doorway and hurried to them.

David, her father's brother, was the image of his father Miles, but had the dark auburn hair of Kitty. 'Tilly, dear niece!' He kissed her cheeks before he greeted anyone else. 'How are you, my precious girl? You grow more beautiful every time I see you.' He leant back to gaze at her. 'What a lovely dress.'

'Thank you, Uncle David.' Tilly hugged him again before turning to her aunt. 'Hello Aunt Eve. Was the trip very terrible?'

'Horrendous!' Eve Grayson smiled sadly. 'And we missed the boys' parade.' She kissed her sons, Patrick and Freddie. 'I'm so sorry, my loves. I did tell your father we should have left yesterday and stayed the night in the city. Armidale is too far from here to make it in time. We left in the middle of the night!'

Grandpapa stood, helping Grandmama and Aunt Connie to their feet. 'Shall we go into the restaurant?'

Lunch was a noisy, jolly affair, as though everyone was making certain that their last meal together would be fun and full of laughter. In the restaurant, the tables groaned under the weight of food and champagne. They were making the most of it, but were not the only ones, as other families in the room were also enjoying the day. There was a fevered excitement in the air. The talking drowned out the pianist playing discreetly in the corner. Black-clad waiters carried silver trays full of drinks and plates of food. Tilly recognised several other families of their social circle, but large potted palms dotted between tables made it difficult to converse with them.

Her grandmama waved suddenly and stood up to receive her brother Rory and sister Mary, who jointly ran a large department store in Sydney. With them were Ingrid and Dan Freeman, old family friends. As more chairs were added and another table commandeered, Tilly escaped the heat and noise of the room and went out into the little courtyard centred in the middle of the hotel. A small fountain gurgled, and tall palms filled the corners.

Hot, she fanned herself with a palm frond from the potted tree next to her, hoping her uncontrollable hair wasn't escaping the hairpins and combs and curling messily around her face.

'It looks like you need a drink.'

She turned to smile at the voice, but her lips never quite made it as she stared at the tall soldier lounging against the brick wall on the other side of the courtyard.

'Would you like me to get you one?' he asked,

26

stepping away from the wall and throwing his cigarette into a brass bin.

Tilly watched him walk closer. He wasn't just a soldier, but an officer. His uniform was cut differently to the boys' standard private uniforms. He wore his dark hair slicked back and had light blue eyes just like her grandpapa Miles; but whereas her grandpapa's eyes only held warmth when he looked at her, this man's eyes roamed her, or possibly assessed her. She swallowed.

'Am I being rude?' he asked, stopping only feet away from her.

'P-Pardon?'

'By offering you a drink? Am I being rude?' His smile revealed one dimple on his left cheek, turning his serious face into something that was so handsome and endearing that she simply continued to stare.

He stuck out a hand, leaving the other in his pocket. 'Luke Williams — apparently I'm Lieutenant Williams of the Light Horse now.' He gave a self-depreciating smile.

She took his hand. 'Matilda Grayson.'

'Grayson? Do I know of the name?' The clear blue eyes seemed to intently search her face, perhaps even her very soul.

Tilly shivered, dismayed at her fanciful thoughts. 'Perhaps not. We're not often in the city.'

'Ah, a country mouse, are you?'

Eyebrow raised, she gave him a haughty look. 'There's nothing mousy about me, sir.'

His gaze flitted over her face. 'I totally agree,

Miss Grayson. Let's go and find a table in the bar and get to know each other.'

'I don't think so. My family is waiting for me inside.' Yet despite her words, she found herself wanting to go wherever he suggested. What on earth was wrong with her? She had flirted before. She'd spent the last few years since turning eighteen flirting with every man, young and old, at Blue Water and nearby farms. She liked the company of men; relished mentally sparring with them. However, this man, this stranger, was no station hand, no neighbourly friend. To propose having a drink with him, alone, was scandalous. Lieutenant Williams was very much a man who played a different game to the harmless one she knew.

'Luke!' A woman sauntered out from French doors, her dress a flimsy vision of soft lemon silk and chiffon. Her hair was the darkest black, cut short and waved. Diamonds dripped from her throat, ears and wrists. 'There you are, darling.'

Tilly tensed as the tall, willowy woman approached, blowing out cigarette smoke. Her long black cigarette holder seemed in danger of slipping from her slender fingers. Tilly had never seen a woman smoke before.

She gave Tilly a disapproving glare and instantly ignored her as she curled her fingers around Luke's arm. 'Everyone is waiting to say goodbye to you. Do hurry up.'

Tilly raised her chin, narrowing her eyes. No one had ever dismissed her in her life. She stuck out her hand to Luke. 'Thank you for the offer of a drink, Lieutenant, but I'll decline and rejoin my family.'

He took her hand in his, bent over and kissed it, all the while watching her. 'It was a pleasure to meet you, Miss Grayson. I hope to do so again.'

His touch sent shivers along her arm, and she quickly tucked it behind her. Without any acknowledgement to the other woman, she walked into the restaurant, knowing with some hidden sense that he watched her. The whole encounter intrigued her.

'Tilly! Do come along. We're getting into the cars.' Oliver helped her to collect her hat and bag.

Although the journey was short, a mere mile to the docks from the hotel, the cars were driven at a walking pace as the crowds shifted from the streets and down to the docks where the ships waited to sail out of the harbour and take the boys away.

On the quay, Tilly held tight onto Oliver's hand as the group edged their way closer to the ship. Around them couples were embracing, and fathers hugged children, warning them to be good for their mothers, while women cried for husbands, sons and brothers. Bands played, filling the air with joyful music; but when the ship blew its horn long and loud, the scene became a little desperate as last hurried and emotional farewells were given.

Tilly stood to one side, near the walkway to the ramp, waiting for her boys. The same cluster of nurses she saw from the hotel walked past her and up the ramp, all smiling and waving. Tilly watched them, fascinated by the thought that those young women, the same age as her, were leaving their homes and going overseas with no family in attendance. To have such freedom bedazzled her.

One by one, the boys came to stand beside her until they were all together.

She straightened Johnny's slouched hat to tease him. 'Now, Johnny Jessup, you make sure you keep warm. You know how you hate the cold, and the winters in Europe can be bleak, or so I'm told.'

Next, she took Samuel's hands in hers. 'Look after yourself. I'll visit your parents every week.'

'You're the best, Til.' He squeezed her in a hug.

Turning to her cousin Patrick, she glanced at his kit. 'Have you got the scarf I bought you?'

Patrick hugged her tight. 'I do, Cousin, even though it's not regulation uniform. I'll keep it tucked out of sight.'

Freddie laughed at him. 'You'll be too busy shooting at the enemy to feel the weather!'

She cupped Freddie's cheek. 'No messing around over there, Freddie; I know what you're like. I want no reports that you've been locked up for not saluting an officer or some such nonsense.' She kissed him quickly, the tears she'd held back all day threatening to spill.

Drew pushed his glasses up further along his nose and gave her a gift. 'It's only paper, but it's good quality. For all the letters you'll be writing to us.'

'Thank you, Drew. That's so thoughtful. I'll

30

write to you often.' Her lip quivered, but she lifted her chin and swallowed the tears back.

Big Max wrapped his arms around her and lifted her off the ground for several moments. They both couldn't speak, then he let her go and walked straight up the ramp. It was enough.

Gabe stood before her, his eyes red. 'Well, this is harder than I imagined.' He gave a watery grin. 'Don't think I'll miss you, because I won't. It'll be good to get away from you and your bossiness,' he joked, but his voice broke on the last word.

She held him tight. 'I'll miss you every second,' she whispered, squeezing her eyes shut to stop the flood of tears. 'Stay safe . . . ' Her voice cracked.

Finally, Oliver was the last to embrace her. 'I'll be back, Til.'

She couldn't speak, her throat was too clogged with emotion, so she just nodded and hugged him again.

Stepping out of his arms, she tried to find composure as she looked at the men who had been her band of brothers all her life. 'I want letters, lots of them, from you all. Promise me.'

The ship's horn blew again, and puffs of black smoke belched from its funnels as the boys walked up and away from her. Her vision blurred and she hastily wiped her eyes, not wanting to miss a moment.

'Do I get a goodbye like that too?' Luke Williams stood beside her, staring up at the ship's decks filling with khaki men. He wore his hat now, with a jaunty feather and a turned-up side. He looked dashing.

Yet Tilly felt wretched, and this handsome man failed to lift the heaviness from her heart. 'Goodbye, Lieutenant Williams.'

'No kiss or embrace?'

'Absolutely not. I don't know you.' Then she remembered the woman at the hotel. 'I'm certain you received your own special goodbye.'

He grinned, the dimple appearing. 'A man can never have enough goodbyes when he's off to war.'

'If that's where you're going, then you'd better hurry.' She nodded to the sailors moving about near the ramps, throwing off ropes.

'You're beautiful even with eyes red from crying.'

She stared condescendingly at him.

Taking one step, he paused and faced her fully. The blue eyes gazed at her intently. 'I will write to you. Where do you live?'

'Blue Water Station, Grafton,' she answered impulsively, unable to break eye contact.

Then he was gone, swallowed up in the flotsam of soldiers eager to be on board and start their journey.

'Are you all right, dearest?' Her grandmama came to hold her hand. She wasn't crying, but simply stood and looked up at the heaving decks above.

Tilly straightened her shoulders trying to be strong like her grandmama. 'No, I'm not all right. And I won't be until they are all home again.'

4

Gallipoli, Turkey, July 1915.

Oliver shifted the weight of his rifle, flexing his right leg a moment before taking up position once more against the sandbags. He kept lookout in a seven-foot-high trench, balanced on a stony ledge they called the fire-step. Further down the line, other soldiers did the same. The order to go over the top would come soon. The pink light of dawn was slowly replacing the lavender blue of the night sky as the sun rose. The heat would bake them for another day.

The noise was deafening as the huge guns boomed from the ships riding at anchor out in the strait. While they waited for the navy to finish their bombardment of the ridge above, most of the men sat smoking, reading letters and chatting.

Oliver let his mind wander. He thought of the letters in his pocket from home and how he could possibly reply to the questions his family asked. They had been as surprised as he was that their ship had been diverted from going to England and instead sailed to Egypt. Months of training at a camp outside Cairo hadn't prepared them for the disastrous landing on the shores of Turkey. A back way into Europe was the idea. Yet all it had achieved so far was slaughter and barely no advancement off the beaches.

How could he write to them about the numbing effect of watching a fellow soldier die in agony, his guts spilled on the dirt, or the flies that swarmed over everything, feasting off the dead bodies in no man's land where they hadn't been retrieved? Did he tell them of his constant thirst due to lack of water; the unpalatable dry, tasteless food? Should he mention the dysentery, the constant drumming of shelling, the fear of being hit by a sniper's bullet? Or the way every man jumped at the slightest sound, or walked hunched over along narrow sandy trenches hoping not to be the next one hit?

What exactly could he write to them about? The answer was to not write at all.

His excitement on seeing the world and being on adventure had soon dissipated like smoke in the sky. What was more, he had dragged his brother, cousins and closest friends with him into the pits of hell that was Gallipoli. At first, on the ship they had been full of enthusiasm, and landing in Egypt filled him with delight at the new wonders of a foreign country. However, after four months of training in Mena Camp, they'd boarded the ships to cross the Aegean Sea to capture Gallipoli and known nothing but failure.

'All good, Lance Corporal?' Captain Markham asked as he made his way down the trench.

'No movement, sir,' Oliver replied, focusing back on the job at hand, wiping the sweat off his forehead. He still wasn't used to his promotion to Lance Corporal. It worried him he wasn't a private like the others; but Markham, a good man, said he needed junior officers in their battalion and Oliver was a natural choice. Thankfully, he was never far from the lads at all times.

The dusty hilltop above them was silent now. The ships behind them shrouded in a smoke haze as the guns grew quiet. The men knew that the Turks still alive lay in ambush at the top. It was madness to think they could take the rocky escarpment. Battling up sandy unstable slopes while being shot at from high advantage spots filled Oliver with dread. It was suicide, plain and simple.

Looking down the length of men waiting for the whistle to blow to go over the top, Oliver searched for his brother and his childhood friends. Gabe stood fourth man down from him, while Big Max, Freddie and Patrick were further down the line, and Johnny and Samuel stood on his other side. Drew, a quartermaster, was safe on the beach in one of the supply tents that hugged the bottom of the mountain range below them.

Gabe gave him a cheeky grin and the thumbs-up. Oliver nodded in return. Every skirmish they had participated in since they landed on the desolate beach four months ago, he'd worried constantly for his brother's safety. Fretting about Gabe catching a bullet was more stressful than being in the firing line himself. Today would be no exception. A trickle of fear ran down his spine along with the sweat.

Movement further down the line caused him to stiffen. A glance showed the officers making final preparations. A runner sprinted up from the trench below and saluted before thrusting a note at Major Simmons, who saluted and read the scrap of paper.

Captain Markham pulled out his pistol and took a step up onto the ledge, blocking Oliver's view of the major. 'Looks like we'll be off then, Lance Corporal.'

'Yes, sir. I doubt our lot will change their minds despite previous unsuccessful attempts.'

'Nay, man, don't be negative.' Markham smiled. 'What's that old saying? 'Men better than us have made their decisions in ivory towers and who are we to disobey,' or something like that.'

'We should be in France, sir, where the real war is happening, not getting ourselves killed on some faraway beach.'

'I happen to agree with you, Grayson, but we must follow our orders.' Markham smoothed his moustache with two fingers.

The whistle blew shrilly. With a yell, the Australia and New Zealand soldiers in that section scrambled over the trench wall and out into the open side of the mountain. Their objective was to capture the summit, but to get there they had to traverse the side of the escarpment, hidden gullies, the rocky outcrops, the loose sandy soil that took a man's feet out from under him, and the scratchy bushes that littered the slope, and do it all while under fire.

Oliver ran, hunched over, to the nearest boulder and crouched down, waiting for the others to do the same. Their attack brought down a hail of bullets from above, which pinged

36

off the rocks in an ear-shattering crack. The zip of bullets hitting the dirt near his feet urged Oliver to move on. Weaving behind stunted trees and outcrops of rock, he gained ground slowly.

Panting, he knelt behind a large rock and aimed his rifle up. Turks fought aggressively from their advantage points along the top of the ridge. As one Turk raised his arm to throw a grenade, Oliver slowly squeezed his trigger and watched as the man fell back, and the explosion of the thrown grenade killed another two of the enemy.

'Good work. Keep it up,' Markham gasped, lifting his rifle, shooting and dashing off again.

In what seemed an age, Oliver kept advancing, kept shooting, his sight on the top of the ridge that never seemed to get any closer. The heat intensified as the sun climbed higher. Sweat mingled with dust coated him like a second skin. His throat felt on fire, but to stop and drink could cost him his life, and so he pushed on. His unit made some ground, foot by foot, yard by yard.

A bullet nicked his upper arm. The sting of it grazing his skin halted him momentarily until he saw Gabe firing further up, and he hurried to get to him.

'Are you all right?' Oliver fell down beside his brother, who was wedged in between two large rocks.

'I'm fine. You?' Gabe squinted at him. 'You're bleeding.'

'It's a scratch. Have you seen the others? I got separated from them.'

'I was with Patrick and Freddie for a while.

Last I saw, they were with Captain Markham along the next gully.' Gabe's face was streaked with sweat and dirt. He ducked as a bullet struck the rock beside him. 'They've seen me — let's go!'

Together they scrambled down and to the right to hide behind a large boulder.

'Bloody hell. It's madness.' Gabe breathed hard, reloading his weapon.

'Slaughter, more like,' Oliver murmured, kneeling. He sighted another Turk heading down between two outcrops and shot him. 'We'll be overrun soon, and out of ammo.'

'Have you heard the whistle to retreat or dig in?' Gabe asked, taking another shot at the enemy.

'Not yet, but we aren't making any more ground here now. We can't reach the top. I'm thinking they'll make us dig in. Any advancement is better than none.'

More men from their unit scrambled up behind them, taking cover along the steep cliff which overlooked the sea at their backs.

'Here they come.' Gabe fired at the advancing Turks, who seemed to pop up like rabbits. 'It's like hunting at home.' Gabe, steely-eyed, pulled his trigger again.

Oliver glanced at his brother, surprised by how quickly he had matured in the last four months. Before, he'd been laid back and a happy-go-lucky kind of guy; but now, steadily firing, he appeared calm and efficient and not at all bothered by the act of killing.

A bullet pinged near Oliver's head, jarring his

thoughts back to the present. Angry at being fired at, he took aim and shot back. He saw at least ten of the enemy in a cluttered group, trying to make it down a gully towards them. 'They're coming closer!'

'Not bloody likely.' Gabe stood and threw a grenade in their direction before ducking back down again. The explosion silenced their section of the attack.

Oliver waited, signalling for the others to stop firing. No movement ahead. From other parts of the cliff the battle carried on, yet in this sector a quiet eeriness descended.

'Are they all dead?' Gabe whispered.

'We're going to have to find out.' Oliver turned and signalled for the others to advance with him. 'Careful now.'

Spread out, slowly picking their way between gnarled bushes and jagged rocks, they inched forward. It took some time to creep up to the area from where the enemy had been firing. They breached the rise and lay flat on their stomachs as the ground levelled out before them for a hundred yards.

'Turk trenches on the other side?' Gabe asked.

'Must be.' Oliver peered keenly at where evidence of digging could be seen. 'I can't see anyone moving about.'

'They could be lying in wait.'

Oliver looked along the line of his men laying in the dust. 'Right, we need to make a decision. Either go ahead and check out that trench or go back and wait for others.'

Private Jones, a young man barely old enough

to shave, wiped the sweat from his upper lip. 'You're the highest rank here. It's your decision.'

For the first time, Oliver cursed his promotion, such as it was. He'd got it for rescuing two men in the dark one night while under the fire from an enemy sniper. 'Gabe, you go back and find Captain Markham or any CO and tell them where we are and how far we've got.'

'No.' Gabe didn't look at him.

'No?' Oliver asked in surprise. 'What do you mean no?'

'I'm not leaving you to raid a trench. I need to watch your back.'

'Shut the hell up, damn you, and do as you're told. That's an order.'

Gabe glared at him, his mouth in a tight line. 'I said no.'

'Look, you little shit, I'll — '

'Lance Corporal, there's movement ahead.' Private Jones pointed with his rifle.

Oliver stared, wishing he had binoculars. He saw two Turks at the end of the trench where it disappeared into scrubby bushland. A moment later, another man emerged and passed them boxes of ammunition before the first two pulled back a cover and revealed a machine gun pointing straight to the right of where Oliver lay hidden.

Frowning, Oliver twisted back and crawled on his stomach to the edge of the ridge and looked over to the right. Below, Captain Markham was encouraging men to climb up the slope.

Heart racing, Oliver scrambled back to his men. 'The others will walk right into that machine gun. Gabe, get down to Captain Markham now, and warn him. Hurry!'

This time, seeing the urgency on his brother's face, Gabe, always quick on his feet, clambered down over the ridge, fast and low.

Oliver studied the terrain to their left. It was not as wide and flat as the ground directly in front of them, but dipped and curved around a large outcrop of rock.

'Are we going back?' a ginger-haired youth called Olsen asked suddenly.

'No, we aren't. Listen, I think we should go to the left and try to get into that trench. If we can come up from behind those gunners, we can disarm it before Markham's men come over the top.' Oliver didn't wait for them to raise an objection, and quickly scurried off behind some bushes and kept heading left. Rustling behind him let him know the others had followed.

He made it to the large rocks without being seen and waited for the others to join him. 'Fix bayonets. Equal numbers on each side once we're in the trench. Last person watches our backs,' he whispered.

The entrance to the trench lay ten feet away. Listening, he couldn't hear any talking. He crept from the rock and, hunched low, crossed to the trench and stepped down into it. It was clear of the enemy, so Oliver lead the men on until he came to where the trench cut sharply to the left. With his back to the dugout wall, he inched his head around to see what lay ahead. Empty. The next stretch of trench was devoid of soldiers.

41

Heart in his throat, he signalled for the others to follow him as he slipped into the next trench, at the end of which it again cut sharply, this time to the right. Here, the harsh rocks of the land jutted out, giving the Turks small ledges to stand on to see over the top. Beyond the next stretch of the dugout, Oliver expected to see the gunners.

Stealthily, he crept closer, every sense on alert. He was conscious of the need to make as little noise as possible. He could hear voices now, the foreign sound of Turkish. He signalled to the men behind to be ready. Rounding the last corner, Oliver raised his rifle. His finger on the trigger, he stormed in at the enemy. He shot two of them before they were aware of his presence. The third soldier grabbed his rifle, but Private Jones, standing beside Oliver, shot him dead.

'Spread out and keep your eyes open.' Oliver indicated to two other privates to collect up the machine gun just as they heard the sound of running. 'Get down!'

The men dropped to crouch low in the trench, expecting a wave of Turks to attack them.

'Lance Corporal Grayson, are you having a picnic?' Captain Markham asked him from above. 'Come on, man, we have work to do securing this section.'

Oliver sagged against the sandbags, the strength leaving his legs for a moment in the relief it was his own side. 'Yes, sir.'

Gabe appeared above him on top of the trench. 'Get up, you lazy sod.' He laughed and disappeared from view.

Swearing names under his breath at his

42

brother, Oliver nodded to his men to follow him out of the trench.

5

Blue Water Station, August 1915.

Tilly pulled the black motor car over to the side of the gravelled driveway in front of the house and turned off the engine. She grinned at her grandmama. 'Well, what do you think?'

'I think you are very clever,' her grandmama said, climbing out of the car. 'It was nice to get out of the house after days of rain.'

'Agreed.' Tilly glanced up at the cloudy sky, hoping they'd seen the last of the rain and the cold weather, but she doubted it.

Her grandmama wrapped her shawl around her closer. 'Does this mean you'll be giving up your lovely horse and riding no more?'

'No, of course not. But now I've successfully learned to drive an automobile, I can take us to Grafton to do the shopping. We don't have to rely on anyone, especially now the men are off to war.' Tilly came around to her side and together they went up the steps to the veranda of the sprawling house.

'I think being on the busy roads of Grafton with horses and carts and people will be a trifle more difficult than our quiet tracks on Blue Water.'

'I'm going to ask Papa if I can go tomorrow.'

'Ask me what?' Her father came out of the front door and joined them on the veranda, where her grandmama had stopped to sit on a white cane chair.

'Can I drive the motor car into Grafton tomorrow please?' Tilly hugged his arm and smiled sweetly up at him. 'I'm tired of driving around the stock yards.'

'I believe, my dear daughter, that it is *my* car bought by *me* for *me* to drive. You're never out of it! I wish I'd never taught you how to drive now. I've had it less than two months and you've driven it every day.' He sat at the table and opened the newspaper.

Tilly sat beside, refusing to give up. 'You always say to do something well you have to practise. That's what I've been doing.'

'I'm surprised there is any petrol left,' he muttered, frowning at the headlines.

'Please, Papa. You know I'm an excellent driver. You've taught me so well, and it gives me something to do while the boys are away.'

'There must be other more suitable occupations to while away your time, surely?' He looked at his mother. 'Mama? Can't you give her things to do, sewing or embroidery? Household accounts?'

'Household accounts?' Grandmama frowned. 'That's my job, always has been since I married your father. It's the one thing I have left to do. Are you wanting to take that away from me?'

'No, of course not,' he soothed, his expression contrite. He flicked the newspaper straight again and bent his head to read.

'Besides,' Grandmama continued as she rang the little bell on the table, 'Matilda is a lost cause

45

in trying to make her adopt ladylike hobbies. It's always been a struggle and you know it. She was brought up with boys. I fear there is no going back now.'

The maid, Nancy, appeared from inside, and Grandmama ordered afternoon tea to be brought out.

Tilly wouldn't let the subject drop. 'I'll purchase fuel for the car out of my own spending money.'

'It's not about the petrol costs.' Adam rubbed his chin. 'I'm not sure about you driving so far, poppet. It's a long way. The roads are bad after recent rains.'

'Please, Papa. I can go to the shops for everyone.' She looked appealingly at her grandmama. 'And to the post office. There may be mail from the boys, and we won't have to wait for Mr Rogers to deliver it on his weekly rounds.' She hoped that might be the winning card.

'It would be good to have our mail,' Grandmama agreed. 'Mr Rogers isn't due for a few days yet.'

Her father let out a breath. 'You think I should let her drive to Grafton?'

Grandmama shrugged one shoulder. 'Not on her own, obviously. But she's not a child. What harm can she come to?'

'She could crash the motor car and hurt herself!'

'I'm a good driver!' Tilly defended hotly. 'Grandpapa even said so yesterday when I drove him to the bottom paddock and back.'

'Oh, why do I bother arguing? You two always

gang up on me and get your own way.' Her father eyed them suspiciously. 'Very well, but you're not going on your own. If there's no one to go with you, then the answer is no.'

Tilly grinned and winked at her grandmama, who just laughed.

★   ★   ★

The following morning, with Adelaide sitting happily beside her, Tilly drove the motor car over the rough dirt roads through the native bushland towards Grafton. Years ago, her grandfather had forged a track through the scrubland, cutting down trees and building wooden bridges over shallow creek beds to create a usable road from Blue Water to the Grafton township.

'I'm so glad you can drive your father's automobile, Tilly,' Adelaide said, bouncing on the seat as they went over a hole. 'It saves us waiting for one of the station hands to go into town.'

'I know. The freedom of driving is rather intoxicating, like drinking too much champagne!' Tilly laughed. She'd always got on well with Adelaide, who was similar in age to what her own mother would have been had she lived. In a way she was a mother figure to her, and she could tell her things that she wouldn't mention to her grandmama or Aunt Connie. Adelaide was light-hearted and funny. She had never married, instead bringing up Max and Drew as her own children when their parents had died, as well as being a companion to her mother.

47

'Did Aunt Kitty not want to come?'

'No; Grandpapa has a slight cold and she wanted to stay with him, though he hates her fussing about him. I'm certain he'd rather she came with us, but she wouldn't.'

'I wanted to bring mother will us, but she refused. I left her happily knitting socks for Drew.'

'I have wool on my list to buy,' Tilly mentioned, steering around the carcass of a dead wombat.

'I'll get it with mine. Mother has given me a list an arm long of things to purchase.' Adelaide held on to the seat as they bounced over another rut in the road. She flashed Tilly a cheeky grin. 'Do you think you'll receive another letter from your lieutenant?'

Smiling, Tilly shrugged and changed gear to slow down as they rounded a bend in the road. 'He isn't *my* anything.'

'Yet he's written to you several times.'

'I wish I hadn't told you anything about him.' Tilly's stomach flipped a little at the thought of Luke Williams writing to her again. His first letter had been full of witty comments about fellow soldiers as they'd sailed away from Australia. He had made it his business to meet Oliver and Gabe on board the ship, but they were in different infantries, and so he'd had little time once they landed in Egypt to socialise with those outside of the Light Horse.

His following letters were full of the sights of Egypt. He wrote such long letters, over several days, and in them he had shared with her all of his training, his boring lectures and officer meetings. He mentioned his horse, Monty, and how well she had adapted to her new surroundings, though he'd not mentioned why a mare had a male name such as Monty. He'd made her laugh with descriptions of how the Aussies were behaving in Egypt, the way camels spat at people, how the market traders tried to sell a person anything and everything if they became too interested in their stalls. Luke had filled her head with wonderful details of exotic foods from a faraway land.

He'd told her much more than any of the boys had done with their letters, even Oliver, whose letters were scarce; if one did arrive, it was for her father, barely more than a short note saying he was well. Tilly knew they were busy fighting a war she knew nothing about, but it frustrated her that Oliver didn't write as frequently as the others did.

Adelaide adjusted her hat after another bounce had shifted it sideways. 'Do you want the lieutenant to be your anything?'

Tilly braked sharply as a kangaroo jumped into the road ahead and quickly hopped away. 'I barely know the man.'

'Letters help with that, though. In a letter he'll tell you things he wouldn't necessarily say to you in person, so you'll know more about him than you did before.'

'He'll stop writing soon.'

'Why do you think that?' Adelaide frowned, brushing the road dust off her grey skirt.

'Because I've not written back to him,' Tilly

replied matter-of-factly.

Adelaide stared at her. 'Why ever not? He's been writing to you for nearly a year now! Oh Tilly. Why haven't you replied to him?'

'Because I doubt I'll ever see him again. It's sheer folly to make an attachment to someone right now.' Though she was sad at the thought. She enjoyed his letters and reread them often. But she didn't want to grow a fondness for someone who might not return. She had enough people to worry about.

'This stupid war.' Adelaide held on to her straw hat as they went over a bumpy patch of road. 'I miss the boys terribly. The cottage is so quiet without Max and Drew. Ma and I hate not having them there.'

'The whole station feels strange, like everyone is holding their breath. I feel as though my life is on hold. That I'm just waiting, doing nothing but waiting.' Tilly gripped the steering wheel tightly in annoyance. 'I'm so restless it makes me mad! I cannot set my mind to anything.'

'This war needs to end,' Adelaide said resolutely.

A light rain shower accompanied them into South Grafton. Tilly concentrated on driving the car onto the little steam ferry that took them across the Clarence River.

'Oh well done, Tilly!' Adelaide applauded as Tilly successfully drove the car off the ramp on the other side of the river and into the wide streets of the main town. She stopped the car on a side street and turned the engine off.

Letting out a pent-up breath, Tilly smiled,

pleased with herself, though her shoulders were stiff from concentrating. 'I need a cup of tea, that's for sure.'

They headed along Fitzroy Street, stopping every twenty yards to say hello to people they'd known all their lives and who always wanted to have a chat. However, before long their spirits dropped as they learned of deaths from a strange place called Gallipoli. Young men Tilly had danced with at social gatherings wouldn't be coming back home; or if they did, they'd be horribly wounded.

They walked along the street noticing the dimmed atmosphere, a marked difference to a year ago when war had been declared and the population had cheered and been full of enthusiasm.

After finding a table in a little tea shop that also sold women's accessories in an adjoining building, Tilly left Adelaide to order tea and sandwiches while she went across the street and to collect Blue Water's mail and to post the letters she'd been given.

Mr Phelps, the old post master, asked after the family and handed her a large bundle of mail. 'I should have left it in a sack for you, Miss Grayson. Can you manage all that? I don't suppose you want to wait for Mr Rogers to do his round.'

'No, we're too impatient.' She gave him a small pile of letters gathered from the family and the right amount of money to pay postage for them. 'I'll be fine, thank you, Mr Phelps. The motor car isn't too far away.'

51

'Motor car? Your father is in town?'

She smiled proudly, then remembered her grandmother's words about those who were too cocky usually always came undone. 'No, father is at home. I've learnt to drive it. I've been practising every day for two months! This is my first trip into town and it went very well.'

'Heavens. We have only a few motor cars in the whole district, and here you are a young lass driving all the way from Blue Water. Your brothers will be envious of you.' He shook his head in wonder as he sorted out her post. 'Wait until the gossips hear about this.'

Tilly laughed. 'I always try to give them something new to talk about, Mr Phelps. I'd hate to disappoint them.' She shifted the pile of mail into her other arm.

Mr Phelps's smile disappeared as he eyed her mail. 'I hope you've received letters from your brothers. There have been some terrible battles just lately. One they called the Battle of Lone Pine. Our boys did us proud, but we suffered heavy losses.'

Her heart sank at the news. 'Have there been many brown envelopes given out in the town?'

'Aye, some. It's a grim business.' He stamped the letters and put them into a sack. 'Give my regards to your family.' He turned away to serve another customer who entered the shop.

'I will. Good day.' Flipping through the large bundle, she pulled out several letters for Adelaide and herself. Her chest tightened a little at the sight of two letters from Luke Williams. She itched to open them but instead slipped them into her small bag.

'Tilly!'

She glanced up to see Joanie Higgins enter the post office, a friend from a neighbouring property to Blue Water. 'How are you, Joanie?'

'I'm very well. I saw you through the window and had to see you. You look wonderful.' Joanie appraised Tilly's dress. 'That colour blue suits you so perfectly.'

Tilly looked down at her lavender-blue dress with cream lace on the bodice and cuffs. 'Thank you. We ordered it when we were in Sydney, when the boys left. I ordered a similar one in dove grey, too. I think Papa was trying to make me less sad and said I could order a whole new wardrobe.'

'I have no time for dresses now, I'm afraid.' She grabbed Tilly's arm. 'I'm glad to see you, Til, as it saves me a trip out to Blue Water when I don't have much time left.'

Intrigued by Joanie's excitement, Tilly smiled at her. 'Oh? What's happening?'

'I leave for Sydney tomorrow.' Joanie grinned, her little elf-like face lighting up. 'I'm sailing to England in a week. I'm going to be a nurse. I passed my certificate.'

'Joanie, that's wonderful.' Tilly gave her a quick hug. She wasn't even aware Joanie wanted to be a nurse, or had studied and trained to become one. Since the boys had left, she'd gone around in a miserable fog of her own making, not wanting to socialise or see friends, or do anything she'd normally do with the boys. Her father's car arrival had changed her outlook somewhat when he'd surprisingly agreed to teach her to drive it. Learning to drive had been the first thing in nearly a year to interest her. She'd made it her mission to become successful at it. Now it paled in comparison to Joanie's achievements.

'Yes, I'm so excited. I'll be nursing our brave boys.' Joanie looked out of the post office window. 'Oh, there's father waiting for me. I must dash, Til. I'm sorry. I've so much to do before I leave.'

'You will write to me, won't you?' she urged, suddenly wishing she was going with her.

'Of course. Make sure you write to me, too, for I'll probably be desperately homesick!' Joanie squeezed Tilly's hand, kissed her cheek and then was away.

Rejoining Adelaide at the tea shop, Tilly sat at the table dejected, passing Adelaide her few letters. 'I just saw Joanie Higgins. She's going to England to be a nurse.'

Adelaide fussed with pouring out the tea. 'How exciting for her. Although I believe it's tremendously hard work. How clever of her to pass her nurse's exams.'

'You knew?' Tilly selected two neat ham sandwiches from the stand and added them to her plate.

'Oh, no, not really.' Adelaide passed Tilly the cake stand with its selection of jam tartlets and Victoria sponge. 'I spoke to Mr Higgins last time he called in to see Uncle Miles. We got chatting, and he mentioned Joanie studying for her exam.'

'You never said anything.'

54

'Sorry, I forgot.'

Tilly stirred her tea. 'I'm jealous, I think. No, I *know* I'm jealous. I'm green with envy. She's going away to be with our boys, while I'm here.'

'Do you want to be a nurse, too?' Adelaide bit into a cucumber sandwich.

'No, not a nurse, but Joanie's doing something worthwhile. What am I doing?' Despair grew as she pondered on the days stretching out before her with no one left to socialise with.

Adelaide gave her a hard stare. 'True. You're bored and restless. I know that feeling. I often wonder what my purpose is. I failed to marry. I earn money because I'm a good bookkeeper for your grandpapa and father, but other than that I'm not doing anything except taking care of Mother.'

'You brought up your brother's sons. That was worthy.' Tilly smiled.

'But I don't feel it's enough.'

'What do you want to do, then?'

'What can I do? I can't leave Mother; she's too old now.' Adelaide paused as two women came to their table. 'Good day, Mrs Nelson, Mrs Potter.'

Mrs Nelson, a ferrety-looking widow and the town's gossip, quickly grabbed a nearby chair and sat herself at their table. 'Well, I'm pleased to see you both, that I am!' She turned to her sister, Mrs Potter. 'Order us some tea, Flo. I'm parched as a desert.' She turned back to Adelaide and Tilly. 'Your family is all well? How are Kitty and Connie? I haven't seen them for some months.'

'Yes, they're well, thank you, but they rarely come into town now,' Tilly answered tightly. She'd never liked this rude busybody.

'I saw your father's motor car in the street. Is he joining you for tea shortly?'

Tilly's jaw clenched. Mrs Nelson admired her father, and ever since Tilly could remember she seemed determined to get some form of affection returned. 'No, he isn't with us. I drove the car myself.'

'Good Lord.' Mrs Nelson's eyes widened dramatically. 'Your good father allowed you to do that?'

'Naturally. I'm not in the habit of stealing my father's car.' Tilly seethed.

'Driving a car ... ' Mrs Nelson blinked rapidly. 'You're very head-strong, Matilda. But then you did grow up without a mother. Now I must speak with you about an organisation I'm starting, and I feel that as a prominent family in this district, you both would want to be a part of it.'

'An organisation?' Adelaide poured more tea, giving Tilly a calming look. 'How intriguing.'

'Indeed it is. I'm a firm believer in helping our brave men. We who are left at home should make it our duty to do whatever is in our power to make their lives more comfortable while they're away.'

'And how do you propose to do this?' Adelaide asked, biting into a piece of cake.

'My sister and I have secured the church hall two days a week to make comfort boxes to send overseas to our boys. We would like to know if

56

you'd wish to join us in this worthy cause.'

'I thought the ladies of the Red Cross were doing such things?' Tilly selected another triangle of ham sandwich.

'Indeed they are. However, I feel we must do more. The ladies of the district feel we can double the good work of the Red Cross. It's our duty.'

'What would you wish us to do?' Tilly asked. Despite her annoyance with the older woman, she was interested in helping the troops.

'Mainly help fill the boxes; but also, if you're able to provide the necessities that will go into the boxes? Cigarettes, socks, gloves, fruit cake, matches, notebooks, pencils, playing cards and all that sort of thing. No alcohol, of course.' Mrs Nelson looked affronted by the mere thought.

'I think that's an excellent idea, Mrs Nelson.' Tilly nodded.

'I knew I could rely on you both.' Mrs Nelson stood as more ladies entered the shop. 'There's Mrs Walker. I need to speak with her. I'll be in touch.'

Left to themselves, Tilly mulled over the idea of the comfort boxes. 'It is a good idea. I wish I'd thought of it.'

'Agreed, but the notion of spending two days a week with Mrs Nelson is a trifle off-putting.'

Tilly grinned. 'Two minutes is more than enough.'

'Maybe we could fill some boxes at home, and save us the irritation?' Adelaide chuckled.

'Yes. Shall we ask for supplies and empty boxes?'

'Wonderful idea, but let's not ask now. I don't want her coming back over here.' Adelaide wiped her mouth with a napkin. 'Did you receive any letters?'

'Two from Lieutenant Williams, one from Gabe, one from Drew. I noticed in the bundle that there are no letters from Oliver, but Papa has one from Gabe.'

'Your lieutenant is still keen, then.' Adelaide turned her letters over. 'One each from Max and Drew. I'm so pleased, though Max's letters are usually no more than a few lines on a scrap of paper. I swear a child of five could write more than him.'

'Same as Oliver then. I do wish he would write more. I worry so much about him. When he was at Kings College, he would write every week, and his letters were so informative and interesting. The silence from him now is very frustrating and makes me angry.'

Adelaide opened Drew's letter and began to read silently. 'Not much to tell you,' she said after finishing the one-page letter. 'The food is still bad, water scarce, the weather hot. Drew writes that Oliver is very busy and doesn't chat much.' Adelaide glanced at Tilly. 'But then Oliver has always been a little more serious compared to Gabe and the others.'

'It's no excuse to not write when the others can manage to do it,' Tilly fumed. 'Shall we go and finish our shopping?' She paid for the meal and led the way out.

'I have to visit the library and haberdashery. Where's my list?' Adelaide searched in her small

58

black velvet bag. 'My head is starting to pound.'

'Let's be quick then, in case your headache turns worse. I'll meet with you at the car in an hour, shall I? As I'm going the other way.' Tilly left Adelaide and crossed the road. She had no real shopping to do, and after depositing the large bundle of mail in the back seat of the car, she headed down towards the river.

A watery sun was drying up the shallow puddles. Close to the water, under the branches of a tall pine tree, Tilly opened Gabe's letter first. He wrote about the fellows he was serving with and the different ways they spent down time. Most read and shaved, and wrote letters home, but he and a few new friends had started turning empty jam cans into hand-held bombs — oh, and he had a knack for gambling. It seemed the men gambled on anything, even such insane things as cockroaches racing. He made no mention of Oliver, only briefly stating that everyone was well. And could she send him some chocolate?

Tilly smiled, her heart aching at how much she missed him. She folded the letter away and took out the two from Luke and opened the one dated first.

Dear Matilda,

You'll be pleased to know, I'm sure, that I'm in perfect health while writing this letter. Since you fail to write to me in return and ask me questions, I am bound to simply tell you things anyway. I am hopeful that you at least wish me well.

She looked out of the water, smarting at his wording. He was plainly put out by her not writing back to him, and his words made her feel awful for being so rude. He had made her feel guilty. She hated that. Why hadn't she written back? Would writing a letter to him be so bad? She couldn't answer her own question. It had something to do with him being so utterly confident in his manner, as though expecting her to fall for his charms.

You may also be pleased to know that I met up with your brother, Oliver, several days ago. My regiment of The Light Horse have been on the Gallipoli peninsula for a few days as support for the infantry. I had the honour of being near your brother in a sector of harsh terrain that made us all wish we were mountain goats. Oliver was heavily amongst the fighting. He has such courage. No task is too big or too small for him. He's been promoted again. He might be aiming for general soon! He is popular with the officers. An educated man like him should have been a commissioned officer. I heard reports that he seems to always be in the thick of things, even volunteering for missions. A true hero — or he has a death wish, I'm not so sure as to which.

I apologise if this news is unwelcome, but I feel you would want to know it. You are not a child to be pandered to, and having a few conversations with your brothers, it seems you are made of stronger stuff than most women. *I hope that is so. I assume your brothers or cousins would not write to you the gory details of being here, but to understand the men that they have become here, then you need to know what they endure.*

We were so very naive, Matilda. To think that we are now doing everything that back home would have us hung . . . it is hard to comprehend.

This war is nothing any of us expected. There is a cruelty about it that is rather shocking. There is no structure, no order once a battle begins. Each man simply has to keep going until he is either wounded, killed or told to stop. The terrain here is desolate, a wasteland fit for no purpose, yet men die on its sandy soil when they should be home with their families.

When you think you are used to it, something happens that shocks you again and you are left thinking, what day will I die? Will it be this day? Which bullet is for me?

Obviously not every moment is filled with such gloom. There are days when we laugh and enjoy the company of our fellow men. We rely on each other implicitly. Each man is the key to the other's survival.

Forgive the black mark on this page. A fly met its end. The intolerable heat is not helping us with the problem. Swarms of them make our lives very difficult. They come fat straight from the battles, and have the canny name of 'corpse flies'. You cannot eat or sleep without the pests bothering you night and day.

Alas, I am unable to continue writing at the moment, as we are off to investigate the enemy's trench system again. I'd like to say that this is a jolly exercise, but it is not. We are making no progress.

I miss my horse. She wasn't allowed to come to these steep cliffs, as she'd be useless here. I am keen to get back to her and see how she fares. She is the one constant in my life — her and writing these letters to you. Whether you answer me or not, I will continue writing as it makes me feel better.

I have no family, you see. My parents are dead, and I am an only child. I thought joining the war would be good for me. I'm not sure why.

My dear Matilda. I wish to call you that. I know you are called Tilly, as Oliver refers to you as that, but I prefer Matilda. I must sign off.

Regards,
Luke Williams

Tilly reread the letter again, then carefully folded the pages and tucked them into her bag. She'd read his second letter tonight in bed.

She sauntered back to the car, her mind a jumble of thoughts. Oliver being reckless? She couldn't understand it. He was the last person she knew to be so. Why was he behaving in such a way? Why? Luke had written of their danger, the fighting, the truth of what they faced. For the first time, she had a first-hand account of what they were going through. She would forever be grateful to him for telling her the truth. Yet now that she had the knowledge, what could she do with it? She couldn't go over there and bring them back, and to speak of it at home would only worry her family even more. It was something she could not talk about to her grandparents. How was she to keep this to herself? She sighed, wishing that it was all over and they'd be home soon.

When she reached the motor car, Adelaide was waiting. Impulsively, Tilly gave her Luke's letter to read on the journey home. 'I'm sharing this with you as there's no one else I can talk to about it.'

They had crossed the river and left Grafton behind before Adelaide spoke. 'I don't know what to make of it. Poor Lieutenant Williams; he seems rather sad. And when did anyone last hear from Oliver?'

'He wrote to Grandpapa last month. One page of nothing of importance, just the weather, the landscape and whatnot. Grandpapa gave it to me to read. It could have been written by a stranger. I've heard nothing from him. Papa receives the odd note, a few lines, which vexes him greatly. Gabe writes regularly, but Gabe's letters are full of antics and jokes about his fellow men. Neither of them say what it's truly like.'

'Perhaps it's so awful they want to spare us.'

Tilly concentrated on the sharp bend in the

road. 'Is it wrong, then, that Lieutenant Williams has spoken so freely?'

'No, not necessarily . . . ' Adelaide pondered. 'Perhaps he needs to write things down, to help him cope with it all. I was talking to Mrs Gardener on the library steps, and her nephew has lost both his legs. He's being shipped back to Sydney. Mrs Wilton at the haberdashery told me that Mr Taylor who works in the butcher shop lost his boy. The telegram arrived last week. This war is ripping families apart. Nothing will ever be the same again. We must not judge our men for what they do, whether they write or not. They're the ones suffering while we're safe in our own beds.'

Tilly banged the steering wheel. 'I can't stand not knowing what's happening. I wish I could go there and see for myself what they're enduring.'

'Well, you can't,' Adelaide said sharply. 'There's nothing for you to gain by going there. It isn't a holiday destination.'

'I'm aware of that.' Yet her heart and mind were at odds. She desperately wanted to see her brothers, to look after them. That was what she was used to doing. The three of them watched out for each other. Now she was left behind and felt adrift. How could she keep them safe?

'Your lieutenant sounds delicious, Til.'

'He's not a dessert!'

Adelaide grinned to lighten the mood. 'Write to him, the poor man.'

Tilly deliberated on the idea, and also the possibility of travelling to Egypt to see the boys. Could she do it? Her father would go mad, for

64

certain. Could she plan the trip without anyone knowing? She had money of her own, so buying a passenger ticket wouldn't be a problem. But would they take her, a single woman travelling alone? Would she be safe? Could a person even get close to the fighting?

Joanie! Joanie was travelling as a nurse. Could she pretend to be one too?

Thoughts and ideas whirled through her head all the way home. Adelaide grew quiet as she reread her letters from Max and Drew.

'We're home.' Tilly smiled at Adelaide as she parked in front of the house. 'And I didn't kill either of us.' She climbed out of the car.

'Or cause any damage. Your papa will be so pleased!' Adelaide grabbed her parcels.

'You're back!' Aunt Connie came out onto the veranda. She waited for them at the top of the stairs; and as Tilly drew closer, she noticed she'd been crying.

'What is it, Aunt Connie?'

Adelaide joined them. 'Mother? What's wrong?'

Connie wiped her eyes with a black edged handkerchief.

Tilly stared at the handkerchief, which was only ever used when someone had died. 'Aunt Connie?'

'Come inside, pet. I've bad news to tell yer.'

6

Gallipoli, Turkey. August 1915.

Oliver dived under the water. It was cold, but refreshing after days in the hot sandy trenches. Under the water he could forget what was above him for a short time, and pretend he was swimming in the river at home. Only this was seawater — clear, salty and cold, not the warm fresh water of his river.

He came up for air and wiped the water from his eyes. He floated on his back, staring at the drift of clouds. It was peaceful out here. No noise, no shouting, no bombs or gunfire. Frowning, he realised it was too quiet. He'd swum out past the breaking waves, away from the other men. His heart skipped a beat at how far he had come. Navy ships dotted the horizon, and further down the cove, smaller boats were ferrying wounded out to the large white painted hospital ships riding at anchor.

Doing the breast stroke, he swam slowly back towards the men. The surf wasn't too rough today, and the waves helped to carry him into the shore. Army supplies and personnel filled the beach. Gabe and the others were sitting around on boxes, playing cards or writing letters home or simply lying naked in the sun. He was their corporal now, and a division had been created between them, probably by his own making. He found it difficult to be light-hearted like they were. He had no patience for playing cards or gambling of any sort. Sitting around drove him mad.

It was as though he had to keep going, had to finish the job — the job that was to win this war and getting everyone home safe. He felt that if he kept fighting, then this whole nonsense would be over quicker, and he lost his temper with those who didn't feel the same. He wished fervently that he could change, that he could laugh and be at ease with the others, but he couldn't. Keeping them safe was a serious business, and he had to stay focused.

Wading out of the water naked, he grabbed a towel, which was rough against his skin, and dried himself before donning his uniform again. He felt cleaner than he had in weeks.

Gabe left his group of card players and joined him. He wore no shirt and his trousers were rolled up. 'You've got to start sleeping more. You look like shit.'

'Thank you for that.' He gave his brother a sarcastic glare. Sleeping well was not something he had mastered out here. Every time he closed his eyes, images rose to taunt him; not the kind he thought he'd have, those of death and blood, but instead he was haunted by home. His dreams were filled with riding his horse along the river, or feeling his grandmama's hand on his arm as she praised him, or Tilly shouting at him, encouraging him to do something adventurous, or her laughing at him over something silly. They were nice dreams that should have comforted him, but instead when he woke, the deep longing for home filled him until he couldn't breathe with the ache of it.

'Captain Markham was searching for you. You're to report to him as soon as you can.' Gabe scratched at his beard stubble.

Oliver looked past him to the card game. 'Are you winning?'

'Holding my own.' Gabe shrugged, squinting in the harsh sunlight. 'Want to join us after you've seen the captain?'

'I'll see what he wants with me first. I'll probably have some task to do. Are the others holding up all right?'

Gabe wiped a hand over his face. 'Freddie has a bit of a limp — hurt his ankle or toe, I don't know which. Patrick has an eye infection, but it's better than yesterday. He is winning at cards, blast him. Big Max is on ammo duty. Johnny is writing home, and Samuel is getting a haircut. Of Drew I don't know, I've not seen him since yesterday, and he looked tired, a bit like you.' Suddenly he saluted. 'We're all present and correct, *sir*.'

'Don't be smart with me, you idiot. I'm concerned, that's all.' He put his hat on.

Sighing irritably, Gabe kicked at the sand. 'We can look after ourselves. We're grown men. You're not responsible for us. I kept telling you that. We worry about *you*!' Gabe made to go, but stopped, his expression angry. 'And for god's sake, write home! They're going mad not hearing from you. You're the eldest. Write home!'

Oliver left him and walked up the sand

towards the line of tents and collections of army stores that littered the beach and hugged the base of the cliff. Gabe's words rang in his ears. Yes, he needed to write home; but whenever he tried, the words dried up and his mind went blank. Sometimes he felt so homesick he believed he would go insane from it. He didn't like thinking of home. Home meant safety, cleanliness, comfort and love. Home meant his family. And he missed them dreadfully.

'Corporal Grayson,' Captain Markham, a tall well-built man, hailed from the opening of a tent.

Crossing over to him, Oliver saluted. 'You wanted to see me, sir?'

'Yes. Walk with me.' They fell into step and headed back towards the beach. 'You'll not be surprised to hear that there's going to be another big push.'

'Not surprised at all, sir.'

'They're trying to take Hill 60.'

'Still?' Shocked, Oliver stopped walking. 'That started days ago.'

'A renewed attack is planned for tomorrow night. I need the men ready and up on the high ground at the edge of the valley by this evening. Sergeant Proctor has dysentery. In fact, I've just come from the casualty station and our unit is greatly depleted. Christ, the whole army on this godforsaken peninsula has something or other wrong with them. We don't need to worry about the Turk's guns; dysentery and exhaustion will finish us all off first.' Markham peered at Oliver. 'You aren't sick, are you?'

'No, sir.'

'You're too thin. Eat, man. I know the food is unpalatable at times, but you must eat. I can't afford to lose any more good men.'

'Yes, sir.'

'Right. Well, assemble the men. I'll meet you in an hour.'

Oliver saluted and headed back to where Gabe and the others were gathered on the beach.

'Oliver.'

Turning at the sound of his name being called, Oliver nodded at Luke Williams. He didn't know if it was deliberate or just by chance that Lieutenant Williams kept stopping him to have a chat. Not that he minded talking to Luke, for the man was decent and intelligent, and he, if no one else, was able to relate comments and jokes to make Oliver smile in this hell hole. He knew Williams was interested in Tilly, but they had become friends as well, for Williams didn't act like most of the other officers and didn't consider himself above his men. Luke Williams was a strange character, and Oliver hadn't fully worked him out just yet.

'Looks like we'll be in the firing line again, my friend.' Luke fell into step beside him.

'No rest for the wicked, it seems, sir,' Oliver tried to joke.

'We should all be called Lucifer then.'

'I wonder if this will be the breakthrough we need.'

Luke grunted. 'It'll be like all the others I expect.'

Oliver stopped outside a quartermaster's tent,

the one where Drew was stationed. A medical officer exited and paused on seeing Oliver.

'Corporal Grayson. I'm glad you've stopped by. Can you get a message to Max Spencer? His brother has contracted dysentery and has just been shipped off to a hospital on Lemnos. It all happened rather quickly, and he was worried about his brother not knowing.'

Oliver's gut tensed. 'Is he bad, sir?'

'Aren't they all?' The other man went on his way.

'Blast!' Oliver swore. Dysentery took men faster than bullets, and Drew was slightly built. Could he handle such a disease attacking his body?

'That's bad luck.' Luke kicked at a stone. 'Is there anything I can do?'

Wiping sweat from his forehead, Oliver nodded. 'I've got to get my unit ready to go up top. Can you find my friend, Max Spencer? He's on ammunition duty. I don't want him hearing this from random gossip, or worse, to go looking for Drew and not know where he is. I'd do it myself, but I don't have the time.'

'Leave it with me. I know I'm not a close friend to Max, but I've met him before, and it's better coming from me than him wondering why his brother isn't at his post. I'll find him. I've got a couple of hours before I need to report to my CO.'

'Thank you, sir. I appreciate it.' Oliver turned to walk away, but hesitated, 'Has my sister written to you yet?'

'No. Still, I'll keep writing to her though.'

71

'My sister is headstrong. She'll have her reasons for not writing, though what they could be is anyone guess.'

'I'll wear her down eventually.' Luke chuckled.

'Good. You do that. I'll see you up top, sir.' Oliver gestured to the top of the looming cliff face above them. 'And thank you again.'

'Just put a good word in to your sister for me.' Luke walked away whistling.

Twenty-four hours later, Oliver, his nerves on edge, waited with the others for their orders to join the battle, which had been raging for a week. Now they were employing a last-ditch attempt to secure Hill 60. If successful, they would then be able to link ANZAC Cove to the British-held Suvla Bay, situated along the coast; but sickness and disease were killing just as many men as the enemy. The soldiers' grumbles at the way the attacks were being handled grew louder with each battle. The Turks always seemed to be a step ahead.

Hunkered down in a shallow hollow, Oliver watched Gabe scuttle his way through the men along the narrow makeshift trench towards him. But before he reached him, the whistle blew and they were charging over the valley, aiming for the hill and the Turks.

The fierce fighting took all of Oliver's concentration. He tried to keep an eye on Gabe and the others, but the enemy's machine guns scattered them all like leaves on the wind. Wave after wave of soldiers headed for the slopes, dodging and weaving, with only one purpose in mind: to reach and take the hill.

Legs burning, Oliver ran a distance, then dropped, fired, and ran again. His chest heaved and breathing became laboured, but he still went on. His kit felt heavier with every step. A quick glance to the side showed that Gabe and Freddie were keeping pace with him. He didn't know where the others had got to.

Ahead he saw the front line attacking the enemy trenches. Oliver yelled to the men to help them out. With renewed vigour, they charged and dropped down into the trenches. Hand-to-hand fighting became the emphasis. Like an instrument of war, he fought his way along the trench, using rifle, bayonet or fists if need be. He fought for his life.

He heard Gabe behind him and kept going. His mind rejected the reality of what he was doing each time he killed a man. All he had to do was hold on to the fear that the next moment he might be the one killed. So he kept on, mindless and without emotion. The dusky faces of the Turks paled into insignificance as he made his way along the confines of the trench, firing and stabbing. Sweat dripped into his eyes. The smell of gunpowder and blood mingled together.

Suddenly from the east, machine-gun fire opened up on them, mowing men down like ducks in a pond. Panic and fear spread. Oliver called out commands until he lost his voice.

'Retreat!' Captain Markham screamed at them above the noise of the fire and the frantic shouts of the charging enemy.

Oliver pushed Gabe back the way they'd come. 'Go!'

Bullets zipped past Oliver. Bodies tripped him up. The men he had killed now lay at his feet, blocking his path. Machine-gun fire hurt his ears, ricocheting around his brain. Confusion reigned amongst the men as soldiers fell in alarming numbers.

He heard a groan from behind. Looking over his shoulder, he gasped as Freddie buckled to the ground. 'Freddie!'

Oliver doubled back and dropped to his knees beside Freddie. He checked his wounds. Blood spurted out from the side of his stomach and he quickly applied pressure. He pulled out his medical kit and tied a bandage around Freddie's waist. He worked as fast as he could to stem the flow of blood, the metallic smell of which filled his nose. 'It's all right, mate. You're fine.'

'Oliver . . . get me back.' Freddie winced in pain.

Panting, Gabe fell down beside them. 'Come on, you can't stay here. We'll be pinned down by fire.'

'You go, Gabe. I'll stay with Freddie.' He raised his voice above the sound of nearby firing.

'Don't be stupid.' Gabe pulled at Oliver's sleeve. 'We'll both take him.'

As they moved Freddie, he screamed in agony.

'No! Stop! Leave me, both of you,' Freddie mumbled. 'I won't make it.'

'Shut up, Freddie,' Oliver snarled like a dog, angry and scared. 'Hold the bandage, Gabe. Apply pressure.' His hands were slippery, covered in blood. 'Freddie, stay with us now. Keep awake. Can you put your arms around our shoulders?'

'We need a stretcher bearer!' Gabe stopped another solider running past. 'Get a stretcher bearer now!'

'Gabe, it's no good. They can't get to us.' Oliver lifted Freddie, who cried out in pain. 'Sorry, old chum, but we're going to have to carry you.'

Gabe snatched up a thin plank from the side of the trench. 'Lay him on this. We can carry him this way.'

They laid him on the plank and heaved him up. Stepping over fallen soldiers, and ignoring the cries of those still alive, they stumbling along. With each movement, Freddie's moans grew. The plank wasn't wide enough to keep Freddie stable; the slightest movement to either side and he was in danger of falling off.

'This won't work, Gabe. It's too far, and it's slowing us up. Put him down.' Oliver gently lowered his end of the plank. He took his kit off and threw it at Gabe. 'Help get him on my back.'

'On your back? You'll not make it ten feet that way.'

'Just do it! Cover us.'

With Freddie draped over his back, Oliver hung onto his arms at the front and doggedly stumbled through the trench over bodies and away from the machine gun. In the mayhem of the retreat, he tried not to think of Freddie's groans and his weight, which seemed to grow heavier with each step.

'Let me take him for a time,' Gabe urged as they hurried across the valley.

'No! We can't stop.' Panting, Oliver held on to

Freddie's arms and, head down, kept going even though his legs felt on fire and his chest burned.

'Oliver!' Suddenly Big Max was there. He lifted Freddie off Oliver's back as though he weighed nothing more than a child.

The relief was immense. Oliver's knees buckled. He fell to the ground, sucking in air. Over his head he heard voices and the receding battle. He tried to stand, but couldn't; his legs refused to obey. His throat was as dry as the sandy dirt he knelt on.

'Drink.' A canteen was thrust into his hands and he drank thirstily. Looking up, he found Luke Williams grinning down at him. 'Well, that's another story to tell Matilda.'

Oliver closed his eyes wearily. Was it even possible to feel this tired and still be alive?

'Come on, old mate. You've done enough for one day.' Luke dragged him to his feet and with an arm around him for support, helped him back to their own trenches.

'Freddie? Gabe?' Oliver muttered.

'Gabe has gone with Freddie to make sure he's all right. Max carried him to the casualty station. He must have the strength of ten men.'

'Yes, something like that.' Oliver stumbled. 'I need to find out how the others are.'

Luke propped him up closer to his side and held him tighter. 'You, my good fellow, are going to lay down and rest, and hopefully sleep for a few hours. I'll find Gabe and we'll check the others. It's a mess out there; a right shambles. My men have been withdrawn, too; we all have. We didn't take the hill.'

Shoulders slumped, Oliver focused on putting one foot in front of the other. 'Why are you helping me? I don't need a nursemaid.'

'I think we differ on that at the minute, mate. Besides, I'm getting into your good books because I fancy marrying your sister when all this is over.'

'She doesn't even answer your letters.'

A delighted grin split Luke's dirty face. 'But she will!'

7

Blue Water Station. October 1915.

Tilly stood by the grave. The dirt had sunk a little as it continually settled. It looked ugly with all the bunches of flowers dying upon the mound. Impatiently, she started bundling up the bouquets into a pile. A slight breeze lifted her hair off her nape where it had escaped the net she'd roughly put it in that morning. The mild wind carried away the dried petals past the other neat gravestones and down the slope towards the river. She watched the drift for a while, her mind numb.

When she'd finished her task, she laid the fresh wildflowers she'd brought with her at the bottom of the gravestone and gently ran her hand over the newly carved words. *Adam Gabriel Grayson.*

She still found it hard to believe her father was dead. A sudden heart attack had taken him before he hit the study floor. Her grandpapa had tried to revive him, but the effort was futile, and all it had done was tire him out so much that they thought he'd be the next one they'd lose.

Somehow, both her grandparents made it through the funeral. However, it had taken its toll on them; on everyone. Blue Water wasn't the same. With her grandparents old and seemingly overnight turning frail, her father now dead and buried alongside her mother, and all the men gone to war, Blue Water lay withered like a ghost town. The frenzied pace and the jolly yet hardworking atmosphere had been replaced by a gloominess that shrouded the land like an impenetrable grey cloud.

Depression weighed on her like a cloak, heavy and unshifting. In the six weeks since her father's death, her world had turned upside down. Gone were her carefree days. Instead, she spent each day without any real thought or purpose, wandering without achieving anything useful. Her grandparents leaned on each other, both wrapped up in their grief. She had no one.

'Tilly.'

She turned to see Adelaide walking up the grassy slope towards her. 'Yes?'

'The mail has been delivered. You've received a letter.' From the pocket of her black mourning skirt, Adelaide withdrew an envelope and passed it to her. 'I thought you might want to read it up here.'

Tilly looked at it. A letter from Luke. The familiar spread of warmth flooded her body at the sight of his handwriting. She had begun to depend on his letters. He was her link to everything happening over there. His voice that shone from the words written on the page were enough to comfort her, for a short time anyway.

'Did you receive any news about Drew?'

'He's recovered from the dreaded dysentery and back on the peninsula at Gallipoli. Aunt Kitty said your uncle David has written saying

Freddie is recovering well. He's been transferred to an Australian military hospital in Cairo.'

'Our poor boys.' Tears welled, but she fought them back. She had done so much crying in the last several weeks that she couldn't cope with any more.

Adelaide sighed and tiredly wiped her face. 'I'll leave you to it. I've much to do.'

Tilly frowned. 'Much to do? Like what?' She had nothing to do. Was bored out of her mind, actually.

'Well, since your father . . . ' Adelaide glanced at the gravestone. 'I've all the bookkeeping to do. And with your grandpapa not himself just yet, I've taken on more work regarding the running of this place.'

'What do you mean?'

'Blue Water doesn't run by itself, Tilly,' Adelaide snapped. 'Who do you think has to organise the buying and selling of the stock, of the feed, of paying the wages, and all the bills? There's so much correspondence with the Sydney businesses, I can't think straight. Nor do I know it all, which is frustrating. Your Uncle David was a Godsend when he was here for the funeral, but since he's returned to Armidale . . . ' Adelaide rubbed her face, the distress clear in her eyes. 'I try to not disturb your grandpapa, but I might have to, for the letters are piling up. I need his signature for many things. Stumpy asked me about the breeding programme, but I don't have the answers. There are mares in season, and Stumpy wanted to know if we'd hired the services of a stallion. I just don't know!

Your father did it all.'

Shocked, Tilly placed her hand on Adelaide's arm. 'Oh, Adelaide. I'm so sorry. I had no idea at all. Why didn't you tell me?'

'You're grieving for your father. Besides, you've never been interested in the business side of things. And why should you be? You're the daughter of the house; you had no need to know.'

Like a slap in the face, she took a step back, understanding the words Adelaide didn't say. She lived a privileged life. And although she'd liked to go mustering with the boys, and play at being a station hand, the truth was she was spoilt. Adelaide was right; she had no idea about the importance of money, of paying bills, or the finer details of how Blue Water was run. Her family was wealthy, and she took it for granted. It all just happened so smoothly, like a well-rehearsed magic trick, that she'd never thought of what went on behind the scenes.

Adelaide squeezed her hand. 'I have to get back. Mother is upset. She hasn't heard from Max or Drew in a while. I told her I wouldn't leave her for very long. Adam's death has shaken her, too. He was like her son as well. She watched him come into the world.'

'I'll come back with you, and you're going to teach me everything about running this place.' Tilly fell into step with her, their arms linked.

'No, really, Tilly, there's no need. I shouldn't have spoken — '

Tilly stopped. 'There's *every* need! I'm ashamed of myself, leaving you with it all to do. I

81

didn't even know what you actually did, in truth; not properly. I'm disgusted that I've sat around bored all these years when you could have been relieved of some of the burden.'

'You weren't bored when the boys were here. You were always with them and doing something. Your father and your grandpapa ran Blue Water splendidly. So don't blame yourself. It all worked very well until . . . '

'Well, I'm going to help you now. We'll do it together.' They continued walking across the fields back towards the house.

Adelaide chuckled. 'You don't know what you're letting yourself in for! It's a thankless task, believe me.'

By the end of the afternoon, Tilly's head swam with figures and information. She was dumbfounded by the effort and knowledge it took to run a property the size of Blue Water, plus all the businesses in Sydney. There were investments and shares, land sales, taxes, wages, building work, repairs, and so much more she was afraid she would forget.

She washed and changed into another black dress for dinner. She hated black. Weeks of wearing the colour depressed her. Luke's letter sat on her dressing table unread. She would read it in bed tonight as a treat to herself.

Entering the dining room, she kissed her grandpapa on the cheek and then her grandmama before taking her chair. The three of them made a sad picture. A room which usually was so full of people and voices seemed too quiet, too serious now.

Her grandpapa poured her a glass of white wine, his hand shaking a little. In the weeks since his son's death, he'd aged dramatically. He'd always worn his age well, but now he looked like the old man in his eighties that he was. The energy had gone from his body and the light from his eyes, which seemed a dimmer blue; while her grandmama appeared even smaller, if that was possible.

'What have you been doing today, dearest?' Grandmama asked as they sipped pea and ham soup with fresh warm bread rolls.

'I've been helping Adelaide. She's struggling to cope with the workload in the office, so I've asked her to teach me.' She glanced at her grandpapa. 'Is that all right with you?'

A deep sadness filled his eyes. 'If you want to do it, Princess, then go ahead.'

'We thought it would take some of the burden off you.'

'That's kind of you.' He played with his food, seemingly not hungry. 'I don't have the energy right now to deal with bills and whatnot.'

Tilly smiled lovingly at him. He'd lost a lot of weight and looked tired. 'You mustn't worry about Blue Water. Adelaide and I will see to the running of it.'

'If there are things that you don't understand, you must come to us and ask for help, though.' Her grandmama patted her hand, her diamond ring flashing in the light. 'Without your father and the boys, we must work together. We can't ask David to come here. He has his own farm to run.'

'Yes, I know. But he's helping with the Sydney businesses. Adelaide has received letters from him about it. I want to learn it all. It'll be beneficial to have someone in control until Grandpapa feels up to it again, and the boys return home.' She swallowed on the last word, for they all knew it was not certain they would return. Nothing was certain about anything anymore.

'I'm not feeling well, Kitty. I think I'll go lay down for a while.' Grandpapa left the table with an apologetic smile, his soup barely touched.

'He's very weary these days,' Grandmama said when he had left the room. 'I can't bear to see it. He's always been so vigorous. To see him like this breaks my heart.'

Tilly held her thin hand. 'He just needs to rest some more.'

'He does nothing but sleep.' Grandmama stood. 'I shall go visit Connie for a bit.'

'What about your dinner? You must eat, Grandmama. I worry about you both.'

'Don't worry about us, my dear. We're just old and tired. Adam's death and the boys being in constant danger has affected us more than we ever expected. It's all been a bit of a shock.' In a rustle of black crepe, her grandmama left the room.

Despondent, Tilly finished her soup and then picked at her plate of roast chicken and vegetables. She drank the rest of her wine and poured another.

'Are you all finished, Miss Tilly?' Nelly the

84

housemaid asked, coming in with a tray. 'Wold you like dessert?'

'No, thank you, Nelly; and yes, I'm finished. Please send our apologies to Mrs Bramwell. Dinner was delicious as always, but my grandparents are a little tired tonight.' Tilly, taking her glass of wine with her, retired to her room.

Sitting on the cushioned window seat, she looked out at the dusk descending on the gardens and opened Luke's letter.

Dearest Matilda,

I am writing this sitting on a little ledge on the side of a cliff overlooking the sea, out of the cold wind. It's relatively safe from gun fire as the Turks in this area are being kept back on the other side of the valley.

The news of your father's death shattered your brothers, cousins and your friends enormously. I happened to be with them when Oliver received the news. It was a bad time for them, and I felt at a loss how to offer any assistance in their grief. Mourning is such a private emotion. Gabe dealt with it by getting drunk and in trouble. No one knows how he managed to get his hands on the alcohol, though I think Drew was involved somehow. Anyway, he caused a fight, and lord knows how Markham got him off the charges. He was due for a promotion, but naturally that was squashed. Oliver was the opposite and hardly spoke to anyone for days.

Your brothers and friends are a good group of men. I like them greatly. In this small cove we are often able to get together when we are pulled out of the lines. Gabe is a man very much like me. We find much to laugh at. Oliver, unfortunately, is very serious. Yet he is intelligent and interesting to talk to about all subjects when he stops for a moment to rest. I respect him.

The weather has turned bitingly cold. There is no comfortable situation here. We are either sweltering in the unbearable heat in summer, made more intolerable by the lack of rations and water (I have seen men come to blows over the dispute of a can of water), or we are shivering in the freezing cold, which is what we are enduring at the moment. It is a forsaken place. Why anyone would want to die over defending it, I have no idea. If it was mine, I'd say have it! It's nothing but sand, rock, and barren wasteland.

I feel dreadfully tired, dear Matilda. We don't sleep well. The constant noise of men living close together and the shelling and the guns makes for poor bed partners. We are often very hungry and thirsty, but mainly we are just tired. When dawn breaks, we feel as though we have slept only for a minute or two.

You will have had news that your cousin Freddie was wounded. Oliver carried him out of the trenches under fire. Gabe said it was more frightening trying to get back safely than it was going into the onslaught. Drew was down with the dreaded dysentery but is back with us after his stay at the hospital on Lemnos.

I have a hole in my boot. My socks are held together by my rather pitiable darning. My needlework skills leave much to be desired. I've never had to do it before, as there was always someone back home to do those tasks for me.

It is the little things like these that make us miss home so greatly. A cold beer, watching a thunderstorm without getting wet, walking down a street with a straight back, not jumping at every shadow, a pretty lady's smile.

I suppose I should scramble back up to the top of this cliff and rejoin my men. My moments of peace are over and I must return to my duties.

If you should not receive another letter from me, it is not my doing.

Until next time, sweet Matilda.

Luke.

For some time, Tilly sat watching the falling night, seeing her own reflection in the glass.

Luke. He sounded as lonely as she felt.

Luke.

His name did circles in her mind. For the first time, he sounded despondent. She read the letter again. Yes, this was definitely more downbeat than his previous ones. But then, was that so surprising? How long could he and the men take such punishment? It wasn't natural.

Jerking to her feet, she sat at her dressing table and picked up her pen. She wrote to the boys every day, in rotation, but she had never thought to add Luke to that list.

He deserved better than that.

Dear Luke.

Forgive me. I should have written long before this and I am ashamed I did not. I cannot tell you why exactly. I suppose in my mind I didn't want another person to worry about. Yet, your letters arrive with regularity and you have forced me to think of you; to worry. I was annoyed by this to begin with, only now I feel the need to write to you and let you know that I am listening.

I am here.

You tell me how it is there. I appreciate it immensely. I NEED to know. Spare me no niceties. I want all the details. I am strong. I have to be.

I have begun learning how to run our cattle station. My grandpapa is an old man who has taken his eldest son's death badly. So I will take over and see what I can do to continue the operations of the station. My dear friend, Adelaide, is teaching me the book-keeping side of things. Together we will keep this place running smoothly in readiness for when the boys come back.

You must come back. All of you.

We who are left struggle to go on without our loved ones beside us. Blue Water feels like an abandoned town. The women who work and live here dread the arrival of the mail. The stockmen are very few now, and mainly those who failed medicals or who are too old to enlist. We all band together to keep our spirits up, but it is difficult when there are empty chairs at the dining table.

I could never have dreamed that this would become my life now. Days go by without meaning. Special occasions are barely acknowledged because it doesn't feel the same without all the family here. I envy those families who have no one in the war. How relieved they must be.

Please keep writing to me, Luke.
Best regards,
Tilly (Matilda)

8

Cairo, Egypt, February 1916.

Walking the crisp neat paths of the convalescent hospital, Oliver scanned the wounded soldiers sitting on wooden deck chairs in the lush gardens. Birds chirped above his head as they flew from rooftop to rooftop. A calm orderliness prevailed, and he liked that. To be off the peninsula lightened his step.

Amongst the palm trees, he saw Freddie clad in pyjamas, lying on a long sun chair. A book was open on his legs, but he was watching a nurse tend to another man and didn't see Oliver approach.

'I observe there are some distractions here, cousin?' Oliver joked.

Freddie grinned and shook his hand. 'Too many, too many. How can a man get better when he has everything to gain by staying ill and being cared for by these angels?'

Oliver glanced at the nurse nearby. She looked up and smiled at him and for a moment Oliver returned her smile, staring into her brown eyes.

'That's Nurse Hutton. Isn't she divine?' Freddie eyed her appreciatively.

Nurse Hutton turned to him fully and gave him a glare. 'None of your nonsense, Private Grayson.' She smiled as she tucked a blanket around his legs. 'Who's your visitor? I haven't met him before.'

'My cousin, Corporal Oliver Grayson.'

'*Sergeant* Grayson.'

Freddie's eyes widened. 'Sergeant? Well blow me down. Congratulations!'

Nurse Hutton smiled. 'Congratulations. It's a pleasure to meet you, Sergeant. Will you stay for afternoon tea? It'll be served shortly.'

'I will, thank you.' Oliver couldn't take his gaze from her lovely face, which was heart-shaped with full lips, and those brown eyes that laughed at him. He noticed her uniform was that of an Australian nurse, and for some ridiculous reason that pleased him. She was from home.

He watched her leave to attend other patients and only remembered Freddie when the other man poked him in the ribs. 'Hey!' he complained.

'Well, are you here to see me or ogle the nurses?'

Grinning, Oliver pulled a chair across the grass and placed it beside him. He hadn't felt so relaxed in a very long time. 'When are they discharging you?'

'I don't know. It can't be soon enough. Despite the lovely nurses, I'm sick of this place. Why?'

'Are you healed enough to rejoin us, or are they sending you home? Patrick didn't know when I asked him yesterday; that's why I thought I'd come and see you today and find out.'

'I'll not be going home, no fear of that. As if I would leave you buggers and toddle off!' Freddie frowned and touched the bandages around his waist. 'It's still as tender as blazes sometimes, but

91

I can walk and dress myself just fine. I couldn't throw down a steer just yet . . . ' He laughed softly.

Oliver's heart twisted at the mention of home; of the times they would all challenge each other to thrown down steers single-handedly and who would be the best at it. Usually Big Max took the title. 'It's good to see you, mate. I'm sorry I don't come as often as I should.'

Freddie closed the book on his lap. 'I understand. You have duties. It's fine, though, as the others come and make me laugh. I'm sure they're trying to burst my stitches. Patrick and Big Max are here daily. How's Drew — any word?'

'Gaining strength, but that last bout of dysentery nearly put him six feet under.'

'Poor sod. To get it once is bad enough, but twice? Unlucky.'

Oliver took his hat off and ran his fingers through his hair. 'He was back at ANZAC Cove for only two weeks, but he was so thin and weak. It's not surprising he succumbed to another bout of dysentery again. I was frightened he wouldn't make it, I can tell you.' Oliver sighed. The last few months had been full of worry over Freddie and Drew and family back home coping with the death of his father, the shock of which still struck him dumb when he thought of it, which he tried not to do.

Freddie threw off the light blanket and swung his legs over the side of the chair. 'I was pleased to hear you got a medal for saving me. You deserved it. You didn't think of your own safety, but then you never do when it comes to one of us.'

'You're my cousin. I wasn't going to leave you, was I? Uncle David would kick my arse!' Oliver tried to lighten the conversation.

Freddie didn't laugh. 'I'm so glad you all got off that hellhole peninsula without mishap. Patrick told me that the evacuation went well and there were no casualties.'

'The best thing about the whole Gallipoli campaign was the retreat.' Oliver shook his head wryly. 'We crept out of there as quiet as a fox out of a hen house.'

'It was a stuff-up right from the start.' Freddie huffed, opening his cigarette packet and taking one out. He offered one to Oliver, who declined.

'I agree. It was freezing before we left — blizzards, the works. I thought I'd never feel warm again.' Oliver shivered at the remembered the icy pain that had chilled him to the bone and made his body ache. Every man there was exhausted and weary, and the cold just made it all so much worse. 'I can't believe we don't have to go back.'

'So, we live to fight another day then,' Freddie said with raised eyebrows.

'Yes, that's why I wanted to come see you today.'

'Oh?'

Oliver turned his hat by its brim, finding the right words. 'I don't want to leave you behind. I want us all together. But if there's a chance you can go home, you must take it.'

'Leave me?' Freddie's mouth gaped in

surprise. 'Where are you going?'

'France.'

'France . . . ' Freddie echoed in a whisper. 'Straight up?'

'To England first, for more training.' Oliver snorted at the last word. 'As if we need more training after being at Gallipoli.'

'When?'

'In ten days, the beginning of March. We have a week off, and then we start filling the ships.'

'I thought we'd be staying here, fighting in the desert.'

'Nope, the generals in command want us in Europe to strengthen the front lines against the Germans.'

'The *real* war then, hey Ollie?' Freddie grinned, puffing on his cigarette.

Oliver smirked. He hated being called Ollie and knew Freddie did it to peeve him. 'Something like that.'

'I'll be on that ship. Don't you leave me behind, cousin.' Despair filled Freddie's eyes. 'I mean it, Oliver. Don't leave me here.'

'Do you have the chance to go home? Have they mentioned anything like that?'

'I'm on the mend. I get better every day.'

'You have a stomach wound. It's your pass out of this mess, surely? Maybe you can go home. Ask the doctor!' He hoped to God Freddie could go home; it would be one man less he had to worry about.

'No!'

'Listen, Freddie — '

Freddie gripped his arm. 'I'm not going home.

We stay together. Isn't that what you always say? Do not leave me behind.'

'I never left you behind on the battlefield, did I?' He shuddered, remembering that awful day.

'No, and I've not thanked you for saving my life.'

'No need. You're my family.' He put his hat on again. 'I've got to go, but I'll come and see you in a few days' time. You need to think about what you want to do, come with us or go home.'

'I'm not going home.'

Oliver let a deep breath and realised he wouldn't have returned to Australia either. 'Fine, then. You must tell the doctors you're medically fit or they'll not let you rejoin us.'

'I'll convince them, don't worry.'

'Good man.' He patted Freddie's shoulder and stood as Nurse Hutton wheeled over a tea trolley.

Freddie stood next to him. 'She is a vision, isn't she? Has a real nice manner, too, as though each patient is important to her.'

Oliver watched her serve tea to the man in the next lounge chair. Her copious uniform covered her from head to toe, but the apron was pulled in at her slender waist and also showed off her small breasts.

'No tea, Sergeant Grayson?'

Startled, he blushed at being caught staring. 'Err . . . yes, thank you.'

Nurse Hutton smiled as she passed them cups of tea and a couple of biscuits. 'You're comfortable, I hope, Private Grayson?'

'Yes, thank you, Nurse.' Freddie beamed up at

her as he sat back down.

She looked at Oliver. 'I'm afraid, Sergeant, that you'll have to go after your tea. Visiting hours will be over.'

'Of course.'

She gave him a lingering stare, then wheeled the trolley to the next patient.

'So much for you going, then. You were putty in her hands.' Freddie winked, sipping his tea. 'She gets off her shift at four.'

Oliver shook his head. 'I don't think . . . '

'Don't think, man, just ask her out. There's plenty who have tried and failed.'

'What makes you believe I'll be any different?' Oliver murmured, holding the tea he didn't even want.

'You're the only one she's smiled properly at. I was watching.'

'I'll think about it . . . '

★   ★   ★

At four o'clock, Oliver stood outside the main entrance to the hospital. Despite the warmth of the day, he was in full dress uniform. Gabe and the others were visiting a brothel and steam house and had asked him to join them, but he had only wanted to see if he could persuade Nurse Hutton to accompany him to a bar for a drink. He'd managed to deflect their questions about where he was going and slipped away when no one was watching. Now that he was here, he couldn't believe how nervous he was. Sweat beaded on his forehead.

She walked by with another nurse before he realised it. 'Nurse Hutton?'

Glancing over her shoulder, she smiled at him. 'Sergeant Grayson. Can I help you?'

He whipped off his hat. 'I was wondering if you'd do me the honour of having a drink with me? If you're free?'

Silence stretched between them as she made up her mind.

Her fellow nurse nudged her. 'Go on, Jessica.'

'I have washing to do. You know how Matron is,' she whispered back.

'I'll do yours with mine. It'll be fine. I get the stains out better than you anyway.'

Oliver took a step closer and smiled at the friend. 'Thank you, that's very kind.'

She chuckled again. 'It'll be worth it just for that smile. Go on, Jess, or I'll go with him instead!'

Jessica sighed tiredly. 'Very well, I will. But not for a drink. I'm starving and need to sit down. I've been on my feet for ten hours.'

'Then we can get something to eat.'

They fell into step and crossed the road. Oliver didn't know the area that well, but Miss Hutton pointed out a small square along the next street that boasted a little café with an English-speaking owner.

'Wine?' Oliver asked as they took seats under a large grapevine that covered the overhead trellis of the café's outdoor area.

'I shouldn't. I haven't eaten much all day. It'll go straight to my head.'

'Are you very hungry?' He noticed she was rather thin.

'I'm always very hungry and very tired. We don't get to eat a lot, and the days are long and exhausting. By the time we finish our shifts, we're too tired to cook, and our money doesn't stretch to eating out all the time. We live on tea and jam and bread.'

'Lots of food it is, then.' Oliver ordered plates of spiced potatoes, kofta kebabs, fattoush salad and red lentil soup, plus a dish of Om Ali for dessert. While they waited for the food, Oliver filled up their glasses with red wine and offered a toast.

'A toast?' Miss Hutton asked. 'To what?'

'To us. Let's hope this is the beginning to something delightful.' He grinned, barely recognising this feeling of something that could only be described as joy.

She laughed a sweet laugh that filled Oliver with simple happiness. He had the urge to make her smile all the time.

'Tell me about yourself, Corporal Grayson.'

'I'm from New South Wales. My family have a cattle property up north, near Grafton. Do you know it?'

'Your property?'

'No, Grafton?'

'No.'

He gave her a wry smile. 'Anyway, I have one younger brother and sister. Gabe is serving in my unit. Tilly, I hear, is running the property back home.'

'Good lord, how clever of her.'

'My parents are dead and my grandparents are elderly. Tilly has to do it.' He shrugged, throwing off a problem he didn't want to think about. He didn't want the guilt to return right now when he was finally enjoying himself for the first time in over a year.

'She *has* to do it?' Miss Hutton scowled. 'Why does she *have* to do it? Can she not decide if she wants to or not, or must she be told?'

Sitting back in his chair, he gazed at the iciness that controlled her lovely features now. He had offended her somehow. 'Our property is her home. It has to be taken care of and run properly for the future.'

'For when you return to claim it.' She watched him closely.

He pulled his collar out from his neck, wilting under her stern gaze. 'I am the heir, yes.'

'So your sister is doing you a favour by keeping the place going?'

'Well, yes, but it's her home too. She'd not want to see it fall into ruin.'

'You must be so proud of her. She sounds like a strong woman.'

'She is, but I don't want to talk about Tilly.' He felt ashamed that he hadn't written home in months. The news of her running the property had come from Luke Williams, who was beside himself to finally receive a letter from her.

'Why shouldn't we talk about her? She sounds interesting, a woman running a cattle property. She has power and freedom. She can make decisions on her own. That must feel so amazing, so invigorating.'

'Is she more interesting than me?' he tried to joke.

'Are you interesting?'

Stumped for words, he was grateful when the waiter brought out some of the dishes. The aroma of spices filled the air around them. For a while they concentrated on filling their plates and passing the food. Oliver drank his wine and poured another.

'Are you a heavy drinker, Sergeant?'

Blinking in astonishment at the question, he slowly put down his glass. 'No, not really. At home I'd drink a cold beer after a hot hard day's work, and a glass of wine at night with my meal.'

'So you do work then?' she asked, a forkful of potatoes halfway to her mouth.

He stared at her. 'Work? I'm a soldier.'

'I mean before the war.'

He forked up some salad. 'Yes, I worked. I worked hard. My brother and I worked just as hard as the station hands. We did the mustering, the branding, the sorting, the fencing, plus I was learning the financial running of it . . . ' He felt like he was being tested and didn't like it. He thought she was kind and nice, or so Freddie said. Maybe it was a mistake asking her out. Why was she so prickly, as though he had to pass some kind of test?

They ate in awkward silence for a while, before Miss Hutton put her fork down. 'I am sorry. I wasn't being a pleasant guest.' She stared into space, fingers playing with the stem of her glass. 'I'm not usually so abrupt. Please forgive me.'

A thought came to him. 'Are you a suffragette?'

'Was I that obvious?' Her eyes grew wide.

100

'You seemed more interested in taking me to task about Tilly running the station than learning about me.'

'I apologise. Though those things do interest me, but I shouldn't always be so vocal about it with someone who doesn't yet know me.' She smiled in apology. 'I can be a little hot-headed at times. It's a severe failing of mine.'

'None of us are perfect. According to my brother, I'm far too serious.'

'I've a lot on my mind.' She played with her food. 'I received notice today that I'm to go to England and nurse in a hospital in London. I am not very pleased about it.'

'Is that not what you want to do?'

'No, I want to be in France. Matron knew it, as I had requested the transfer, but instead she sent word to those who organise these things and told them I should be in England. I'm a little tired of being told what to do. I know I shouldn't be. I'm a nurse in the army, and being told what to do is my life now. Yet it's very difficult for me to take orders again after leaving home.'

'We all have to take orders.' Oliver sipped his wine.

She drank some as well. 'I became a nurse because I wanted to help our brave soldiers and escape my father, who has no respect for me or any woman. However, it seems I only exchanged one form of control for another.'

'You could aim for promotion. That way you'll start having some power of your own.'

'The matron hates me. There's no promotion under her.'

'Why doesn't she like you?'

'She says I'm too undisciplined to be a good nurse.' She continued eating, her movements short and jerky. 'I am a good nurse, you know. I care for my patients. I don't treat them as numbers like she does. I never put their safety at risk, but I do feel that some of the rules she hands down to us are ridiculous. When a man is dying, does he care if my curls have escaped my cap? Does he care that my boots aren't polished? Does he care if there's an old stain on my cuff?'

'We soldiers have just the same issues to contend with, but there's a point to it. If we didn't follow the rules there would be chaos.'

'Please don't side with Matron, otherwise our friendship will be very short-lived.' She grinned.

He smiled back. 'The matron is the very devil incarnate. There, am I still your friend?' He was pleased when she laughed. 'Is the matron going with you to England?'

'Heavens, I hope not. I'll throw myself over the side of the ship if she does.'

Oliver chuckled. 'That's a bit dramatic, surely?'

'You don't know her.'

'Shall we talk only of happy things? No matron, no army, no hospital, no war, just things that make us happy.'

Miss Hutton raised her glass. 'That sounds like an excellent idea, Sergeant.'

'I'll go first. It would make me happy if you called me Oliver and not Sergeant.'

'Oliver.' She nodded. 'Then I'm Jessica.'

'Now it's your turn, Jessica. What makes you happy?'

She thought for a moment. 'Dancing. Whenever I could, I would escape my father and go dancing. Do you dance?'

'Only if I have a pretty lady on my arm.' He winked and ate some more, relaxing as she smiled back at him. He'd passed the test.

★ ★ ★

The next evening, Oliver waited for her outside of the hospital when she finished her shift.

'Where are you taking me?' she asked.

'Dancing, of course.' He grinned. 'There's a British services club not far from here. They have a band playing tonight.'

'Oh wonderful!' She rested her hand on his arm. 'I'll need to get changed.'

Later, as they entered the club, which was located in an old British colonial building, and were shown a table, Oliver couldn't help but feel proud to have Jessica on his arm. The envious looks he got from the other men in the room made him straighten his back with smugness. Jessica wore a deep red dress which went well with her black curls.

'You are the prettiest woman in the room,' he whispered to her as they sat at the table. He meant it. He couldn't take his eyes of her. Despite the warmth and the press of people, he felt as though she was the only person there. If he could, he would have kissed her right there in front of everyone.

She gave him a steady look, but happiness shone in her eyes. 'Flatterer.'

Oliver silently thanked Tilly for her love of dancing and her badgering of the boys to practise with her on rainy days. He held his own, as Jessica wanted to dance to nearly every tune the band played. With ease, for she was a small woman, he could turn her around the room, light on their feet.

When he begged for mercy to sit down after hours of dancing, he ordered a bottle of champagne and raised his glass. 'A toast.'

'To what?' Her brown eyes sparkled in amusement.

'To being alive.'

'I'll drink to that.' She clinked her glass to his.

They danced until the club closed and the band began to pack away their instruments. Without any music at all, they danced slowly, wrapped up in each other and oblivious to everything around them. When the maître d' politely asked them to leave, they reluctantly pulled apart. Outside, the streets were quiet, the moon low in the sky.

'It's dreadfully late.' The night air was cold. Oliver took off his uniform jacket and put it around Jessica's shoulders. 'Or very early, depending on your perspective.' She smiled.

'Shall we walk?'

'Yes, let's.' She yawned behind her hand.

'You're tired.'

'I am, but happily tired. It's been one of the best nights I've ever had. Thank you.' She stopped and turned to him. On tiptoe, she

104

reached up and kissed him.

In the street light, he gazed at her lovely face, putting it all to memory. He kissed her softly, reverently.

'What shall we do tomorrow?' she whispered against his lips.

'Anything you want,' he replied, kissing her again. The feel of her soft curves played havoc with his concentration.

'A drive somewhere?' She ran her fingers over the buttons on his uniform jacket.

He drew her closer, an ache building in his body for her. 'Anything you wish for.'

After a few hours' sleep, they met up after a late breakfast and Oliver hired a car and driver. From the market they bought fruit, nuts, bread and cheese and bottles of flavoured tea. Once loaded into the car, they sat back and instructed the driver to take them to the pyramids.

They spent a couple of hours wandering around the giant structures, which were busy with other tourists and soldiers. Oliver marvelled at the size of them, how they were built and how they stood proud. The landscape was of two colours, the bleached sand and the blue sky. He paid for a short camel ride around one of the larger pyramids, and laughed as Jessica clung on to the seat while the animal jolted them about.

'I think this camel has one leg shorter than the other three. I feel like my head will be shaken off!' she laughed.

'Perhaps we should have ridden donkeys instead.'

She gave him a superior look. 'We'd have been

closer to the ground if we fell off!'

At the foot of the Sphinx, they shared a picnic. Hawkers cried out their wares, all eager to sell souvenirs of Cairo and the pyramids, but Oliver soon waved them away so they could eat in peace.

'It's hard to imagine that this is winter in Cairo,' Jessica said, biting into an apple.

Oliver nodded. The weather was pleasant for February, a still warm day. He cut up some cheese. 'I doubt England and France will be so accommodating.'

'I'll be going into spring. I imagine England will be full of blossom and flowers.'

Breaking apart the bread, Oliver offered a piece to Jessica.

'After so much sand and desert, I'll be glad for the change.'

Just as they were finishing up, Luke Williams, camera in hand, walked past.

'Lieutenant Williams.' Oliver saluted.

'Captain now, Sergeant Grayson.' Luke saluted back, then grinned. 'I'm not keen on all this saluting lark on our days off, but there's a group of officers over there who would report us if we didn't.'

'You deserve your promotion, sir.' Oliver knew how courageous Williams was in battle. He made introductions for Jessica. 'Care for a drink, sir?'

'No, thank you. I've not long had one.' He held out his camera to Oliver. 'I bought this a few days ago. It's a Vest Pocket Kodak, and I'm as excited as a child at Christmas.'

Oliver studied the little camera and showed it

106

to Jessica. 'I've seen a few soldiers with these now. I wouldn't mind one myself.'

'Well, I doubt I'll ever come back here after the war, so I want to have photographs to remind me. Let me take a picture of you both.'

Sitting closer together, they allowed Luke to take their image. 'There, captured for all time.' He grinned. 'I'll take another, then you'll have one each.'

Oliver stood. 'Show me how to use it and I'll take one of you. You can send it to Tilly.'

'Do you think she'd want one?' Luke jested, but handed the camera over. 'Have you heard from her lately?'

Oliver shook his head. 'No.' He refrained from mentioning his lack of letter writing.

The sun was starting to set when they left the pyramids and headed back into the city.

Jessica rested her head against Oliver's shoulder and yawned. 'Captain Williams is a nice fellow.'

'Yes, he is. I like him.' Oliver cuddled her tighter to him and smiled when she closed her eyes. 'You're tired.' She nodded sleepily. He woke her when the car stopped outside of the nurses' quarters.

'I'm on night shift tomorrow,' Jessica said with another yawn. 'I'll need to sleep a bit in the afternoon, but if you'd like we can meet for breakfast in the morning, and then perhaps do a bit of shopping?'

'Sounds perfect.'

'Breakfast at the café we first went to?'

'I'll meet you there at nine.' Oliver kissed her,

holding her close, wanting her closer still.

As the car pulled away, he wondered how he had lived his life without her in it. After their initial awkward start, they had become closer than he could have hoped for. Jess made him smile and laugh. She pushed the war away for a while, and he was grateful.

★　★　★

In the morning, they had a delicious breakfast of shaksuka with baked eggs, pitta bread and coffee at the quaint café in the square, and recounted the fun of the day before. After many cups of coffee, they eventually waded through the noisy crowds at one of the markets. Spicy aromas and Arabic filled the air. Oliver bought Jess little gifts: a silk scarf, handkerchiefs, and gaudy trinkets from stall holders who he believed had robbed him. Laughingly, Jessica pulled him away as he tried and failed to haggle for the best prices.

'You're rubbish at haggling!' She hugged her parcels to her chest as they walked along.

'I've not had the practice!' he defended, counting his change which he was certain was short.

She laughed at him and went to the next stall that sold shoes. In a few minutes, she had successfully bought them both a pair of brown leather sandals for a very small amount of money.

Sceptical, Oliver glanced at them. 'When will I ever wear these?'

'Who cares? I got them for next to nothing. Send them home, it'll make Tilly laugh.' Jessica moved on to another stall and Oliver glared down at the sandals, knowing they'd never be posted home. To do that, he would have to share what his life was like here, and he wasn't prepared to do so.

★   ★   ★

Their remaining days together flew by too fast, and before Oliver was ready for it, he had to say goodbye to her. A sharp winter wind blew along the docks, and Jess held onto her hat to stop it from being wrenched off her head.

Oliver had got his men together, and they were grouped by the ramp ready to embark. He was leaving for England, then going to war again. The thought frustrated him. Why wasn't the war over already? Surely all this death must mean something? Once more they would all be in danger. He'd been thoughtless and naive when he'd suggested going to war that day by the river at home. He could never have believed what was ahead of them. He and the others had never known danger, not this kind of danger. At home, the biggest worry had been falling off a galloping horse, being gored by a bull, or bitten by a snake or a spider. However, in comparison to being shot at or blown up by a bomb, that seemed like child's play.

They had survived Gallipoli, but now they were headed for the main theatre of the entire war: the battlefields of France. The prospect of what they were to face, and saying goodbye to Jessica, rendered him speechless.

Jessica squeezed his hand. 'You're very quiet.'

'We ought to say goodbye now, and let you get out of this wind, but I don't want to part from you just yet.' He smiled down at her.

'I'm made of strong stuff. A bit of wind won't bother me.'

'Oliver!'

He turned to see Luke Williams edging through the crowd. 'You made it then, sir.'

'Yes, I wanted to see you all off.' Luke looked around for the others.

'They've already been called up on deck. I'll tell them you said goodbye.'

'I have photographs.' Luke pulled out a wad of them from the satchel he carried. 'There's two of you and Miss Hutton, one each, and I've also got these.' He showed them a few photographs he took of all the boys together outside of a café only a few days ago.

'They're great, sir. Thank you.'

'Keep them. I've got others. I've sent similar ones to your sister.'

Oliver gazed at the group photo. All the guys were smiling at the camera. 'She'll adore the one of us all together.'

'Anything to get into her good books, I'm hoping.' Luke laughed.

'Thank you for this.'

Luke shook hands with him. 'Best wishes to you, Sergeant.'

'I wish you were coming with us.' Oliver would genuinely miss him.

'The powers that be wish for the Light Horse to stay here for a bit to control the Suez and move into the desert properly.'

'Not an easy mission.'

'No, but we'll see it through.'

'Well, take care of yourself.'

'And you. Good luck. I'll see you when all this is over.' Luke doffed his hat to Jess and then disappeared into the crowd again.

Oliver took Jessica's hand and led her through the throng of soldiers to a more sheltered part of the dock. 'As soon as you arrive in England, let me know where you're staying. I'll do my best to get some time off to come and see you.'

'I will. I'll be right behind you. My ship leaves in four days.' She stood on tiptoe and kissed him on the lips. Oliver held her against him, feeling a rising heat in his body that only she could put out. He kissed her deeply until the ship's whistle blew, tearing them apart. 'Goodbye, Jess.'

'Until England.'

He nodded, and with one more sweet kiss he left her to join the mass of men ascending onto the decks. He found Gabe and the others standing at the rail.

Big Max patted him on the shoulder. 'You'll miss her.'

Nodding, Oliver searched the crowd on the dock below, looking for her.

'There she is.' Gabe pointed to Jessica, who waved fanatically. 'Everyone wave to my future sister-in-law.' He laughed, and Oliver punched him in the arm.

9

Blue Water Station. June 1916.

With the rain lashing down and the wind tossing
the branches in the trees, Tilly hurriedly closed
the barn door and, head down, ran up the road
towards the house.

'Matilda!' Grandmama yelled at her from the
veranda as Tilly skidded up the wet steps and
shook herself like a dog.

'Blazes, that storm crept up on me. I was so
busy in the barn I didn't realise the weather was
changing so rapidly.'

'Come inside; it's freezing out here.' Her
grandmama, wrapped in a blue cashmere shawl,
ushered her inside the house. 'What have you
been doing out there so long? You've been gone
hours. I was getting worried.'

Tilly shrugged off the long waterproof coat she
wore and gave it to Nelly, who hovered near the
door. 'I've been talking to Larry. The barn roof
has leaks, and some of the fences down in the
holding yard need replacing. Also, the road out
of the station is full of potholes. We need them
filling in, but there's no one to do it. If they get
any worse, it'll be impassable for the cars and
could damage the carts.' Tilly warmed her hands
in front of the fire and wiped the rain off her
hair, which hung raggedly about her face. Her
skirts were a little damp but would dry soon.

'Tim and Billy Woods have both handed in their notice; they're off to enlist in the morning. Tim was waiting for Billy to turn eighteen so they could join up together. Billy is eighteen today.'

'Mrs Woods will be upset.' Grandmama sighed, sitting on the sofa. 'Poor woman.'

'Yes, she said she knows now what we are going through. The worry that unites us all when loved ones are off to war.'

'Shall I ring for tea? I thought Connie might be over by now, but this storm has kept her at the cottage.'

Tilly looked out at the pouring rain. 'Do you want me to go and check on her? Where's Adelaide?'

'I've sent her home. She had another one of her headaches. She looked worn out.'

'She works too hard. She'll be with Aunt Connie, then. I'll leave them to it. Where's Grandpapa?'

'He's reading the newspaper in the study.'

Tilly glanced at the basket of wool beside the sofa. 'We must get on with knitting those socks for the boys. We need to get them sent before the winter starts in Europe; it'll take months to reach them.'

'They may be home by then.'

'I doubt it. The newspaper is full of battles that no one seems to clearly win.' Tilly sat in the wing-backed chair on the other side of the fireplace. She eyed the wool dubiously. Knitting wasn't one of her favourite tasks, and she was terrible at it, especially at making socks.

'Matilda . . . '

She looked over at her grandmama, who wore an anxious expression. 'What is it?'

'I need to talk to you about something that isn't pleasant.' Kitty patted the cushion next to her on the sofa. 'Sit with me for a moment.'

'What's wrong?' Tilly adjusted her skirts as she sat down beside her. 'Has something happened?'

'No, nothing at all; but we need to talk about the possibility of your brothers . . . not returning home. Decisions have to be made, now that Adam has gone.' Her green eyes clouded with sadness.

Tilly recoiled. 'No, Grandmama, I don't wish to talk about it.'

'You'll do as you're told, Princess.' Grandpapa stood in the doorway, leaning on the polished wooden cane he used now. 'This is important, and you must listen. I've been putting it off long enough. This war is dragging on, and who knows when it will end and what the result will be.'

'Very well.' Tilly waited as her grandpapa gently lowered himself into the chair by the fire. She hated seeing him so frail.

He prodded the fire with the iron poker, then gazed across at her. 'Tomorrow Mr Hornby, my solicitor, is arriving from Sydney to help me rewrite my will.'

Tilly shivered at the mention of a will. 'Rewrite it? Why?'

'There are changes to be made because of your father's death. Now listen carefully. If Oliver and Gabe don't return home, or if they're so incapacitated that they're unable to run Blue Water, then the whole property is yours.'

114

Tilly clenched her fists at the enormity of the honour, her heart thudding. 'Mine?'

'Yes.' Grandpapa nodded seriously.

'What about Uncle David?'

'He has his property at Armidale and has no need or wish to live here at Blue Water. He's happy with what he has built himself, just as I was when I built this place. His station is of such a size that he couldn't handle both places.'

'But he's your only surviving son.' Tilly frowned. 'You've discussed this with him?'

'Yes, after your father's funeral and recently in letters. David will receive some stocks and shares, and a few of the Sydney businesses, but he doesn't want Blue Water. He always knew it would never be his, but Adam's, and he feels Adam's children should inherit.' Grandpapa ran his fingers over the end of the chair's armrests. 'Now, of course we want the boys home safe, but we have no say in what happens over there and if they are . . . killed . . . we need to make provisions so that you inherit the property. The businesses in Sydney will be split between you and David.'

'What of Freddie and Patrick?'

'They'll inherit the station at Armidale and all of David's shares, but also receive money from me as well.'

'I don't know what to say.' Tilly glanced at her grandmama. 'Do you agree?'

'Naturally I agree.' Grandmama sat straighter and frowned as if she was offended. 'Why wouldn't I? Just because you're female doesn't mean you can't be a successful land holder. If the boys do come home, well, Oliver is the eldest and Blue Water will be his. However, when your grandpapa and I die, both you and Gabe will receive the parcels of land we own in Grafton and a share in the businesses in Sydney along with David. Should only Gabe return, then Blue Water is his and all the land in Grafton is yours. Do you understand, my dear?'

'Yes, Grandmama.' Tilly felt the tears well and her throat grew tight. 'Thank you, both of you.'

Miles sat forward, his eyes full of admiration. 'You deserve it. You've been running this place since your father . . . left us.' He coughed back his emotion.

Tilly knew he still couldn't speak of his son's death even after all of these months.

He gathered himself and continued, 'You've proven to me how strong and capable you are. You're very much like your grandmama. Every day you remind me of her when we first met. She gave me hell.' He smiled lovingly at Kitty.

'It's a precious and very generous gift you have bestowed on me. Thank you both.' Tilly squeezed her grandmama's hand. 'I won't not let you down, but I do hope with all my heart that my brothers return.'

Miles coughed again. 'Kitty, my love, ring for some coffee — and cake. I fancy some cake.'

Tilly crossed to her grandpapa and hugged him tight, alarmed at how thin he'd become. 'I love you.'

'And I you, Princess.'

★   ★   ★

116

The following morning, with misty rain still lingering outside, Tilly and Adelaide were sorting through tax receipts in the study when the postman arrived. He brought the cold winter weather in with him.

'Would you like a hot drink, Mr Rogers?' Adelaide inquired, taking from him the large mail bag. 'Mrs Bramwell has cooked some lovely lemon curd tarts this morning.'

'A cup of tea is exactly what I need this cold morning, Miss Spencer, thank you, but . . . ' He looked at the bag nervously. 'Reverend Pickering, the new man of the cloth from Grafton, is here.'

Tilly's hands froze where she sat behind the desk. 'Why is he here?' Though she knew the answer. Someone at Blue Water had received a military brown envelope. The government felt that a member of the church should offer to deliver such envelopes in regional country areas where the military couldn't always send someone. She stared at Adelaide, who blinked rapidly, showing her fear.

'He's to see Mrs Johnson.' Mr Rogers twisted his damp hat between his fingers. 'The reverend has many calls to make today. It's easy and quicker for him to come out here with me in my truck, and I'll take him back. Saves bringing out his little horse and buggy in this weather, lessens the chance of getting bogged on the muddy roads . . . ' He flushed at his ramblings.

'Eric Johnson . . . he's dead?' Tilly murmured, relieved it wasn't one of the boys, yet suddenly feeling guilty for it.

'I believe so. The reverend doesn't attend if it's just an injury.'

'Poor Eric.' Tilly had liked Eric; always a funny joke would pass between them in the stockyards. She looked at Adelaide. 'He wasn't very old. I remember little Hattie Johnson baking him a cake for his birthday last year, a week before enlisted. He was twenty-eight, I think.'

'Poor Glenys. She'll be heartbroken. The children will be too young to understand.' Adelaide shook her head sadly.

Tilly stood and gave her arm a light squeeze. 'How frightening. This is the first time Blue Water has been personally touched by the war.'

'Let's hope it is the last,' Adelaide whispered.

'I'll go with the reverend. Glenys might feel better having another woman there.' Tilly walked to the door. 'Is Reverend Pickering waiting in the truck?'

Mr Rogers shook his head. 'No, Miss Grayson. He's on the veranda.'

Ignoring the mail, Adelaide joined her at the door while Mr Rogers left to visit the kitchen, as he'd done many times previously over the years. 'You go talk to the reverend, and I'll tell Aunt Kitty and Mother.'

Straightening her hair and the cuffs on her long-sleeved white blouse, Tilly crossed the hall and took a shawl from the closet. Wrapping it around her, she went through the front door onto the veranda. 'Reverend Pickering, I'm Miss Matilda Grayson. It is a shame to meet you for the first time on such a sad occasion. Please, won't you come inside? It's awfully chilly out here today.'

'Miss Grayson, it is indeed inclement weather.' The reverend, a tall thin man dressed all in black, shook her hand. 'Would you kindly ask someone to show me to the workers' cottages, please? I'd rather not delay in delivering my news.'

'I'll show you.' Tilly drew the shawl over her head and led the way down the front steps.

The misty rain lingered, coating everything in fine droplets like silver cobwebs. Tilly led him across the drive and down a dirt road, past empty paddocks and on to the working heart of the station.

'Did the army take all your horses, Miss Grayson?'

'A good deal, yes. We were allowed to keep the older ones for farm use, but my grandpapa bought a new tractor for the ploughing, which is much easier and faster. We did give up most stock horses though, which is a deep sadness.'

'In times like these we cannot be selfish,' he touted.

They walked on past differently sized buildings that lined each side of the road: feed barns, the blacksmith, storage barns, the saddlery, carriage barns. The cool dismal day seemed to highlight the quietness.

Tilly shivered with cold. 'It saddens me how quiet it is here now. Normally this area is a hive of industry, but our workforce has diminished to only a handful of people.'

'The war has affected all aspects of the country. You're not alone in that.' The reverend gazed about him. 'You don't have a church on the property?'

'No, we don't.' Tilly blushed. 'My grandpapa isn't a believer and has raised his family as such.'

The reverend missed his step in surprise. 'Not a believer? At all?'

'No. My grandfather is a Darwinian.' She grinned, secretly pleased she had shocked him.

'He has a duty to his employees and their families on this station to provide a place to worship, surely?'

'They can travel into Grafton on Sundays if they wish to attend church, but my grandfather wasn't going to build one. He says if the people wanted to pray, then their so-called God should be able to hear them no matter where they were.'

'That's outrageous!' he gasped.

'Is it not true though? Can you only pray in a church?' she asked innocently.

His mouth gaped open and shut like a stranded fish. 'God listens always, in any situation or place.'

'Then we don't need to build a church then, do we?' she said smugly.

He grunted. 'I read that all weddings took place here at Blue Water with my predecessor. Where did they take place?'

'That's true. Behind the house we have extensive and very fine gardens. It's traditional at Blue Water to be married there. Family and workers alike.'

'I also read in the notes left by my predecessor that you have a graveyard?'

'We do, yes, up on the hill behind the house.

120

It's peaceful and beautiful, with a wonderful view of the river in the distance.' She stepped around a puddle.

'But no church . . . '

Tilly's anger rose, but she remained silent and kept walking. She wasn't going to explain her family's decisions to this man.

After the buildings, the road widened to the stock holding yards, but Tilly turned left and, following another smaller dirt road, headed for the little school hut and the workers' cottages on either side.

'Glenys's cottage is the fourth along, on the left,' Tilly said, suddenly remembering the task ahead of her. 'The one with the large gum tree out the front. Usually the children are out playing, but the weather must have kept them indoors today. They'll be driving their mothers wild, I would imagine.' She was babbling and had no idea why. She'd never had to do this before, be present while someone was told their loved one had been killed.

She walked up the narrow path and knocked on the door. From inside she heard a child laugh, and she cringed.

When the door opened, Tilly smiled at Glenys, who stood wearing a long black skirt and a white apron, a dusting of flour on her blouse and face. The other woman's eyes stared past her and directly at the reverend, and all light went from them.

'Can we come in, Glenys?' Tilly asked gently.

★ ★ ★

Much later, as night quietened the animals outside, Tilly sat in the parlour curled up on the settee next to the fire. She held a letter from Luke but hadn't opened it yet. The silence of the room was broken only by the shifting of the burning logs in the grate. She still hadn't become used to the house being so silent in an evening. The missing presence of her father and Oliver and Gabe was large, almost physical. Their personalities left a gaping hole in every room.

She missed them.

She missed her father's steady hand.

She missed Gabe's laughter, his silly ways and his closeness. Whenever she was feeling low, Gabe would be there to take her hand and make her laugh.

And she missed Oliver. She missed the way his eyes would secretly laugh at her; the way he shook his head at her foolish antics. She was devoted to both her brothers, but Oliver was ever there in her life. He had stood beside her, talked to her and listened to her. He could calm her, support her and encourage her. With him she could do anything. Now all that was gone. He didn't even write to her. It was like he'd died when he had sailed away. He'd hurt her, and she didn't know if she could ever forgive him for abandoning her.

'You appear tired, my dear,' her grandmama said, coming into the room. She still wore the deep purple velvet gown she'd worn at dinner.

'I am, a little.' She gave a small smile. 'Have Grandpapa and Mr Hornby retired for the night?'

'Yes, they have, and so shall I in a minute. But first I wanted to make sure you were all right.'

'It was a tough day.' She uncurled her legs so her grandmama could sit beside her.

'You did so well, dearest. That wouldn't have been easy, giving such comfort to Glenys today.'

'It wasn't. I kept thinking of Papa, and of the boys.' Tilly yawned; the emotion of the day had drained her. 'Glenys was awfully brave, Grandmama. She sat there at her kitchen table and tried to offer us a cup of tea, even though her hands shook so bad.' Tilly got up and stood in front of the fireplace. 'Of course I made the tea for her and kept the children busy. I stuffed them full of currant cake that I found in a tin.'

'Good idea.'

'And Reverend Pickering, who I am telling you now I do not like at all, gave her a silly speech about Eric being with God now. What proof does he have of that?' she demanded to know. 'Or that such a god even exists? I wanted to show him the door, truly I did, for God isn't going to keep her company tonight like Eric would have. God isn't going to provide for her children like Eric did!'

'Yes, I know, dear — and do lower your voice, or your grandpapa might hear and will get upset. You know he doesn't like talking about religion. It fires him up and it's not good for his blood pressure.' Grandmama wiped a hand wearily over her face. 'When Connie and I visited Glenys this evening before dinner, she told us she wants to go live with her sister in Brisbane. She'll be able to get work there, and her sister can watch the children. Connie and I and the other wives are going to help her pack up the cottage tomorrow. Your grandpapa is giving her money, enough to tide her over for a good while until she's on her feet.'

'Oh, you never said this at dinner.'

'Well you and your grandpapa were busy entertaining Mr Hornby. And I like to keep dinner talk away from death and war if possible.' Grandmama grimaced. She picked up Luke's envelope from the sofa where Tilly had placed it. 'He's a very regular writer, isn't he, this Luke Williams?'

Tilly gazed at the letter. 'Yes. I've grown so used to his letters. I feel I know him very well. Yet that seems so strange to say, because I don't know him really. I might know his thoughts, but I don't know him as a physical person. Does that make sense?'

'Of course it does. You haven't been in his company enough to know certain things which would make him a whole man. However, you must invite him here, after the war, so we can all meet him. Then, perhaps, you'll find the whole man is worth knowing.'

'I will.'

'Do you write to him a lot?'

'I've started to, though not as much as I should. There are so many to write to — all the boys, Joanie and Luke; that's ten people. It can be exhausting after I've been working all day on the station's books, or out riding to check on the stock.'

'Yes, I understand, but do the best you can.

Those boys need all the small comforts we can offer them.' Her grandmama got slowly to her feet. 'I'm away to bed.' She kissed Tilly's cheek. 'See you in the morning, my dear.'

'Good night, Grandmama.'

Left alone again, Tilly curled up on the settee once more and opened Luke's letter, and was shocked when photos fell onto her lap. She gathered them up and stared at the group photo of all her boys. They were either standing or sitting and all smiling at the camera as though they were doing it just for her. Gabe had his hand up as though waving to her, and Oliver stood at the end, arms folded but smiling. Freddie, grinning, had his hands around Patrick's neck in mock throttle, while Samuel and Johnny were leaning against each other's backs like in some staged comedy show. Big Max towered over them all, standing at the back, and dear Drew sat on a crate with a cup in his hand.

Laughing, they were all having a joke, and she wasn't there to share it. Pain tightened her chest, pain and anger. How could they be smiling and laughing without her? She couldn't! She didn't spend her days laughing and joking. She missed them too much! She couldn't live her life properly without them, but they seemed as though they didn't miss her at all.

Luke had written on the back, 'Your boys send their love. Cairo, Egypt. 1916.' Angry tears welled and spilt over her lashes. She threw the photo to the side.

The next photo was of Oliver and a woman dressed in a nurse's uniform, sitting near the

Sphinx, obviously sharing a picnic. On the back was written, 'Egypt. 1916. Sergeant Oliver Grayson and Nurse Jessica Hutton.'

'Jessica Hutton,' Tilly whispered. She studied the woman having lunch with her brother and wondered about her. She was pretty, with a cheeky smile that Tilly liked; but the hurt remained. They were all together, sharing everything, and even this Nurse Hutton was a part of it!

'What about me?' Tilly snapped, biting her bottom lip to stop herself from crying. Oliver was spending time with the nurse when he couldn't even be bothered to write on a card to her, his own sister!

She felt betrayed and unwanted and forgotten by them all. Blinking back the tears, she sniffed and sat up straighter. Damn them all. She'd show them! She'd show them all that she didn't need them. If they could be happy without her, then she'd be the same. To hell with them!

A knot of anger and frustration built in her chest. No more. No more would she mope around the station thinking about those lot. She'd create a life for herself.

The next photo was of Luke. It was the first time she'd seen him since he'd left in nineteen fifteen. It shocked her how much she had forgotten what he'd looked like. His image had grown distant and blurred. His smile was cocky and his eyes looked directly at the camera, at her.

On the back he'd written, 'With love. Egypt. 1916.'

She felt a tingling glow ripple across her skin

126

as she gazed at his handsome face. Now she had his photograph, she could easily remember his direct blue eyes, the blackness of his hair. Smiling, she traced his jaw with a fingertip. Quickly, she opened the pages of his letter.

My Dear Matilda,

Please forgive the state of my writing. During a small skirmish with the enemy a few days ago, I was shot in the hand, just a nick really, but it makes holding a pen a trifle difficult.

The Suez Canal is under our control, and now our priority is to gain territory in the desert. The Light Horse is remaining here in the East. I am sad at that, as I'd like to have gone to France with the others, but we must do as we are told. Though some men have resigned from the Light Horse and rejoined in the infantry so as not to miss out on being in France. I did think about it, but after a lengthy discussion with Monty — yes, I do talk to Monty — I decided to remain with the Light Horse. Besides, our hats are so much jauntier!

Monty is doing splendidly. If the rumours are true, both she and I are to be tested soon. The desert is no picnic, apparently. If that is so, my letters to you will become sparse, I should think. I have no idea what is ahead of us.

I was out walking the other evening, when the weather was cool and the stars littered the sky. *It was remarkably beautiful, and I had a longing to share it with you. One day perhaps we will, if the fates allow. I think of you constantly. The image I have of you standing on the dock in Sydney will stay with me forever. When we meet again, will you wear that white dress with pink flowers, please?*

I hope you take great pleasure in the photographs I've sent you. My new little camera is so entertaining. I spend hours taking photographs and then getting them developed. I've found an Egyptian man at the local market who will take my film and develop it for me in record time. I may have become obsessed with this new hobby.

I must sign off now, as my hand is paining me. I'm sure seeing the boys' photograph will fill you with boundless joy. Please don't use the photograph of me as a dartboard!

With deepest regards,
Captain Luke Williams.
As you can see, I have been promoted! Apparently I'm rather good at this army stuff.

She smiled at the line about the dartboard, and felt ridiculously proud that he had been promoted. She quickly put the screen around the fireplace and turned off the lights.

In the shadowy light, she slipped into the dining room. The table was set up for breakfast in the morning. She put the photograph of

128

Oliver and his nurse on the table in front of her grandmama's chair, then placed the group photograph in front of her grandpapa's chair. It would please her grandparents to see those. Her grandmama would take them to show Aunt Connie and Adelaide.

She took a last look in the half-light at the group photograph and resolutely hardened her heart to the lingering hurt. It was time she started to live her own life.

Once in her bedroom, she sat at her dressing table and propped up the photograph of Luke against her jewellery box. She pulled out clean paper from the drawer and began to write.

Dear Luke,

I cannot thank you enough for the photographs — all of them. I know they will be much admired by my family, as it has been too long since we've seen their dear faces.

I was most interested to see Oliver with a woman. Is she his friend? He rarely writes to anyone here, so we know nothing of what is happening with him. Gabe writes regularly, as do the other boys. We know they are in France now, after training in England.

She paused and tapped her pen against her chin, staring at his face. A sudden thought came to her, and she continued writing.

I have decided to purchase a camera like

you have done. I will take photos of Blue Water and send them to you. One of myself, too. That way you can see what I write to you about.

Can you send me a photograph of Monty? I hear so much about this horse from you that I feel I should see her.

The war hit us today at Blue Water. For the first time it touched us personally, and not just something we read about in the newspapers. One of our stockmen was killed in action in France, in a battle at the Somme. I was with the widow when the news was given to her, and I can say quite plainly it is an experience I never want to undergo again. Could we be that fortunate? I felt useless in giving Glenys any comfort. How could I understand her pain? She has lost her husband, the man she loved, who she was meant to grow old with, her children's father.

I have lost my parents — my mother's death is a distant memory as I was a little girl when it happened, and my father's death was a shock and a great loss to me; but to lose your husband, the man you love above all others? I cannot imagine the pain she must be suffering. A young widow with two small children to bring up alone. How dreadfully sad and frightening for her.

I do hope it is the last time that the reverend comes here on such a mission. (Actually, I hope to never seen him again. Pompous man!)

I imagine your experiences of this war will be very different to that of the others. You are desert bound and they are in Europe, walking the fields of France. While I sit in the comfort of my home and worry constantly.

The women of Blue Water are knitting socks and making up parcels to send to the boys. I have added your name to the list. Be prepared to accept holey socks, along with other desirables, for I cannot knit very well, much to my grandmama's disappointment.

Well done on your promotion, Captain Williams. I am very impressed and not surprised you have done so well. You seem to me as someone who would hate to fail at anything.

I have not worn that white dress with the pink flowers since that day in Sydney, and nor shall I, until you return home.

Take care of yourself, Luke.

Best wishes,

Matilda.

She reread the letter and quickly sealed it in an envelope. Writing to Luke always made her a little nervous, as though she mustn't reveal too much too him. She didn't understand herself. She didn't understand him. They were two people writing to each other, getting to know one another through words on a page.

A part of her wished he had never written to her, never made her look forward to his letters arriving. She had enough to worry about without another person to invade her thoughts. He'd made her feel concern for him, and it annoyed her.

What if he came back from the war and went off to his own life with not a backward glance in her direction? Or what if he came back and expected something from her that she couldn't give? It was all too maddening!

She quickly undressed and donned her nightgown, her head buzzing with *what ifs*.

After washing her face and cleaning her teeth, she climbed into bed and turned off the lamp. In the shadow-dappled grey light, she stared at the ceiling, recalling Luke's cheeky dimpled grin.

What if he never returned at all?

10

Pozieres, France. July 1916.

Oliver squelched through the mud, inches deep at the bottom of the trench. His ears rang with the constant pounding of the field cannons shelling the village ahead of him. The ground vibrated with every explosion. A pall of smoke hung low in the night sky like a fog, accumulated from thousands of exploded bombs and mixed with the dust of the village's buildings as they were smashed beyond recognition.

'Here.' Gabe thrust a cup of warm tea into Oliver's hands as he reached their section of the trench.

'Thanks.' In the dim moonlight, he looked at each man, their faces drawn and nervous. Snubs of candles stuck into the trench walls gave a wavering light, as though ghosts walked amongst them.

'We'll do all right, lads.' He spoke with more confidence than he thought. As a sergeant, he was now second in command of a platoon. More men, more responsibility.

Captain Markham joined them from the opposite end of the trench. He held a wad of official papers in one hand and with the other he stroked his moustache, a habit Oliver had noted he engaged in before they went into battle. 'Right, men. You know your objective. We are going in quietly, to surprise the first trench. Our barrage will keep at them, and we need to slink through the darkness to get as close to their trench as we can without them knowing we're there. Once the barrage stops, we rush the trench. Understand?' He waited for the information to sink in. 'We must take the village. The enemy is to be pushed back as far as we can make them. Stay together. Watch for German hideouts in the village, and snipers. If we can get beyond the village to their northern line of trenches, then that's what we'll do. It's a big task and I believe we can do it. We've got help from the British Tommies, but the attack is ours. Good luck, men.'

When Markham had gone to speak to the soldiers further along the trench, Oliver visually checked his own men. Patrick and Freddie stood together, smoking a cigarette. Big Max stood next to them, checking his rifle, while Johnny and Samuel were chatting quietly. The new recruits, Jones and Olsen, were on lookout, leaning against the sandbagged walls, their eyes wide in young faces. A sombre atmosphere surrounded them.

Oliver looked at his watch. 00:26.

'Time?' Gabe asked.

'Soon.'

'Why are we bloody fighting in the middle of the night? It's stupid.'

'It's so they can't see us.'

'If they can't see us, then we certainly can't see them hiding in their trenches.' Gabe swore under his breath.

'I don't make the rules, Gabe.'

'We follow like sheep. Who thinks up these bloody battles, anyway? Some general in London somewhere safe, smoking fat cigars?'

'Stop it!' Oliver growled low. 'It doesn't help matters, you bleating like a child. Think of the others. I rely on you to keep the morale up.'

'It's hard to joke when you're heading into a slaughter.' Gabe turned away but then turned back just as quickly. He squeezed Oliver's arm. 'Not tonight.'

'What?' Oliver frowned, not following. 'What the hell are you on about?'

'Not tonight. It's not our time to go tonight.'

'Gabe — '

A whisper carried down the trench to get ready. Oliver nodded to Gabe, and they unslung their rifles and held them against their chests. All the men in the trench stood poised to go over the top.

Oliver looked at his watch. 00:30. 'Let's go,' he whispered down the line, his stomach in knots. 'Keep low.'

In the mad scramble over the top of the trench, Oliver encouraged the lads to be quiet. Hunched over, he weaved and dodged across no man's land as the ground shook beneath his feet. Ahead, the continued shelling lit up the night's sky in gold and white, highlighting the black line of the enemy's trench they were to attack.

Blood pumping, he tripped over the barbed wire before he saw it. Cursing, he landed on his knees. Wire cutters were in his belt, and for a moment he was all fingers and thumbs trying to extract them.

'Oliver!'

He jerked at the sound of Gabe's muffled voice. He tugged himself free of the wire, his uniform tearing at the struggle. He crawled further along the roll of barbed wire.

'I'm caught,' Gabe whispered. 'I can't find my cutters.'

'Lie still.' Oliver pinned him down in the dirt and climbed over him to the wire. The air grew quiet as the barrage stopped its pounding of the village.

'Shit.' Frantic at being caught out in the open, Oliver hurriedly cut the barbed wire, his fingers bleeding from the little spikes.

Once Gabe was released, Oliver pulled the wire roll away, creating a gap. He called to other men to come this way. A fireball exploded at the edge of the village. The sudden light gave Oliver and the men a glimpse of the hell before them.

Running as fast as he ever had in his life, Oliver spurred the others on. In twenty yards, they jumped or fell into the Germans' trench and created havoc.

Oliver fired compulsively at anything that moved. One German raised his gun to shoot him, but Gabe shot him first.

'Clear the trench,' Oliver yelled at his men. 'Check the dugouts.'

With cries of enthusiasm, the men shot the enemy or fought in hand-to-hand combat with bayonets.

A German came out of a dugout and stabbed

at Oliver with his bayonet. Oliver twisted to the right just clear of the blade, and without thought punched him in the face. The soldier reared back. Oliver aimed and shot him.

'Grenade going in!' Gabe shouted, pulling back the curtain on the dugout.

Oliver stood aside to let Freddie throw a grenade in. The explosion deafened them for a moment, but they had no time to think about it.

Bodies littered the duckboards as they advanced down the length of the trench. In a rush, they cleared their section, and with another shout, Oliver urged them over the top again, to head for the village. Bullets zipped past him or thudded into the ground by his feet. He felt a sharp sting on his neck, but kept running. In the dark they stumbled on the uneven ground, falling into craters made by shells. Oliver flinched each time a bullet hit the ground near him.

Reaching the back gardens of the village, he indicated to his men to kneel and take cover behind fences or walls. Gun shots came from the damaged cottages, eerie in the darkness.

'Can't see a damn thing,' Patrick complained from his spot near a crumbled wall.

'Advance. Stick to any cover you can find.' Oliver rushed forward to the side of a barn with no roof. Inching along its stone wall, he waited for the others to join him, and then they hurried through an open gate and into a cobbled courtyard. The farmhouse stood bleak and ruined to the right. To the left remained the rear walls of a cottage, the front of it collapsed into a large shell hole.

A shot rang out.

'Sniper!' Gabe yelled, his rifle aimed at a window in the farmhouse's loft, the only part of the building not blown to bits.

'Bomb it,' Oliver ordered.

They dashed forward, grenades in their hands, and as a group they all threw them up at the loft space. The blasts echoed in the courtyard.

'Take cover!' Oliver ran back against a small broken wall. He waited to see if the sniper shot at them again; but the loft, smoking heavily, started to disintegrate, as the destroyed walls could no longer hold it up. With an almighty crash, the rest of the farmhouse collapsed into rubble.

'Let's go.' Oliver, knowing the sniper would be dead, led the men across the main road to the other side. There was nothing left of the village to show what it once was. Not a single building remained intact. No trees, no signs of life; just desolate debris, blackened stumps and waste ground.

Climbing through rubble and dodging shell holes, Oliver led the men onwards across crater-strewn fields. Ahead, bombing continued on the German trenches. The noise deafened them. The ground shook. Dirt rained down on them like hail, pinging on their tin helmets.

'Sergeant!' Markham and several men advanced on them from the right, appearing out of the smoky gloom like apparitions. 'You made it then, Grayson,' he called over the booming noise of the shelling. 'Well done.'

'Sir.' Oliver paused and turned to his men. 'Take cover,' he ordered, and dropped low into a shell crater with the captain. 'Are we to remain here, sir?'

'No, Sergeant. We're to continue, and take more trenches.'

Oliver nodded, resigned to his fate. He drank thirstily from his flask.

'We take the first of these northern trenches and advance as far as our barrage.' Markham ducked as a shell burst not far from them. For a moment the black night lit up golden. 'I'd like that first trench taken before dawn.'

'Yes, sir.'

'However, the Huns know we're here. We should expect heavy bombing to come from them. We need to hold this village until our relief arrives.'

'Yes, sir.'

'Right, let's do this.'

Crawling up the side of the crater, Oliver called to the men to advance.

Over ground chewed up by bombing, strewn with barbed wire and dead bodies, he guided and encouraged them onwards. Yet before they'd gone thirty yards, they were in the Germans' sights, and a bombardment of bullets and machine-gun fire descended upon them.

Yelling at his men to take cover once again, Oliver stumbled in the dark and down a hole. On one knee, he took aim. Their returning gunfire added to the chaos of the falling bombs. The countryside lit up with bursts of explosion as the ridge where the Germans were entrenched felt the full power of the allied cannons, and in return the Germans shelled them back.

Gabe scrabbled into Oliver's crater. 'We can't stay here, Oliver. We're too exposed in this field with this wind.'

Oliver peered ahead, noting that the rising wind was shifting the smoke haze away from them and giving both sides a clear view. 'Get the men moving. We take the trench tonight!'

Oliver raced on, knowing Gabe and the others would follow him. Noise clouded his mind. Everywhere men were falling. Screams and shouts of the injured were ignored as they raced to their objective.

Landing in the trench with a bone-jarring thump, Oliver had no time to take stock of his surroundings as German soldiers rushed to overwhelm him. Fighting hand to hand in the confined space of the walled trench, he fought methodically, bayonetting or shooting any enemy he saw. With one section of the trench clear, he paused for a moment to catch his breath, his eyes frantically searching the darkness for Gabe and the others.

'You bloody idiot!' Gabe rounded a corner, chest heaving. 'I could have shot you. Why must you go off by yourself? It's dumb and dangerous! Stop being a bloody hero!'

'Casualties?' Oliver panted.

'Peterson got one in the head. Wilkins is out there, dropped when we left the village. Campbell got knocked in the gut. He's bad. One or two more are missing, but I don't know for sure. I think Johnny copped a scratch on his arm. There's plenty with wounds of some sort. It might be easier to ask who's left whole.'

'Sergeant!' Markham jumped down into the trench. 'Get your men to wait here. We need reinforcements before we go any further. Understood?'

'Yes, sir.' Oliver ducked as a shell hit further up the trench and showered them with stones and mud. He tasted dirt in his mouth. 'What about the wounded?'

'Sort them out as best you can. We're stuck here, pinned down by the German cannons. Take a roll call if possible.' Markham thumbed in the direction of the destroyed village. 'Their cannons have got range on the village; they'll find us soon enough. I'm trying to get a line established back to headquarters. I need a runner, though; the previous one is gone.'

In the waning moonlight, Oliver looked at the weary faces of his men. Most had fallen down where they'd stopped.

'I'll go, sir.' Patrick edged past Gabe and the others.

'Good man.' Markham scribbled down a note and thrust the paper at him. 'Wait for a reply. As quick as you can, soldier.'

Oliver frowned, not liking that Patrick had volunteered. He'd told them back in Gallipoli to never volunteer for anything, as it was usually an ugly task that had to be done. He grabbed his cousin's arm. 'Keep your head down.'

They watched Patrick scramble up the side of the trench and disappear into the night.

'Rest your men, Sergeant, but post lookouts.' Markham glanced about the trench. 'Keep your eye out for any information the enemy might have left behind. I'll be further along, in the next bend.'

'Yes, sir.' Oliver turned away. 'We're here for a bit, men, so let's clean the place up. I want sentries every five yards. Bodies over the top.'

With their last remaining strength, they lifted the dead bodies of the Germans up and over the trench, which built the walls higher and gave more protection. Oliver organised an area for his wounded, taking an interest in Johnny's arm, which had the scraping of a bullet from wrist to elbow. 'Can you move it?' he asked while a medic bandaged it.

'Aye, I'll be fine.' Johnny winked and lit a cigarette. 'I'll get it cleaned up properly when we're out of the line.'

'Lord knows when that will be,' Samuel said, sitting down beside Johnny and offering him some water. He looked at Oliver. 'Are we here for the night?'

Oliver nodded. 'I should think we'll raid the next trench at dawn, so get some sleep.' They flinched as another shell exploded and screams came from further down the trench.

'We're sitting ducks here.' Samuel shook his head, disgusted.

'We need reinforcements to continue the advancement.'

'Well, where are they?' Johnny asked. 'We can't take that ridge by ourselves.'

'Want to make a bet?' Oliver said sarcastically,

wiping the dirt off his face with a handkerchief. 'Sleep now.'

He left them and, hunched over, made his way down the trench, checking on the men he passed, most of whom were asleep despite the constant shelling. He reached Gabe and Freddie, both of whom were standing up on the fire-step on lookout duties. 'Any movement?'

Gabe glanced down at him. 'Can't see a thing in this haze. The wind has changed direction and it's blowing towards us now.'

'Get some sleep, Ollie,' Freddie said, without taking his eyes off the smudged line of the ridge they were meant to take. 'We'll wake you if there's anything.'

'Wake me in an hour.' Sighing, and suddenly feeling as old as time, Oliver sat down on the opposite step and leaned back against the sandbagged wall. He could do nothing until they got their orders. He hoped Patrick had made it to safety. His gut growled with sudden hunger, but he couldn't stomach another tin of bully beef right now.

Closing his eyes, he thought of Jessica. If he had the energy, he'd have read her latest letter again that he carried in his pocket, but it felt like too much effort right at that moment. Not that he needed to read it to remember the words, for they were imprinted in his memory. He smiled sleepily, recalling the sunny spring day in London when he had gone to the hospital she worked at and taken her out for lunch.

One day. That was all they had been able to steal from the war. One day. He had only managed to get two days' leave after weeks of training on Salisbury Plain, and she had succeeded in changing her shift at the hospital to meet him in Piccadilly. They'd gone to a fancy restaurant and eaten a wonderful lunch before walking around Green Park and visiting the gates of Buckingham Palace. Later they'd gone to a show in Leicester Square before saying goodbye at the entrance to the nurses' lodging where Jessica lived. It had been a perfect day, and Jessica was as lovely as ever, and when he kissed her . . .

'Oliver! Jesus, man, wake up.' Gabe shook him roughly awake.

For a moment he didn't know where he was. Blinking in the pale light of dawn, he scrambled to his feet, instantly alert. 'What's happening?'

'Captain Markham is coming. Patrick is back.'

Oliver, his mouth dry, took a quick swig of water from his flask and threw a bit into his face to freshen himself up.

'Sergeant Grayson, have the men stand ready,' Markham instructed, smoothing his moustache. 'A British regiment is in place to the east of us. We attack in five minutes.'

'Yes, sir.' Oliver issued the order to be passed down the line. 'Check your ammunition.' He patted Patrick on the back. 'Stay at the back. You must be done in.'

'I'm all right.' Patrick's haggard face belied the statement.

Oliver checked his watched and turned to Gabe with a scowl. 'I told you to wake me in one hour, not three!'

Shrugging, Gabe grinned. 'What are you going to do about it? Put me on a charge?'

'I'll knock your block off one of these days, brother.'

'I'd like to see you try!' Gabe laughed at him.

Making their final preparations to attack and quickly eating their rations of bully beef, the order to go over the top came quicker than expected. Oliver led the charge again, this time in the pink morning light. Gunfire started the moment they cleared the trench. The objective was the ridge ahead, but between them and that high ground were entrenched and well-armed Germans intent on mowing them down with their machine guns.

Like a repeat of the night before, the ground they gained was to a cost of many lives. Oliver ducked and weaved, yelling commands until his voice grew hoarse.

After an hour of little progress, they found the energy for another push. The landscape was pock-marked with craters. A breeze lifted the smoke, exposing the broken line of men attacking. Biplanes from both sides flew overhead, fighting their own battle as well as dropping bombs.

Throwing himself into a hole, Oliver gasped, his throat raw, his limbs heavy from running with his kit on his back. He jerked as someone landed beside him. Olsen.

'Keep going, Olsen,' Oliver urged, but the boy didn't move.

Shaking him, Oliver rolled him over, ready to shout at him, when he saw the boy no longer had

145

the right side of his face. Blood, muscles, shattered skull and brain matter glistened in the morning light.

Retching, Oliver stumbled up the side of the hole and ran on, not caring if he was shot. He kept running, blind to the machine guns in front of him, to the men falling down beside him. He shot on the run, tripping and stumbling on the uneven ground.

He fell into a trench and shot wildly. The empty click of his pistol brought him out of his stupor. Ammo, he needed ammo. Panic tightened his chest. German voices came from further down the trench.

Scrambling, frantic, Oliver found a dead German's gun and started firing, using a wooden support post to hide behind. The voices stopped.

Slumped against the sandbags, he watched in a daze as his men jumped down into the trench. Someone was firing and he tried to focus on who, but a flask of water was thrust into his hand and he drank instead.

'Are you on a death wish or something, Sergeant?' Captain Markham asked, coming to sit beside him.

'No, sir.'

'Well that was insane, charging out in front like that. You're either stupid or very brave, I'm not sure which yet.'

'Olsen is dead, sir. He was no more than a boy, just seventeen.'

Markham sighed. 'We're very light in numbers, Grayson. I'll need a report on who's left.' He got to his feet again. 'We'll secure this trench and wait for relief. Ammunition is running very low. Have the wounded sent back, and it's just rations until communications get established and they send the food wagons up to us.'

'Yes, sir.'

'Keep up the good work, Grayson.' Markham patted him on the back and left him.

Gabe and Patrick took his place, slumping down into the dirt. Oliver peered at them, looking for injuries. Like him, they were filthy. Gabe was bleeding a little from the temple. Patrick looked fine. 'The others?'

'Made it through.' Gabe pulled out his bandage kit and applied it to Oliver's bleeding neck. 'Hold this while I tie it, you bloody mad fool.'

Oliver glowered at him and held the bandage at the side of his neck, not remembering he'd been hit, but now his neck stung like hell. 'Just a nick?'

'Aye, the Germans spared you your good looks it seems.' Gabe grinned, his face streaked with grime. 'You'll never be as handsome as me, of course, even if you're a sergeant.'

11

Blue Water Station, September 1916

Tilly straightened her aching back and surveyed the vegetable garden. Rows of neatly turned soiled stretched out before her. To the right were winter vegetables; cauliflower, cabbages and onions.

'You need a rest, my dear.' Grandpapa sat on a chair, repainting the picket fencing white again. Where he could, he mended broken panels.

'I'm fine. I've nearly finished anyway.' A cool breeze lifted the hair from her forehead. Spring hadn't completely arrived, and today was cool with a slight wind blowing the tops of the gum trees.

'Give the soil a week to settle, then we can plant the seeds.'

'And watch the rabbits and wallabies eat them as they sprout.' She sighed and leaned her spade against the fence. Fighting the elements and the native wildlife seemed a never-ending task — that was one thing she had learnt over the years living in the country. One minute they wouldn't have enough water as the lack of rains would dry out the storage tanks and the river, the next minute they'd have too much and were in danger of flooding. A dry summer would bring the danger of bushfires, or a long cold winter would kill off early spring-born calves and delay crop planting.

'I'll replace the netting to keep them out.' Grandpapa stood, his knees creaking. 'Let's have some coffee.'

She nodded, took off her gloves and apron and joined him to walk back to the house. 'You haven't worn yourself out, Grandpapa?'

'A little, but I'll have a nap this afternoon. Don't tell your grandmama, or she'll not let me out of the house again for weeks.' He grinned at her, which reminded her of Gabe, and her heart twisted a little.

'It's our secret. But you mustn't do too much. I can finish the painting once the seeds are sown, or I'll get one of the stockmen's wives to do it. I'm sure they could all do with earning a few more shillings. Old Jim will be back at work by then.'

They strolled past the laundry buildings towards the back of the house. Grandpapa paused at the junction of another pathway leading down to the holding yards and barns. 'I need to talk to you about the mustering.'

Tilly frowned. 'I didn't think we were doing it this year. We don't have enough good stockmen, and those layabouts we got last year were hopeless.'

'I've changed my mind. I've been thinking about it for days. It doesn't sit well with me that we aren't doing it. We didn't muster enough cattle last year, with most of our men gone. And you're right, the new stockmen we employed had no idea. But I simply cannot rest easy at the thought of not doing one this year.'

'But how? Those men were worse than useless. They simply wanted a place to hide away on instead of enlisting and doing their duty.' It still maddened her that they received scores of men looking for work when they should be overseas at the front.

Grandpapa nodded. 'Yes, I feel the same. Anyway, the old hands did their best last year; it wasn't enough though. Disease and bad breeding will result, you know that.' He paused by the rose garden and looked at her fully. 'We can't afford to allow our herds to diminish in both pedigree and numbers. Plus it *is* income, our main income.'

Tilly thought rapidly, anxious at the worry in his eyes. 'But we have even fewer men this year. How can we get all the cattle brought in?'

'That's what we have to plan, Princess,' Grandpapa said as they reached the veranda where Kitty and Aunt Connie sat with a tea tray.

'I was just about to send Adelaide for you both.' Her grandmama's eyes assessed how tired Grandpapa appeared.

Sitting down, Tilly watched her grandmama, knowing she would have something to say if he had overworked himself. 'We've done enough for today,' Tilly spoke before he grandmama had the chance to rebuke them.

'Good, you'll wear yourselves out,' Aunt Connie said, passing around a plate of oat biscuits.

'There's no one else to do it.' Tilly shrugged. 'With the men gone, we need to do work that normally we wouldn't do.'

150

'I've done plenty of manual labour in my time.' Grandpapa accepted a cup of coffee from his wife.

Grandmama gave him a sharp look. 'Yes, but you were younger then, not an old man.'

'I'm not dead yet, woman.' He sipped his coffee. 'Tilly can't do it all by herself. Old Jim White can't do everything in the garden either, not without help.'

Tilly added cream to her coffee. 'Old Jim wanted to dig with me today, but he was bothered by his arthritis, so I set him the task of sorting out the seeds in the greenhouse. It's warmer in there and he can sit down if he chooses.'

Adelaide came out onto the veranda. 'The postman came while you were busy in the garden. No letters today, I'm afraid.' She took a seat and poured herself some coffee.

'No news is good news,' Grandmama mumbled, nibbling a small piece of soda bread and butter.

Tilly bit into an oat biscuit, disappointed she'd not heard from Luke in months. That was why she hadn't wanted to get involved with him, so she wouldn't miss the letters that never arrived.

Grandpapa sat straighter in his wicker chair and looked at Tilly. 'I think we should put an advert in the newspaper for qualified stockmen.'

'But that might take a while, Grandpapa.'

'We have no option. The old hands can only do so much. It's not fair to ask them to sit in a saddle and sleep rough for weeks on end.'

'I don't think they would mind,' Grandmama

151

spoke, cutting more slices of bread for Miles and buttering them for him. 'They're made of strong stuff.'

'No.' Grandpapa shook his head. 'They can't handle hard riding now. Too many years in the saddle and of back-breaking work have ruined their bodies.'

'I'll go.' Tilly surprised herself with the words.

'You can't do it alone, Princess.' Grandpapa chuckled.

Adelaide put her cup down. 'She won't be alone. I'll go with her.'

'You?' Aunt Connie spluttered. 'Yer've never mustered cattle in yer life.'

'But I can ride a horse. I can learn the rest.' Adelaide shrugged as though it was no big deal.

Tilly grinned at her, getting excited by the prospect of them mustering together.

'Even so . . . ' Grandpapa eyed them both. 'Two women can't bring in hundreds of cattle by themselves.'

Selecting another biscuit, Tilly placed it on her plate, her mind whirling with a hundred crazy thoughts. 'We're late in mustering, you said it yourself. So instead of waiting another month for men to see our advertisement, respond and be interviewed, why don't I go into town tomorrow, ask a few families who they can spare? I might be able to start the muster by the end of next week. The old hands can bring in the cattle close by, and Adelaide and I can go further afield.'

Grandmama gave her a tender smile. 'Darling, I know you've done it before, but you had plenty of men to do all the hard work. You mainly just rode. This would be very different. You'd be gone for weeks. You'll be sleeping rough and eating the same food every day. It's long days in the saddle in all weathers.'

'I can do it, Grandmama.' With each passing minute, the idea grew more thrilling. She could do this. She'd show everyone that a woman could bring in a muster. She was determined to be successful.

Grandmama poured out more coffee. 'Yes, I'm sure you could, maybe for a day or two, but weeks on end?'

'Trust me. Let me see who can come and help us first. If I can get a few good men, then I see no reason why we can't muster.' She sat back and drank her coffee, pleased with her idea and eager to get started.

Her grandparents exchanged a look, and Grandpapa grinned. 'She really *is* you all over again!'

⋆ ⋆ ⋆

Five days later, Tilly stood in the middle of the large barn which housed the carts and carriage, plus her father's motor car that she now claimed as hers. She read through her list one more time, and checked it off against the contents of the cart. A bag of salt, a sack each of flour and oats, a jar of dried yeast, jars of jam, sack of tea, large tins of sugar and coffee, small barrels of salted meat, rice, a crate of cabbages, beans and potatoes, and finally bedrolls, enamel cups, plates and cutlery, pots, frying pan and kettle.

She glanced up as old Jim White, the head gardener, came in and added a long bunch of onions tied on a string to the back of the cart.

'You'll need these, miss. They weren't put in the crate.'

'Thank you, Jim.' She wrote *onions* at the bottom of the food list.

'Have a good trip, miss.' He touched his flat cap and hobbled back towards the house on legs bowed with age.

'Miss Grayson.'

She turned and smiled at Stumpy, Blue Water's head stockman, who although in his early sixties, still worked as hard as any man half his age. 'Yes, Stumpy?'

He walked to the cart and rested his arm on it. 'A new fella has just rode in on the back of the postman's truck. He says he's looking for work.'

'What kind of work?' she asked. Was he just another layabout dodging his duty to serve his country, or a returned soldier wounded out of the army?

'He looks fit and healthy to me. Says he can ride and has worked on stations before, up in Queensland.' Stumpy scratched his grey hair under his filthy wide-brimmed hat that Tilly had seen him wear all her life. Stumpy was part of Blue Water as much as the buildings and animals. He'd worked for her grandpapa since he was a boy.

'How old is he?'

Stumpy shrugged. 'Late twenties perhaps, maybe older. His hat was pulled down low, couldn't tell much.'

'Should we employ him on the muster?'

Swatting a fly away, Stumpy screwed up his face in thought. 'We have what, five new men from Grafton? Me, you and Miss Adelaide. We could do with another one, especially if he's experienced. Then we can leave Larry and a few youngsters here to see to everything while we're gone.'

'Very well, employ him, Stumpy. Give his details to Miss Adelaide.'

'Will do.' He pointed to the cart. 'I'll add another bedroll for the newcomer.'

'Thank you.' She added the extra bedroll to her list and continued marking off what had been packed. Extra bridles, reins, saddle blankets, horse shoes, tools, salves and ointments, bandages and iodine.

'There you are.' Adelaide came into the barn carrying a large bag. 'I thought to bring this down now to save time in the morning.

'Oh good. I'll put mine in as well later.'

'I hope I'll have enough clothes. I assume we will get filthy out there.' Adelaide placed the bag in the cart.

Tilly tucked her notepaper and pen into her skirt pocket. 'Are you sure you want to come? It'll be tough, hot and dirty work.'

'Of course.'

'Did you bring your headache medication?'

'Yes, that was the first thing I packed. Don't worry. I'll be fine.'

'I'm allowed to worry. You'll struggle if you get one of your migraines out there.'

'Tilly, stop fussing. I can look after myself.

155

Besides, I'm looking forward to going and getting out of the house for a while. Anyway, you can't go alone with all those strange men. It's not like how it used to be when you knew everyone and had the boys with you.'

'I'd have Stumpy with me.'

Adelaide pulled a face at her. 'I'm going. I won't change my mind.'

'I'm glad, actually. I think I'll enjoy having you with me.' Tilly gave a final look at the well-stocked cart. 'I'd best get back to the house. Grandpapa has several old maps showing the extents of Blue Water he wants to discuss with me before dinner.'

'He's very nervous about this, you know.' Adelaide fell into step beside her as they walked back up the dirt road towards the house. 'It's a big task, bringing in herds of cattle.'

'I'm not worried. We can do it. I'm going to enjoy the challenge.' She smiled at Adelaide, believing every word. She had no doubt how hard it would be, as she'd mustered before with the boys, and knew of the long dusty days in the saddle. But she needed to do this; it was important to her. If she could successfully bring in the muster, then Blue Water's finances would remain stable, and it would show the whole district that she just wasn't a simple daughter from a good family, but someone to be reckoned with. If the boys didn't come back, then Blue Water would be hers, and she had to know it inside out.

Crows called loudly in the eucalyptus trees, and Tilly looked up to watch them. Their cry was such a forlorn sound. The sun warmed her, and she felt the need to swim in the river, but it wasn't warm enough for that yet. Spring had barely begun.

Walking up the steps to the veranda, she paused before opening the door. 'Stumpy said the postman has been?'

'Yes, but he brought no letters again, just bills.' Adelaide sighed in disappointment. 'Are you taking your new camera?'

'Yes, I think I might. I can take the photographs when we stop each day. Grandpapa would like to see parts of the station he's not seen in a long time.'

'One more sleep.' Adelaide grinned.

Early the following morning, just as the mist was lifting and the sun edged over the distant hills, Tilly stood on the veranda and hugged her grandparents and Aunt Connie. She had her oil-skinned coat on over her riding culottes and shirt, and she wore her wide-brimmed hat, looking like a worker more than the daughter of the house.

'Don't take any risks.' Her grandpapa hugged her, his veined hand touching her cheek gently. 'Stumpy knows what he's doing. Follow his lead.'

'Yes, I will. It'll be fine. Don't worry.' She couldn't keep the excitement out of her voice. For the first time in two years, she felt she was doing something worthwhile. Bookkeeping and running Blue Water when it was working at half strength didn't really inspire her. There was nothing stimulating about adding up accounts and writing cheques, or issuing instructions to people who already knew how to do their jobs. She wanted to do something new and exhilarating.

Adelaide quickly kissed them all. 'Goodbye Uncle Miles, Aunt Kitty. Don't mope, Mam.'

Aunt Connie bristled. 'I shan't mope. I've never moped in my life! Just don't fall off the daft horse.'

'Look after each other.' Adelaide followed Tilly down the front steps to their horses waiting below.

Once mounted and with a final wave, they rode down to the holding yards to where Stumpy and the others sat on their horses, waiting for Tilly to lead them away from the homestead. Behind them, a retired stockman named Jonas would drive the horse and cart holding their supplies.

'All set, miss?' Stumpy asked, adjusting the reins in his hands.

'I am. Is everything ready to go?' She looked around at the men, and further away to the few women and children who were awake and braving the brisk dawn air to watch them depart. Usually their husbands would be on this cattle drive, but not this year.

'All ready, miss.'

She glanced around at unfamiliar faces. A few of the new men were returned soldiers, wounded and not able to fight anymore, but who could still work. She had felt sorry for them when meeting them in Grafton a few days ago with Stumpy. One man was terribly scarred along his face, while another man had been shot in the chest and lost a lung, but could still ride a horse. The third man had been shot through the arm and could no longer use it well, but he said he'd needed the money and he could sit a horse enough to muster. The last two were stockmen from out west, who were enlisting as soon as this muster was finished.

Her gaze rested on a total stranger, and she realised he must be the fellow who had arrived yesterday. He slouched in the saddle, a rolled cigarette hanging from his bottom lip, his hat pulled low, shadowing his face. He touched a finger to the brim of his hat in acknowledgment and she stiffened, offended at his insolence.

'Let's go, Stumpy.' She kicked her horse forward, forgetting the man and instead embracing the sense of freedom.

12

London, October, 1916

In the late afternoon sunshine, Oliver waited outside of the gates of the nurses' quarters. He checked his watch again for the tenth time in as many minutes. He was early. Tall trees lined the street; their leaves had turned pretty shades of red and orange. He stared at them in wonder. After months of seeing nothing but churned-up fields, dirt and mud and dust, this delightful avenue appeared a little unreal. It seemed even more uncomfortable to not have a rifle in his hand. His hands felt lost, empty, and he quickly stuck them in his trouser pockets.

Back home in Australia, October meant spring, blossom, rebirth, the weather warming up ready for summer. The muster would be done and there would be parties and Christmas preparations. A wave of homesickness washed over him. How he wished they were all home again.

Although he was desperate to see Jessica, he didn't feel right leaving Gabe and the others at the hotel. Their plans for the next two days were to get as drunk as possible and to eat, sleep and find some available ladies. They didn't need him, not in London. They were safe here. Even still, it felt strange not being with them, not watching over them.

So once he'd bathed and shaved, he'd left them to it. Last month he'd been commissioned in the field to lieutenant. As an officer, he'f needed a new uniform from the numerous tailors in the city, who were happy to supply all that he needed. The filthy rags he'd worn leaving France weren't fit to be seen in, especially not by Jessica.

After being kitted out, he spent the morning shopping and sent Christmas gifts back to Australia for his grandparents and Tilly, Aunt Connie and Adelaide. He hadn't done that last Christmas, stuck on the rocky cliffs of Gallipoli. He hoped the gifts would make up for not writing to them.

Now he waited to take Jess out for a meal and dancing. Normal things — the things normal people did. However, it all felt anything but normal.

From the other side of the street, two young nurses walked out of the gates and down the road, talking happily with young innocent faces. They were so clean-looking. Despite scrubbing himself in the bath that morning, Oliver still felt the grime on his skin, the itch of flea bites.

'Oliver,' Jessica called from another gate further up the road.

He held up his hand in acknowledgement and walked to meet her. His heart thumped the closer he got to her. She was beautiful. Her black curls sprung around her head, escaping from under her straw hat, and her smile stretched wide just for him.

On the last step between them, she flung

herself into his arms, and he squashed her hard against his chest. She smelt of flowers and fresh linen.

He kissed her soundly. 'I'm sorry, I thought it was the other gate.'

'No matter.' She kissed him again, her eyes filled with tears. 'I've missed you.'

'And I you. So much.' He kissed her again, never wanting to let go. When they came up for air, he slipped her hand through his arm and stared down at her. She wore a lavender dress with a straight skirt and white lace ruffle on her chest. A white fox fur cape covered lay over her shoulders. Excited, his stomach tightened at the thought of spending time with her, of kissing her again and holding her close. 'Are you hungry?' he asked.

'Always!' She laughed, and the sound soothed him like nothing else. 'It's too early for a meal. Shall we have a cup of tea first?'

'Sounds like a good idea.'

'How long do we have?' she murmured, the smile leaving her face.

'I have to report back tomorrow night.' Oliver said, as they strolled to the end of the terrace and headed down Queens Gate, another wider main street filled with little cafés and shops. It wasn't as busy as other places like Oxford Street or Piccadilly Circus.

Jessica squeezed his arm. 'So little time. But it's better than nothing.'

A loud bang shattered the air. Oliver dropped to the footpath, automatically reaching for his rifle and discovering it wasn't there. He grabbed at Jessica, who stood watching him in surprise. 'Get down!'

'Oliver, dearest.' She crouched down beside him. 'A motor car backfired.'

'A motor car?' He glanced around the street as the panic subsided, leaving him feeling foolish. People stared and walked past with pity on their faces.

Slowly he stood, though still on edge. His heart raced. 'I'm dreadfully sorry, Jess.'

'Nothing to be sorry about, at all.' She slipped her hand through his. 'I see it all the time. I have patients hiding under beds some nights. Do you feel all right?'

He nodded, adjusted his hat, and gave her a thin smile. 'It took me by surprise. I didn't expect to hear such a loud bang here in the street.'

They selected a small café and went inside. Choosing a table by the front window, they ordered tea and a variety of biscuits.

'We've only got shortbread and sandwiches, sir,' the waitress said, her eyes downcast. 'It's difficult to get supplies for all that we usually offer.'

'Shortbread will be perfect, thank you,' Jessica answered. She took Oliver's hand in hers across the table and smiled at him. 'Shame we don't have any brandy to put in your tea.' She chuckled, then grew serious. 'You look tired.'

'I am. I can't remember the last time I had a decent sleep. We nap when we can, wherever we are. It's noisy all the time. The slightest sounds wake me. Some of the men can sleep through

163

anything. I don't know how they do it. I wish I could. And when I do sleep, I dream. It's easier to stay awake sometimes.' He shrugged. 'But I'm not the only one who's exhausted. We all are. You as well, I imagine. It mustn't be easy working long shifts and seeing all that you do.'

'Oh, I'm made of strong stuff. At least I'm not in danger, not like the medical staff in France near the battle lines. I feel a fraud compared to what they endure.'

'You won't transfer to France, will you?' He was worried at the thought of her being closer to the fighting.

'No, I don't think so. I'm needed here, but it's tempting to see how they work in the field hospitals.'

'Please don't. I couldn't cope with another person to worry about.' His stomach clenched at the thought.

She squeezed his hands. 'No need to worry; I'm staying here in London for the moment. How's your family, Gabe and the others?'

He rubbed his thumb over her fingers and took a deep breath to steady himself. He still felt shaken. 'All good. The boys will be running wild all over London tonight, I should imagine.'

'It'll do them good. And poor you chose to spend your leave with me.' She winked.

'I know I got the best deal.' He smiled.

'Good answer.' She laughed and let go of his hands as the waitress brought over their pot of tea, milk, sugar, teacups and saucers and a plate of pale shortbread cut into fingers.

'Have you been writing home like you

promised me?' Jessica asked, pouring out the tea into two cups.

'A few times.' He added milk to his cup and passed it over for her to use. He didn't want to be reminded that he was remiss in writing home. 'I sent a letter to Grandpapa this morning, telling him that we're in London. Though by the time it reaches him, we'll be back in the trenches. I informed him of my commission.'

'We must celebrate your promotion tonight. I just had a thought — why don't you send your grandfather a telegram? They would all enjoy that so much.'

He thought for a moment, wishing he had done so. 'I think I will actually, tomorrow. Yes, I'll send a telegram.' He thought of Tilly, and another wave of homesickness rolled over him.

'It's been hell over there, hasn't it? So many battles,' she murmured, eyeing the other few customers seated at tables nearby.

He snorted, biting into the shortbread. The sweet flavour was so good after front-line rations. 'We don't expect anything different now. It's madness, all of it.'

She sipped her tea. 'There's nothing you can say that will shock me, as I see it all as well.'

'True, but you don't have to live through it.' He snapped a shortbread finger in half. 'You can return to a clean bed, you're safe. No one will shoot at you, or send bombs your way.'

She grabbed his hand again. 'I know, my darling.'

'Let's talk about something else.' He drank his

tea and tried not to think about France, the mud, the death and destruction. 'Do you like living in London?'

'I do.' She nodded eagerly, black curls bouncing. 'It's modern compared to Sydney, don't you think?'

He grinned at her enthusiasm. 'Yes, I suppose it is.'

'The shops here are far superior to the ones in Sydney, but apparently the shops in New York even put London to shame. Imagine!'

'Perhaps we could go to New York for our honeymoon?'

Her hand stopped midway to her mouth and the shortbread landed with a thud on the plate. 'Honeymoon?'

'It was just a suggestion. You might want to go elsewhere.'

'You want to marry me?' Her brown eyes were wide in shock.

'You think it's a bad idea?'

'We've only known each other a short time. We spent time together in Cairo, then one day here before you went to France, and now today. How can you possibly know enough about me to want to marry me?'

'Don't forget about all our letters. I feel I know you very well by now from those. When this crazy business is over, I want to take you back to Blue Water and spend our lives there together.' He wiped his mouth on a napkin, upset that she wasn't as overjoyed by the idea as he was. 'Obviously, you don't feel the same. I understand that.'

'Marriage is a serious step, Oliver. It can't be decided lightly.'

'Agreed. This isn't something I impulsively thought to mention. You're all I think about, night and day.'

Her shoulders softened and she took his hand again. 'When the war is over, we'll marry.'

For a fleeting moment, he wondered if he'd survive the war. The odds weren't great. Then he thought of something else. 'Only if I'm whole. If I'm disfigured or missing bits, then I won't marry you or anyone.'

'Oliver . . . '

He jerked to his feet. 'Shall we go?' He went to the counter and paid the bill.

Once outside, Oliver sucked in a deep breath. He felt light-headed. He'd asked, no he *suggested*, that they should get married. What had he been thinking? He had no right to do such a thing, and so callously, in a café! For God's sake, was he insane? Why didn't he choose a more romantic setting? Why did he even mention it in the first place? Yes, he'd thought of it, but how could think of a future when they didn't know if he'd survive the next week or month?

'You're angry with me,' Jessica stated as they walked along the street.

He stopped and placed his hands on her shoulders. 'No, I promise you I'm not. Quite the opposite, in fact. Forgive me. I was rash and uncouth. It was stupid of me to even mention it.'

Jessica reached up and gently laid her hand against his cheek. 'I'm honoured that you would

167

wish to marry me. Truly, I am.' She stood on tiptoe and kissed his lips softly. 'I love you, Oliver Grayson.'

He gathered her against him in a bone-crushing hold. He'd never said the three words he should have said at the beginning. 'I'm the world's biggest fool, my darling. I should have started by telling you that I love you, and I do, most whole-heartedly.'

She laughed, wrapping her arms around his neck. 'You're a fool, but you're my fool. Now let's do something; anything!'

'Shall we see a show? Then enjoy a meal and some dancing?'

'Yes, yes and yes!' She kissed him again. 'Let's laugh all night!'

Oliver spotted a hansom cab driving towards them and shot out his hand to hail it down. He bundled Jessica inside and asked the cabby to take them to Leicester Square.

'Will we be able to obtain some tickets, do you think?' Jessica asked, snuggling up to him.

'If we aren't choosy as to what we want to watch, I'm sure it'll be fine.' He kissed the top of her head.

'Oliver?'

He wrapped his arm around her shoulder. 'Yes?'

'Tonight, later, after we've done every-thing . . . ' Her fingers played with the lace at the front of her dress. 'I was wondering . . . thinking really . . . whether you'd want to . . . '

He smiled at her. 'Want to what, beautiful girl?'

'Get a hotel room ... the two of us ... together ... '

He stared into her eyes, seeing the honesty there, and the suggestion. He hardly believed it. 'You want to — '

'I do.' She blinked rapidly for a moment. 'If you do, of course.'

A warmth spread through him like slowly melting wax, pushing away his fears and his thoughts and leaving him with a sense of love and need. 'Yes, my darling, I most certainly do.'

13

Blue Water Station, November 1916.

Tilly squinted in the sunshine and pulled her hat down lower to shield her eyes. Dust swarms picked up by the wind swirled around the valley, coating everything with a fine layer of grit to limit visibility.

Hot and windy, the heat of early summer sapped her strength. A large herd of cattle plodded slowly in front of her. For weeks she'd been mustering, learning so much, more than she thought she would.

Stumpy was her saviour. He told her vital information regarding the land, how to read landmarks to not get lost, or if she did, how to find her way again. He taught her how to look for stray beasts in the hills, and to secure the cattle at night, plus a host of other things she might never remember. Between him and Adelaide, she had made it through the weeks of being saddle sore, of backache from sleeping rough, of boring food and brackish-tasting warm water.

She felt she'd aged — that she had started this muster as a girl and was returning as a woman. Authority weighed on her, the responsibility a partner to her accountability. She pushed on when others thought she'd flounder. She'd dealt with injuries, crossing streams, the heat and the flies and petty squabbles. Yet for all that, she enjoyed each day. When the sun rose, she was eager to get up and get going again. She took photographs as often as possible so that this, her first proper muster, was captured on film and would always be evidence of what she'd achieved.

'Miss Grayson!'

She turned in the saddle, one hand on her thigh. 'Yes, Stumpy?'

He pointed to the other side of the valley. On the wind she heard the shouting of the stockmen, urging their horses up the slope.

'They've found another bunch,' Stumpy called to her.

She raised her hand in acknowledgment and continued on, guiding her horse around a large boulder and through knee-high grass. The stockmen on the other side of the valley disappeared over the ridge. Minutes later, a lone cow came over the top, followed quickly by several more.

Although tired, happiness filled her as she watched the stockmen bring more cattle into the herd. This muster was proving a great success. More cattle than she thought possible were being rounded up and driven back towards the holding yards near the homestead.

For a moment, she thought of home, still more than three days' ride away. They'd covered hundreds of miles, more than she'd known existed. Obviously she'd grown up knowing Blue Water was immense in size, a fact her grandpapa was so proud of, but until now she'd never ridden to the very edges of it. Other farms had been bought over the years, all adding to the power and stature of Blue Water. She thought of her father, and how amazed he would be at her undertaking such a journey. She wished the boys could be here to see her.

The sound of thundering hooves got her attention, and she smiled to see Adelaide rein in beside her. 'How are you going?'

Adelaide nodded. 'We'll be making camp soon. There's water up ahead, Jonas told me. He says it's the best place to camp for the night.'

'Good. I'm done in for today.'

'You and me both.' Adelaide sighed. Her hair hung in a straight plait down her back, the same as Tilly's. They'd decided that fashion wasn't needed, and wearing old clothes and plaited hair was just the thing when bathing was difficult.

They rode in silence for a while, content to watch the cattle. At times, the other stockmen had to break away from the group and bring back cows that had strayed from the herd. The wind tossed the branches in the eucalyptus trees, silencing the birds.

'I can't believe we've been away from home for five weeks.' Adelaide stretched her back. 'Although my body is very aware of it. I think I'm too old for this kind of work. I'll stick to my accounting in future.'

'You've not had one headache while we've been out here.'

'Yes, that's one good thing at least.' She laughed lightly. 'It must be all this fresh air and not having my nose continually stuck in books.'

'And look at the weight we've lost.' Tilly grinned. 'It shows how spoilt we were with Mrs Chalmers's cooking.'

'Yes, I miss her cakes!'

Tilly grinned. 'That's why we've lost weight, no cake!'

Adelaide gave her an assessing look. 'You were thin enough to start with. Now you're positively skeletal. You're all right, aren't you?'

'Yes, of course.' Tilly waved her concerns away. 'So much exercise and basic food will do that to a person.' She glanced over to the stockmen riding on the far side and behind the herd. Her gaze searched and found the one she was looking for. Rob Delaney. She shivered despite the heat.

He kept his distance from everyone. He did as he was told, but made it clear he didn't want to be a part of the group. He ate and slept separately from the men and spoke only when he was directly asked a question. He worked hard, that couldn't be faulted. Yet Tilly felt uneasy about him. Often she would look up to find him watching her. She didn't quite understand her feelings. Perhaps it was because he was so private. No one knew anything about him. He was a mystery, intriguing.

'Look, Jonas is stopping the cart. I'll go help him set up camp.' Adelaide trotted away.

Tilly reined about and headed to where Stumpy and the men were guiding the herd towards a natural curve in the hillside. By a group of eucalyptus large trees, she realised there was a waterhole fed by a running stream trickling down from the hills above. Sheltered from the wind, Jonas had picked the perfect spot to camp.

She dismounted at the edge of the waterhole to let her horse drink. Further up the stream, the cattle gathered at its edge to drink thirstily, snorting and slurping the water. The smell of cow dung and animals filled her nose. She longed for a deep bath with lovely soft soap. Washing out of a bucket never made her feel clean.

Jonas came to stand beside her. 'They'll be fine here tonight. Good shelter here, Miss Grayson,' he said, bending by the stream to replenish the water butt. 'I'll have a fire going shortly and boil water for some tea,' he added, walking away.

'Thank you.' She knelt and splashed water onto her face repeatedly, washing away the grime and dust. From the west she noticed clouds racing on the wind. Before they had been fluffy and white, now they were steel grey and angry.

'That storm will be interesting.' Rob Delaney stood behind her, one foot resting on a large rock.

Standing, Tilly patted her handkerchief around her wet face, surprised he had spoken to her. 'Yes, though I hope it continues on its way without bothering us.'

'I doubt it. We're up too high.' He took his hat off and tilted his head back to look at the changing sky. His dark hair was flat from wearing a hat all day. 'Storms love the mountain ranges. It'll dump rain here before heading out to sea.'

'You seem to know plenty about it.' She felt

174

ridiculously pleased that he chose to speak to her.

'University. I obviously learned something.' He had brown eyes that suddenly softened as he looked at her.

'Heavens, I wasn't expecting you to say that.' She felt a little flustered at his nearness. Delaney's handsome face was finely structured, his body slight and not very muscular. He didn't have the big powerful arms that most stockmen had from years of wrestling cattle and riding stock horses.

'You weren't expecting that I went to university?' He glanced down at the grass and back up to her. 'You don't know anything about me, Miss Grayson.'

'Well, you've hardly made yourself amiable to the group.'

'I'm here to work, isn't that what you pay me for?'

Her eyes narrowed as she studied his features. His nose was a little too thin, she decided. He looked nothing like a stockman; he looked too controlled, too smart in appearance. When the others were dusty and sweaty, he seemed cool and clean. Though he could do the work and ride better than anyone in the group, he didn't share the easy camaraderie with the other men as she was used to seeing.

'Where do you come from?' she asked, her mind working quickly, trying to figure him out.

'Melbourne, originally.' His gaze intensified as he stared at her.

'You're a long way from home.'

He shrugged. 'It's no longer my home.'

'Why are you here? If you have an education, you must have suitable finances behind you.'

'I did, yes.'

She waited for any further information, but when he gave no more, she prodded, 'But no longer?'

'No.' He took a step closer. 'I would very much like to kiss you.'

She took a step back in shock at the abrupt turn of subject, and nearly trod into the water. 'I think not, Mr Delaney.'

'I think you want me to. You're frightened, that's all,' he said softly, almost as a caress.

Heart thumping, she raised her chin. 'I can assure I'm not frightened in the least.'

'Then kiss me, or let me kiss you like you've never been kissed before.'

Shocked, she glared at him icily, not used to being wrong-footed so easily. 'You're being terribly rude.'

'Am I? To want to kiss a beautiful woman?' He lifted his arms out wide. 'We're surrounded by nature, and it's natural that I to want to kiss someone who I find attractive and interesting. This is life. You should embrace it.'

'I'll embrace it another time, thank you very much.' Leaving her horse to graze, Tilly went to find Stumpy on legs that were not as strong as she would have liked them to be. She needed to clear her head. Rob Delaney overwhelmed her. For weeks he had hardly spoken a word, and then when he did, it was about kissing her! The impertinent fool. She should have sacked him!

Stumpy dismounted near the camp. 'Ah, miss, I think we might get a storm tonight.'

'Shame. We've been blessed with agreeable weather all these weeks.' She spoke calmly, but her gaze kept Delaney in sight.

'The cattle should be all right. They're sheltered a bit. We might have a difficult night of it though, if the storm turns violent.'

'We'll stay vigilant tonight then.' Tilly walked into the middle of the makeshift camp.

With the herd nestled into the curve of the hillside, happy to be grazing and not walking, their bellows began, which would go on until dark. The men were finding wood to stack near the fire and and logs to roll into a circle for everyone to sit on. Adelaide made the damper bread dough, ready for the coals, while Jonas chopped onions and salted meat for the pot. Food supplies were low now as the muster was nearing the end. The odd rabbit was shot to supplement the meals, and the fresh meat made a nice change.

Stumpy brought a cover from the cart and wrapped it over the stacked wood. 'Fellas, this storm that's brewing might hit us tonight. We'll need to keep the horses close by, hobbled. I'll take first watch of the herd after dinner.' He turned to Tilly and Adelaide. 'I suggest, Miss Grayson, that you and Miss Adelaide sleep under the cart tonight. You'll be drier there if the rain starts.'

Used to having dry weather the entire muster, Tilly simply nodded, knowing Stumpy spoke from experience. She spied Delaney standing at the back of the group, his eyes on her. She shivered.

Jonas placed the pot on an iron stand over the flames. 'I'll make sure the goods in the cart are covered and protected, miss. If you place your ground sheet underneath the cart and then your bedrolls, you and Miss Adelaide should be fine and dandy under there.'

'I'll do it now.' Tilly got to work making a comfortable bed under the cart, thankful to have something to do. The tops of the trees swayed fiercely, the branches creaking. The wind was gathering pace as the sun slipped behind the western hills. She tucked her hat under the produce crates in the cart before strapping the oilskin canvas down again. The horses, hobbled by the river, nervously whinnied, sensing the storm.

'Dinner will be a quick affair tonight, lads,' Jonas called, his voice taken by the wind. He threw chopped onions, sliced potatoes and beef onto the hot pan, and added Adelaide's damper bread to the coals.

Hungry, Tilly sat on a log and watched him. Her stomach growled at the smell of frying onions. She ached from being in the saddle all day and longed to eat and curl up in her bedroll, but the brewing storm worried her. If it frightened the cattle and they bolted, all their hard work would be undone and they'd have to spend another day gathering them all back again.

Within half an hour, they were eating hot food by the light of a few oil lamps. Adelaide sat next to Tilly on a log, while the men spread around the fire. Thunder rumbled like a giant beast above their heads, and lightening flashed above the hills. The horses jostled skittishly.

'I don't think many of us will sleep tonight, Stumpy,' Tilly said, drinking her tea.

'No, miss.' Stumpy gazed up at the purple evening sky. No stars twinkled. Heavy dark clouds dropped low as daylight faded altogether. The cows' bellowing hadn't lessened with darkness.

'If you need extra hands to watch the herd, I'll do it.'

'Actually, miss, I'd feel better if you and Miss Adelaide stayed under the cart. I'll have enough to think about without the concern of you being in the middle of a storm.' Stumpy threw the last of his tea away. 'I'll saddle up. That lot might calm down better seeing me out there. With this wind, the fire needs to be put out now we've eaten. We don't want to start a bushfire.'

The camp settled down for the night. The men smoked and chatted while Tilly and Adelaide used the rest of the warm water to wash themselves. Large drops of rain started to fall, splattering the ground and making the fire coals hiss and spit.

'Let's get under the cart.' Adelaide grabbed her things and crawled underneath. 'Good lord, I'm too old to be on my hands and knees.'

Following her, and despite her worries about the cattle, Tilly chuckled. She placed a lamp up by their heads so they could see. 'It's a bit cramped.'

After a struggle, and both of them hitting their

heads, they lay flat on their backs inside their bedrolls, watching the men take cover where they could, or simply wrapping oilskin coats over themselves.

'It's going to be a long night, I think,' Tilly murmured, staring up at the bottom of the cart only inches away from her face. She jumped as suddenly Rob Delaney bent down beside her and peered in.

'Room for one more?' he inquired.

'No, there isn't!' she snapped.

'Call me if you need me.' He withdrew and walked away, whistling.

'He's a strange one,' Adelaide said sleepily, squirming into the bedroll more comfortably.

Tilly turned her head and watched him walk to the other side of camp, holding a lamp. 'I don't know about him. There's something intriguing.'

'What do you mean?'

'I don't really know.' She couldn't explain it, only that he had caught her attention, and despite herself, she thought too much about him. She wasn't sure if he excited or repelled her.

Adelaide yawned. 'We'll be home soon, and he'll be gone on his way again.'

Thunder boomed overhead, making them jump.

'That one hurt my ears,' Tilly laughed.

Moments later, lightening forks lit up the sky, throwing the landscape into stark profile. Rain poured down in a torrent. The wind blew it underneath the cart. Tilly adjusted the canvas

180

sheet over them. She was getting damp and cold.

'We'll not sleep in this.' Adelaide sighed.

Lying on the ground, Tilly felt the pounding of the rain through her body. Thunder crashed again. Some of the horses whinnied and snorted. The rain seemed relentless, coming down in sheets, blocking their view of the other side of camp and quickly gathering into puddles.

A shout came from somewhere, and Tilly sat up quickly and banged her head on the bottom of the cart. 'Damn! Blast!'

A loud crack and a crash above them drowned out any other noise. In a heartbeat, Tilly was lying flat on her back again and the cart was pressing down, crushing her chest. She screamed. Her arms were pinned down by her side. Instinct made her want to push the weight off her chest, but she couldn't move. Moaning coming from the left kept her still for a moment as she listened.

'Adelaide?' she whispered, every breath hurting. 'Adelaide?'

'Til . . . '

'I can't move, Adelaide.' She couldn't see her. The lamp had gone out. Turning her head just slightly, Tilly heard desperate shouts and yells now.

'Miss Grayson!'

'Oh my god!'

'Get them out!'

She carefully turned her head again to look down towards the end of the cart. Someone was there, but she couldn't see who it was in the dark. 'Help us!'

'We are, miss, we are. Hold still.'

'I can't breathe properly — please help.' Water trickled by her head, wetting her hair. 'Hurry.'

'Miss!' Another voice came from above her head. 'A tree has fallen on the cart. It's broken. We have to lift the tree off somehow.'

Tilly shivered, cold and wet. A tree was on the cart, breaking it on top of them. 'Adelaide, did you hear what he said?'

Silence.

'Adelaide?' Tilly moved her head to the other side, searching the dark for any movement. 'Adelaide?'

'Tilly . . . I'm hurt.' Her voice was barely a whisper.

'They'll get us out. You'll be fine. Lie still.' Concentrating, she moved her hand a little and felt material. 'Can you feel my hand?'

'No.'

Outside of their black cocoon, Tilly heard loud voices and the splashing of running feet through puddles. She lay as still as possible, trying not to panic, even though breathing was difficult.

Suddenly, creaking came from on top of them. Scared, Tilly wanted the men to stop in case the whole thing came crashing down further, crushing them totally.

Light filtered through to her. A lamp was placed close to her side of the cart. A face appeared. Rob Delaney.

'Won't be long now. We've tied two horses to the tree. We'll pull it off the cart and then drag you both free.'

'Be quick, please.'

182

More voices shouted instructions. Stumpy's booming voice gave orders and he cursed fluently. A great tearing, crunching sound came directly above her face. The dim light exposed the broken cart on top of her; it rested at an angle on one wheel, which had shattered and held only by a few spokes. The cart shuddered and squeaked. She closed her eyes, expecting it to fall further on top of her and kill her.

With a sickening lurch, the cart jolted. Tilly felt the weight on her chest push down. She screamed, bracing herself for further impact. Then suddenly she was released. She lost her breath for a moment and panicked. Beside her, Adelaide groaned.

Yells and shouts were all around the cart now. Bits of wood fell on Tilly's face.

'Grab my hand!' Rob Delaney's voice came clear. He crawled under the cart to her side. His hands felt over her body. 'Give me your hands!'

Without waiting for her to respond, he grabbed her arms and pulled. Mud and water sloshed around her, covering her clothes as she was dragged free. Rain, finer now, hit her face. She sucked in great lungfuls of air, yet still felt she couldn't breathe. Delaney sat her up. She grasped his shirt, unable to speak or breathe.

'Calm down! Calm down!' Delaney placed his hands on both sides of her face. 'Calm down,' he said soothingly. 'You're safe. Breathe. Slowly. That's it. It's over.'

Light-headed, Tilly focused on breathing. Tears burnt hot behind her eyes. The panic receded a little, though she still felt she couldn't take enough deep breaths.

Movement caught her attention, and she watched Stumpy pull Adelaide free of the ruined cart.

Rob wrapped Tilly up in a waterproof stockman's coat and thrust a tin cup into her shaking hand. 'Drink it.'

'Adelaide?'

'Stumpy's looking after her. Drink.'

She tasted the brown liquid, hoping it was tea, but it smelt of rum. It tasted vile and burnt her throat. She shook so much she was in danger of dropping the cup. The storm was abating now; the wind was dying and the rain had lessened to a slight drizzle.

Rob bent down in front of her and softly rubbed a damp handkerchief on her cheeks. 'Are you hurt or bleeding anywhere?'

She trembled with shock and cold. Under the waterproof coat, she was soaked through. 'No, I don't think so. I just couldn't breathe very well.'

'The pressure of the cart on your chest.'

She stared over to where Adelaide remained unmoving on the ground. 'I need to see her.'

Rob helped her up and she trod through the puddles to Adelaide's side. She knelt down and held her hand, pleased to see Adelaide smile at her.

Tears ran down Adelaide's face. 'I'm fine. My legs took the weight, but I'm fine now.'

Stumpy, who knelt with Adelaide's head and shoulders on his lap, shook his head. 'You both had a lucky escape, that's for sure.'

'Are her legs broken?' Tilly asked Stumpy.

'No, I've felt for broken bones like I do with the horses. They seem fine, just a few cuts. I'd say they'll be badly bruised for a couple of weeks, though. You'll be sore as blazes tomorrow.'

'Thank you, Stumpy,' Adelaide murmured, sipping rum.

'I'll send one of the men home at dawn. They can get there faster on their own and bring back another cart, or even the truck. It might make it, and then you can both go home in that.'

Tilly immediately refuted the idea of going home, although she longed for it. She wanted to see her grandparents and hug them. However, she needed to see this muster through. 'We can send Adelaide, though.'

Adelaide struggled to sit up. 'No, you won't. I'll be all right shortly. I'll make any decisions about me, thank you very much!'

'As you wish,' Stumpy grumbled, and moved out of the way for Tilly to come closer. 'Right, miss. I'll leave you to it and get back to the cattle.'

'Thank you, Stumpy.' Tilly hugged Adelaide to her and spoke over her head to him. 'Have they scattered much?'

'No, not really. Some of the lads can round up the stragglers. We can control them.' He stared at the demolished cart. 'I'll send one of the lads home for another cart.'

'Can we not divide the contents and pack them on the horses? There's not much food now. Is it possible? It'll save losing one man. Besides, if my grandparents hear the news of an accident, they'll worry, and I would like to spare them that.'

Scratching his whiskery chin, Stumpy sloshed over to the cart and peered in at the squashed and broken contents. 'I suppose we can. There's less than I thought, now that tree has damaged most of it.' He turned to Jonas. 'Can you still ride, old man, now your cart is firewood?'

'Aye, course I can!' Affronted, Jonas spat into the mud. 'And less of the *old*, too.'

While Stumpy issued orders, Jonas unwrapped the canvas from the wood pile and started another fire. Tilly helped Adelaide to stand and gingerly walk closer to the fire, as they were both shivering from being wet and cold.

'I'll have a hot cup of tea in your hands soon enough, miss,' Jonas said with determination as the flames struggled in the damp conditions. 'The wood is dry. It won't take long once it catches properly.'

Rob Delaney laid out a ground sheet and had salvaged their bedrolls from under the cart. 'They're damp, but not too bad. The fire will dry you out soon enough.'

He helped Tilly to make Adelaide comfortable. 'Do you need me for anything else?' His expression was serious, yet his eyes sent her another message.

'No, thank you, Mr Delaney,' Tilly dismissed him and turned away, unsettled by not only the events of the night but him, too.

He bowed with a smirk and walked away into the darkness.

'That man never addresses you properly. Have

186

you noticed?' Adelaide looked at her. 'He thinks he's your equal. Keep your distance from him.'

Tilly stared into the growing flames, feeling the heat on her face as she remembered his gentleness when he wiped her cheeks, and remained silent.

14

Somme, France. November 1916.

Oliver entered the wooden barn and made his way through the men to the central black iron stove in the middle of the room, the only heating they had. Outside, rain fell heavily, blanketing the landscape, accentuating the ugliness of shattered buildings and villages nearby.

'Hot chocolate.' Gabe poured out brown liquid from a tin kettle into an enamel cup and pushed it into Oliver's hands as he sat down on a wooden chair.

'How did you manage to get that, or shouldn't I ask?' He sipped at the drink, thankful for the warmth, though it only tasted mildly of chocolate.

Gabe smiled. 'Don't ask. How did your few days of officer training go in London?'

'Some lessons were dull, like teaching babies to suck milk. We already know how to fight. But other lessons were interesting. I managed to get some good up-to-date maps. Though travelling back in this awful weather wasn't a picnic.'

'And how's the lovely Jessica?' Gabe wiggled his eyebrows suggestively. 'Is she still allowing you to paw her?'

'Shut up, man. And I don't paw anybody.'

'Ah, Australia's greatest lover sits before me!' Gabe slapped him playfully on the shoulder.

'At least I've got a woman, brother!' Oliver raised his eyebrow at him.

Gabe gave him a rude gesture.

Oliver had thought about nothing but Jessica all the way back from London. He'd been fortunate to be sent to London again for training so soon after his leave. Markham had pulled some strings so that he'd attended the training in London and not in France. He'd only had one night with Jess, due to her hospital shifts and his duties to attend the lectures, but they had not wasted any time at all. Those moments together in his hotel room had been the best of his life, and he'd hated leaving her.

'Is she coping all right, then? Jessica, I mean,' Gabe said seriously. 'Those nurses are so busy. Did you spoil her?'

'Yes, she's fine. Thin and tired, but happy enough. And yes, I spoilt her as much as I could. Food restrictions are hurting the people over there too. There are long queues for all kinds of food in London. Dismal, really.'

Putting Jessica and London out of his mind, Oliver stared around at the men, who were in various stages of relaxation. Some were playing cards while others were talking quietly, sleeping, or writing letters home. He knew Big Max was on leave and had travelled to visit Drew, who had pneumonia and was at one of the field hospitals. Patrick and Freddie were on patrol duty, and Johnny and Samuel were on mess duty.

Oliver frowned at his brother. 'Weren't you meant to be on wood detail? I saw the roster before I went away.'

'I was, but then I realised my talents were better suited to other things. I paid Smithy to do it for me.'

'And what did you do instead?'

'I got my hair cut, had a shave, cleaned my boots, that sort of thing.' Gabe rested back against his chair.

'Gabe, we all have to do our share.'

'What difference does it make who does it, as long as it gets done? Smithy needed money, I had some. It was a fair trade. The wagon is full of duckboards for the trenches up the line, so all is shipshape. Do you like your chocolate? It's not as nice as back home. No sugar in it.'

Oliver shook his head at his brother, but what could he say? Gabe got through each day of this dreadful war by his wits and his charm, and good luck to him.

'Mail has got through, by the way.' Gabe pointed to a few letters on the small wobbly table in front of them. 'None for you, I'm afraid.'

'Before I left, I received one from Luke Williams and one from Grandpapa. I don't expect another too soon.' He drank more of the hot chocolate, wishing he'd been able to have another night with Jess. He missed her dreadfully. She was his link to the world beyond France. For the next few months, until he could beg for another leave, he'd have to rely on letters. He knew she was very busy and too tired to write each night after her shift, but the selfish side of him wished that he could receive a letter every day.

190

'Williams? How is he doing in the desert?'

'It's hot and dry and sandy.' Oliver gave a glimmer of a smile. 'The opposite to here.'

'The bullets will be the same, though.' Gabe drank more of his drink. 'What I wouldn't give right now to be on the back of a horse in the sun and dust.'

'And having a cold beer on the veranda afterwards, listening to the kookaburras laugh.' Oliver refilled both their cups.

'And telling Grandpapa how we had got on, then listening to his stories of what he used to do as a young man.'

'Smelling the eucalyptus trees after the rain.' Oliver closed his eyes, remembering.

The door opened and Captain Markham walked in, bringing with him a blast of cold damp air. 'Rest easy, lads, as you were,' he said as they shuffled to acknowledge his presence. He made his way over to Oliver. 'Is that chocolate I smell?'

'It is, sir.' Gabe refilled his own cup and passed it to him. 'Have mine. I'll leave you two to it.'

Once Gabe had left to join the others, Oliver glanced at Markham. 'I'm thinking you might have some news to tell me, sir?'

'We're moving up the line in the morning.' Markham cradled the cup between both hands. Water dripped from his coat and hat.

'There's a push on?'

'No, not yet. It's more a case of keeping the line steady. We're relieving another unit. Normal stuff.' Markham drank deeply. 'By the way, I received good reports on you from the training. Well done.'

'Thank you, sir.'

Markham stared into his cup. 'I don't have to tell you the state of the trenches in this foul weather. Morale will be low with it coming up to Christmas. Keep a close eye on the men.'

'Yes, sir.'

'We expect the fighting to be mild over the winter.'

Oliver added another piece of wood to the fire. 'After Poziers, I sure hope so.'

'Well, you never can tell with the army, but fingers crossed both sides stay in their own trenches for a while.' Markham drained his cup and placed it on the table. 'Right, I'd best be getting on. Assemble the men in the village square at 0600. News coming through is that the roads are so bad it takes hours just to travel a couple of miles. We all need a good sleep tonight!'

True to Markham's prediction, the next morning Oliver and the men trudged wearily through the churned-up mud-filled rutted roads in pouring rain towards the trenches. After four exhausting hours, Markham halted the men to rest and eat.

'We're only halfway there,' Oliver told Big Max and the others as they huddled together to protect each other from the slanting rain.

'I've never seen so much mud in all my life,' Patrick moaned, trying to shield his tin of bully beef from filling with water.

Oliver tipped his head to the side so the rain

dripped away from his food. 'Apparently this area was drained long ago. However, the mass shelling of it has destroyed the drainage channels, and with all this rain, it's reverted back to as it once was — a swamp.'

'I can't feel my feet anymore,' Johnny murmured, looking miserable.

'When we get to the trench, you must dry your feet and rub them with oil to prevent trench rot.' Oliver suddenly heard a horse neighing.

'Look, it's the food cart! The horse is stuck.' Freddie hurried back down the road to where a horse and cart had slipped into a shell hole filled with sludge and water. The weight of the sinking cart was dragging the horse down. The driver had jumped off and sunk up to his knees in mud. He was stuck as much as the horse, and both were sinking further.

'Cut the horse's harness!' Oliver bellowed, running to help. While some of the men pulled the driver free of the sucking mud, Oliver, Gabe and Big Max grabbed at the panicked horse's bridle and tried to pull it out of the hole.

'Use your bayonet, Oliver,' Gabe shouted, cutting through the harness with his own. 'It'll drown otherwise.'

Hacking at the harness, Oliver felt himself sinking in the thick mud. His boots and puttees were covered with dense cloying sludge. The horse was tired, and its thrashing to climb out of the hole had slowed. The whites of its eyes showed fear.

'Hurry!' Gabe yelled.

Oliver strained, but felt himself sliding down

into the hole, the water and mud inching up his legs. 'Watch yourself, Gabe. Don't sink too far in; it's like quicksand.'

With most of the men helping, they strained to pull the horse out of the shell hole, but the effort was wasted. Without ropes and a pulley or more men to heave, the horse remained stuck with the water and sludge now up to its neck. The incessant rain made everything slippery and more difficult.

Gabe kept straining, his face red and up to his waist in thick mud. He was in danger of being stuck too.

'Enough!' Oliver let go of the bridle and jerked his legs up and out of mud, only to sink in and nearly fall on his back. 'We can't save it. Enough.' He looked at Gabe, still struggling to gain precious inches. 'Let it go, Gabe.'

'No, we can do it!'

'No!' Oliver nodded to Big Max and Patrick, both of whom let the harness go, and the horse sank further down.

'Damn you! Pull!' Gabe yelled.

Out of nowhere, a shell whistled over their heads and burst only twenty yards away, destroying a tree stump. The men ducked, cursing as they were showered with clods of mud. Another shell screamed overhead, landing with a sickening boom.

Oliver yanked himself away from the shell hole, rain in his eyes. 'Right, all of you, let's go, on the double. We need to get out of their range.'

'Oliver, the horse!' Gabe yelled.

'Damn it, Gabe.' Without thought, Oliver pulled out his pistol and shot the horse between the eyes. 'Now get the hell out of there! Now!'

Big Max silently pulled a shocked Gabe out of the hole.

Plodding through the mud, his face twisted in anger, Gabe glared at Oliver. 'You shot it — why? For god's sake, we could have rescued it.'

'No, we couldn't. We tried and failed. Now get going before we're all blown up!' Oliver pushed him away as he came to stand nose to nose. 'I said go!'

Another shell exploded metres away. Mud and soil pelted them.

As they ran up the boggy road in the pouring rain, Johnny turned to Oliver. 'You said you wanted adventure.'

'Shut up,' Oliver snapped.

An hour later, dispirited and cold, wet and miserable, Oliver led the men into the reserve trench. Captain Markham left them to go and converse with the officer in charge, and Oliver indicated for the men to find somewhere to rest. Looking around at the water-filled trenches, he sighed at the thought of sleeping in these conditions.

Finally, the rain ceased and the men sighed in relief. Oliver took off his helmet to scratch his head. The temperature had dropped, and he shivered.

'How long are we in the reserve trench for?' Freddie asked, trying to light a damp cigarette.

'A day or two, I should think. Then we'll move

further up the line.' Oliver cupped his hands around the lighter's flame to help him.

'Gabe's in a filthy mood, cousin. I'd stay clear of him if I was you.'

'I intend to.' Oliver snorted. 'I wasn't going to risk everyone for the sake of an old nag.'

'It's cut him up pretty bad. We've seen mates blown to pieces and we've got on with it, but for some reason that horse dying has upset him more than anything else.' Freddie puffed vainly on the cigarette, but it went out. 'Christ! I hate this bloody war!' He threw the cigarette into the mud and stomped away.

Glancing over at a sullen Gabe, Oliver rejected the idea of talking to him and went to wait for Markham and their orders.

By nightfall, they were settled in their section of the reserve trench, having relieved a British unit who deserved a well-earned rest. Oliver listened to the men's grumbles, but nothing could be done about the harsh conditions. The trenches held a foot of water and mud. Walking anywhere required effort and stamina. Fire-steps were used to sit on, or sleep on, and Markham agreed that they'd have to make do for now and use anything they could to get up and out of the mud.

In the quiet of darkness, Oliver found Gabe and sat beside him. They'd not talked since leaving the horse.

'The Germans haven't fired a shot since we arrived,' Gabe murmured. 'They must be as miserable as we are in these conditions.'

'I'm sure they are.'

'You can't fight a war in mud. It's not sensible.'

Oliver stared up at the stars in the black sky. 'No, it's not sensible at all.'

'Both sides will die of hypothermia instead of bullets.'

'It'll be a quieter way, that's for sure.' Oliver sighed deeply.

Gabe adjusted his position on the fire-step. 'I was talking to some of the Tommies as they moved out, and they said most men were down with trench foot and pneumonia. We didn't have to worry about that in Gallipoli, did we?'

'No.' Oliver yawned, thinking about the lectures he'd sat through about fighting in France. Trench foot was a major concern in the army. Soldiers' feet could balloon to twice their size, which could lead to toe or foot amputation. A soldier who couldn't walk couldn't fight. He wiggled his toes in his own boots and glanced across at Gabe's boots covered in mud. 'Just make sure you change your socks and dry your feet as often as you can, and rub oil into your feet every day.'

Gabe grunted and shifted his position again. 'My arse is numb.'

Across the other side of the trench, Patrick snored. Oliver wished he could fall asleep so easily.

'You should get some sleep, brother,' Gabe said as if reading his thoughts.

'I will soon. Look, I wanted to talk about today and the horse . . . '

'Don't. There's nothing to be said.'

'I did the right thing. It was suffering and would have drowned, or been blown up. We had to get out of there.'

Gabe pulled his coat tighter around his neck. 'I know. It's just that . . . oh, I don't know. It's the *waste* of it all. An innocent animal.'

'Yes.'

'I can cope with just about anything except animals getting hurt.'

'I know.'

'It didn't help that last night I had a dream I was riding Sugar across the paddocks near the river back home. Then today, that horse, the fear in its eyes . . . ' Gabe kicked at the mud. 'I just wanted it to be free, out of that stinking hole.'

Knowing that words were useless, Oliver sat silent, staring down at the mud covering his boots and puttees.

'I want to go home, Oliver,' Gabe whispered.

'We all do, mate, we all do.'

15

Blue Water Station. February 1917.

Tilly opened the two top buttons of her white shirt and fanned herself with her hat. A simmering heat haze enveloped the land, turning everything dry and brown. Even the birds were quiet, content to sit on branches high up and catch any slight breeze. The shade under the eucalyptus tree did little to offer respite as she leant against the trunk. Her horse nibbled the brown grass, but soon ignored the scant tufts and instead rested quietly; every now and then, with a jingle of the bridle, he shook his head to ward off the gathering flies.

She had spent the morning riding along the river for some miles, checking its flow and depth. As the main water supply for the animals and crops, it was important the rains came soon. The water level was low, but not dangerously so. Now, as the summer sun was at its highest, she'd stopped to eat the beef sandwich she'd brought with her.

From her skirt pocket, she pulled out a letter from Luke. His letters didn't arrive as regularly as before, but they still got through to her. Guilt filled her. Luke Williams hadn't been at the forefront of her mind for a while. Rob Delaney had eclipsed him. She tried to reason the change in her head.

Rob was here in the flesh.

Luke was a man in a letter thousands of miles away.

True, she knew a lot about Luke. Through his letters, he revealed more about himself than he realised. Whereas she knew nothing about Rob, despite him living on her property and seeing him every day. However, Rob made her laugh. His reserved manner when he'd first arrived had gone, although he still didn't get along with the men. He behaved as though they were beneath him, and that caused resentment and hate. She didn't like discord among the men, but despite the chats she had with him regarding his behaviour, nothing changed.

Only with her did he drop the condescending act, and in response she found herself listening to what he had to say. He sought her out and entertained her with interesting facts about all sorts of things. The more time she spent in his company, the more she liked him. His accidental touches sent her senses spinning for more of him. Yet he never asked for more than just her time.

Did he find her attractive still? He'd not mentioned wanting to kiss her since the muster. Why didn't he try? He'd had many opportunities on the long walks they took, or the quiet moments when they worked together somewhere on the station. She must have shown him that she'd be responsive to his advancement. She longed to be kissed properly. She ached to be held by a man in a passionate embrace. Was that so wrong? She was at an age where most women were married by now. Yet with living so far away from towns, and people and the young men away to war, the prospect of such a thing happening seemed as unattainable as flying to the moon.

With a deep sigh, she opened Luke's letter.

Dearest Matilda,

Forgive my lack of correspondence lately; we have been on the move quite a lot and are not always able to have letters sent. I've been involved in some desert reconnaissance, which eats up my days and nights. I cannot tell you how much I abhor the paperwork one has to do in the army!

I'm writing this letter from a beachside town in the middle of nowhere which goes by the name of El Arish. (I can mention this because this letter will not be seen by the censor, as I have a civilian friend who works for a newspaper. He will post it to you directly once he arrives in Sydney.)

Anyway, yesterday we completed a battle and took the sandy village of Magdhaba that the Ottomans fled from. That statement makes it sound so simple, doesn't it? But it wasn't.

To arrive at Magdhaba, we had two nights of solid travel. (It's cooler to ride during the night than in the heat of the day, obviously, but it also hides us from the enemy.) Even so, the long nights of riding are exhausting for man and beast. When we reached Magdhaba, the fighting was fierce, terribly so. The Ottomans know how to defend!

We were faced with six redoubts (little forts hidden outside of the town) and the enemy was so very well entrenched it took all of us — British, New Zealanders and Australians — fighting out of our skins to gain ground.

We found that we had to ride under fire right up to the redoubt and then dismount and engage in the battle at close quarters with rifles and bayonets. The men were brilliant. I have nothing but admiration for them all. Such spirit. Even in desperate and unforgiving conditions, the they do their very best.

I've taken a bullet in the leg, a slight thigh wound. Nothing too serious. I'm at the makeshift hospital they've created in this town. I call it a town, but it is nothing more than a village in the sand. Everything is the colour of sand here — the ground, the buildings, as far as you can see. It is so monotonous. The only colour comes from the blue sky and the blue Mediterranean when we can see it.

That said, there can be a virgin beauty sometimes. An orange horizon, or the wind rippling across the dunes. Still, I'd swap it all for home this very moment. I'll take some photographs for you, since riding is out of the question for a few days until I heal a bit.

In your last letter, you wanted to know

details of my home in Australia. Well, I can tell you that I have a house in Vaucluse, right on the harbour. From my study window, I have a beautiful view of the ships riding at anchor.

However, I also have a farm in a beautiful green valley. A day's drive from Sydney, going south west, you come across a place called Kangaroo Valley. It's full of steep cliffs and glorious mountains, winding rivers and greens plains. My farm is nestled in a hollow at the bottom of a small mountain. Dairy cattle farming works well there. I have a man in charge who looks after it for me, and when I am tired of doing business in Sydney I return there and relax.

I want you to see both of my homes. How is your family and Blue Water?

'Ah, I found you!'

Tilly jumped at the voice, but smiled as Rob Delany dismounted from his horse and walked towards her. 'I didn't hear you ride up.'

'You seemed engrossed in your letter.'

'I was.' She thrust Luke's letter back into her pocket.

'And I've spoilt it for you.' His smile didn't reach his eyes, one of which she noticed was slightly swollen and bruised.

'You've been hurt?'

He touched his cheek. 'It's nothing.' He shrugged and stepped closer.

'What happened?' She frowned. He was quiet and reserved, but when he did speak, his opinion

203

usually rattled some of the others and offense was taken.

'I'll tell you later. First, I must kiss you.'

Speechless, she allowed him to gather her into his arms and do so. His lips were demanding, his tongue seeking. She accepted it, and judging by his soft moan she was doing the right thing.

'I want you, Tilly,' he whispered against her mouth, his arms tightening about her.

Suddenly she stepped away, needing air and some semblance of thought. Finally, he'd asked what she'd wanted him to; but now he had, she wasn't sure if she should give it. Did she want to marry this man?

He stared at her, his hands still holding hers. 'Well? Have I shocked you?'

'Yes. No. I don't know.' Her heart raced in her chest.

'Do you want me?'

She blinked trying to clear her mind and think rationally. He had appeal. Was good-looking and intelligent. 'Do you love me, Rob?'

'What is love?' He kicked at the dirt with the toe of his boot. 'I want you. Isn't that enough?'

'Is it? I have no idea. I'd like to marry for love.'

His eyes widened. 'Marry?'

'Isn't that what you're asking?' She held her breath, waiting for his answer. Had she got it wrong? Were his advances false? Did he think she was free and easy and not worth marrying?

'I . . . suppose so . . . Yes, all right then. Let's get married.' He smiled abruptly as if the idea delighted him beyond measure.

Tilly collapsed against the tree. 'Really?' She

204

could barely believe it.

'Why not?' He leant against her and kissed her deeply. 'I think it's a brilliant notion.'

The heat of the kiss built and she clung to him, her body responding, even if her mind wasn't fully committed. Eventually she broke away.

'What will your family think about it?' she asked, hoping he'd be more revealing about his background, for she knew so little about him.

He kissed her neck and her legs went weak. 'I think it's none of their business.'

'Rob?' she murmured as he nibbled her earlobe, which sent delicious tingles over her skin.

'Mmm?' He cupped her cheek and kissed her deeply.

'I want you too,' she whispered when they parted.

'I know you do.' He released her and moved away. 'But now isn't the time, my darling girl.' He took her hand and guided her back to her horse. 'You need to tell your family.'

She balked a little at that. Her grandparents would be surprised. Lord, *she* was surprised. But as he kissed her again, she banished those thoughts and melted against him.

★   ★   ★

Later, as the family were taking an evening drink on the veranda after dinner, Tilly mentally prepared herself to speak of her decision to marry Rob. She'd spent all afternoon thinking it over and still hadn't come to terms with the suddenness of it. However, her body ached with a need she didn't fully understand, though she knew Rob could fulfil it. Did it need to be more than that? Was lust enough reason to marry? How else did a woman sate the hunger for a man, unless she married him?

'There is something I need to tell you all,' she said quickly, glancing at her grandmama, grandpapa, Aunt Connie and Adelaide, hoping she had their attention before she lost her nerve.

'Oh?' Grandmama sat up a little straighter, a smile on her face in anticipation.

Tilly couldn't meet her eyes and instead looked at Adelaide, whose puzzled expression nearly made her falter. She took a deep breath. 'Yes, you see, I'm . . . that is . . . we . . . ' Good lord, what was the matter with her?

'Princess?' Grandpapa lowered his reading glasses and put down the newspaper. 'Has something happened?'

'Yes. Not bad, though. Good in fact . . . ' She swallowed and felt the sweat break out on her forehead. Her stomach rolled as though ready to expel the lovely dinner she'd just eaten.

'We all like a bit of good news,' Aunt Connie said, sipping her coffee.

'I'm getting married.' There, she'd said it, and it was out in the open.

Stunned silence greeted her words. She stared at her family, willing them to be happy for her.

'Married?' Grandmama said in a quiet tone that everyone knew belied her actual feelings. 'May we know who this lucky man is?'

Adelaide jerked forward, smiling. 'Has Luke Williams proposed in one of his letters?'

Tilly stared at her, a guilty flush crept up her neck. 'Luke? No . . . no, he hasn't.'

'Not the captain?' Grandmama frowned, puzzled. 'Then who?'

'Rob Delaney.' Tilly chanced a glance at Adelaide and saw the horror on her face.

'Who is Rob Delaney?' Grandmama asked, her whole body completely still.

'One of our stockmen,' Adelaide muttered.

'A stockman?' Grandpapa frowned.

'Are you in trouble?' Grandmama said.

Tilly frowned at her. 'Trouble?'

'Is there a baby on the way?'

'Kitty!' Grandpapa reprimanded harshly.

His wife glared at him. 'What? Don't be a fool, Miles. It happens, you know it does.' She gave him a pointed looked and he nodded.

Tilly clenched her fists, annoyed her grand-mama had suggested such a thing. 'No, Grandmama, there isn't.'

Grandpapa leaned forward. 'Then why, Princess? Who is this man? Why have we not met him formerly?'

She shrugged, not enjoying being under his scrutiny. 'It's all been rather sudden.'

Grandpapa's blue eyes softened. 'This Delaney fellow, he was one of the men who helped you when the tree fell on the cart, wasn't he? But you mustn't think you're obligated to him in anyway.'

'I'm aware of that. I'm not a child. However, since then, he and I have become friends.'

Aunt Connie sniffed, disgust written on her

face. 'He's taken advantage, that's what he's done. He's no one decent if he can't introduce himself to your family. Why, he only lives a two-minute walk away. Could he not find the time to come and talk to your grandpapa like a gentleman?'

'He's no gentleman,' Adelaide murmured.

'My thoughts exactly,' Aunt Connie declared.

'Connie,' Grandmama warned under her breath, but her green eyes flashed her own irritation. 'What do you know of him, Matilda?'

'He's intelligent. He went to university in Melbourne; that's where he's from.'

'And his family?' Grandpapa asked.

'He doesn't mention them, really.'

'I would like to talk to him, if I may,' Grandpapa said, standing. 'In the morning.' He briefly touched Kitty's shoulder. 'I'll be in the study for a little while.'

An awkward silence descended on the women. Tilly's stomach churned. It had not gone to plan. Though what had she expected? She had shocked them.

'I'm off to bed.' Aunt Connie stood with the aid of her walking stick. 'Are you coming, Adelaide?'

'In a moment, Mam.'

Grandmama also stood. 'I'll retire too, I think.'

'Grandmama?' Tilly reached for her hand. 'Have I disappointed you?'

Grandmama's stiff shoulders relaxed slightly. She smiled and patted Tilly's cheek. 'No, dearest. But we're surprised, that's all. We had no warning. We haven't even seen you and this

208

Mr Delaney walking in the gardens or anything like that. He should have come to speak to your Grandpapa, and he didn't.' She kissed the top of Tilly's head. 'Give us time to adjust to the news.'

Left alone, Adelaide moved chairs and sat closer to Tilly. 'I swear if you'd said you were running away to join a travelling show, I couldn't have been more shocked! Rob Delaney! Him!'

'What's so wrong with him?' she replied defensively.

'Have you not got eyes in your head?' Adelaide demanded hotly. 'He's hated, Tilly, hated by the men. Stumpy told me only yesterday he had to break up another fight with him. If we weren't so short of workers, he'd have booted him off the property months ago.'

'He's not like that with me!'

'Of course he wouldn't be. Don't be so naive, you're cleverer than that.' Adelaide stared at her. 'Have you been intimate with him, is that it? Do you feel you have to marry him now?'

'I haven't. We've only kissed.' An anger was building inside her.

'Then why, for heaven's sake?'

She jerked to her feet. 'Because I'm lonely! I'm missing the boys. They might never come home, any of them. If this war continues, there'll be no men left! I want to be married to a whole man, someone here right now, who can help me run this place. I want to feel a man's touch, *his* touch. There's something about him that makes me tingle inside, and I like feeling like that. It excites me.'

'You don't have to marry the man to have a little fun.'

'Why shouldn't I marry him? Why is it so wrong?'

'Because we know nothing about him. He rolls up here with nothing and barely talks to anyone for weeks, and when he does start talking it ends up in fights. How can you believe he'll make you happy?'

Tilly walked to the veranda rail and looked out over the dark landscape. 'How can anyone when they marry?'

'Well usually they're in love to start with. That helps them through the tough times.'

'What do you know about it, anyway? You've never been married,' Tilly snapped.

'Have sense, Tilly!' Adelaide strode to her and gripped Tilly's hands. 'This man will become part of our family. He'll live in this house, sit at that table with your grandparents. He'll be involved in decisions.' She paused. 'What will your brothers think if — when — they come home?'

'I don't care what anyone thinks.' She said it automatically, but her voice shook a little at the mention of Oliver and Gabe. They would not like Rob, she knew that for certain.

'Then you're being immature.' Adelaide let go of her hands. 'I'm going to home to bed; my head hurts again. Perhaps you should think long and hard about this decision. And while you're at it, think of poor Luke Williams. The man thinks only of you. And although I've never met him, only through his letters you let me read, I still

210

think he's worth ten of Delaney.'

Annoyed, Tilly's temper flared again. 'I've never promised Luke Williams anything. All we do is write letters. Damn letters, that's it. He's not here. I'm not keeping myself for a man I met once two years ago. You make more out of it than it warrants.'

'Really? Then ask yourself this. If Luke came here tomorrow, which man would you choose?' With that parting remark, Adelaide walked down the steps and away across the gardens.

Long after Adelaide had left the veranda, Tilly sat thinking. The lamp attracted moths and mosquitos but she didn't really care. Her head spun with the events of the day. Rob Delaney wanted to marry her. So did Luke Williams, or at least he hinted of it after the war. Only, Luke was in the Middle East fighting a conflict he might not survive, and despite him writing to her for the last two years, did she ever think marriage was going to happen between them? No, she didn't. She dared not think that far ahead in case he was killed. Did it make her a bad person to want to live in the present? With a war on, there wasn't a future, not really. And how did she know waiting for Luke was the right answer?

Rob lived here. He wanted her now. If the boys didn't return home from France, he would help her run Blue Water.

She turned out the lamp and went inside, ignoring the little voice in her head that asked what she would do if all the men returned home, including Luke Williams.

16

Hindenburg Line, Lagnicourt, France.
April 1917.

Accepting the note from the runner, Oliver saluted and walked back through the gate. Head down against the driving sleet, he hurried across the farm courtyard to the little house his men were nestled in. At the door, he paused to knock the mud off his boots and eye the surrounding buildings that comprised a half-burnt barn, a dilapidated cow byre and a broken chicken coop. Sentries were posted at the gate and beyond the barn. He looked at the dull grey sky and cursed the foul weather. He was tired of being wet and cold and uncomfortable because of it.

Opening the door, his nose twitched as the smell of a stale odour, of unwashed and damp men squashed in a confined space.

'Everything all right, Oliver?' Patrick asked, cleaning his rifle.

'Yes, all quiet.'

'For the moment,' Freddie added, yawning.

'Let's hope it stays that way.' Oliver stepped over to Gabe, who sat in the corner.

'Tea.' Big Max thrust a cup of tea into his hands as he passed.

'Thanks.'

Gabe, using a small axe, chopped bits off a wooden door that once was part of the chicken coop. 'How are the Brits?'

Oliver read the note. 'They got a battering last night, apparently, but held the line. So the runner just told me.'

'That was all the noise, then, and the reason we couldn't get to sleep?' Gabe added more wood to the fire, which crackled and fed out a circle of heat.

'That's it. Our orders are to hold this position.'

'The mail was delivered while you were on your rounds. One for you from your delightful nurse.' Gabe grinned, handing the letter to Oliver.

Tucking the letter into his breast pocket, Oliver anticipated the happy feeling of reading Jessica's letter later. He had managed to see her last month. She had earned a week of leave and crossed the Channel to meet him in Calais. He'd begged Markham to let him attend some training lectures not far from the town and had been given twenty-fours. With no thought of attending any lectures, he'd met Jessica and they'd snatched one wonderful night together before he'd dashed back to his unit the next morning.

'And Tilly has written to me,' Gabe continued. 'The letter is dated in January. God only knows why it's taken this long to reach me. She said she'll send photographs in the next letter, which I haven't received. Oh, and the muster is in. The cattle sold for a good price.'

Surprised, Oliver lowered his cup. 'They mustered? There are men still there? I thought everyone who was able had gone to fight?'

'Tilly led the few they have, Stumpy and a few

213

wounded soldiers who've been sent home. Apparently Adelaide helped as well.'

'Adelaide?' He shook his head and tried to fathom it. 'Tilly led a muster?'

'She's more than capable.' Gabe shrugged and added more splintered bits of wood to the open fire. 'She's done enough of them with us in the past. Stumpy would have helped her. She mentioned that they had a storm and a tree fell on the cart that she and Adelaide were under. They're both all right, though.'

'Good God, they could have been killed,' Oliver murmured, staring into his cup. He, and not his sister, should be home working the station. He had wanted the excitement of war, making the other men want it too, when they should have been home. His guilt grew. Would this war ever end? He should be home.

'Don't worry about Tilly, she'll be fine. She says the old folks are all good, too. Grandpapa is slowly coming to terms with Father's death.'

Oliver nodded sadly, thinking of his father and his dear old grandpapa. His father's death was just one more thing he put to the back of his mind.

'Oh, and news closer to home.' Gabe pointed to Samuel, who was sitting in the corner with his Lewis machine gun in pieces. 'The Lewis is out of action. Jammed tight, and we can't fix it. You'll have to send for another one. Samuel is heartbroken.'

'I'll send for another one.' Oliver scratched his neck. 'I'll be glad when Markham gets back from HQ tomorrow.' He pulled his notebook out of

214

his pocket. 'I'm tired of all this paperwork.'

Suddenly the door flung open, and Johnny stood there bleeding from a wound at the side of his head. 'Attack! Germans!' In one movement, the men grabbed their rifles and helmets.

'Where, Johnny?' Oliver pushed his way through the men to the door.

'In the field beyond the barn. They must have moved up during the night. I didn't see them until they just shot at me.' He shook, with fear on his face.

Cautiously, Oliver edged to the doorway. No firing. Silence. He peered around the door. The hair stood up on the back of his neck. The yard was clear. Down the rutted drive, the other sentry crouched by the wooden gate, not daring to cross the open space back to the house.

'Gabe, I want five men to get to the barn, one in the chicken coop,' Oliver whispered.

'Let's go.' Gabe led the men quickly past Oliver and out into the yard, hugging the walls of the house before sprinting across to the barn.

Oliver looked at Patrick, the best shot in the unit and their sniper. 'Can you get to the well behind the house? It'll give you a clear view beyond the buildings. You'll be exposed. If it gets too hot, get out.'

Patrick nodded and slipped out past Oliver, sidling along the house until he was out of sight.

Left with just Big Max and Johnny, Oliver peered out again, watching Gabe and the others getting into position. A shot rang out, cracking the silence. Then another.

'Max, you stay here. Get on the radio and tell

HQ what's happening. Defend the others if they have to run back. Johnny, come with me.'

As Gabe and the others opened fire, Oliver left the safety of the house, and with Johnny at his back, ran down to the gate and joined the soldier there. 'Have you seen anything?' he asked, squatting down.

'No, just heard shots from the barn.' The soldier, Philips, looked nervously around.

'I don't like it. They could surround us.' In the gloom, Oliver peered at the adjoining fields and along the road. He couldn't see any enemy on this side of the farm. A ditch ran alongside the road all the way to the next village.

'Are we outnumbered?' Philips asked.

'I don't know. Probably.' Oliver watched the fighting happening near the barn. 'The only protection we have is this ditch and that small wood half a mile up the road there. It'll be the retreat point if need be.'

Gunfire started in earnest. Turning, Oliver watched as a small band of Germans rose out of a shallow dip in the land and advanced on the barn.

'You two stay here. Get in that ditch and out of sight; fire on them if they break through into the yard. Watch your backs in case they flank us.' He hurried up the driveway and across the yard to the barn, where the men were firing rapidly. One man fell, and then another. Germans seemed to be everywhere. Reaching Gabe's side, Oliver fired his pistol and brought down one enemy soldier.

Bombing could be heard from a few miles

away further up the line near the village. Oliver cursed and fired again. 'It's a proper attack on different advance points.'

A bullet struck the wooden barn wall next to his head. He ducked and fired back.

'Oh shit.' Gabe groaned and crumpled to the ground.

'Gabe!' Oliver pulled him by his coat collar further into the barn. He frantically searched his brother's body, fear filling him at what he'd find. Blood started seeping through Gabe's uniform jacket on his left shoulder.

'It's nothing.' Gabe grimaced, taking his medical kit out of his pack with one hand. 'I'm all right. Finish them off.'

'There's too many.' Hurriedly pulling out the bandage, Oliver tied it to Gabe's shoulder. 'Put pressure on it. I'll be back shortly.'

Creeping back outside, Oliver hid behind the wall as in the distance, another wave of Germans came over the rise and headed their way. It was suicide to stay now.

'Retreat to the gate! Go now!' Oliver yelled at those who remained alive. 'Freddie, help me get Gabe.'

Pulling Gabe up between them, they ran out of the barn and down the yard under fire. Samuel joined them, turning back every now and then to shoot at the enemy, who stopped at the barn to fire upon them.

Big Max came out of the house, firing, then took Gabe up over his shoulder like a fireman and ran down the driveway. Oliver blessed his friend's strength.

At the gate the men assembled, hunched down in the slight ditch by the dirt road. They were missing four men, one of them Patrick.

'We have to wait for my brother.' Freddie gripped Oliver's arm. 'I'm not leaving him behind.'

'I have to get Gabe to safety.'

'Stuff that!' Gabe scowled at Oliver. 'My shoulder is fine; I've just been clipped, that's all. This arm is numb, but I can still shoot with my right. Don't you dare think of me. We're not leaving our cousin behind.'

Oliver turned away. 'Johnny, how's your head?'

'Fine.' Johnny stared resolutely back at the farm. 'We need to find out about Patrick.'

Freddie reloaded his ammunition. 'Oliver? Hurry, man. We need to get him.'

Oliver rubbed his forehead, thinking of the best action. 'Right. Gabe and Johnny will stay in this ditch and cover us. Big Max and Samuel will go out to the left towards the barn; and Freddie, Philips and I will go to the right to the house.'

'Look!' Samuel pointed. 'There's Patrick!'

They all watched as Patrick made a run for it down past the house; he was firing wildly behind him as he ran.

'Cover him!' Oliver yelled. They opened fire on the enemy, filtering out from the barn and following Patrick. In horror, they saw Patrick stumble and fall to his knees. He scrambled back up and ran a few feet, then fell once more and lay still.

'No!' Freddie launched out of the ditch and sprinted toward him.

'Cover them!' Oliver screamed.

Freddie, dodging bullets, dragged Patrick back. The Germans took shelter against the farmhouse, and the small respite was enough for Freddie to get Patrick to them.

'Is he alive?' Oliver asked as they helped Freddie to pull Patrick into the ditch.

Crying, Freddie hugged Patrick against his chest. A bullet through the throat had killed him. Blood soaked over his uniform, mixing with splattered mud.

'Oh, Christ! No!' Gabe gripped Patrick's hand, his face full of anguish. 'Not Patrick.'

Bullets pinged into the dirt around them as the enemy shot at them. Angry and upset, the men fired back.

Suddenly, Philips keeled over next to Gabe, struck in the head. Dead.

Oliver, his mind racing at the predicament they were in, quickly took Philips's personal belongings and then gathered up Patrick's and pocketed them in his jacket. 'Freddie, we have to move!'

'I can't leave him!'

'He wouldn't want you to stay and die too. Think, man!' Oliver gently but swiftly took Patrick out of Freddie's arms and laid him in the mud. 'When we can, we'll come back and get him. I promise. But we have to go. We're outnumbered. We'll all die if we stay!'

'How the hell are we getting out of this?' Gabe asked between shots. His eyes were red from unshed tears.

Oliver couldn't look at him; he had to stay

219

focused on getting them out. Grief would come later. 'We're going to stay in this ditch. It carries on past the wood to the next village, but for now, that wood is where we want to be. It'll offer some protection.'

'I'm out of ammo,' Johnny mentioned in panic.

Oliver swore. He took the ammunition from Patrick's pack and passed it over. 'Let's go. Keep low.'

Freddie, his face set like stone, gave a last lingering look at his brother and joined the others as darkness began to fall. Oliver touched Patrick's leg in farewell. He couldn't think about him right now. He heard the Germans talking and hurriedly followed the others along the ditch. The dismal weather had brought darkness early and for once he was grateful for it.

His spine tingled as they crept along the ditch. The German voices could be heard behind them. As the last person in the line, Oliver expected a bullet between his shoulder blades at any moment.

It seemed to take forever to reach the wood. However, when they were within fifty yards of it, the whine of bombs filled the air. Abruptly the wood shattered. Shells rained down on it, turning the trees into large splinters. The air exploded with light, noise and debris.

'Take cover!' Oliver yelled as the ground vibrated beneath them with every blast.

Flattened against the bottom of the ditch, water and mud splashed their faces. The dank smell of brackish water filled Oliver's nose.

Broken trunks and branches, clumps of dirt and rocks landed on them. The men groaned in pain. Their ears rang with the blasts.

'We can't stay here!' Oliver knelt up, searching the other side of the road for enemy; believing it clear, he encouraged the others to follow him across into the field.'

'Oliver, stop!'

'What?' He turned and ran back to the ditch. 'Come on!'

'Oliver, Samuel's been hit.'

In the dark, Oliver made his way along the ditch to where Gabe and Johnny were huddled over Samuel. On seeing him, Oliver baulked, then quickly schooled his expression. Samuel lay with a two-foot-long piece of tree branch sticking out of his chest.

Bombs fell again, lighting up the darkening sky, and revealing in gory detail the injury Samuel sustained.

'We have to get him to the village.' Johnny wrapped bandages around Samuel's chest and the piece of wood to stabilise it.

Big Max helped Johnny. 'There'll be a casualty clearing station nearby, surely.'

In a break between bombs falling, they suddenly heard the sound of running. Instinctively, they crouched down.

'Is it our lads or Germans?' Gabe whispered, peering over the side of the ditch.

Oliver stared out, heard a voice and relaxed a little. 'Our guys. Come on, fellas. We'll join them.' Oliver scrambled out and helped Gabe up beside him.

'Stop! Who's there?' a voice called out from further up the road.

'If we were the enemy, we'd have shot you by now!' Gabe called. 'Idiots.'

A British soldier ran up to them, his unit behind him. 'I'm Lieutenant Isaac. Where's your commanding officer?'

'I'm it at the moment. Lieutenant Grayson from the — '

'No time for that now. Get your men out of there. The Germans have taken the village and we need to retreat down this road.' The British officer edged away.

'No point in that,' Oliver told him. 'The farm was taken from us. We'll be shot at the minute we go by.'

'Blast.'

'I suggest we cut across the fields. Do you have a map?'

'Yes, much good it'll do us. Every known feature is blown to bits.' Isaac pulled it from his breast pocket just as another bomb exploded in the wood. 'Damn them,' he muttered tiredly. 'Let's go, and I'll check the map when we're out of range.' He turned and signalled to his men. 'It's chaos out there. Fighting all up and down the line. We held on for as long as we could.'

'I've got wounded.'

Isaac sighed. 'I left mine behind at the casualty clearing station.' He pointed in the direction they had come from. 'It's that way, behind the village. That's if it hasn't been moved. News would have filtered to them that Lagnicourt was lost. They

222

were preparing to evacuate as we left.'

'I've got to get my men there.' Oliver saluted. 'Good luck, Lieutenant.'

'And to you, Grayson.'

Oliver indicated to his men to break away from the British soldiers, and with the bombs lighting the way for them, they headed in the opposite direction.

Big Max carried the top half of Samuel and Johnny took his legs, but the weight of the wood pressing his chest belaboured Samuel's breathing. He moaned feebly, trying to be quiet and not draw attention to them. Oliver held on to Gabe, who'd lost a lot of blood, while Freddie, ghost-like, walked behind them.

They skirted the bombed and broken village as silent as shadows, and turned away from the buildings to take the road towards the next village of Vaulx. After walking a mile or so, they saw a small column of soldiers, Australians.

'They're a sight for sore eyes,' Gabe murmured.

The column paused and drew to one side to let Oliver and the others go by.

'Is there a hospital further down?' Oliver asked one of the officers.

The officer nodded sympathetically, his gaze roaming over the sorry little group. 'Yes, keep going. It's on your right along the next bend.'

'Are you heading for Lagnicourt?'

'That's right. We heard the Germans took it. We've been told to take it back.'

'Give them hell,' Gabe cheered half-heartedly. The movement made him clutch his left arm.

'We'll get bandaged up and come and help you as soon as we can.'

'We'll manage, fellas. You lot go get some rest.' The officer nodded his goodbye.

Oliver kept walking, listening to the tread of boots on dirt as the column marched away, wondering how many of those men would make the trek back again.

Around the next bend, a field held a few tents and an ambulance truck parked next to them. Wounded men were being loaded into the ambulance, while others sat or lay quietly in the dark waiting their turn.

Quickening their step, the tiredness leaving them, the men hurried to the first tent as a nurse exited it to meet them. She went straight to Samuel, holding her lamp high. 'What is his name?'

'Samuel Jessup. My brother,' Johnny told her.

'Take him in. The doctor is inside. Who else?' Her accent was upper-class British, her expression kind.

'We're fine,' Gabe said. 'See to Samuel first.'

She paused and peered at his raggedly bandaged bloodstained shoulder. In the golden light of the lamp, she gazed at Gabe then at Oliver. 'Your friend has already gone, I'm afraid.'

Oliver bowed his head as though a great weight pressed on top of it, pushing him down through the earth. Yet, to combat that, a huge rage was building.

Gabe swore violently. He and Oliver looked up as Johnny came out of the tent with Big Max's arm around his shaking shoulders. Big Max shook his head in a silent message to the others and led Johnny over to sit on a small stack of upturned crates.

'Patrick and Samuel in one night.' Gabe's voice broke a little. 'I can't believe it.'

The nurse put her hand on his arm. 'Come inside with me. I'll get the doctor to take a look at your shoulder.'

Relieved of his brother's weight, Oliver swayed.

Freddie came to stand next to him, his eyes vacant, the stare cold and detached. 'I need to go back and get Patrick.'

'We will, I promise.' Oliver took out his notebook and systematically started writing his notes. Anything was better than processing his loss.

'No, now.' Freddie's voice was deep and low. 'I'm going now. I'm telling you, not asking permission.'

'The farm is occupied. There are Germans everywhere. I'll inform HQ and sort it out.'

'We bloody left him! *You bastard.* You made us leave him!' Freddie's anger replaced the ghost-like stare. As quick as lightening, he punched Oliver on the chin.

Reeling back, shock and pain numbing his mind, Oliver cradled his jaw. Anger thudded through him. He wanted to hit Freddie back, but restrained himself for he was in danger of not stopping. 'I did what I had to do. I'll not apologise. It had to be done to save the rest of you,' he said through clenched teeth. His jaw throbbed like hell.

'Bullshit!' Freddie went to hit him again, but Big Max grabbed him from behind in a bear hug and refused to let go.

'Enough, Freddie. That's enough.' Big Max relaxed his hold. 'We'll go and get him when we can. We'll bury him next to Samuel.'

'No, we won't! The bastard army will send us elsewhere, and Patrick . . . Patrick will rot there . . . '

Oliver walked away. Nothing he could say would lessen Freddie's grief. And he was probably right. If the Germans held the farm for a long time, there would be nothing of Patrick left to retrieve. Their barrage would blow the area up and Patrick would be scattered to the four winds. It happened all the time. They all knew it, had all seen it. Whatever he said to Freddie now would be empty words.

His head pounded from the punch and his mind whirled from the deaths of one of his cousins and one of his childhood friends. He'd have to write to his uncle David and tell him what happened to Patrick. His letter would be more comforting than the official telegram from the War Office. He'd have to write to the Jessups.

He paused next to the ambulance, trying to think rationally. If he could get to a town, he might be able to cable his grandparents with the news. He could imagine Tilly and his grand-mama driving out to the Jessups' farm, ready to give them support, to try and ease the pain. His grandparents would go to David's house at Armidale to help and share with them their grief. Their first grandchild to die. Tears built behind his eyes, but he shook his head to clear them. There was no time for emotion.

Staring into the black night, listening to Johnny and Freddie comfort each other with whispered words, he wondered how many more of them wouldn't make it home.

17

Blue Water Station, April 1917.

The accounting figures blurred before Tilly's eyes. Try as she might, she couldn't concentrate. Sighing, she closed the ledger and leant back in her chair. The ticking of the clock on the mantel was the only sound in the study. Beyond the door came the soft voices of the maids as they cleaned the dining room.

She was pleased her grandparents and Aunt Connie were returning from Armidale today. They had stayed longer to be with Uncle David and Aunt Eve, who had taken Patrick's death hard. She and Adelaide had returned home a few days ago. Adelaide was suffering dreadfully with her headaches, brought on by so much crying. Tilly had accompanied her home to rest.

However, the house was too quiet. She had too much time alone in the evenings to think of things, and thinking did nothing but bring heartache and worry. Mourning enveloped the house again. Her grandparents seemed to grow even older as they absorbed the news that one of their grandsons was dead, and happening only eighteen months after her father's death, it was too much. She feared any more bad news would finish them off.

The floorboards creaked and she looked up to see Adelaide standing in the open doorway. In

228

her hand, she held a bundle of mail. Tilly stared from it to Adelaide's face.

'It's all right. Nothing official. Just bills and letters.'

'Oh, thank God.' Tilly let out her held breath. She dreaded the postman arriving.

Adelaide put the bundle on the desk. 'Aren't you getting ready to drive to Grafton to pick everyone up?'

'Yes, soon. They aren't arriving until this afternoon.'

'I think the rain will hold off.' Adelaide looked out of the window, one hand on her head.

Sorting through the mail, Tilly glanced at her. 'What's the matter? Another headache?'

'Yes. It started this morning. I can't seem to go a day or two without having one.' Her pale face was drawn in pain.

'You should see the eye doctor again. I read that constant headaches might mean you need new glasses. I think you should get your eyesight rechecked and try different reading glasses.'

'Yes, I'll make an appointment with the eye doctor in Sydney who I went to last time. Though the long trip is off-putting.' Adelaide adjusted the curtains a little.

'I'll come with you. We can stay with Aunt Mary and Uncle Rory. We'll go shopping.' Tilly smiled, trying to cheer her up.

'Perhaps. Though at the moment, the thought fills me with dread. I'm struggling to function normally here at home, never mind in the crowded rush of Sydney.'

Opening up one of the letters, Tilly grimaced

229

at the tax bill. 'You'll feel better in a day or two.'

Adelaide rearranged the position of a vase filled with late pink roses. Their petals were dropping onto the lace doily underneath. 'Dinner last night was interesting.'

Tilly's fingers paused over the letters. Last night she had invited Rob to join her and Adelaide for the meal. It had been great to start with, as Rob entertained them with stories of his university days. He had dressed in his best shirt and trousers, and complimented the food and the wine. She'd been thankful he'd made the effort, and relaxed as the night progressed. Rob had charmed her and Adelaide, and for the first time since announcing her decision to marry him, she felt it might actually work between them. That was until later in the evening when the conversation turned to the war, to the loss of dear Patrick and Samuel, and innocently Adelaide asked Rob what was his time in the army like. He had quickly replied that he was tired and snapped them a good night and left. His conduct had puzzled Tilly, and embarrassed her.

'His behaviour was rather odd at the end, don't you think?'

'I think perhaps it's a touchy subject and he doesn't want to discuss it,' she defended him.

'What was his injury that sent him home? Has he told you?'

'No. I don't know what it was.' A coldness seeped into Tilly's heart. Rob never mentioned why he was no longer in the army, or anything about the war. He changed the subject every time she mentioned it.

'Stumpy tells me he refuses to talk about the war with any of the men as well.'

'Maybe it reminds him too much of the horrors of it.' Tilly opened another envelope. 'And why are you talking to Stumpy about Rob?'

'They spend the most time together, working all day. Stumpy's a good judge of character, you know that.'

Tilly played with the silver letter opener. 'You don't want me to marry him, do you?'

'No, I don't.'

'Why?'

Gripping the edge of the table, Adelaide sighed. 'I think you're marrying him for the wrong reasons. You're marrying him because you're impatient. You want to secure someone before all the suitable men are killed. To be frank and honest, I think you're frightened the boys won't come home and you'll be left here alone to run this place when your grandparents are buried up on the hill.' Adelaide gazed at her. 'Am I wrong?'

Tilly turned the letter opener end to end and remained silent, hating the words Adelaide spoke.

'Do you love him, Tilly?' Adelaide came closer to the desk. 'I mean really love him?'

Her chest tightened. She didn't like being put on the spot. She didn't have the answers. 'I don't know. It's too soon to have such feelings. Surely they grow in time?'

'Your parents' marriage was made of love. Your mother and father were devoted to one another.

231

Your father wasn't even able to replace your mother when she died. What does that tell you?'

'Well, what about Grandmama and Grandpapa?' she snapped back. 'They didn't have an ideal start to their life together. They fought and had misunderstandings. Grandmama even left him to be with Aunt Mary for a while.'

'It's not the same and you know it. Miles adored Kitty from the first moment he set eyes on her. He's told us all the stories of how much he wanted to make her his, even though she was as stubborn as a mule. My mam backs him up word for word. Yes, it might have been a fiery relationship at the start, but something was there underneath forecasting the great love they have for each other. Do you feel that for Delaney? Do you feel a burning desire to spend the rest of your life with him?'

'Every relationship is different, Adelaide.' Tilly jerked from the chair, uncomfortable with discussing the subject any longer. 'I can't predict how my relationship with Rob will go, I'm not a fortune teller.' She left the desk to walk out of the room.

'Here, you forgot this.' Adelaide searched through the bundle of mail and handed a letter to Tilly.

Taking it, Tilly's chest tightened as she recognised it was a letter from Luke Williams.

'His letters are becoming more frequent again. Is he out of the desert?'

'I don't know.' She felt guilty for not writing to him in many weeks. 'I need to get ready to drive into Grafton.'

Once upstairs in her bedroom, Tilly sat on the window seat and stared at the envelope with its foreign stamp mark and Luke's writing. She sighed deeply. What was she to do about Luke? How could she tell him that she was engaged? She couldn't upset and disappoint him while he was fighting for his life. And a stupid silly part of her didn't want him to know. She didn't want to lose his friendship; it was too important to her.

Not that she deserved it. What had she done to earn his devotion? Nothing!

She thumped the seat, annoyed that she was at odds with herself. Why had she allowed this situation to happen? Usually she knew exactly what she was doing in her life. True, it was a little mundane at times; but the war and the boys leaving had thrown everything upside down, and she hadn't been prepared for the changes it would cause. She hadn't been ready to be left to deal with things that had never concerned her before. Her life had been carefree and happy. Now it was fraught with responsibilities, deaths and the unknown.

Suddenly hearing the clopping sound of horse hooves and the rumbling wheels of a cart, she slipped the letter under her pillow and went downstairs. Her grandparents and Aunt Connie were coming up the veranda steps.

Tilly stared at them. 'You're home? But I was about to drive to Grafton to collect you.'

'I know, my dear, but we arrived in Grafton earlier than expected.' Grandmama kissed her cheek and waved back to their neighbour Col Higgins, who was unloading luggage from his cart. 'Col saw us and kindly offered us a lift to save you the bother of driving out to us.'

Tilly went down the steps to speak to Joanie's father. 'Good to see you, Mr Higgins. How is Joanie getting along?'

Col took off his hat and smiled. 'She's doing all right, thanks, Tilly. She writes saying how busy she is over there. The nurses are in great demand.'

'I posted a letter to her only last week.'

'She'll be grateful for it, I'm sure. She misses home and we miss her. Right, I'll be off then, Miles.' He shook Grandpapa's hand. 'I'll see you all next week for dinner.' He waved his goodbye and climbed up onto the cart.

'Thanks again, Col, and think about buying a motor car.' Grandpapa grinned.

Col waved and urged his horses on down the drive.

The smile slipped from her grandpapa's face as he took Tilly's hand. 'We need to talk later, Princess. Once we've rested from the journey.'

'Yes, Grandpapa.' Subdued and wondering what he had to tell her, she followed them inside into the parlour while two maids came out and gathered the luggage.

'How are Uncle David and Aunt Eve? They'll miss you.'

Aunt Connie sat down on the sofa and drew off her gloves. 'Suffering. There's no other word for it.'

'They'll cope. They have to, as we all do.' Grandpapa put on his glasses and picked up the pile of mail sitting on the side table near the fireplace. 'I'll be in the study. I'll have my tea in there, please.'

'Any problems?' Grandmama asked Tilly as Adelaide joined them and welcomed them home.

'No, none at all.' Tilly looked worriedly at the empty doorway. 'Is Grandpapa all right?'

Grandmama sighed. 'He's not, no. He's lost his eldest son and now one of his grandsons while he still lives. It's not meant to be that way, dearest. Old people aren't meant to bury the young.'

'Damned war,' Aunt Connie muttered. 'It needs to stop. We want our boys home!'

When the maid brought in the tea tray, Tilly poured a cup and took it into the study. 'Did you want something to eat, Grandpapa?' she asked, placing the tea on his desk.

'No, my dear, thank you.' He looked over the rim of his glasses at her. 'Sit down, will you?'

She returned to the door and closed it before sitting on the chair placed at an angle near his desk, though for many weeks she now thought of it as her desk. 'What is it?'

'You know I spent my whole adult life building Blue Water into a profitable station, and with the businesses in Sydney and other interests, I've gathered a small empire to my name.'

'Yes, Grandpapa, I know.'

He shuffled some of the letters on his desk. 'Now I have to be careful who gets their hands on all this. It is a lot of money and responsibility. My goal was always to hand it down to my sons, and they in turn hand it down to their children and so on. It's the Grayson legacy.' He took a sip

235

of his tea, his hand shaking ever so slightly. 'With your father's death, you three receive a greater share of Blue Water. We've discussed all this before, haven't we? You know what you'll inherit?'

'Yes, Grandpapa.'

'I've spoken to David at length about this, and he's still happy and wealthy enough with his own property and businesses that he doesn't need or want a stake in Blue Water. He will, of course, receive an inheritance sum on my death.' He paused and shook his head as if to clear it from memories or dreams. 'If Freddie dies too, David will have no son to inherit his property at Armidale. Eve has only distant relatives, so he's written in his will that it all goes to you and Gabe. Oliver has Blue Water. Are you following me, my dear?'

'Yes, Grandpapa.' Her mouth was dry though, and she concentrated on every word he said. She disliked talking about death and inheritance. It made it all seem so real.

'This means that if Freddie, Oliver and Gabe are killed, you are the sole heir to everything — both properties. You'll be an extremely wealthy woman.'

'I see.' She sat forward on her chair. She'd never considered her uncle's property. 'But there are a lot of ifs, Grandpapa. The others have to die for me to inherit it all, and I hope they don't.'

'I know that, Princess. We all hope that. However, I have to safeguard you.'

Tilly frowned. 'Safeguard me against what?'

'Fortune hunters.'

'Oh!' She leaned back and nearly laughed. It sounded so ludicrous. Fortune hunters! Then abruptly she tensed. A cold shiver ran down her back. Instinct made her stomach clench. 'You have more to tell me, don't you?'

He nodded sadly. 'Since you announced your intention to marry Delaney, I had to arrange for some background checks on him.' He held up his hand to ward off any protest from her. 'I had to. You must understand how important this is to the whole family and to the survival of everything I've achieved.'

Gripping the edge of the chair, she forced herself to remain seated. 'What did you find out?'

'I've been waiting for this report.' He tapped a thick document that lay on his desk. 'Rob Delaney has never been in the army. He refuses to join up. He's a conscientious objector.'

Tilly's heart seemed to plummet to the bottom of her shoes. 'Are you sure, Grandpapa? He's never mentioned being an objector, or spouted his ideals about the war, not like I've seen the protestors do. Perhaps your information is wrong?'

'His name was recorded at a rally in Melbourne at the beginning of the war.' Grandpapa picked up the document and read bits briefly. 'But that's the least of his, and our, worries. He's wanted by the police regarding enquiries about a robbery in Melbourne. His first wife died in childbirth, and he took her inheritance and spent it all. In Melbourne, he's a known gambler and ladies' man. He has large debts which he cannot pay.' Grandpapa dropped the document as though it was filth in his hands. 'The man is a rogue, possibly a felon, and not the man you think he is.' He glanced at her and took off his glasses. 'I'm sorry, my dear.'

She sat very still. 'I knew none of this, Grandpapa, I promise you.'

'I didn't think you did. I didn't expect him to be honest with you and tell you of his sordid past.' He sipped more of his tea and took a deep breath. 'Now if you still wish to marry him, I'll have to change my will. I cannot tolerate a man like him becoming a part of everything I've worked so hard to create. You'll be taken care of, don't worry. However, you won't receive as much as you would have done, and there will be restrictions and rules so that Delaney can't get his hands on this family's money.'

'I see.'

'We have to make sure he's marrying you for you and not what he can gain. I'm sorry, Princess, but I have to do it this way.'

'I understand.' She felt sick.

'I wish I didn't have to tell you all this. I wanted the man to be decent and worthy of you. He is not. Before I went to Armidale, I spoke to Stumpy and the other men, but my own opinion is one I've trusted all my life; and when this man didn't make himself known to me, despite working on my property, then I knew his measure. So I had to prove it.' He passed her the file on Delaney. 'It's yours to read.'

'I don't need to read it.' She glanced at it with distaste. 'I believe you.' She felt numb.

Grandpapa leaned back in his chair. 'It is your decision, Princess. If you still want him, then that's up to you.'

She smiled half-heartedly in reassurance, wishing it was all a horrible dream. 'There'll be no marriage, Grandpapa. I'm certain of that.'

'Thank God.' He peered at her. 'He's a wanted man. What do you want to do?'

'After embarrassing myself? I've no idea.' She wanted to cry, yet an anger was building and she clung onto that instead.

'Nonsense! You have nothing to be ashamed of. He's a scoundrel.'

'I was weak. He deceived me.' She gripped her hands to stop them shaking. 'I was so foolish. Adelaide warned me, but I thought I knew better. I'm so stupid.' She stood and walked to the door in controlled movements. 'I'd best confront him, hadn't I?'

'No, you don't need to. I can have him thrown off the property. You never have to see him again.'

'Oh, I think I do need to see him.' Rage was building and it needed an outlet. She stopped at the door, her fingers clutching the handle. 'You needn't worry, Grandpapa. If I'm the only Grayson left, you can be assured that I'll take control of everything you've built; and no one, *no one*, will take it from me.'

She stormed out of the house and down the drive towards the farm buildings. The sun was setting and a light misty rain hung low on the distant ranges. The holding yards were quiet, but she heard the sound of general talking near the men's quarters and headed for those behind the stables.

'Hello, my pretty girl.' Delaney detached himself from the group of men sitting outside their huts smoking and drinking ale.

'Don't speak to me in such a way.' Tilly cringed that he called her that in front of the others. She felt humiliated enough without the men laughing behind their hands at her. Did they think she was his plaything? Had she lost their respect?

As Delaney came nearer, she saw him properly for the first time — with new eyes. Yes, he was handsome, but his smile never reached his eyes; and she realised he always appeared to be watching and assessing everyone and everything. There was a rigidness about him, a controlled coldness.

'I need to speak to you.' She walked away from the huts and around the corner of the stables, not waiting for him.

'Is something wrong?' he asked when she stopped and faced him.

' 'What battalion were you in?'

'Pardon?'

'What was your injury that got you discharged from the army?'

He stepped back, edginess in his eyes. 'I've never said I was injured.'

'No, we all assumed. You let us assume! Why else would an eligible young man not be overseas fighting?'

'I never made out I was a returned soldier.'

'No, but you let us believe it and didn't say

anything to the contrary when it was suggested. You've kept yourself aloof so you didn't have to answer questions!'

'It suited me to let the others think that.' He shrugged, unconcerned.

'Because you couldn't face those who'd returned wounded! Those fighting to save your life.' She could happily hit him.

'Not mine. Australia is far enough away.'

'You're a fool to think that!'

'Listen, I'm not over there fighting because I chose not to,' he sneered, folding his arms across his chest. 'I don't believe in getting shot at by strangers who have nothing to do with me.'

Any tiny spark that remained for him spluttered inside her and died. She lifted her chin in revulsion. 'So you're a coward, then?'

'No! I simply don't care to shoot at other men for no reason and only because the government instructs me to do so. Why is that wrong?'

She gave him a look of disgust. 'I haven't the time or the energy to continue this argument.'

'Just because your saintly family and friends have gone to die doesn't make it right!'

Loathing filled her. 'How *dare* you speak of them! They're fighting to save us from tyranny.'

'Hardly. The Germans don't want this country, they want Europe!'

'Then you're stupid as well as a coward, and I'm not the one who supposedly went to university! But I guess that's a lie as well?'

'No.' His expression hardened. 'Anything else?'

'I've learned many things about you today. But

even if I hadn't been informed of your previous wife, your gambling and debts, what you just said now would be enough for me to demand you to leave. So go. This minute. You're fired.'

'I don't think so.'

She blinked in surprise. 'What did you just say?'

Delaney grabbed her by the arms and shook her like a rag doll. 'I said, I don't think so! At least not without some compensation.'

Her eyes widened and he laughed. 'No, I don't want you, as tasty as you might be. I want money, and I'll get it. Why else do you think I came here? I did my research. I wanted to find a daughter from a wealthy family who had brothers overseas and who would, with luck, be killed, leaving the daughter all alone and very rich! But I underestimated you. You're not a silly ninny who does embroidery all day.' He jerked her along beside him. 'Come on.'

'Where are we going?' She shook with fear and anger, each emotion fighting to consume her.

'To the house.' With his grip tightening on her arm, she had no choice but to be marched back to the house, and with every step she hated him more.

'We don't keep money there.'

He chuckled. 'I'm not after loose change.'

The lights were on as dusk filtered shadows across the gardens. Delaney pulled her up the stairs and through the front door. They heard talking in the parlour, probably her family waiting to for her to join them for dinner.

Delaney pushed her into the room. Four faces

stared at them: her grandparents, Aunt Connie and Adelaide. Tilly closed her eyes briefly in humiliation.

Her grandpapa was the first to react, and he stood stiffly, his expression like granite. 'By the aggression with which you entered this room, Delaney, I do believe this isn't a polite social call.'

'You've done a check on me, haven't you?' Delaney glared defiantly at Grandpapa. 'And you made me out to be someone unsuitable for your precious granddaughter.'

'You aren't,' Adelaide muttered, looking pale but fierce.

Delaney stared at each person in turn. 'You think it's going to be that simple to get rid of me? Not a chance.'

'What do you want, then?' Grandpapa grounded out between clenched teeth.

'He wants money,' Tilly murmured with disgust and abhorrence. 'It's all he ever wanted.'

Aunt Connie banged her cane on the polished floor. 'Of course he does, the scum.'

Delaney stiffened at the insult. 'Well, let's get down to business then, shall we?'

Grandpapa made towards the door. 'Come into my study.'

'No!' Tilly yanked her arm out of Delaney's hold as he went to turn. 'You'll give him nothing, Grandpapa!'

Angered, Delaney grabbed her shoulders. 'If I leave here with nothing, then I'll besmirch your reputation countrywide. I'll spend every day for the rest of my life planning how to ruin you.'

243

Fury built in Tilly. 'Do your worst, you piece of filth. As if anyone would believe you anyway. Who are you? You're nothing but a nobody!' She kicked at his legs and pulled away as he released her. She wanted to scratch his eyes out. 'Now get out and get off our property!'

'You're calling my bluff?' He turned to Miles and laughed. 'Good luck trying to get this one married off by the time I've spread the word. Rumours spread faster than bushfire in this country. I'll make her out to be a dirty whore who lifts her skirts for every man in the district.'

Grandpapa took a step closer to him and said very softly, 'Get out before I shoot you and bury you where no one will ever find you.'

'Shut up, old man.' Delaney spat on the floor at Grandpapa's boots. 'Don't think you've heard the last from me.' He turned for the door and stopped to laugh in Tilly's face. 'I'll ruin you and your precious Blue Water. You just watch me!' He stomped from the room, the front door banging behind him.

Once he'd gone, Tilly started shaking.

'Brandy, Miles, quickly.' Grandmama gathered Tilly into her arms and sat her on the sofa. 'It's done with now, sweetheart.'

'I was so blinded, Grandmama. All I thought was that he was here right now, whole and handsome. Someone who'd be mine to help me run this place in the future in case my brothers didn't come home.'

'We all can do foolish things at times, dearest.' Grandmama took the glass from Miles and gave it to her. 'Drink this.'

'I'm sorry to have brought that man into our home.'

'Don't worry about it. You weren't to know.'

She looked up at Grandpapa. 'Can Delaney ruin us?'

He snorted in contempt. 'No, of course he can't, and he knows it. He's all blather and hot air. I'll write to every farmer in the district and those I know further away and tell them to not employ him. His words will fall on deaf ears, dearest. Our friends know you; they won't believe him.'

'They might. They know I've always preferred being with the boys over indoor occupations like their daughters have. None of my friends would consider bringing in a muster, or learning to drive a motor car . . .'

'Matilda, enough.' Grandmama gave her a stern look. 'Our friends understand you might be a bit uninhibited — you have been since you were a child — but none of them would believe a filthy word Delaney says. Don't worry.'

She nodded, but wasn't totally convinced. 'I think I'll have an early night.'

Aunt Connie patted her hand. 'Shall I have a dinner tray sent to you?'

'I'm not hungry, thank you.'

Tutting, Aunt Connie raised an eyebrow. 'I'll organise a tray for you anyway. *He's* not worth starving over, and I know how much you like your food.'

Tilly took the brandy upstairs to her room and sank onto her bed. One of the maids had lit the lamp beside it. Slipping off her shoes, she curled up underneath the quilt and sighed deeply.

Thoughts whirled around her head like a merry-go-round. How could she have been so stupid? So dumb! She'd thrown herself at the first man to touch her. Now she was a laughing stock. The men in the yards would be discussing her, and likely never take her seriously again. How could she manage the station if they thought her to be a rash girl who played about with someone as low as Delaney?

She felt the heat rise in her cheeks at the humiliation; then she plumped up her pillow, and her fingers touched Luke's letter. She stared at it for a long time. She had thrown his affections to one side without thought. What kind of person did that? She'd been self-centred and thoughtless.

Opening the envelope, a small photograph fell out. The tears gathered and she didn't know why, as she stared at Luke's handsome face and his wry smile as he stood next to his horse, Monty. His eyes drew her attention and the humour which always seemed to be lurking there. So different from Delaney's coldness. She shivered. How had she got it so wrong? How had she allowed herself to be swept away by a rogue of a man just because he'd showered her with attention? Was she so shallow? So desperate?

She suddenly screwed up Luke's letter and threw it into the corner of the room, unread. Picking up his photograph, she thrust into the bedside drawer and slammed it shut.

Undressing quickly, tears running down her cheeks, she donned a nightgown. Hairpins

246

scattered across the rug as she pulled them out in jerky movements, annoyed with herself at how Delaney had played her like a puppet. But more annoyed with herself for allowing him to get away with it.

Climbing back into bed, she ignored the knock on the door and turned off the lamp. Emotion welled, filling her throat. Hot tears burned behind her eyes. She wanted her old life back, when her father lived, her brothers were here, she didn't have to take responsibility for the station, and she didn't have to worry about people dying and leaving her. A sob escaped at the thought of her grandparents dying, and Aunt Connie; and if the boys didn't come back, who would she have? She'd be alone with just Adelaide. She closed her eyes and begged for sleep to escape her thoughts and the foolish actions that had made her a laughingstock.

Snuggling under the blankets, she wallowed in self-pity. One night. She'd cry for one night only, and in the morning she would put all this nonsense behind her and in the past, where she would forget it ever happened. In the morning she would be strong and worthy of her grandparents' trust again. She could run Blue Water by herself, she knew she could!

Another sob escaped and she gave in to the tears and cried until she had none left and her head throbbed.

She woke abruptly, a light shining in her eyes, blinding her. Half asleep and confused, she scrambled up in the bed. She blinked to focus and stared, horrified. Delaney sat on her bed.

His hands were under the quilt, on her inner thigh. He jerked a hand out from under the blanket and over her mouth and nose before she had a chance to scream.

'No, pretty one. You're mine tonight, to do with as I please, and you'll not say a word. Understand? That's my payment.'

She moaned in her throat and squirmed, trying to edge away from him. He cut off her breathing and she bucked, desperate for air.

'I want compensation for not getting the money I was hoping for.' He grimaced, hate in his eyes. 'Your grandpapa ruined it all. No one would've been any the wiser. I could've helped you run this place. We could've been happy!'

She shook her head, trying to speak, but his hand prevented any words.

'I'd have worked hard here; not too hard, obviously, but enough to be successful. Your brothers aren't coming home; and if they do, who's to say they will be whole in mind and body? You and I could've had it all. We could've had children to keep you busy. It would've been perfect. But it still can be.'

She frowned. The smell of tobacco from his fingers was in her nose.

'Listen. We could go away together, just the two of us. Disappear. You could be free. Imagine that. No more running this place, being tied to it. I'd make you happy, Tilly. Think about it.' He kissed the top of her head. 'Your grandparents love you, they wouldn't want you to go without, so we'd have something to start again with. You like me, I know you do. I've seen it in your eyes that you want me to touch you. You liked it, didn't you? We can have that.'

Her eyes widened in fear as behind Delaney an image rose in the shadows. She blinked as Aunt Connie lifted up her cane and wacked it hard on top of Delaney's head repeatedly until he grunted and slumped against Tilly.

Stunned, sickened, she pushed him off the bed. He landed with a thump on the floor.

'Are you all right, Tilly?' Bent over panting, Aunt Connie held her chest. Her grey hair escaped the pins holding it. She looked like a crazed woman, bent over wheezing in her dressing gown.

'Have you . . . have you killed him?' she whispered.

'No, not likely, just knocked him out,' Aunt Connie rasped, one hand on the bed to hold her upright.

Tilly peered over the side of the bed. Delaney lay in a heap, a trickle of blood seeping out of his hairline and down his face. 'How did you know?'

'I saw him from my bedroom window. He crept past the cottage and across the gardens, and I knew he only had one thing on his mind.' Aunt Connie sneered as she looked at him. 'Now we need to get rid of him.'

'How?'

Aunt Connie put her cane on the bed and straightened. 'We'll drag him downstairs.'

'You can't do it, not with your heart. I'll drag him.' Tilly climbed out of bed, warily stepping past Delaney and wrapping her silk dressing gown around her. She shivered from shock.

Aunt Connie kicked at his legs, disgust on her face. 'Filthy scoundrel. Thinking he could defile you. I wish I'd killed him.'

'Shhh. Don't say that. He's not worth going to jail for.' Tilly glared down at him, feeling nothing but revulsion. She didn't think she could touch him.

Aunt Connie grabbed her cane and pointed at Delaney. 'Take him by the ankles. We'll have to be as quiet as we can. We can't wake your grandparents. They've had enough to cope with.'

'And you talk nonsense, Connie Spencer.' Grandmama, dressed in her nightwear, stood in the doorway. 'I'm stronger than I look, always have been, and after fifty years of friendship you should know that by now.' She barged in and glared at the unconscious Delaney. 'I feared something like this would happen. That man was never going to go quietly. I've been listening for any sound.'

Tilly couldn't stop shaking. 'I'm sorry it's come to this.'

Grandmama smiled wryly. 'It's life, my dear Matilda. Now, put your boots on and go get Stumpy. He'll help us. We have to get rid of this scum before your grandpapa wakes up.'

18

London, June 1917.

In the warm late-afternoon sunshine, Oliver strolled arm in arm with Jessica through Hyde Park. A dog barked while children ran about with diligent nannies watching from iron benches. Outside of the park, the heavy traffic noise competed with hawkers touting their wares and the general humdrum of a busy city.

It seemed unnatural to Oliver to be walking so freely and without fear of bullets or bombs whizzing through the air. He'd arrived in England only that morning, travelling by ship from the French coast to Dover, and from there by train to London. He, with the men, had been given three days' leave. The others had found a pub and seemed ensconced there for the duration, but Oliver wanted to see Jessica and surprise her. Luckily for them both, she had managed to obtain a day's leave too. She was well liked at the hospital, and not having family in the city, she often volunteered to work extra shifts to let the other nurses go home.

'Shall we get — '

'Would you like to — '

They both spoke at the same time and laughed gently, leaning into each other, savouring the closeness.

'You go first,' Oliver said.

Jessica bowed her head, then with a sigh she looked straight into his eyes. 'I need to talk to you. It's important.'

'Oh? What is it?' He frowned, and then spying an empty bench under a tree, he guided her to it and stood waiting for her to speak.

Fiddling with her small black bag, Jessica seemed nervous and uncomfortable. It was very unlike her, and Oliver swallowed, his mouth suddenly dry.

'Jessica? You're worrying me!' he burst out when he couldn't take her silence any longer.

'I'm sorry. I don't know how to say this.'

'Say it straight out.' He braced himself for bad news. 'Do you want to stop seeing me, is that it?' The thought made his heart drop to his boots.

'What? No!' Brown eyes wide, she stared at him. 'You — you don't want that, do you?'

'Of course I don't.'

Her shoulders relaxed slightly. 'Good, because I think you're going to be stuck with me.'

He had no idea what she was talking about. Laughter came from a group of young boys running across the grass near them. He watched them, they reminded him of himself, Gabe and the lads when they were younger. The innocent times they grew up in before they became men who killed . . .

'Oliver! Did you hear me?'

He jerked back to the present. 'Sorry. What did you say?'

'I told you I was pregnant.'

The whole world narrowed to just her face, to her worried expression, to the tears filling her eyes. Pregnant? That meant a baby. A baby? His mind went blank.

'Oliver, please say something,' Jessica begged.

'I . . . I . . . ' He couldn't form a coherent thought.

'I know you're shocked. I was too.' She placed a hand on her stomach, and he saw the small roundness of it where usually she was reed thin.

'Jess . . . ' God, he couldn't breathe. He pulled at his shirt collar.

'You don't want it, or me now?' She stood up, her eyes bright with unshed tears and a budding anger smouldering in them. Her lips tightened into a white line. 'Fine! Don't bother yourself with this problem then. I'll . . . I'll . . . manage . . . ' She turned away, fumbling in her small bag for something while mumbling under her breath.

Oliver grabbed her arms, spun her back to him and crushed her to his chest. He held her tight, needing to feel her against him. 'I'm sorry.'

'Let me go!' Jessica glared up at him. 'I don't want your pity. I thought I could rely on you, that you loved me and — '

'I do! I meant I'm sorry for my reaction. It was just a surprise. I never expected it.'

'Nor I, but here we are.' She stepped away and stiffly sat back on the bench, half turned away from him.

'Jess, look at me.' He sat beside her and took her hands in his. 'We've only been together a few times.'

'It only takes once!' she fired at him. 'Do you think it isn't yours?'

'No! No, not at all.'

'Good. Because I've only done that with you. It was the night we had together when you came to see me in Calais, a few months ago. Do you remember that night? Or do you sneak away for a few hours with loads of women?'

'No! Never! Not at all. I love you!' He squeezed her hands, somehow trying to get through to her what he couldn't articulate. 'No woman has ever had a second glance from me since the moment I met you in Cairo.'

'I hoped that was the case. I'm in love with you, Oliver. I'd never even look at another man!' She huffed, her body stiff.

'You truly love me?' A warm glow spread throughout his body. A lightness lifted his shoulders, and for the first time in a long while he felt a happiness that made him smile, and if he was honest, want to cry.

'Yes, I do, most desperately.' Jessica glowered at him, still not ready to forgive him.

'I love you too.' He kissed her softly.

She raised an eyebrow, unconvinced. 'Really? This . . . us . . . won't work if you don't. I don't want false promises, Oliver. I can't live my life being unhappy. It's not fair for me or you or this child. I've seen it happen with my own parents. I know how terrible marriages can ruin people. It eats away at the person they once were and they become mean and ugly and — '

He bent down on one knee and took her hand. 'Marry me, Jess, please.'

She sucked in a breath. 'You mean it?'

'You're all I want. You know that. I mentioned

once before about marriage. I'm serious. I want you forever.'

She gave him a watery smile. 'Yes. Me too.'

Oliver stood and hugged her too him. 'I still can't believe it.'

'We need to get married quickly. I'm already showing, Oliver. The matron will see it soon. They'll send me home. You know the rules. Once a nurse marries, she has to resign.'

'Come on. Let's go find my brother and Major Markham. He'll know what we can do.'

'*Major* Markham?'

Oliver nodded, smiling. 'Yes, Markham's promotion came through last week. He deserves it.'

'Shall we get an omnibus or walk?'

He kissed her on the nose. 'Let's walk.'

Hand in hand, they strolled out of the park and along busy Knightsbridge Road into the heart of the city.

'I'll get you a ring, Jess,' Oliver said as they waited on a corner for motor cars and horse and carts to pass. 'I have money in an account here in London. My grandfather set it up for me, and one for Gabe, and my cousins in case we ever needed money in an emergency. I believe he thought that should we lose the war, we might need it to get back to Australia. My grandpapa thinks of everything.'

'Do we have enough time?' Jessica put a hand to her face, her eyes bleak. 'We don't know when you'll get leave again.' She looked up at him, her delicate face sad. 'I'll have to leave you. I can't stay in London once the matron finds out. I'll need to return home to Australia, to my father . . . ' She shuddered. 'He'll be relentless about what I've done. It was bad enough when I went away to train as a nurse, then I left to go to Egypt. He thinks no decent woman would behave in such a way. Now this . . . '

Ignoring the noisy traffic, Oliver turned to her. 'You can go to Blue Water, to Tilly and my grandparents.'

'Will they want me? They don't know me. Have you even *told* them about me? You barely write a letter a year to them!'

'Of course they'll want you.' He squeezed her hand, and they quickly crossed the road while there was a break in the traffic. Walking along, he admonished himself for not writing to his family more, for not telling them about Jessica, though he knew Gabe had mentioned her in his letters home. They'd be so surprised. Guilt filled him for his neglect of those he'd left behind. He missed them so much. He should have written more, especially to Tilly, but pride and arrogance and guilt stopped him every time.

Ahead he saw a sign for a post office. He pointed it out to Jessica. 'I'll send a telegram. Tilly and my grandparents will be happy to have you, I know it.'

Jessica nodded. 'I suppose if they don't, I shall have to return to my father's house, if he'll allow me through the door.'

'He sounds a charmer, Jess.' Oliver frowned. She rarely mentioned her family, but when she did it was never anything pleasant.

'His hatred of his life, the choices he made,

made him into a monster. When my mother died, he turned that hatred on me. I don't want to go back there, Oliver, especially pregnant and unmarried.'

'He sounds like an evil fool, and I don't want you there either.' He kissed her tenderly. 'You're mine now, and you'll always have Blue Water as your home. We'll get married before my leave is over.'

★ ★ ★

Four days later, with amazing speed, and lots of strings pulled and red tape removed, Markham had managed to arrange a day's extra leave for Oliver and Gabe, so Gabe could stand as his brother's witness at the wedding. On the last day of their leave, in a small church near the hospital where Jessica worked, Oliver married the woman he loved. He wished his family and the men he served with could have attended, and he knew Tilly and his Grandmama would have enjoyed the moment.

The ceremony took less than twenty minutes, conducted by a vicar. Oliver kissed his beautiful wife, who wore a duck-egg blue suit and a small white hat with a short delicate net covering half of her face. She looked beautiful. He felt the proudest and luckiest man alive at that moment.

'Thank God for that!' Gabe roared when the vicar turned away to lead them to sign the registry. They had asked the woman who played the organ to be the other witness.

'Be quiet, Gabe,' Jessica chuckled as Gabe

257

kissed her cheek. 'He's done the impossible and married us in record time.'

Oliver shook Gabe's hand. 'Yes, and I've paid him handsomely for the privilege. I don't want him changing his mind!'

'Let's sign the register, then it's legal.' Gabe pushed them on. 'Drinks are on me!'

With no one else there to celebrate with them, they went to a noisy pub on the corner of the next street. Gabe ordered sandwiches, beer and a small glass of sherry for Jessica. The pub was crowded with soldiers on leave, and the air was thick with cloying cigarette smoke. Gabe announced to them all that they were a wedding party, and the men cheered and clapped. One soldier started playing the piano, and the landlord opened a bottle of champagne.

'A proper party!' Gabe yelled above the noise as Jessica was repeatedly kissed on the cheek and Oliver's hand shaken until he winced.

'Are you all right?' he asked Jessica, concerned, seeing her pale face.

'Of course she's all right.' Gabe answered before she could speak. 'She's a Grayson now. I've gained another sister. Heavens, I thought one was more than enough. Now I have two!' He pulled a face at that and then laughed when Jessica slapped his arm.

'Will I like Tilly?' Jessica asked Gabe. 'Oliver says I will, but I know you'll give me an honest answer.'

Gabe took a deep drink of his beer. 'Well, the truth is, my sister has a temper that goes off like a firecracker, a very short fuse.'

'Gabe,' Oliver warned.

'No, no, hear me out. Her temper is foul when riled — she gets it from our grandmamma — but she's one of the finest people you'll ever meet. If she likes you, or loves you, she'll be your best friend forever.' Tears came to Gabe's eyes. 'I miss her.' His voice broke and he turned away.

'I'll be with her soon, and I can tell her that.' Jessica took his hand and kissed his cheek. 'I'm an only child, but today I've gained a brother and sister, and I couldn't have asked for better. Now, let's enjoy this time we have together.'

Gabe took the pint out of Oliver's hand. 'Dance with your beautiful wife, brother.' He grinned tearfully and pushed them together.

Amidst the laughter and cheering, Oliver danced with Jessica as the piano player filled the pub with jaunty music. For nearly two hours, everyone forgot there was a war on, and the impromptu party grew in numbers as strangers entered the pub and remembered what it was like to have fun.

At six o'clock, Gabe hurried back to their lodgings and grabbed their kits. He'd meet them at Victoria train station.

'It was a lovely day.' Jessica smiled, tiredly as they entered the station. They'd taken a cab from the pub and sat quietly together, kissing and holding each other.

'It was.' His chest grew tight, knowing he was leaving her.

Her eyes were troubled. 'One more week and I'll be on a ship to Australia. I can hardly believe it. Going home.'

'Don't work too hard on that hospital ship. You'll need your rest.'

'I'll take care of myself, don't worry. But I'm strong, and I couldn't ignore the fact that I could be of use sailing home on a hospital ship. Doctor Annis made it happen for me, and by doing so, I've saved myself the fare home.'

'I would've paid for a cabin on a liner.'

'I know.' She reached up and kissed him. 'Let me do this my way. Once the baby is born, I'll be content to be a simple wife and mother.'

He laughed. 'I'll hold you to that.' At the gate, Oliver held her close. 'Are you sure you have all the details about how to get to Blue Water?'

'Yes.' She ran her hands over his shoulders and chest, touching his jacket's buttons in slow movements. 'And I know to telegram Tilly when I reach Sydney to let her know when I'll be travelling to Grafton so she can collect me. I won't be staying long with my father, just a night or two. That's all I can stand of him.'

'If he's unreasonable, go straight to Grafton. Someone there will take you out to Blue Water.' He kissed her desperately, not wanting to leave her. 'I'll miss you.'

'And I you.' She gripped his arms. 'You must stay safe, Oliver. I need you to come home to me.'

'I will.' He crushed her to him, emotion tight in his throat. How could he let her go? He was dreadfully torn. The army needed him, his men, his wife, his family at home. It was like his mind had shredded into pieces of guilt and there was nothing her could do to fix any of it.

The train whistle blew, making them jump. There was a rush of soldiers climbing aboard and of carriage doors slamming.

'Oliver!' Gabe hung out of a window, halfway down the train. 'Over here.'

With a nod to the porter, who allowed Jessica to join Oliver on the platform, they quickly walked down to the carriage.

Jessica reached up and kissed Gabe's cheek. 'Take care of yourself and my husband.'

He grinned. 'I will. Give my love to the family when you see them.'

The whistle blew for the final time.

Oliver turned her to him and kissed her, gathering her up close. 'Write to me every day, even if there's nothing new to tell me.'

'You too! Go quickly now, or it'll leave without you.'

'I wish I was coming with you instead.'

'Soon, my love. We'll be together again soon.'

He nodded, and after one more lingering kiss, he jumped into the doorway as the train shunted down the platform. He made his way through the press of soldiers, his footsteps heavy, his heart even heavier. He found Gabe, who moved away from the window to let Oliver take one last look at his new wife.

Jessica, her black curls escaping her hat, had to run down the platform, keeping pace with the slow-moving train.

'I love you, Mrs Grayson,' he shouted.

'And I love you, Oliver Grayson!'

19

Blue Water Station, August 1917.

Frost-covered grass crackled under Tilly's boots as she crossed the lawns to Connie's cottage. Winter still held a strong grip on the countryside, and she pulled her coat around herself more tightly in the cool morning air. Birds squawked their dawn chorus from the eucalyptus trees, and in the distance came the odd cow's bellow. She loved early mornings, when only nature was awake and the rising sun created beautiful colours in the sky of coral and lavender. Normally she was so busy in the mornings she couldn't take advantage of the peace, but today being Sunday, the station staff slumbered later, and those already up were quiet in respect to the others.

Winding through the garden paths, she stopped to pull out random weeds growing in the white gravel. The gardens were never at their best in winter, and today they looked tired and dismal. Old Jim White, the head gardener, was feeling his advanced years; and with the lack of manpower to do the labouring for him, the gardens had become neglected. Tilly's grandmama did as much as she could, but it hardly made a dent in the work that needed to be done. Was it only three years ago when the gardens blazed in colour? So much had changed, so many faces gone.

Carrying on along the path, she came to the white wooden cottage, and after a brief knock on the back door, entered the quiet dwelling. Aunt Connie sat at the kitchen table, a fire roaring in the hearth, the crackle of the wood and the ticking of the carriage clock on the mantel the only sound.

'Morning.' Tilly kissed her cheek, the skin paper thin.

'Morning, my lass.' Aunt Connie lifted the tea pot. 'Would you like some?'

'Please.' Taking off her coat, Tilly hung it on the brass hook on the wall. 'How is she this morning?'

'Not good.'

Tilly looked down the hall in the direction of Adelaide's bedroom. Unexpectedly, two days ago, after complaining of her head hurting, Adelaide had fallen unconscious to the study floor. She'd not left her bed since. 'Is she awake?'

'Not yet. The draught Doctor Halton left for her to take is strong; it makes her very sleepy. Do you want some breakfast? There's toast, or I can make you some porridge.'

'Thank you, but no. I've had some eggs already.' Tilly sat at the table and added sugar and milk to her tea. 'Did you talk to her about going to the hospital in Sydney?'

Aunt Connie sighed, crumbling a piece of toast on the plate. 'I tried last night. I talked until I was blue in the face, but she won't budge on her decision. She refuses to go. She says the doctors can't fix her head. Kitty tried talking to her as well, but it did no good.'

'What about her reading glasses? Maybe she needs stronger lenses. That might stop the headaches.'

'Her headaches have been a constant thing for years. You know how she gets; changing her glasses makes no difference. Adelaide believes it's just her, the way she's made.' Aunt Connie added more tea to her cup and stirred slowly.

'But if she'd go to the hospital in Sydney and have one of those X-ray things Doctor Halton mentioned, then she might be cured of them.'

'He scared her by mentioning that if the X-ray showed something, then they could cut it out. He believes she may have a tumour.' Aunt Connie's hand shook as she placed the teaspoon on the saucer

Tilly eyes widened in surprise and a little fear. 'A tumour?'

'The word horrifies me, so I can't imagine what Adelaide feels.'

'Cut out a tumour from her head? They can do that?' she whispered, barely able to comprehend such an idea.

'Apparently, though I don't like the sound of it.' Aunt Connie looked at Tilly in sadness. 'She's getting worse, Tilly. I'm worried fair to death about it. She's lost so much weight in the last few weeks. Yesterday evening, she couldn't see properly and wasn't making sense when she talked.'

'Yes, I noticed.' Sadness filled Tilly.

'She has no appetite or energy. Doctor Halton said if she doesn't make the trip soon, she might become too weak to do it at all.' Aunt Connie wiped a tear away. 'It's like she's fading away right before my eyes and I can't do anything about it.'

Tilly reached out and gripped Aunt Connie's thin hand. 'I'll talk to her. I'll convince her to go to Sydney.'

Aunt Connie sniffed and nodded. 'Go and see if she's awake. I'll make up a tray for her.'

Tilly left the kitchen and walked down the hallway to the bedroom on the right, which was Adelaide's. She paused to look through the open door of the bedroom opposite, Big Max and Drew's room. Their things were still in place, as though they were only out for a morning ride and hadn't on the other side of the world for the last three years. How she missed them. She missed Big Max's quiet presence and Drew's deep, serious conversations.

Turning away, she entered the room and crossed to the bed. She hardly recognised the fragile figure resting in the dim light as her dear friend. 'Adelaide?'

Slowly, Adelaide opened her eyes, which took a moment to focus. Her lips lifted into a tiny smile in a face as white as the sheets she lay on. 'Til . . .'

Sitting on the chair by the bed, Tilly took her hand gently and stroked it. 'Aunt Connie is making up a breakfast tray for you and I want you to eat it all. We need you strong and well again.'

Adelaide blinked.

Alarmed at her frailness, Tilly tidied the sheet and blankets to keep herself occupied. 'And I need you in the study. I'm getting behind with the accounts without you there. Grandpapa has offered to go through some of the bills for me as the pile is stacking up.'

'You'll . . . need . . . to teach . . . Jess . . . ica . . . '

Tilly stiffened at the name of her brother's new wife. The whole family had been surprised when Oliver telegraphed them the news of his marriage to Nurse Hutton. He'd not mentioned her in the odd letter he sent to grandpapa. Now here she was on her way to live with them! A stranger. She was so angry with Oliver for dumping this outsider on them.

'Til . . . '

She softened her shoulders and relaxed enough to smile at Adelaide. 'Yes, I'll teach her.'

'You must.'

Tilly rose and opened the curtains, letting in the pale morning light. 'Though lord knows what we'll do with her. She's from Sydney, a town girl. I bet she can't ride, or shoot, or swim. Oliver must be crazy to think she'll last out here.'

'Teach her . . . everything . . . '

'Why couldn't she have waited until Oliver came home? Why did she have to come here first, alone? Does she have no family? We don't know her.'

Aunt Connie came into the room. 'Then we *will* get to know her, poor lass. She'll be frightened like mad coming into this family without Oliver here to help her.' She turned to smile at Adelaide. 'Are you feeling better, my lass?'

266

'Yes . . . ' Adelaide murmured, and they all knew she was lying.

Tilly stood at the end of the bed. 'We should heed Doctor Halton. He says you must go to Sydney, so I'll arrange it.'

Adelaide started to shake her head but winced instead. 'No.'

'It's for the best, please,' Aunt Connie begged.

Adelaide's hand lifted slightly towards her mother. 'I'll . . . die here.'

Tilly gasped, reeling at the words. 'Don't say that! Don't you dare say that! We just need to rid you of these headaches! Then you'll be better.' She paced the room, hardly able to contain her anxiety. This was getting out of hand. She'd not lose another member of her family. 'Listen, I'll make arrangements with Uncle Rory and Aunt Mary in Sydney; we can go there. The doctors will — '

'Mam . . . ' Adelaide's eyes beseeched her mother. 'Please. No Sydney . . . '

Taking a deep breath, Aunt Connie clasped her daughter's hand. 'If that's what you want.'

'No!' Tilly stepped closer, pain squeezing her chest. 'No, it isn't right to speak like this, of dying. How preposterous! She has headaches, that's all. They weaken her, but she'll be fine again soon, she always is. This time last year we were preparing to go on the muster. We've another one coming up. You have to get better!' She spun for the door. 'I'll send for Doctor Halton. We'll talk to him again. He might know of something else we can do. I'll be right back.'

She ran from the cottage and along the paths,

267

refusing to give up hope. Tears of frustration and anger blinded her. Rounding a bend that afforded a view over the fields, she skidded to a halt to stop herself from knocking over her grandmama.

'Why are you running, Matilda?' Grandmama snapped, her face full of worry. 'Adelaide?'

'I'm sorry. I was hurrying so I can send for Doctor Halton.'

'Has she turned for the worse?'

'She won't go to Sydney and she's talking of dying here. Dying! I'm not having that!' Hot tears blurred her vision. 'She's giving up without even trying! We need to do something, anything!'

'Dearest.' Grandmama took her arm and led her to the wooden bench further up the path. 'Adelaide is very ill.'

'But she can be fixed.' Tilly adjusted her navy skirts as she sat down, tears dripping onto the material. A deep pain burned in her chest at the thought of losing Adelaide.

Grandmama sat beside her. 'That isn't strictly true. An operation might be successful in Sydney, but it might also fail. There's no sure way of knowing. Such new equipment is not failsafe.'

'How do you know this?'

'Doctor Halton spoke with your grandpapa yesterday before he left. X-rays are still experimental. If it's a tumour, they have to locate it in the brain, and that's very dangerous. Even if she survives the operations, there's no way of knowing if she'll be herself when she wakes up.'

'It must be worth a try though, surely?' Tilly

demanded, unable to fathom why everyone was so eager to give up. 'If we get her to Sydney, then it gives her a chance.'

'She doesn't want to go, and we need to honour her decision. She's been given all the facts and made her choice.'

'She's not thinking straight. She's in pain, and no one thinks straight when they're in pain. If we just take her, I'm sure — '

'Matilda, enough!'

Tilly stared down at the white gravel beneath her boots. 'Why would she choose to die and leave us?'

'Because she's in terrible pain. It's wearing her down. You know how she used to be with one of her headaches; she'd be in bed for two days. Now they're getting more frequent, and the pain can't be controlled so easily. Doctor Halton is having to give her morphine. Adelaide told me last night that she couldn't make the journey to Sydney; she doesn't have the strength, or the will.' Grandmama squeezed her hands.

'Without proper tests, how can we be sure that she can't be cured? Doctor Halton may be wrong. How can he be sure it's a tumour?'

'Years of medical practice, I suppose. And he's written to colleagues.'

'I won't believe it.'

'You have no option but to believe it and deal with it the best you can. This is Adelaide's choice. We aren't living her life.'

Tilly gazed out over towards the horse paddocks. A low mist hovered over the acres of grass. 'How long does she have, then?'

'Doctor Halton thinks she has months, if it's a tumour. He can't say for sure. All he can do is keep consulting with his colleagues who study in that field.'

'And if she goes to Sydney? We can just take her; it's not as if she's in a position to run away from us.'

'The journey alone might be too much for her, never mind the operation. And we won't do it without her consent.'

'Then we shall pay for those special doctors to come here.'

'No.' Grandmama wiped the tears from Tilly's cheeks. 'This is Adelaide's decision. Not ours.'

In the distance, a stockman rode away from the stables, probably to check on the cattle pasturing a few miles away near the river. Tilly watched him until he was a mere speck on the horizon. Her mind felt dazed, numb.

'Let's go and help Connie. She needs us.' Grandmama stood and waited for Tilly to join her for the walk back to the cottage.

Tilly linked her arm through her grandmama's. 'So much has happened in the last few years since the boys left. I'm exhausted by it, Grandmama. I don't know how you do it at your age.'

'I have no choice, my dear. I wake up and I get on with it. Just as you do. What alternative is there? We have a good home, money, and a wonderful family. All that gives us a stable foundation to keep going when we think we can't.'

'I don't feel I can cope with any more deaths.'

270

'We have no control over that, my dear. We simply have to carry on.'

'You're so wise.' Tilly kissed her cheek. 'You know, I feel like I was raised by three women — you, Aunt Connie and Adelaide. I was lucky, wasn't I?'

'That's true, really. Adelaide is the same age as your mother. They were good friends.'

'I never thought of Adelaide as a mother figure, but more of a much older sister. Strange, isn't it? When she's twice my age.'

'Yes, but she's always been young at heart.'

'She laughs a lot when she's not in pain. On the muster last year, she was incredible. She made me laugh so many times.'

'Probably to help you not worry too much. Organising that muster was a big undertaking; that's why Adelaide went with you — to help you. Well, that and to have an adventure. Perhaps she knew it would be her last one.'

'She certainly got that. It's not every day a tree falls on you!'

Grandmama chuckled. 'Absolutely!'

'I just can't believe this is happening, Grandmama, I really can't.'

'I know, my dear. It's difficult to comprehend how Connie and I are still going, and yet we've lost a son each, and now Connie will lose Adelaide.'

'Soon Aunt Connie will only have her grandsons left.' Tilly sighed deeply.

'Connie has us.' Her grandmama sniffed, her eyes teary.

Tilly faltered. Grandmama rarely cried, yet in

the last few years it seemed it was all she had done. 'We need to make Adelaide's last months as happy as possible, Grandmama.'

'We will, darling.'

At the cottage door, they paused and looked at each other in understanding.

★ ★ ★

The following day, Tilly ate her late lunch from a tray while working in the study. She'd spent the morning out in the yards with her grandpapa and Stumpy discussing the breeding programme they wanted to start with a new bull that needed to be purchased. Miles and Stumpy had agreed that it was time to introduce new blood into the herds.

When rain had sent them indoors, her grandpapa decided to attend to his correspondence while Tilly opened the account books, the worst task written on her list to do. There was nothing pleasing in adding figures and writing down expenditures. It bored her senseless. Instead, she thought she might write a letter to Luke. She'd not had the courage to write to him since the Delaney fiasco.

A knock on the open door preceded Penny, a young maid who had begun working in the house the previous week. 'Excuse me, Miss Grayson.'

'Yes?'

'The delivery truck from Spalding's Grocers has arrived.'

Tilly sighed and bit into her ham sandwich. 'I

don't need to know about that, Penny, thank you. Mrs Chalmers will sort it out. She knows what to do.'

'Yes, I know that, miss. Mrs Chalmers sent me to tell you that Mrs Grayson has come in the truck.'

Tilly frowned, not understanding. 'Mrs Grayson?' Her grandmama? Then realisation dawned. There was a new Mrs Grayson now. Oliver's wife. 'But she was meant to send word that she was coming!' Annoyed that she wasn't better prepared, Tilly snapped the account books closed.

Penny lingered at the door, a nervous expression on her face. 'I've given her a towel to dry off, as she got wet; it's pouring still. She's waiting in the drawing room. The fire is lit in there.'

'Thank you, Penny. Make up a tea tray, please.' Tilly dropped her sandwich and stood. Would Jessica like her? Would she like Jessica? What would she do if this new wife of Oliver's was a horrible mean-spirited woman? What if the woman hated Blue Water? So much depended on them getting along. Stomach clenching, she left the desk.

Glancing at the mirror on the wall by the door, she tidied her hair, which as usual escaped its net. She wore a navy skirt and a white blouse. 'I look like a schoolmarm,' she tutted to herself, wishing she was wearing one of her finer day dresses. It seemed forever ago that she took pride in her appearance. She'd not been to a party or dinner dance since before the war started. Her

273

ball gowns were gathering dust.

Tilly's heart thrummed faster as she walked down the hallway to the front of the house. In the doorway, she stopped and stared at the small woman standing in front of the fire. She had her back to Tilly, so all she could see was black curls beneath the brim of her wide black hat, and she wore a long dark green coat that nearly touched the floor.

'You're here. My brother's wife . . . ' Tilly croaked, her voice suddenly lost.

Jessica turned quickly, her smile tentative. 'Yes. I do apologise for not sending word. I had no time to . . . ' Her hand lifted to her face, hovered for a second, then lowered again. 'You must be Tilly?'

'Yes.' Entering the room, Tilly studied the other woman. She was tiny, swamped by the large coat and wide hat. The rain intensified outside, bouncing off the drive and making a thundering noise as it hit the veranda's tin roof.

Tilly dithered on the spot, not knowing if she should go find her grandparents or sit down, but then Jessica turned her head a little and Tilly saw the bruising on her face. 'You're hurt?'

'Oh, it is nothing.' Jessica pulled her hat brim down lower. 'I . . . I fell.'

That Jessica couldn't meet her eyes made Tilly suspicious. 'You've married my brother. We're family now. We have no lies in this house.' She'd said it more harshly than she intended, but she'd have no more strangers lying to her; she'd had her fill with Delaney.

Jessica's chin jutted up, defiance sparkling in

274

her eyes. 'I think it was a mistake coming here.'

'Why? This is my brother's home. You're his wife. You belong here now,' she snapped, wondering why she was speaking so awfully.

'You don't owe me anything. We're strangers.'

'We are. But for Oliver's sake, we must learn about each other.' Tilly watched the expressions change on Jessica's face from wariness to sadness. She softened. 'How did you hurt yourself?'

'My father was drunk and he hit me. He wasn't impressed I'd married a soldier without him knowing.' Jessica boldly stared at Tilly, showing the dark bruising around her left cheek and the half-swollen eye.

'Your father . . . ' Stepping forward, Tilly tried to find words of comfort, but Penny arrived with the loaded tea tray and she busied herself pouring out tea to buy time. This poor woman had been beaten by her father for marrying Oliver. It was unconscionable to her that could happen.

'Shall I take your coat, Mrs Grayson?' Penny asked.

'I — I, er . . . yes.' Reluctance showed in every movement as Jessica unpinned her hat, then took off her gloves and shed her coat, revealing her pregnant stomach.

'Oh my!' Tilly gasped, as Penny scarpered with the hat and coat. 'You're having a baby?'

'I was hoping Oliver would have told you by now.'

'Huh, my brother tells us nothing!' Shocked, she stared at the rounded stomach. 'Even Gabe didn't mention it, and that's so unlike him.'

'I'm sorry this has been such a surprise to you. May I sit?' Jessica looked pale and ready to faint.

'Yes, of course.' Tilly handed her a teacup. She couldn't stop staring at Jessica's stomach.

'The baby is the reason why we married so suddenly.' Jessica blushed. 'Though I'm not ashamed. I love Oliver very much, more than I thought I ever could love a man, and I know he loves me too. He truly is the best person I've ever met,' Jessica babbled, tears shimmering. 'And I know he adores you and misses you more than he can say. It's terribly hard for him, and them all, to be away from you and the family. He's told me so much about you all and Blue Water. He misses home a great deal.'

Her words poured over Tilly like a balm, soothing her hurt and anger at what she felt was Oliver's abandonment. The tears she hadn't cried for her brothers' desertion now flowed freely.

Jessica sat forward on the sofa and leaned towards her, her own eyes brimming. 'I'm sorry. I didn't mean to upset you.'

'You haven't, not at all.' Tilly gripped Jessica's hands in hers. 'You've brought my brother back to me, in a way. He doesn't write, and I miss him so much. For you to say those words . . . I've not seen them in three years! Yet you've spoken to him and spent time with him and Gabe recently. You can tell me things about them.' She could barely speak for the sorrow filling her. 'I want my brothers back.'

'We both do.' Jessica smiled, her bruised face

276

causing her to grimace. 'And I've always wanted a sister.'

Tilly grinned, wiping her eyes. She was warming to this woman her brother loved.

'Your smile is exactly like Gabe's.' Jessica smoothed her skirts.

'Yes, people have said that before.' Tilly took a deep breath to compose herself. She was so tired of crying. She'd hardly ever cried before this god-awful war started.

'You should be so proud of them, Tilly, of all of them. I've never met such a good bunch of men before. They take care of each other.'

'They're all brothers. They grew up together, we all did. My grandparents will come in shortly. You'll make them happy by being here.'

'They won't mind about the baby?' Jessica sipped her tea.

'Heavens no.' Tilly glanced at Jessica's stomach again. 'They'll be thrilled. We haven't had a baby in this house since Gabe was born. It's something to look forward to.'

Jessica relaxed with a sigh and took another sip. 'I've been so worried.'

'So were we. The news shocked us that Oliver had married and you were on your way to live with us. We couldn't take it in.'

'It was all done in a rush. Oliver had limited leave and had to call in favours for us to be married in such a short time.'

Tilly offered her a plate a sandwiches and small delicate scones. 'And you're a nurse? I'm right in that, aren't I?'

'Yes. I was serving with the Australian army,

but once you're married you have to resign.' Jessica bit into a beef sandwich.

'And you couldn't stay in London to be closer to Oliver?'

'Not really. I know no one in London and I didn't have the money to cope on my own with no wage coming in. It would have taken a long time for the army to organise Oliver's pay to come to me, and then I didn't know if it would be enough to live on, at least not anywhere decent.'

'But Oliver has money.' Tilly added cream to her scone. 'Our father left us an inheritance.'

'Oliver told me that, but I didn't want him to use it. I felt I needed to come back to Australia. I stupidly thought my father might become a better man towards me now that I'm married and he'll be a grandfather, but it was wishful thinking on my part.'

'Any man who can hit his pregnant daughter is a scoundrel.' Tilly bristled. 'I'm sorry, but it's true.'

Jessica's expression fell. 'Yes. He's always been the same. A bully and a drunk.'

Disgusted, Tilly stiffened. 'Well, we'll look after you and the baby. Your home is here; you're a Grayson now.'

Jessica visibly relaxed, and her smile was genuine. 'Thank you. I'm so relieved — and I'll work. I can use my nursing skills here on the station, and clean and do whatever else needs doing. I'll pull my weight, don't worry about that.'

Tilly glanced up as her grandparents entered

278

the room. 'Look, Jessica has arrived!'

Introductions were excitedly made, and Penny brought in another tea tray.

'You're very welcome here, Jessica. And you're having a baby. How wonderful!' Grandmama said, her fingers held to her mouth in awe. 'Miles, we're to be great-grandparents!'

'Good gracious, woman, you make us sound instantly ancient.' Grandpapa gave Jessica a welcome kiss on the cheek.

'You *are* ancient, but I'm in my prime!' Grandmama laughed.

'That you are, my love.' He grinned, kissing the side of her head.

Jessica turned to Tilly. 'And now I know where that cheeky grin comes from.'

20

Broodseinde, Flanders. October 1917.

In the grey light of dawn, with sheets of rain blighting the landscape, Oliver waited with his men for the signal to advance. He shivered as water dripped off his helmet and trickled down his neck. Absentmindedly, he watched the rain splash the muddy puddles at his feet, wishing he was miles from here and in the heat of Australia, and preferably in Jessica's arms.

'I swear I'll never get used to this rain and mud,' Johnny grumbled beside him, trying to lift his boots clear of the sloppy sludge.

Big Max shifted his stance on the other side of Oliver but remained silent.

'Gabe is well out of it today,' Freddie added, drawing on his cigarette. 'Lucky bugger.'

'He had a tough night of it last night,' Oliver said, watching the other men down the row. They appeared as miserable as he felt. 'Gabe looked dreadful when he came back an hour ago.'

'Did they lose anyone on the raid last night?' Freddie pulled his large waterproof cape over him, better to shield against the weather.

'Yes, two. Arthurs and Rodman.' Oliver squinted against the driving rain, which now came at them at an angle. 'Gabe told me it was a near thing that they all weren't killed or captured. A German advance party saw them break from the wood. Gabe said it was only the clouds covering the moon and making it so dark that saved them, and they were able to get back to safety.'

Johnny swore, and cupping his hands, tried to light a damp cigarette. 'Trench raids are dangerous at the best of times, but in this disgusting weather they're murderous. The mud stops you from running. Freddie, do you have a dry cig? Mine are useless.' He swore again and threw his cigarette into the mud.

'Hey, don't waste them! I could have dried that out,' Freddie grumbled, passing his own packet to Johnny.

Oliver lifted his head, listening. The monotonous booming of the big guns continued. The ground vibrated under their feet. He waited for a pause in the thundering shellfire and distinctly heard the whistle, muted in the downpour. 'Let's go, boys.'

As a group they moved off, cold, wet and dismal. Yet they wouldn't want to be anywhere else. Together they were brothers, and the need to watch out for each other was stronger than the need to be safe.

'Our objective is to take eighteen hundred yards,' Oliver told Johnny and Max as they squelched through the mire. 'The barrage will move up every hour.'

Freddie slipped over in the mud and swore. Big Max helped him back up. In torrential rain, they advanced until a storm of enemy machine-gun fire opened up on them.

'Take cover!' Oliver yelled as the men

scattered for shell holes. He jumped down the slope of one hole, the sides slippery, and he had to scramble for footholds before he landed in the pool of thick murky water at the bottom. Freddie, Big Max and Johnny joined him.

'Jesus wept!' Johnny shouted, waist deep in mud. Big Max pulled him up before helping Oliver and Freddie.

Oliver wiped mud from his pistol. 'Are you all right, Johnny?'

'Aye.' He grimaced, trying to scrape the cloying sludge off his body.

Squelching his way back to the top of the hole, Oliver peered over the edge. Wiping the rain out of his eyes, he focused on the trenches in front. A wide area of no man's land stretched before them, strewn with rolls of wire, deep craters and uneven wasted ground. Beyond that were entrenched Germans and their machine guns.

'Another bloody suicide attack,' Freddie murmured, ducking as bullets zipped into the mud around them.

'Shut up, Freddie,' Oliver snapped. 'Let's just get it done.' He watched for a moment as other soldiers further down the line battled forward. Some made it through, plenty did not.

But the momentum was swinging the Allies' way. They needed to take advantage of it and go with the push. The roar of bombs landing in front of them hurt their ears. Dirt thrown up by the shells showered them like hail.

Oliver looked to the left and saw that Jones, one of the men in his unit who used the Lewis machine gun, was lying injured, but alive.

'Freddie, get over to Jones and take the Lewis gun. Set it up in the next hole. I want you to cover us as we move forward.'

'Right-o.' While Freddie crawled out of the hole, slurping through the mud on his belly, Oliver, Johnny and Max opened fire until Freddie reached Jones and gave the thumbs-up.

'We're going to head that way,' Oliver said, pointing to the right, 'and take that trench.' With a signal to Freddie, who opened fire on the trench, Oliver urged his men onwards.

They only got a few feet when Johnny was shot in the head. He dropped like a stone. Stunned, Oliver jerked to a stop. Big Max cried out and bent to tend to him. Oliver just stared.

Freddie landed with a thump in the mud beside them, firing randomly to give them cover. 'Oliver, get down, for Christ's sake! I'm running out of ammo.'

He was jerked down by Freddie, shaking him out of his stupor. He closed his eyes momentarily, trying not to look on the shattered head that only moments before was Johnny. Their Johnny. No, not again. Not another one.

'Oliver!' Freddie yelled into his face.

He blinked, clearing his head. The world crashed in on his senses once more. His heart was in his throat. Grief and rage combined into a madness in his head. Bullets zipped past him. Bombs exploded. The rain washed his face.

Max was holding Johnny, rocking him like a baby. 'Max . . . Max leave him, come on!' Oliver desperately tried to pull him away as bullets smashed into the ground around them. They

283

would all die this day.

'No! I'll take him back.' Big Max bent to pick Johnny up, but a bullet went through his thigh. He howled in pain and buckled into the mud beside Johnny.

Crouching low, Oliver pulled out his medical kit and wrapped a bandage around Max's thigh. He yelled for stretcher bearers until his throat went hoarse. Freddie gave them cover, but out in the open they were sitting ducks for the German gunfire.

'Go!' Big Max gave Oliver his ammunition and pushed him away, his eyes half closed with pain. 'Go. I'll be fine!'

'I'll come find you later.' Oliver squeezed Max's shoulder. With a last look at Johnny, he and Freddie ran to catch up with the others, who had successfully taken the first line of trenches.

⋆ ⋆ ⋆

Later that afternoon, after hours of fighting, Oliver led those of his unit able to walk back to safety behind the lines. Another battalion had taken over their hard-won position as their relief. Exhausted, and in charge of six captured German prisoners, Oliver chatted quietly with Markham as they tiredly plodded back to the village they were billeted in. Around them, soldiers of the British and Commonwealth armies milled about, some coming out of the line and others preparing to go into it. The potholed dirt road was edged with horses and carts and motor trucks filled with either supplies or wounded. Those village buildings still standing were temporary accommodation and officers' quarters. From somewhere the smell of cooking drifted over to them.

Oliver's stomach rumbled and he couldn't remember the last time he ate a decent hot meal. 'Are all our dead and wounded accounted for, sir?'

'Yes.' Markham nodded, lighting a cigarette before offering the pack to Oliver, who declined. 'We'll need new recruits before we move out again. We're greatly diminished.' Markham spoke between puffs of a cigarette. 'Losing some of our fellows has hit us hard. Then we have many wounded who won't be back for some weeks, either. However, we're out of the line for a while until we wait for new orders. It'll give us time to recover and bury our dead.'

Oliver wiped his eyes wearily. Another funeral. This time Johnny's. It still hurt him that Patrick's body hadn't been retrieved as he promised it would. The enemy held that area, and Oliver hoped they would have done the decent thing and buried him. Samuel was buried in a makeshift cemetery on the side of the road near the casualty clearing station with the other wounded soldiers who'd died.

Markham took a final puff of his cigarette and threw it away. 'I know you'll want to see Max, but I can't say it'll happen. I need you here.'

'That's fine. I'll write to his brother, Drew; he's a quartermaster further down the line. He'll find out which hospital he's been taken to and visit.'

As they neared a transport truck, Markham stopped the silent march of men too weary to chat and went to talk to the driver. After a few minutes, he returned to Oliver. 'I need to report in. You'll see that the prisoners are loaded into that truck. The driver has the paperwork. Our men need food and rest. Come and see me in an hour for the debrief.'

'Yes, sir.' Oliver walked back to the men and the small group of prisoners. He nodded to the truck driver, a thin man with a bristling moustache. 'These prisoners are going with you.'

'Yes, sir.' The driver signalled to the guards, who waited in the doorway of a building.

Oliver stood watching the prisoners, some no more than teenage boys, climb up onto the back of the truck. They looked as dirty and miserable as Oliver's men.

'That's it for them.' Freddie, eyes dimmed from exhaustion and cradling a bandaged hand, smoked a stub of a cigarette. 'They're out of it. I wish the rest of them would hold their hands up, too; then we can all go home.'

Sighing, Oliver gave the order for the men to go wash and eat. He turned to Freddie. 'I've got to find Gabe and tell him about Johnny.'

'I still can't believe it.' Freddie shook his head.

'Oliver!' Gabe came out of a cottage further down the street. 'I just heard you were back. You look like shit.' He glanced at Freddie and then back to his brother. 'Everyone all right?' he asked hopefully.

Feeling the depths of despair rise in his chest, Oliver shook his head. 'Johnny . . . '

286

'No!' Gabe gasped, wide-eyed. 'Oh God no. Not Johnny.'

'The Jessups . . . they've lost both sons . . . ' Oliver closed his eyes in sadness and swore violently. It was too unfair. The Jessups were lifelong family friends. Johnny and Samuel's grandmother, Alice, had travelled from York with his grandmother and Connie fifty years ago. The Jessups farmed the neighbouring property that had been his grandmother's, and the two families were joined by a deep friendship. His grandmother and Aunt Connie would be devastated.

Oliver swore again at the loss and the futility of it all. There'd be no welcome home at the Jessups' house when all this nonsense was over.

How would he be able to face any of them? Yet, perhaps he need not worry about that, for who was to say that any of them would return home?

'Max got caught in the leg.' Freddie squinted through the cigarette smoke.

'Bad?' Gabe asked. 'Is he being sent home?'

Freddie stubbed out the cigarette on his boot and threw it away. 'I doubt it. A clean shot through. A month and he'll be back, knowing Big Max.'

'Will we be burying Johnny here? Can we get him?' Gabe struggled to speak.

Oliver nodded, depressed at the thought. 'Yes, Markham organised for our men to be brought back before we left the field. The stretcher bearers were working as we left. The burial will be first thing in the morning. I'll go sort it out now.'

Gabe, with tears in his eyes, grabbed Oliver's arm. 'Come sit for a minute first. The food wagon's just been brought up.' He thumbed over his shoulder to the cottage he'd just left. 'They've got hot stew in there, and bread.'

Oliver looked down at his hands, which were filthy. 'I need to wash . . . ' Emotion clogged his throat. He couldn't break down, not here, not yet.

A weak setting sun broke out from behind the grey clouds and bathed the village in a soft fading light. Above them, a biplane flew overhead, its low hum drifting on the air.

Oliver raised his face and watched the plane, wishing he was sitting up there in it and flying away. 'There were eight of us. The men from Blue Water Station. Eight men. Now we're five.'

21

Blue Water Station, December 1917.

A dry heat, which sapped the energy from both humans and animals alike, baked the countryside. Even the birds were quiet in the motionless eucalyptus trees; not a hint of breeze blew to shiver the branches. The grass had turned brown and brittle.

Tilly rode her horse, Ness, alongside the Orara River, where it snaked through a shallow valley a mile from the house. The water depth was recorded in her notebook at different points. Her grandpapa was meticulous about writing everything down and encouraged Tilly to do the same. Historical documentation was important for the future of the station. However, she was taking photos too. Grandpapa could no longer ride the boundaries, so she did it to show him, and he'd mention if things had changed.

She twitched the reins and rode on towards the house, her mind flitting from thought to thought. She kept her eyes peeled for any sign that Delaney might hiding, waiting to pounce on her, but so far they had heard nothing from him. On that fateful night, Stumpy had tied him up, driven him to Grafton and put him on the first boat heading for Sydney. He'd not been seen since. Most days she forgot about him; it was only at night, if she heard a sound, that she'd sit up in bed, watchful.

Ness checked her footing as they rode down along the river bank. Large wombat holes littered the sandy edge, but she didn't see any of the fat furry beasts. Rabbit warrens also studded the bank, but the heat of the day had driven them deep underground. Above her head a kookaburra laughed, its call loud in the peaceful quiet of the day.

Her thoughts turned to home as naturally as she shifted the reins and led Ness away from the river. Poor Adelaide lingered; her deterioration had been swift and distressing in the last few weeks, to a point where now she was bedridden and rarely lucid. Doctor Halton kept most of her pain at bay with morphine. Aunt Connie hardly left her side, which worried Grandmama greatly, for she was growing weak too. Jessica's nursing skills were heaven-sent. She cared for Adelaide with attention and kindness, talking to her about Egypt and London, keeping her company to give Aunt Connie a rest.

Tilly loved her sister-in-law with a devotion that surprised her. Jessica fitted into the family as though she'd always been a part of it. She was the sister Tilly never had. With Jessica she could be free with her thoughts and emotions. She'd told her about Delaney and Luke. Together they worried over the boys' safety, the future of Blue Water and the old folks' fragility. Yet despite the anxiety they shared, they also rejoiced in a closeness that delighted them both.

Ness tossed her head, knowing she was nearly home to a good feed of hay, and bringing Tilly's mind back to the present. Her gaze drifted over to the other side of the river in the direction of the Jessups' farm. She still could not believe that Johnny and Samuel were dead. The boys she'd grown up with. How was it even possible? Two healthy young men, full of life and energy, snuffed out like candles. The group would never ride out as whole again. The parties they'd had, especially when Freddie and Patrick came over from Armidale, were legendary in the district. The barn would be cleared out and tables of food and drink set up. Stockmen would create a makeshift musical band, and they'd sing and dance until dawn. Tilly was never short of partners and would laugh until her cheeks ached.

Would they ever have those happy times again? The day they'd found out about Johnny's death and Big Max's wounding remained etched on Tilly's mind. Her grandparents had comforted Aunt Connie, and then Tilly had driven them over to the Jessups' farm. Paul Jessup, who had grown up with Adam and David, had barely acknowledged them, his eyes blind to everything but the grief which gripped him. His wife, Rachel, a dear woman Tilly admired, served them tea and put on a brave show. The poor woman had lost her two sons, yet she smiled at Tilly and hugged her close, encouraging her to talk of the boys and the fun they'd had growing up.

A shout from one of the stockman made Tilly turn in the saddle. The men were breaking in a new colt. A dust cloud hung over the stockyards as the horse tried to assert his independence.

Tilly rode Ness into the stable block and saw Jessica waiting for her. Dismounting, she stared at her sister-in-law, who looked hot, tired, and hugely pregnant. A shiver of dread tingled down her spine. She would be very glad when both Jessica and the baby were safely through the ordeal of childbirth. 'Why are you out in this heat without a hat on?'

'I just popped down to see if you were about. Stumpy told me you were out riding the river, then we saw you returning, so I thought I'd wait.'

Stumpy came out of the nearest stable, his eyes red. 'Here, miss, I'll take Ness inside for a rub down; you go on up to the house.'

'Thank you.' She stared at Stumpy as he took Ness away, knowing he'd been crying. Stumpy never cried. 'Is it Adelaide?' Tilly asked Jessica, taking off her riding gloves and hardening her heart against bad news.

'She's worse today, Til.' Jessica sighed, linking her arm through Tilly's to walk back. 'I've told Stumpy that I don't think she has long.'

Tilly digested the news with a sickening feeling. A lone cry of a crow filled the still hot air. For the first time, she hated the sound. 'Poor Stumpy. I think he's been in love with Adelaide for years. If she'd been well, he'd have asked her to marry him.'

'Really?' Jessica looked surprised. 'He's a dear man.'

'Yes. They've known each other for such a long time, obviously, but when we went on the muster they grew close. I don't know why Stumpy waited so long to ask her, and now it's too late.'

'Such a shame.' Jessica rubbed her round belly. 'I'd have liked the baby to have been born so Adelaide could see him.'

'You always call the baby *him*. It'll be a girl, you'll see.'

'It'll be a boy. He's been lazy like a male and not in a hurry to come out.'

They skirted the house and headed across the lawns to Aunt Connie's cottage. Relieved to be out of the sun, Tilly took off her wide-brimmed hat and wiped the sweat from her brow. The cottage was dim, cool and quiet.

'You go through. I'll make some tea.' Jessica stirred the low coals in the Aga to boil the kettle.

At the doorway to Adelaide's bedroom, Tilly paused and smiled at her grandmama and Aunt Connie, both of whom sat on either side of the bed. 'Is she awake?'

'She's in and out.' Aunt Connie stood with a creak. 'Sit with her for a bit while your grandmama and I have some tea and stretch our legs.'

'I need to wash.'

Aunt Connie waved away her concerns. 'Adelaide won't mind a bit of dust on your clothes.'

'Jessica's in the kitchen putting the kettle on.' Tilly sat on the chair and took Adelaide's cool hand in hers.

In the quietness of the room, Tilly relaxed. She gazed at Adelaide, who lay silent. Grey liberally sprinkled her dark hair, and her breathing hardly moved the sheets over her thin body.

Adelaide's fingers twitched in Tilly's hand. She leaned forward. 'Adelaide?'

Adelaide's eyelids flickered, then opened. For several seconds she stared up at the ceiling, before moving her head slightly and smiling at Tilly. 'You look hot . . . '

Tilly grinned. It was the first coherent sentence Adelaide had said in weeks. 'I am. I've been out riding the river. I need a bath.' Unlike the others, Tilly refused to act as though Adelaide was made of spun sugar, and behaved with her as she normally would. 'Do you want anything? A drink?'

'To talk . . . '

'All right.' Tilly leaned back in the chair, enormously pleased that Adelaide was rational. 'Talk away.'

'Prop . . . me up.'

Tilly retrieved another pillow from the chest under the window and, gently lifting Adelaide up, she placed it behind her shoulders. 'Comfortable? Have some water.' She helped her sip water from a glass which stood on the bedside table. Delighted that Adelaide was sounding better than she had in weeks, Tilly couldn't stop smiling. Perhaps she was getting better.

'Thank you.' Adelaide took a deep breath. 'I must talk to you.'

'I'm listening.'

'I need you to make sure Mam is watched over after . . . I'm gone. She'll be lonely . . . worried over the boys.' The effort of talking showed on her pale face and laboured breathing.

'We'll watch her, don't worry about that. Grandmama won't leave her side.'

'I want you . . . to have the things I didn't have . . . marriage and babies.'

'Who's to say I won't have those things?' she said light-heartedly, but Adelaide was starting to fade before her eyes.

'I know you . . .' Adelaide closed her eyes for a moment and took some time to gather her strength. 'Delaney has made you harder, emotionally, and . . . you're stubborn . . .' Adelaide held Tilly's hands in a feeble hold. 'Don't end up alone. Don't be like me and watch everyone else have a family while you stand on the sidelines.' A tear slipped out of the corner of Adelaide's eye and she dragged in a deep breath, wincing as the pain hit her. All colour left her face. 'Write to Luke. Take a chance . . . on him. For me . . .'

Tilly stared down at their joined hands, swallowing back emotion. She didn't want Adelaide talking with such finality. 'I will.' She'd stopped writing to Luke since the fiasco with Delaney, though his letters still came at least once a month. The last one stated he was deep in the desert and that the Ottomans had defeated them in some major battles. He sounded low with none of his usual banter, and *still* she had hardened her heart against him.

'*Matilda* . . . please? He doesn't deserve your silence . . .' Adelaide's voice waned as she became exhausted, her spell of being awake coming to an end.

'Rest, Adelaide.'

A flash of annoyance came into her eyes and she struggled to sit up. 'I'll be doing enough of that soon enough. Listen to me! This will be the last time I'll be able to advise you . . . as your mother would have wanted me to. He's a good man, Matilda . . . '

Tilly held her hands up in the air in surrender, knowing that she only called her *Matilda* when she was cross with her. 'All right, for you I will.'

'Promise?'

'I promise.'

'Good.' Adelaide flopped against the pillows like a rag doll, her breathing raspy. She glanced at the writing desk in the corner of the room. 'There's pen and paper . . . '

'What, now?'

Adelaide smiled gently and closed her eyes, sleep claiming her once more.

With a huff, Tilly stomped over to the desk and sat down. Grabbing the pen and a sheet of paper, she thought what to write.

Dear Luke,
How are you? I am well. Adelaide is dying! I hate it! I hate it all!

She wrote uncaringly, in sharp jerks, then felt bad and stopped. Behaving like a spoilt child would help no one.

She peeped at Adelaide and muttered an unladylike word under her breath. She didn't want to care about Luke or any man, or be open to being made to look a fool again. He'd been on

296

her mind, but she'd refused to think of him. But she had promised.

Taking a deep breath, she started screwed up the paper and started on a new page.

A sudden need to be honest with him filled her. She had nothing to lose anyway, and if she managed to scare him away then so much the better!

I must apologise for my lack of letters. I have no excuse, except to say I felt the need to distance myself from you due to some foolish notion that maybe you were not the man for me. A stockman (RD) who was working here caught my attention, but he led me false. I thought he could be someone I could rely on. I was wrong. He humiliated me.

My foolish behaviour inhibited me from writing to you or thinking about any man in a favourable way.

My trust and confidence are broken.

As you know, I have been left at home to oversee the running of this station, and I have risen to the challenge; and if I am honest, I have for the most part enjoyed doing it. However, the fact remains that the men I love — my brothers, my cousins and my childhood friends — all left me, including my father. Then you were added to that list — another man who wasn't here. Through your letters you made me care for you.

After RD disappointed me, I felt an

overwhelming sense of injustice. I was angry, and I took that anger out on you by not writing. It was stupid and selfish of me. I am sorry.

My dear friend Adelaide has shown me the error of my ways. She says I must give you a chance to prove yourself. So I will. Though you may not want to correspond with me after reading this letter and learning that I fell for another! That will be your choice, and any decision you make I will accept.

To catch you up on our news (unless you have already heard from Oliver), I can tell you that Oliver married Nurse Hutton, as you would recall her; the woman you met in Cairo with Oliver. She is here living with us, and I am so thankful for it. Jessica is a wonderful addition to our family, and by Christmas we should have the celebration of her baby being born. I am to be an aunty. I'm deliciously excited by the prospect.

Sadly though, this news is the only happy information to report. Our dear friend Johnny has joined his brother Samuel in another French grave. My sweet cousin Patrick has also been lost, devastating us all. (If the boys write to you still, you may already know this news.)

The happy group you met in Egypt has shrunk in size and attitude, Luke. Gabe could always be relied on to make us laugh with his letters full of witty comments about things he'd seen and done, and the funny observations of others, but even he has changed. His letters are perfunctory now, and Oliver sends none at all to me. Jessica receives letters, but they are short and mainly ask questions. He reveals nothing of himself. Do you hear from him?

I fear for them all. The things they, and you, have witnessed must be horrific. How can you all return to normal lives?

I suppose it must be up to us who have remained behind to help you readjust.

How is Monty? When will you be out of the desert?

I will sign off now. I have nothing else left to write about, and I should be in the study writing cheques to pay the bills. My grandpapa is having terrible trouble with the arthritis in his hands this week and can't hold a pen to write his signature.

She paused and reread what she had written. Was it enough to regain the friendship they had? What would he think of her now? Would he be shocked? Perhaps he'd want nothing to do with her after her silly dalliance. The anger left her as suddenly as it had arrived, and she felt deflated and sad.

Do you forgive me, Luke? Have I disappointed you? I will understand if I never hear from you again.

Stay safe.
Fond regards,
Matilda.

Standing up, she folded the letter and stuck it in an envelope.

She went to the bed and kissed the top of Adelaide's head. 'I did it. It's up to him now.'

Adelaide didn't stir, but her hand twitched slightly.

Leaving the room, Tilly went into the kitchen to find Aunt Connie reading the newspaper. Jessica and her grandmama had left.

'Is she sleeping?' Aunt Connie asked.

'Yes, but we had a chat.'

'You did? Oh, how marvellous. She's not been clear in anything she'd said for days. Oh, I'm so pleased!' Aunt Connie's eyes came to life. 'What did she say?'

'She bullied me into writing a letter to Luke Williams.' Tilly waved the envelope in the air. 'I did what she asked.'

'Good. It's a start.'

'A start of what?'

'Of getting on with your life again. You need to get Delaney out of your head, lass. Adelaide saw him for what he was. Afterwards, she told me how worried she was about you being involved with him.'

With a sigh, Tilly sat at the table. 'I should have listened to her. She's a good judge of character. She saw Delaney as the waster he is. I didn't.' With a fingertip, she traced the pattern of the lace tablecloth. 'I suppose that's why I've written to Luke. I've explained my actions, and well, I hope he understands. I'm not even sure I understand it all myself.'

'You were wanting to recapture what you'd

lost, lass. There's nothing wrong in that. You thought Delaney could replace the boys, that you could have some excitement back in your life, and his presence would lessen the hole they'd left.' Aunt Connie patted her hand. 'And if this Luke fellow doesn't understand, then he's not right for you either.'

'I wonder if Delaney made good his threat to disgrace me with gossip.'

Aunt Connie huffed. 'He wouldn't dare! He'd know your grandpapa would make his life a misery. Miles will have eyes and ears on this fellow. The minute he surfaces, your grandpapa will know about it.' Aunt Connie closed the newspaper. 'No, that scoundrel has gone to ground, you mark my words. He'll be looking for another poor sod to mess with.'

'I thought perhaps he'd come back. I find myself listening to sounds at night.'

'He's a coward. He'll be moving on to someone else by now.'

'That makes me feel even worse. That I really did mean nothing to him.'

'Don't spend another moment thinking of him, lass. He's not worth it.' Aunt Connie slowly got to her feet and started to tidy away the tea things.

'Leave that, I'll do it.'

'Thank you.' Aunt Connie kissed the top of her head. 'I'll go sit with Adelaide for a bit. She might wake up and want a chat with me for a few minutes.'

Tilly rose and gathered the tea things. 'She wants to know that everyone will be all right after she's gone. She's worried about you. It's only natural.'

'She doesn't have to worry about me. I'll be fine. I'll survive until the boys come home, then I'll die happy and join my loved ones.'

'You know I don't like talk like that, Aunt.' Tilly scowled at her.

'It's life, my lass.'

'Have you heard from Max or Drew today? I forgot to ask before. I went riding early and I've not seen the post.'

Collecting her basket of knitting from the side dresser, Aunt Connie nodded. 'Yes, I received a letter from Max this morning. He's healed enough to be discharged from the hospital, and he was getting ready to rejoin Oliver and the others. He said it was good seeing Drew, who got some leave to stay with Max for a couple of days.'

'I'm glad his leg has healed.' Tilly put everything onto a tray and put it on the sideboard, ready for one of the maids to clean when she came down from the house.

Aunt Connie shook her head. 'I'm not. I wish it had been bad enough for him to be sent home.'

'He'd not want to leave them, you know that. Right, I'd best go. I have a whole afternoon of work to do.' Impulsively, Tilly kissed Aunt Connie's cheek. 'I'll pop back later.'

'All right, my lass. Jessica said she'll be back shortly. She's gone to one of the stockmen's cottages. I think one of the children down there has hurt his arm, fell out of a tree or something.'

'She does too much!' Tilly took her hat from the hook and put it on.

'Aye, she does, but you can't tell her. It was a good day when that lass got out of the grocer's truck, I can tell you. Oliver is a lucky man.'

'I agree. He'd better appreciate her, too.' Tilly left the cottage and headed for the house, feeling lighter of spirit than she had in a long time. She looked down at the envelope and smiled, hoping Luke would write back. If he was the man she hoped he was, then perhaps they had a chance once the war was over. Perhaps . . .

'Tilly!' Jessica called to her from across the lawn.

'What is it?'

Before Jessica could reply, she bent double and groaned.

'Jessica!' Tilly ran across the grass, her heart thumping nearly out of her chest. She skidded to a halt beside her. 'The baby?'

Jessica gripped Tilly's arms. 'Help me inside, will you? And send for Doctor Halton.'

22

Hazebrouck, Flanders, April 1918.

The heat of the sun warmed Oliver's face. A crow's harsh call disturbed the quiet, then Tilly's laughter drowned out the bird and he smiled. What was she laughing at? Something Gabe had done, probably.

'Oliver!' She called him. She was always so bossy. 'Oliver!'

He jerked awake, ready to give Tilly a piece of his mind. But Gabe stood there, not Tilly. He was disorientated for a moment until he realised Gabe wore a dirty khaki uniform and he was in France and not back home.

'I thought you were dead. I couldn't wake you.' Gabe scowled at him. 'We're moving out. Markham is looking for you. Something's happened.'

'All right.' Oliver rubbed his eyes, not fully awake. 'I can't remember sleeping like that for ages. I had a dream that Tilly was laughing then calling for me, but the calling was you. It seemed so real. Her laughing was so clear, as though she was standing next to me.'

Gabe shook his head. 'Stop twittering. Come on. Markham is in a strop about something.'

They hurried from around the side of the barn, where only an hour previously Oliver had sat down to rest in the sunshine.

Markham's shouting could be heard before they saw him. Last night when they had billeted in the small village, it had been quiet. The few French occupants who'd remained in their homes had praised their arrival and offered them warm food. This morning, though, the lane which ran through the centre of cottages was rammed with trucks and soldiers.

Oliver saluted Markham, his gaze darting from left to right. Soldiers, supplies and ammunition were being loaded onto the trucks at a furious rate. A large canon drawn by six horses came thundering by, swirling dust. Above them dotted in the sky like large birds were Allied biplanes which swooped and dived.

'Orders, sir?' Oliver asked.

Markham paused in writing in his notebook. 'We've got to get to Hazebrouck, five miles away, and defend it and the railway. The Germans have broken through. They're heading for the coast. It's desperate. We've got to stop them. The railway is vital to us. We can't lose it.' Markham barked an order to a passing solider, then turned back to Oliver. 'We have to hurry. The British divisions are under pressure, and it's up to us to swing this push the other way before they cave. Messines has already been lost.'

'Yes, sir.' Oliver's heart sank. They had taken and held the town of Messines only days before. Now all that fighting and death were for nothing.

'Get the men loaded. We're in for a nasty time, Grayson. We won't let them take Hazebrouck.' Markham sighed deeply and stroked his moustache. 'You know what to do. Let's go.'

Lying in the shallow ditch he and his men had just dug, Oliver squinted in the sunshine at the fields stretching out before him. Ahead lay the village of Meteren, and behind their line was the small town of Hazebrouck, the German objective. But for the enemy to get to Hazebrouck, they had to go through the Australians.

On the slight breeze came the acrid smell of gunpowder, blood and a hint of pungent mustard gas. More than once in the last few months, they had worn gas masks during an attack when the Germans sent over gas bombs.

'Here.' Gabe fell down beside him and passed him a canteen of water.

'Thanks.' Oliver drank deeply, then remembered to save some for later. Who knew when they'd receive rations again. 'Are the men all right?'

'They'll do. Big Max's leg is giving him some discomfort, but he never complains. I only know of it because he winces when he walks. He came back too early. Freddie's giving last-minute instructions to the new recruits. Poor buggers. They've only been with us a few weeks and now find themselves in the thick of things.'

'Best way for them to learn, as we did at Gallipoli.' Oliver checked his watch.

Gabe stared out over the fields to the right. In the distance, near the village of Merris, a bombardment of shelling descended in a continual harassment of the British troops. 'Jesus. When is it our turn? This sitting around is driving me crazy.'

306

'Any minute now. Look.' Oliver pointed to the dark smudge on the horizon, which they knew to be a line of enemy soldiers advancing.

Gabe snuggled down further into the ditch. 'Come on you bastards, let's be having you.'

Oliver peered down his line of men, all hunched into the shallow trench, armed and ready. 'Hold your fire until I give the signal,' he called out to them.

'Lieutenant Grayson.' Markham, bent low, was hurrying to him. 'The Tommies are getting a drubbing but holding the line to the south, only word has come through that Armentieres has fallen.'

Gabe swore.

'Hazebrouck will not fall, do you understand?' Markham's eyes were bright with determination.

Oliver gave a ghost of a smile. 'No, it won't.'

'We go down to the last man. Understood?'

'Understood, sir.'

'Good.' Markham nodded and kept moving down the line.

Oliver watched the dark smudge move closer, his breath tight in his chest. 'Well, brother, looks like we're in for a tussle.'

The German covering barrage began, and in reply the Allied big guns fired back. The ground shook as bombs exploded in front of them, as yet the range not on target. Explosions hurt their ears, and they had to shout to be heard.

Gabe glanced at Oliver. 'We're not dying today. We've got to get home and see your son. I'm an uncle!'

Oliver smiled at the thought of his son, Alfie.

Letters from Jessica and a photo from Tilly had arrived a month ago, showing him the beautiful baby who was his son. He could scarcely believe he was a father. It didn't seem real, not yet. But then everything back home no longer seemed real. It was as though he'd dreamt that other life where he was clean and wore nice clothes, where he ate good food and received a kiss from his grandmama. He had a dreadful fear that even if by some slim chance he did return home, it would not be as he left it, because he was no longer the person he'd been.

A shell landed twenty yards in front of the ditch. Oliver and Gabe ducked. Rocks and dirt sprayed the men.

'Their cannons are finding range,' Gabe said, squinting through the smoke haze.

'We're not moving,' Oliver said stubbornly. 'Here they come!' He gave the signal to open fire and the air shattered with gunfire.

Wave after wave of German soldiers advanced. It soon became carnage. Bodies lay strewn over the fields. Oliver and the men could barely miss a target, such were the numbers that kept walking towards them. When the enemy managed to make it to the allied line, fierce hand-to-hand fighting erupted.

Without thought or reason, Oliver shot at the enemy, his mind focused on only one thing — to keep the Bosche from getting past them. As the battle raged on, there were small pauses when the German soldiers regrouped, allowing Oliver and his men to have a drink and bandage up any small wounds. Casualties were driven away by ambulance to the nearest casualty clearing station.

'We're doing well,' Gabe said, leaning onto the back of the ditch in a lull of the fighting. 'The Bosche know how to put up a respectable fight.'

'I'm worried about our ammunition levels. We need supplies.' Oliver hunted around the ditch, looking for extra ammunition left behind by those men who had been killed or wounded.

'I could do with a beer.' Gabe wiped his rifle with a rag. The men around him murmured in agreement.

'We all could.' Oliver wrote in his notebook the day's actions so far.

'Lieutenant Grayson!' A call for Oliver came down the line.

Craning his neck to see who wanted him, he spotted a young solider, newly arrived from back home and who looked no more than sixteen even though he said he was eighteen.

'It's the boy soldier.' Gabe grinned.

'Lieutenant Grayson!' the youth shrilled as he made his way through the men.

'Private Dowling, do not shout for me like I'm a dog,' Oliver told him wearily, tucking his little notebook away in his jacket pocket.

The private stumbled to a stop before Oliver. 'Yes, sir, sorry, sir, but you've got to come quickly,' he squeaked, his voice not fully broken yet, and Oliver wondered if the boy was barely fifteen. 'Major Markham has been hit.'

A shiver of dread tingled down Oliver's spine. Grabbing his pistol, he looked at Gabe, and behind him sat Big Max and Freddie. He leaned closer to Gabe. 'This is your section now.'

'Go,' Gabe said, coming to full alert.

With anxiety clawing at his innards, Oliver jumped out of the ditch and hurried behind the youth to the far end. A rumble of speculative whispers from the men followed Oliver. They'd been with Markham for four years. He had earned their respect.

Taken back into a small treed area, Markham lay surrounded by medics working diligently to stop the blood flowing from the wound in his chest. Oliver knelt by his head. The metallic smell of blood filled his nose. 'It's Grayson, sir.'

Markham opened his eyes, but they were unfocused and dazed with pain. 'Notebook . . . '

Oliver reached into Markham's blood-soaked uniform jacket, and from the inside pocket pulled out the thick notebook filled with instruction notes from high command. 'Got it, sir.'

'The men are yours now . . . ' Markham struggled to breathe, the rasping sounds horrible to hear.

One of the medics, his hands covered bright red in blood, called for more bandages, but the desperate look he gave to Oliver spoke volumes.

Markham gasped. The blood from his throat ran out of the corner of his mouth. The life seeped from his eyes, and his body went limp. He was gone.

Oliver tensed. Sadness washed over him; sadness and anger. Another good man dead.

'Lieutenant Grayson, there's movement from the enemy.'

Oliver blinked, his mind at odds with the knowledge that Markham was no longer his superior officer, no longer in charge. He was. At least for today.

'Lieutenant Grayson!'

With a mental shake, Oliver tucked the notebook into his breast pocket and gave out orders to fill the line again. Men ran back into position in the ditches. Running along behind them, Oliver encouraged them to give all they had. They wouldn't lose this ground. He owed it to Markham.

'Right, lads,' Oliver shouted down the line of men, all poised with rifles ready. 'Let's show them what Australians are made of, shall we?'

A roar echoed across the land.

★   ★   ★

When their relief came three days later, Oliver blearily led his men out of the front line. The enemy had abandoned their attempt to take Hazebrouck, the Australian defence being too strong, the losses too great.

Sleep deprived, exhausted, filthy and hungry, the men trudged the dirt roads, the sun warm on their backs. Once in the town of Hazebrouck, they made their way to the railway station and waited for orders.

Dropping where they stopped, most of the soldiers slept on the platform while others happily allowed the grateful French villagers to tend to them. Food, basic and wholesome, was pushed into grimy hands; and bloodsoaked bandages were changed for new ones, usually torn strips from women's petticoats and bedsheets.

Oliver, so fatigued he could barely hold his pencil, wrote in his notebook, spoke on the radiophone to his superiors and caught up with letters he needed to send to dead men's families. A station porter gave him use of a little office, big enough for just one man to sit in. Gabe brought him tea, bread and a thin soup prepared by old village women who smiled and nodded and forced food onto anyone who stood still long enough.

His eyes watered from tiredness, but he knew he had to complete his paperwork. He needed to write to Jessica, too. He'd only managed to scribble a few lines in a week and wanted to finish the letter to her. She'd be worried, not having heard from him. He closed his eyes for a moment, thinking of her; replacing the images of death and destruction for her sweet cleanness, her gentle smile and soft touches. He'd not see her until the end of the war, whenever that was, and he didn't know how he would bear it.

From his pocket he took out the photo of Alfie and touched his little face. Would he ever see his baby son?

23

Blue Water Station, July 1918.

'Alfie, do stop eating grass!' Tilly laughed, uncurling his little chubby fingers from the tuft. 'I know you're clever, getting yourself over there.' She picked him up and brought him back to the middle of the blanket she had positioned between the graves.

'There you are!' Jessica called as she came up the slope.

Tilly kissed the top of Alfie's head. 'Look, your mother's here. Show her how far you can get.'

'I wondered where you two had got to.'

'Yes, here we are.' Tilly jiggled Alfie up and down on her knee. 'I thought that since it's a lovely day for a change, I'd take him out while you were busy with Mollie Sanders. How is she?'

Jessica sat on the edge of the blanket and gave Alfie a kiss. 'I think it's just a sprained ankle. It's not broken, thankfully. I wasn't sure for a while. But the swelling is going down now we have her leg elevated.'

'She must be relieved.' She passed Jessica a small tin of oat biscuits.

'She said she was chasing the children out of her garden, as they were trampling her plants. She won't be working in the dairy for a week or two.' Jessica wrapped her shawl around herself tightly as the breeze blew a little stronger up on the slope. Above their heads, the branches of the big old gum tree that offered wonderful shade in the summer creaked and swayed.

'Watch him, Jess; watch how he tries to bring his knees up.' Tilly indicated to Alfie, who at seven months old was doing his best to crawl. 'He wants the grass at the end of the blanket. He knows it's there. I'm always so amazed at everything he does.'

'He's growing so fast, Til.' Pride glowed in Jessica's eyes. 'He's the image of Oliver, too.'

'Oh yes, there's no doubt who his father is, that's for sure. But I see Gabe in him when he's being cheeky.' Emotion welled in Tilly as she thought of her brothers.

'Alfie has the Grayson grin, there's no denying that.' Jessica snorted.

'He has everyone wrapped around his finger!' Tilly laughed. 'Grandpapa thinks he's the best baby ever to be born, I'm sure of it.'

'Did you mail those photographs of Alfie and Miles? Oliver will be thrilled to see them.'

'I did, yes. They went in the post this morning.' Tilly nodded sadly and looked over to the newest grave — that of Adelaide, who had died four months ago. 'Last week I took a photograph of Adelaide's headstone, one each for Drew and Big Max. Grandpapa said it was macabre, but I think they'll want to see it. I also took a sneaky photograph of Aunt Connie and Grandmama sitting on the veranda. I sent that to them, too.'

'Anything from home will be cherished, I've told you that. All the soldiers treasure things from their families.' Jessica brought Alfie back from the grass and sat him on her knee.

'You don't think I'm strange for bringing Alfie up here, do you?' Tilly asked, getting up to tidy the vase of flowers that had topped over on the uneven ground of Adelaide's grave. The soil was still settling and winter rains had caused it to sink more.

'No, I don't think so. He's too young to even know where he is. As long as he's with someone he knows and trusts, that's all that matters to him.' She smiled down at Alfie as he tried to suck her dress sleeve.

'I feel he should grow up knowing these wonderful people who were his family. My mother and my father are grandparents he'll never get to meet.' Tilly wandered between the graves, filled with sadness. 'My father would have adored Alfie.'

'I wish I had met him. He sounds like a wonderful man.'

'Oliver is very much like him, whereas Gabe takes after Grandpapa.' She ran her hand over her father's headstone. Behind his grave stood Charles and his wife's grave. 'Aunt Connie has lost her son and daughter-in-law, and now Adelaide. Big Max and Drew have to return.'

'They all must return, those who are left.' Jessica rocked Alfie in her arms as he grew sleepy. 'Have you heard from your Luke?'

Tilly bent and pulled at some weeds near her mother's headstone. 'No. I think he's lost to me.'

'You shouldn't have told him about Delaney. The man isn't worth mentioning. You had nothing to hide or to feel ashamed of, but he isn't important.'

'And yet I told Luke everything like a fool.' Tilly angrily tugged at the weeds.

'There's still time. A letter might turn up even now. It might have got lost or been held up.'

Tilly turned to her, her temper flaring. 'No, Jessica, a letter hasn't got lost or held up! He's not written. Not one letter this year! I've been writing to him every week since December when I wrote to him about Delaney, then I wrote about Alfie, then Christmas, and on and on like a damn stupid idiot!'

'Til — '

'It's now July! July!' She tugged hard at a stubborn bit of grass that suddenly gave way, and she fell backwards onto her bottom with a thump. Tilly swore like a stockman.

'Matilda!' Jessica reprimanded. 'Do you want Alfie's first words to be *those* kind of words?'

Getting to her feet and rubbing her backside, Tilly scowled at her sister-in-law. 'Well, he'll learn them soon enough living here!'

Jessica stared at her, then burst out laughing. 'Oh my, you are a card!'

Tilly, her temper gone as quickly as it had come, laughed with her. 'Come on, let's go back. He's asleep.' She took Alfie from Jessica so she could stand and grab the blanket and biscuit tin.

'How many biscuits did you give, Alfie?'

'Just one . . . '

'Really?'

'Maybe two . . . ' Tilly gazed down at her darling nephew and hugged him closer. 'We have

316

to build him up to be big and strong. I want to buy him a pony soon.'

'Oh, Tilly!' Jessica shook her head in amusement. 'He's only seven months old.'

'Never too young to get in the saddle.' Tilly kissed his blond head as she cradled him and walked back down the slope. 'We all rode early; Grandpapa insisted upon it.'

As they reached the gardens, a figure stepped out in front of them. Jessica gave a small scream, and Tilly instantly held Alfie tighter as they faced him. Dressed in a long filthy coat and with uncut lank hair and a straggly beard, the man glared at them, his hat pulled low.

Tilly stared. A familiar tingle of fear shivered down her back. Delaney. 'What do you want?' she barked at him, frightened.

He chuckled. 'That's rather straight to the point, isn't it? What about 'how are you'?'

'You aren't welcome here,' she grounded out through clenched teeth.

He remained very still. 'You're not going to get rid of me so easily.'

'Who is this person, Tilly?' Jessica asked, standing closer to her.

'Delaney.'

'Give me the baby.' Jessica's eyes widened, sending a message to Tilly. 'I'll take him inside.'

He advanced on them a step. 'You'll stay right where you are, lady.'

Tilly's temper ignited like tinder. 'Let her take the baby inside. You're not going to stop her!' She passed Alfie, who still slept, over into Jessica's arms. They gave each other a small nod.

317

Jessica edged around the garden bed and walked very fast towards the house.

Tilly watched her reach the safety of the veranda and then faced Delaney. Her hands shook, so she tucked them behind her back. 'There's nothing for you here. I thought we made that clear before.'

'I want money.'

'You've come to the wrong place.'

'I need enough to leave the country. I'm going to America.' Delaney wiped a hand over his eyes. He looked tired. 'Listen to me, Tilly. I don't want to do you or anyone harm. Just get me some money and I'll be gone. No one needs to know. Meet me in Grafton tomorrow at noon, then you'll be free of me.'

'Did all your plans to get ill-gotten gains from another poor woman fall flat?' she sneered, hating him for the weak rogue that he was and for making her feel this fear again.

'It's your fault I'm reduced to this state!' he snapped. 'If you'd listened to me, I could've made you happy.'

'No you couldn't. It would have been false, and in time we'd have been miserable.' She raised her chin. 'I didn't love you. I thought I did but I didn't. And you don't love me.'

Behind Delaney, Tilly noticed her grandparents come onto the veranda with Jessica. Sensing her distraction, Delaney turned and saw their audience. 'Ah, the family.' In a sudden movement, he pulled out a pistol from inside his coat pocket and aimed it at Tilly's head. 'Tell them to go inside.'

318

A cold finger of terror went through Tilly like ice in her veins. 'Delaney, please!'

He stepped closer and grabbed her, putting the pistol to her throat. 'Get your grandfather to give me some money and then I'll be gone. Do it!'

Shaking, feeling the cool barrel on her skin, she nodded. 'Grandpapa!' she called out, and her grandpapa hurried down the steps.

'No! Stay where you are, old man!' Delaney yelled.

'Grandpapa, he wants money.'

'I'll get it.' Her grandpapa returned into the house.

Tilly closed her eyes at the despair on the faces of her family. Why was this happening? After months of thinking he would return, and then when he didn't, she'd finally accepted he was out of her life. But her instinct had been correct. Only, he'd taken longer than she expected. She'd been stupid to let her guard down.

Grandpapa emerged from the house, money in his hand. 'Here, Delaney, there's one hundred pounds. Take it and go!'

Tilly gasped at the amount.

Delaney snatched at the money. He checked it quickly. 'Excellent. That'll do nicely.'

'Let Tilly go,' Grandpapa hissed, anger blazing in his eyes.

'I think not.' Delaney smirked like the devil he was. 'She's coming with me.'

'No!' Grandpapa shouted.

'Don't try to follow us, old man.' Delaney, holding Tilly tight to him, edged backwards.

Tilly tripped on Delaney's feet. He lost his grip on her as she wobbled and nearly fell.

Grandpapa sprang forward. A shot rang out, then another.

Tilly was thrown to the ground, banging her head on the lawn and jarring her body. Grass filled her face. Delaney, laying on the lawn beside her, writhed in pain. She couldn't make sense of it all. He had the gun; why was he hurt?

'Tilly!'

'Is she hurt?'

'Miles!'

'Oh god . . . '

'Jessica, is Delaney dead?'

'Send for the doctor . . . '

'And the police . . . '

Tilly raised herself up into a sitting position. Her family fussed around her. Her head swam. Voices echoed. She tried to focus. Then something made her turn and look at the man standing at the edge of the group.

Luke Williams held a rifle in his hand.

★ ★ ★

The tea, heavily laced with brandy, tasted disgusting, but Tilly sipped at it under orders of everyone who happened to glance her way. She'd cradled the cup so long it had gone cold in her hands, but nobody took it from her.

People filled the parlour. Her grandparents, Aunt Connie, Jessica, Stumpy and Doctor Halton. The maids hovered, refilling empty teacups. By the door stood Luke Williams.

Tilly had been sitting on the sofa near the fire for what felt like hours, not really listening to the talk, not really knowing what was occurring. All she could think of was that Luke was here at Blue Water. She kept wanting to stare at him, but dared not, for none of it could be real. This all had to be a dream, surely. Would the numbness go, and she'd wake up at any moment and be in her bed?

A commotion at the doorway made her glance that way. Two policemen, one of whom was a friend of Gabe's and who had been medically unfit to join the war, entered the room. She smiled at him tearfully, wishing it were her brothers returning.

The talking became subdued. She couldn't make out what was being said. She watched them all, like players on a stage. No one came near her. She wanted to stand up and make them talk to her, but she didn't have the energy or the inclination to move. Such apathy was foreign to her.

Grandpapa's voice rose. Tilly hated it when he was angry, as it was such a rare thing, and the more potent because of its infrequency. Suddenly, Luke was led away. Her heart somersaulted. She jerked to her feet, spilling cold tea down her dress.

He glanced back at her and smiled, the same smile she'd gazed at in a photograph for three years. Then he was gone with the policemen.

'Dearest.' Jessica took her arm, gentle and soothing, and sat her back down. 'Everything will be all right.'

'Am I dreaming?' she whispered, not really daring to speak aloud.

'Unfortunately not.' Jessica touched her cheek softly. 'Do you wish to lie down?'

'No, thank you.' She found the courage to ask the question which swirled in her head. 'Is Delaney dead?'

'No, just wounded in the leg. Doctor Halton has seen to him. He's been taken to the hospital in Grafton. He's under arrest, so when he's able, he'll be taken to jail until his trial. However, Captain Williams has also been arrested for shooting him.'

Tilly let the words flow over her. It was astonishing to be mixed up in such a scandal. Another question begged to be aired. 'I want to know why he was here.'

'Who? Delaney?'

'No. Captain Williams.'

In a ruffle of skirts, Grandmama sat down beside her. The talk in the room quietened. She clasped Tilly's hand. 'What a day. How are you feeling, Matilda?'

'I'm fine.' She didn't believe it herself, but it didn't matter.

'Let me tell you what happened. While you and Jessica were out with Alfie, Captain Williams arrived without warning. We had a lovely chat. He's a very nice man. We'll make sure he is acquitted over this issue. Your grandfather will hire the best lawyers for him, though I don't think the captain is without means himself, of course.'

'Why is he *here* though?'

Grandmama smiled. 'To see you, naturally.'

Tilly's heart leapt. 'Is the war over?'

Sadness filled her grandmama's green eyes. 'No. Captain Williams has been invalided out. He got severely wounded near Gaza, around Christmas time. That's why he's not written to you and you weren't informed, because you're not next of kin. He was very ill. He's only just returned to Australia.'

Grandpapa, standing by the fireplace, came over. 'We were talking, waiting for you to return, when Jessica rushed in telling us about Delaney threatening you in the garden. I sent for Stumpy, but the captain asked if we had a gun here. I gave him my rifle hanging up in the study.' Grandpapa wiped a shaky hand over his eyes. 'The captain snuck out the front door and along the veranda and around the side of the house. He's a soldier. He knew exactly what to do.'

'Luke shot Delaney.' Tilly's stomach heaved.

'It was either that or Delaney shooting one of us again.' Grandpapa plucked at his jacket sleeve, showing a tear. 'He just missed me.'

'Oh, my lord!' It was all too much to take in. Tilly stared in horror at the torn sleeve, then abruptly vomited into the potted palm by the sofa.

24

Epehy, France, September 1918.

'Another bloody battle.' Gabe crouched next to Oliver, a cigarette hanging from the corner of his mouth.

Oliver looked at him. The blasts of continual shelling of the village ahead lit up the night sky and threw shadows onto the men's faces. Their barrage had been shelling the German-held village since midnight, five hours ago. Once it stopped, they were to attack.

'It's just another battle, like all the others. It's one more to finish and gets us closer to going home to the family.' Oliver nodded over his shoulder to where their new officer stood talking to a British major. 'I'm more worried about him.'

Gabe grunted. 'Less said about him, the better.'

Big Max, who stood on the other side of Gabe, took out his water canteen. 'He needs to stay behind and let us get on with it.'

Oliver stared at the scene before them as dawn broke and wondered how this battle would go. Since Major Markham's death, they'd been pulled out of the front line for some time and only had involvement in light skirmishes. However, even in those, their new young officer, Captain Cornell, proved himself to be raw and incompetent. Cornell refused to listen to wiser heads, and the plummeting morale was due to his arrogance and indifference.

Silence descended. It always seemed louder after the bombardment. It wasn't just quiet, with the normal morning chorus of birdsong missing. It was tomblike, as though everything was dead or stunned. A hush enveloped the land like a thick blanket.

A sharp whistle blew.

Oliver sucked in a deep breath. He looked at Gabe, who gave a nod, and they set off. In a line, they walked the fields towards the rubble of what had been the village. No one spoke as they trod over chewed-up earth, avoided broken tree stumps, rolls of barbed wire and gaping crater holes. The sun rose, casting a pale light of pink and gold, etching the carnage in muted relief against the disappearing night.

A hundred yards from the village's outer buildings, gunfire opened up on them. Oliver ordered the men to the ground. They returned fire. Keeping low, Oliver indicated for the men to move up into the ruins of the village.

He hated clearing out villages. There was always the chance a sniper was hiding, an unseen demon ready to take out an individual; and if the Germans had had time to lay them, bomb traps as well.

'Keep vigilant,' Oliver called down the line as they crept along narrow cobbled alleys between broken old stone buildings. As they ran out into the main street, shots rang out from the opposite side.

'Take cover,' became the call up and down the

road as the men hid behind garden walls, upturned carts and anything that would afford them some protection.

'Grenades!' Oliver shouted to the men closest to him. In a prepared movement, they hurled their grenades across the street into the buildings. As the blasts erupted, Oliver and the men hurried across and into the smoking edifices. Close-range fighting ensued. From cottage to shop, they entered each crumbling ruin and fired at will. Shouts and yells, gunshots and exploding grenades filled the air. Smoke reduced visibility.

'They're surrendering!' Gabe pointed his gun to three Germans he'd found in a front room of a cottage. The enemy threw down their rifles and held up their hands.

Oliver and Freddie swept from room to room, house to house, rounding up those Germans who surrendered and shooting those who did not.

'Get them all into the middle of the street!' Oliver told Gabe and Big Max as they herded several of the enemy out of a house.

Further down the road, more enemy soldiers were being brought out of the rubble.

'Lieutenant Grayson!' Cornell marched up to Oliver. 'What is the meaning of this?'

Oliver frowned in confusion. 'Sir?'

'Why are you stopping? We're to keep going!'

'We have prisoners, sir.'

'Tie them up and leave them. We've got to keep moving beyond this village. We've got the Bosche on the run!' Cornell spat as he spoke.

Zealous, unproven and impulsive, he was the worst type of soldier to Oliver and the seasoned men.

'We can't tie them up, sir. They have to be sent back to — '

'Are you arguing with me, Grayson?' Cornell sneered. 'Do you want to be put on a charge?'

'This is not the way to do it, sir,' Oliver tried again.

Cornell pulled out his notebook and called for a runner. He scribbled on the paper and tore it off, shoving it at the young man. 'Take this back to headquarters.' Cornell looked at Oliver. 'Why are you still standing there? Get the prisoners into one of the buildings and tie them up. We'll leave one man to watch them. I've sent a note to headquarters telling them about our success.'

'One man to guard? We have at least fifteen prisoners, perhaps more.' Loathing for the man filled Oliver. 'They could easily overpower him.'

'Only if they get free, Grayson. Make sure they do not!' Cornell stomped away from him, calling out orders for the prisoners to be put in the small school at the end of the road.

'I'm going to have to shoot that little prick,' Gabe said, lighting a cigarette.

'You'll have to get in line, brother.'

Oliver turned to search for Big Max, and found him getting a drink out of a communal tap by the road. 'Maxie boy, you're it.'

'I'm what?' he asked, wiping water off his chin.

'The guard. You're the biggest person we have, so it might deter them from getting free.'

Big Max rolled his eyes. 'Thanks.'

'Sorry. It's not my idea. I'd send them back with a detail covering them.'

Walking together, they went down to the school and entered the only building in the street that was mostly intact. It had four walls but no roof. Amid the rubble, eighteen prisoners with hollow faces and blank stares sat and made no protest about being tied up.

'How long am I to watch them for?' Big Max asked, his rifle resting in his arms.

'Until the British come and get them, which hopefully will be soon. A runner has been sent.' Oliver glared at the prisoners, but the dejection in their manner relaxed him somewhat. They looked done in. No life flickered in their expressions. They sat, miserable and finished. Their war was done.

Oliver made his way back to the men, ignoring Cornell, whose gaze followed him back up the street.

'All sorted?' Gabe asked when he joined him and Freddie.

'I don't like leaving Big Max alone with them, but Cornell is running this show, not me.'

'The Tommies will be here soon.'

Cornell blew his wretched whistle again. The unit moved off, leaving the village for the fields on the other side and to hunt down more Germans.

They'd only reached the far end of the first field when shots rang out from a small coppice wood. Hunkering down, Oliver signalled to open fire.

'Stop! Stop!' Cornell shouted, nearly getting

his head knocked off as he stood to yell at them.

'What's he doing?' Gabe stared in amazement.

Cornell came running up behind the line of men. 'No firing until I give the command.'

'What?' Oliver, lying in a shallow furrow, glared up at him. 'Sir, the Germans are in those trees. We have to shoot back.'

'I want prisoners. More prisoners. Understand?' Cornell's fevered eyes darted from man to man as he dropped to one knee. 'Get in there and bring them out. You three, you do it.' He pointed to Gabe, Freddie and a young new recruit called Taylor.

'Are you trying to get us killed?' Gabe spluttered where he lay on his stomach.

'Don't be insolent or you'll be on a charge, Corporal.'

Gabe shrugged. 'Then put me on a charge. But I'm not going into that wood without firing my gun, and I want full cover.'

Oliver swallowed his fear that their officer was a complete idiot who would get them killed. 'Sir, I think if we split up and flank the German position, we — '

'Did I ask for your opinion, Lieutenant?' Red spots of colour spread across Cornell's cheeks as his temper grew. 'I want those three men to go in and get some prisoners. The Bosche are on the run. Hurry now; they could already be gone.'

Oliver clenched his jaw in frustration. 'I'll go with them.'

'No, I want you here.' Cornell turned to smile coldly at Gabe. 'Off you go, then.'

'Sir, this is suicide,' Oliver grounded out

angrily. 'At least give them cover fire.'

Cornell raised an eyebrow. 'Your brother is clever enough to work this out, isn't he?'

Turning his back on Cornell, Oliver shifted over the grass to where the three of them were about to sprint towards the trees. 'Listen, don't run in a straight line; zigzag. If it gets too hot, drop to the ground. We'll come and get you.'

Gabe nodded but kept his gaze fixed on the small crop of trees, whose leaves turned glorious shades of gold and amber as the sun shone. Without another word, Gabe, Freddie and Taylor scrambled up and started running.

With his heart in his mouth, Oliver watched his brother, his body tensed, waiting for him to be hit. A deep fury was building in his chest at Cornell. He gripped his pistol, trying to keep calm.

When a shot rang out, Oliver half jumped in the air, ready to sprint forward. Young Taylor, only nineteen, fell with a scream.

'This is bloody stupid!' a voice up the line rang out.

It was enough for Oliver. 'Attack!' He was the first on his feet and running towards the coppice and his brother and cousin, who had disappeared amongst the trees. He paused briefly by the fallen Taylor, who gave him the thumbs up, even though he was bleeding from the hip. Oliver called for stretcher bearers and kept running.

Leaving the bright sunlight for the dappled shade of the trees, Oliver dropped to one knee on the carpet of fallen leaves to let his eyes adjust. Behind him, the others did the same. On

330

high alert, Oliver scanned the tree trunks, looking for any movement. 'Fan out!' he whispered harshly.

There was no sign of Gabe or Freddie. Panting, hardly daring to blink in case he missed something, Oliver inched forward, gun raised.

The trees thinned, allowing sunlight to penetrate. Falling leaves drifted down sedately. A bird flew out from above their heads, making the men jump. Beyond the trees, fields opened up once more, and in the far distance, Oliver could just make out the steeple of a church.

'There they are!' Arnold, a lance corporal recently returned from hospital, held field glasses to his eyes and pointed. 'The Bosche are on the run.'

'Can you see Gabe or Freddie?'

'No, sir.'

'Keep searching.'

'Lieutenant Grayson!' Cornwell barked, coming up to Oliver.

Oliver flinched. Was the man never quiet? 'Yes, sir?'

'You went against my command! I gave you no order to run into these trees!' Spittle flew from his lips. 'This will not go unpunished.'

'As you wish, sir.'

'Here's Gabe and Freddie!' Arnold caught their attention.

Oliver turned to see his brother and cousin running like crazy back into the trees. 'Where the hell were you?'

'We thought we could bring a few more down. They're headed for the next village.'

Cornwell pushed forward. 'Grayson, I told you I wanted prisoners!'

Gabe squared up to him. 'Aye, sir, you did. But they weren't sitting here waiting to surrender. When they saw us, they took off.' He gestured to the village they could glimpse on the horizon. 'My guess is that they have reinforcements in the next town.'

'Right, well, let's press on then.' Cornwell stared at them all.

'We don't have a barrage hitting them this time, sir.' Oliver stated the obvious, trembling with anger. 'Report our position and see what headquarters want us to do. We can return to the village and hold it.'

'I don't need to be told by headquarters, Grayson! This is in my training! We'll keep going on.'

'We don't have any support!'

'There are British divisions on either side of us!'

'Have they advanced as far as we have?'

Cornwell raised his chin, loathing clear in his eyes. 'I said we're to take the next village. And we will. Are you going to disobey me again?'

Oliver was about to reply when they heard the familiar diving drone from above. A bomb exploded nearby, cracking the trees like matchsticks.

'They've got back and told them our position!' Oliver yelled at the men. 'Get out of the trees!'

Bombs landed with every step they took. The smell of burning timber, gunpowder and earth filled the air. Oliver felt the hair on the back of his neck stand on end as the trees exploded into fireballs about them. A man fell beside him, shrapnel piercing his leg. Oliver and Gabe took an arm each and hauled him up between them and kept running. Then they heard the distinctive popping sound of gas bombs landing.

'Gas!' Oliver lowered the man he was helping and pulled out his gas mask. Once it was on, he helped the wounded private to put his on as Gabe did the same. A smoky green mist curled around them as they got the private back on his feet and started running again.

'Back to the village?' Gabe panted through his mask.

'No. Into the field.' Oliver shouted to be heard over the mask and the pounding of the shells. 'If Cornwell wants us to attack again, then we need to go around the trees, not bloody straight through like normal. After four years of war, do they never learn?'

'Does it look like those in charge have learned anything?'

Reaching the centre of the field, Oliver ordered the men to lie down. 'Is everyone out of the trees?'

'No.' Freddie knelt, regaining his breath, which sounded harsh through the mask. 'Cornwell got struck by a falling branch.'

'Is he dead?'

'I think so, but not sure.'

Oliver swore and watched the green mist to see which way the wind was blowing the hazardous gas. 'We'll have to go back and find out.'

'Oliver,' Gabe warned, knowing the decision wasn't popular with the men.

'I know he's hated, but we can't leave him.'

The bombing had stopped, but on such a windless day the gas lingered like a deadly pall over the field. Oliver glanced around, hoping to see signs of the British forces. He wanted to rip the gas mask off. He hated wearing the damn thing and felt he couldn't breathe with it over his face.

'Right, come on then.' Gabe got to his feet once more. 'I'm sick of running today. Just thought I'd share that with you, brother.'

'You stay here; you're in charge.'

Gabe shook his head. 'Nope. I'm coming with you.'

'Gabe — '

'Stop bloody arguing with me. I'm coming, and there's an end to it.'

Oliver swore under his breath. 'Freddie, you're in charge until we get back. Masks are to stay on until I say otherwise!'

Oliver and Gabe ran back to the coppice and entered the wreckage of the trees. What had been a beautiful shady grove now resembled a nightmare in which a giant had picked up all the pretty trees and thrown them down again as blackened broken stubs.

They found Cornell pinned down by a tree trunk at the edge of a shell hole. Oliver knelt and felt for a pulse. 'He's dead.' Sighing, he took Cornell's notebook and personal effects. 'I'm getting rather fed up with searching through dead men's pockets.'

'As long as they aren't mine, I don't care.' Gabe lit a cigarette, then remembering he wore a mask, stubbed it out in disgust. 'I hate this bloody war!'

25

Sydney, October 1918.

Tilly lifted her face to the sun as it broke through the clouds. The cool breeze coming off the harbour chilled her, but she didn't want to return to the hotel just yet. Her grandpapa would still be napping, and she didn't want to disturb him. The journey from Blue Water to Sydney had taken it out of him, and then sitting in court all day yesterday had added to his exhaustion. An old man in his eighties shouldn't have to go through such an ordeal; but he, along with Jessica and herself, had to attend the trials of both Delaney and Luke as witnesses.

A ship's horn tooted in the harbour, making Tilly jump. A mist of salty water churned up by the passing boats sprayed her face and made her hair curl under her hat. She still wore the clothes she'd gone to court in that morning. Between visits there, and seeing family and friends, she and Jessica had managed to do some shopping. The soft green of her dress, highlighted by white lace at the cuffs and throat, suited her colouring, and she wanted to look her best for Luke.

Sadly, they hadn't spoken since he'd been arrested three months ago. He and Delaney had been transferred to Sydney, and she'd had no way of getting in contact with him. He had been released on bail, but he hadn't written to her, and she hadn't known where he would be to write to him. She knew of his army address, not his home address; only that he had a house in Vaucluse on the harbour, and a farm to the south in a place called Kangaroo Valley in the country.

In the grand court he had smiled at her once, but kept his attention on his lawyer and the judge. She had listened intently when he was questioned, and hearing his strong confident voice again after so long seemed bizarre. He had worn his dress uniform and looked so handsome and imposing. His voice carried the room. She'd been mesmerised by his presence and his manner. This man had possibly saved her and her grandpapa's lives. Luke was no longer a name in a letter, but real and here. It pleased her enormously to have him home safe.

However, the enjoyment of seeing him was tempered by the shame of having her name on society's lips. Her stomach churned every time Delaney's name was mentioned, and her cheeks grew hot with humiliation. Delaney had actually done what he said he'd do: ruin her reputation. The trial had made the newspapers. The public knew of her indiscretion with a stockman, of him returning to blackmail her family, and of the shooting. The scandal had rocked their society, and she wondered if the shame would ever fade.

When she had stood shaking in the witness box, she thought she would die from the disgrace, but Grandmama had told her before she left Blue Water that Graysons held their heads up, no matter what. So in the daunting

337

courtroom she had stood straight and tall and talked clearly. It helped that she soon became angry at the questions and the finger pointing, for in anger she could stand straight and tall; anger kept her firm. She had concentrated on her grandpapa's face, not daring to look at Luke or Delaney.

What did Luke think of her now? Would he walk away and never look back?

The silence from him told her the truth. He hadn't sent any letters to her since his arrest. But could she blame him? She had embarrassed him in all this mess.

'There you are. I thought you might be down by the water.' Jessica came to stand beside her. 'It's taken me an hour to find you. How are you?'

'I'm fine.'

'Miles is awake and wanting to go back to the courthouse. Captain Williams's verdict will be read out soon.'

'I don't think I want to go. What if he gets jail time? I can't face him.' Tilly shivered. 'I'm a coward, aren't I?'

'No, of course not. Don't think that way. You've been through a lot. You've dealt with the death of your father, the boys being away, Delaney and running Blue Water, and now this court case. Give yourself some credit and value.'

She leaned her shoulder against Jessica's. 'The last time I was in Sydney was to see the boys onto the ship. Perhaps I saw you too.'

'Me?' Jessica pulled away to stare at her. 'How so?'

'I saw a group of nurses, twice. Once walking past the hotel and then again at the dock, boarding the ship. I was so envious. They were going away to be useful, to have an adventure.'

'It isn't any kind of adventure I'd recommend, Til.' Jessica looked out over the water. 'Seeing young men mutilated and die, often in agony, is not something I'd ever want to go through again.'

'I want to go home, Jess. I want Luke free and I want to go home.' She sighed sadly. The joys of Sydney were lost to her on this trip.

'You're cold. The sun has gone behind the clouds.' Jessica hugged her. 'Let's go back to the hotel.'

They walked away from the quay and up the busy street, passing shops and buildings. Before crossing over at the next corner, they paused to let a brewery cart go by pulled by six big black horses.

Jessica linked her arm through Tilly's. 'I want to go home, too. I miss Alfie.'

'You should have stayed with him. I feel guilty you came without him.'

'Why should you? I was called as a witness. It was my choice to leave him behind. You needed my support, and I couldn't do that with the worry of looking after Alfie in a strange environment. Anyway, Alfie is fine, and being spoilt by Kitty and Aunt Connie. He has the household staff wrapped around his fingers, too. No doubt Mrs Chalmers is feeding him into a big fat lump!' Jessica laughed.

The noise of the city replaced that of the ships

in the harbour. Instead of the calls from sailors and the blast of ship horns, now their ears were accosted by the rumble of street traffic, horses and carts, automobiles and the cry of traders. The wind picked up and was funnelled down the streets, and they had to hold onto their hats.

They entered the hotel's foyer and nodded to the front doorman. 'Miss Grayson, your grandfather is waiting for you in the lounge.'

'Thank you.'

The lounge area was on the other side of the dining room, past the little palmed courtyard where Tilly had first met Luke. They found Grandpapa sitting in a large wing-backed chair by the fireplace, a glass of whiskey next to him.

'It's early in the day for that, isn't it? Tilly joked, kissing his cheek. 'How do you feel after your nap?'

'Much better.' He received Jessica's kiss with a smile. 'Where have you two been? More shopping?'

'No, down by the water.' Tilly sat on the twin sofa opposite him and ordered a tea tray from a passing waitress.

'I've telephoned your grandmama. Everyone is fine at home.' He sipped his whiskey. 'Alfie is doing grand, I'm told.'

'Oh, good. I was thinking of telephoning them tonight, if you don't mind.' Jessica held her cheek. 'I have the most terrible toothache.'

'Being out in the wind wouldn't have helped.' Grandpapa nodded wisely.

'Perhaps visit a dentist before we return home?' Tilly said. 'Didn't the boys go to one in

George Street, Grandpapa?'

'I believe — ' Grandpapa stopped mid-sentence to stare past them. 'Good lord.'

Turning around on the sofa, Tilly's heart seemed to stop in her chest. Luke Williams walked with a limp through the groups of people standing in the foyer and reception area.

'How is that possible?' Jessica whispered. 'Did we get the time wrong to go back to the court?'

'I thought it was starting again at three o'clock.' Grandpapa checked his pocket watch and slowly got to his feet, beaming a smile as Luke came closer. 'This is a most welcome surprise, Captain.' He shook Luke's hand vigorously.

Tilly simply stared.

'We're so happy to see you, Captain.' Jessica nudged Tilly discreetly. 'We were about to head back to the courthouse.'

Luke, dressed in full uniform, smiled down at Tilly. 'Matilda.'

One word. Her name. It was enough.

As though her heart and mind had been frozen on the day of the shooting, they now came alive. Tears filled her eyes and blurred his form.

She was aware of Jessica and her grandpapa leaving them alone, of Luke sitting down opposite her and taking a quick gulp of the whiskey her grandpapa had left. Blinking away the tears, she gazed at him. Her heart thumped, her stomach clenched, and her mind whirled with unspoken questions. His blue eyes seemed bluer than she remembered, his smile just as

341

cocky. And she knew she wanted to never stop looking at him.

She dragged in a ragged breath. 'They let you go?'

Luke nodded, signalled to a waiter for another whiskey, then turned back to her. 'I was found not guilty. Once the army got involved, it was soon sorted. It might have been a different story if I had killed him or shot him anywhere other than his leg.'

'But you weren't trying to kill him, were you?'

'A soldier's instinct is to do that, yes. He had a gun in his hand. Thankfully, sanity prevailed and I aimed for his foot, hoping it would knock him off balance and you could get free of him.' Luke shrugged.

'I'm so grateful. If you hadn't done so, Grandpapa would have shot him or been killed himself.' They owed Luke so much.

'The court believed the same. It's done now. Finished.'

'No, not until we know what will happen to Delaney tomorrow when his verdict is read out. What if he's found not guilty?'

Luke leaned forward, his eyes earnest. 'He won't be. My lawyer believes he'll go to jail for some years at least. He was charged with attempted abduction, and he shot at your grandfather with intent. Then there are other offences he's committed in the past. The police in Melbourne enjoyed catching up with him, I think. He'll be lucky if he doesn't do at least ten years.'

An invisible weight left Tilly's shoulders, one

342

she didn't realise she'd been carrying. She plucked at her green skirt. 'Soon I'll be able to sleep better at night.'

The waiter returned with his whiskey as the waitress placed a tea tray for three on the small table in front of Tilly. She busied herself with pouring out cups of tea even though Grandpapa and Jessica had disappeared. Doing anything was better than sitting there staring at Luke.

'Perhaps I should have tea instead of this.' He pushed the glass of whiskey to one side.

'Oh I think you deserve it after everything. It mustn't have been pleasant the past few days in court.'

'A necessary evil.' He smiled as she handed him a teacup.

'One which we can never repay you for.'

'I don't need repaying. You aren't indebted to me, Matilda.'

She nodded. 'Thank you.'

'When do you return to Blue Water?'

'In two days. Grandpapa has businesses here in Sydney, and he wants to meet with managers and his solicitor before we return. I wouldn't be surprised if it is his last venture to Sydney.'

'It's a long trip for a man of his age.'

She had an idea. 'We're to have dinner with Uncle Rory and Aunt Mary tomorrow. Would you like to join us?'

'Would your family mind?'

'Not at all. You'd be most welcome.' She smiled warmly at him.

'I'd like that. I wish to spend as much time as possible with you.'

'Will you come back with us to Blue Water?' she asked impulsively, not wanting to say goodbye to him.

Surprised, he stared at her. 'Is that what you want?'

She looked straight into his eyes. 'Very much so.' Then she had a sudden thought which chilled her. 'Or are you to be sent overseas again?'

'No, I'm not. My war is finished. My leg is too damaged.' Luke reached across the table and took her gloved hand in his. 'This is not the homecoming that I dreamed about and planned in my head for the last four years.'

'No. And I'm sorry to have ruined it.' She liked that he held her hand. It gave her hope that he didn't hate her, or blame her for his arrest.

'It wasn't your fault.' He tapped his leg. 'In my dreams, I walked down the gangplank to meet you waiting for me at the bottom. Instead, I was carried off on a stretcher not knowing what day it was.'

'I wish I'd known.'

'I should've made you my next of kin.'

Her chest swelled at his words. How could he have such faith in her after all this time, when she had wobbled so often? 'Were you wounded only in the leg?'

'No, I was shot through the stomach and shoulder, too. I developed a fever just to add to the misery.' His smile became bittersweet.

'Oh, Luke. I had no idea.'

'I know. How could you?' He took a deep breath. 'Anyway, I like a challenge. Fighting for your life puts so much into perspective.'

'I imagine it does. Then, after all that and you regain your health, you come to see me and end up being arrested. I'm so very sorry.' Guilt riddled her.

He chuckled. 'True, I wasn't expecting that kind of welcome, but well . . . ' He stared down at their joined hands. 'I needed to see you and talk to you. To make you real in my head.'

'And I wasn't wearing the white dress with the pink flowers on it as I promised I would on the day you came home.' She tried to make it sound light-hearted, but instead she sounded forlorn.

'No.' He smiled, his gaze sincere. 'But it would do perfectly for a wedding dress in the summer.'

His words shocked her and her hand slipped from his, but he gripped it tighter.

'No, Matilda. I've waited for years to touch you. Let me hold your hands and ask you to marry me properly.'

'You don't know me, Luke. Not really.'

He leant forward, closer, his eyes softening with emotion. 'I think I know you better than anyone. Four years of letters. I've told you everything about me, and whether you know it or not, you've revealed a great deal about yourself, too.'

'Enough for you to know that you want to marry me? I doubt it,' she scoffed.

'Sweetheart, I have a lifetime to prove to you just how well I know you; and what's more, we've years ahead of us to continue the education.'

Feeling a mix of emotions she couldn't

345

identify or control at that moment, she straightened her shoulders, ready to do battle, but left her hands in his. 'What about Delaney, and my ruined reputation? People are talking! I was mentioned in the newspaper. What will your friends and family say?'

He sat back and laughed. 'Let people talk. Those who are whispering behind their hands I don't care about. My friends know about you. They know about my hopes of having you as my wife. I'm sure I've bored them to death over the last few years telling them about you in my letters.'

Surprised, she stared at him. 'You have?'

'I have.' He grinned that cocky grin she loved. 'And I'm not marrying Delaney or your reputation. I'm marrying you, Matilda Rose Grayson, of Blue Water Station. The woman who's stubborn and hot-headed, spontaneous and vivacious, but who's also kind and loving and loyal.' He leaned forward again and gripped both of her hands. 'That's the woman I know. That's the beautiful woman I'm going to marry.'

'Gracious, you got a lot from a few letters!'

He laughed and kissed her hand. 'Trust me, darling. Before very long, I'll know you inside and out.'

She tingled at his meaning and impulsively leant over and kissed him, not caring they were in a public place. 'Welcome home.'

26

France, November 1918.

Oliver stared at the note in his hand, then looked at the runner and back at the note again. 'Are you sure this is correct?'

'Aye, sir.' The young lad nodded eagerly, holding his bicycle by the handlebars. 'I've come straight from Headquarters.'

'Do you know what this says?'

A smile split the lad's face wide. 'Oh aye, sir. Us runners have been pedalling like mad all morning to get to all the posts and to let the officers know. The telegraphers have nearly split their fingers trying to get the messages out.'

'Then let's hope the Germans know, too.' Oliver patted the lad's shoulder in thanks and walked back into the cottage in a state of numbness.

The men were relaxing in various states. Some were eating breakfast, cooked by the lady who owned the cottage, while others were shaving, and some still slept on the floor. They had been rotated out of the front line last week after making great progress with pushing the Germans back past the Hindenburg Line. They were staying in this village, which had become the reserve line, some miles back from the front. Further down the street, a selection of French, British, Canadian and New Zealand

347

troops were also billeted.

'Oliver, look what Madame Du Pont has done for me.' Gabe held up his uniform shirt, neatly darned and washed.

Oliver gave his brother a sour look. 'Madame Du Pont is not your maid, Gabe. This is her cottage, her home. She's not here to skivvy for you, or anyone.'

Gabe tried to appear innocent. 'She wants to do it. She says I'm like her son. She hasn't seen him for two years. Taking care of us makes her happy.'

'Do we have orders?' Freddie interrupted them from where he sat by the window, cleaning his rifle.

'Yes, we do.' Oliver stared around at the faces he knew as well as his own. For four years he'd been with this group of men. Some had gone and been replaced, but the truth was he'd die for any one of them. He swallowed the sudden lump in his throat and cleared it. 'All divisions on the front line are to harass the enemy until eleven am. We personally are to stay here until further orders.'

'We're going back into the line soon then, as relief?' Freddie swore.

'Another big push is coming, what's the bet?' a private adding logs to the fire grumbled.

'I'll have clearer orders in an hour, but for now we're to stay here.' Oliver glanced at Gabe. 'I need to speak to you, and Big Max, and you, Freddie.' He left the cottage and walked into the small garden at the side to wait for them to join him.

'What's the problem?' Gabe said, tucking his shirt into his trousers.

Oliver looked at the three faces, still not believing the words he'd read on the note he still held in his hand. 'You're to keep this to yourselves, but we're going home.'

The colour left Gabe's face. 'What are you saying?'

Oliver went to speak and tell them about the note, but Freddie stepped forward. 'Do you mean desert?'

'What?' Gabe gasped. 'Are you mad? We aren't cowards! We can't desert the army!'

'We'll get shot if we're caught. But perhaps we can do it.' Freddie scowled. 'Have you got a plan? There's food in the old woman's pantry we can take with us.'

Gabe rounded on him. 'I'm not stealing from her. She's been good to us!'

Oliver smiled at them, seeing their confusion and their panic. 'Do you not want to go home?'

'Oliver.' Big Max, always the quiet one, put his hand on his shoulder. 'We can stick it out. We don't need to do this. We can't desert. I won't.'

Oliver shrugged. 'Well, I'm going. You lot can stay here if you want.'

Wiping a hand over his face, Gabe appeared ashen. 'Brother, listen — '

Unable to help himself, Oliver burst out laughing. The shock on their faces made him laugh even more.

'My god, he's lost it!' Freddie eyes widened in fear. 'He's gone mad.'

'Oliver, please!' Gabe seemed close to crying

or throwing up at what he obviously believed was Oliver losing his grip on reality.

Trying to calm down, Oliver wiped laughter tears from his eyes. 'There's a ceasefire, you idiots. At eleven o'clock.'

'Ceasefire?' Gabe frowned. 'What are you talking about?'

'Ceasefire,' Big Max echoed.

'Are you sure?' Freddie demanded, angry now.

'Are you joking with us? Gabe snapped.

'Believe it. It is true. Germany have surrendered.' After his laughing fit, Oliver felt suddenly tired — elated but tired. 'It stays between us until eleven, when it becomes official.'

'Is it really true, though?' Freddie asked.

'The Germans could change their minds,' Gabe added, still looking worried.

'They won't. They're finished,' Big Max said quietly. 'More and more prisoners are being captured every day. I've talked to some of them, those who could speak English. They and their people back home are starving.'

'Yes, they're demoralised,' Oliver said, passing them the note he'd been given. 'They've surrendered. We're going home, lads.'

'Oh God!' Freddie dropped to his knees with a sob.

Gabe swore long and loud; and then with a whooping yell, he tackled Oliver to the ground before pulling Big Max and Freddie down too. 'We're going home!'

Squashed under their heavy bodies, Oliver laughed, crying for them to get off him, yet so happy he could barely contain it.

'You deserve a good beating!' Gabe laughed. 'I thought you'd gone mad and wanted to desert!'

'I know. It was so funny seeing the look on your faces!' Oliver grabbed his brother in a head lock.

'Ha ha, very funny.' Gabe wriggled free and slapped Oliver's cheek hard. 'You've been a misery guts for four years and suddenly you want to be the joker?'

Oliver wrestled him over onto his back. 'Come here, brother, and give me a big sloppy kiss!' He tried to kiss Gabe, who roared his disgust.

'You fellows there! What's going on?' a British officer on the other side of the garden wall shouted at them.

They all quickly sat up and saluted. Gabe grinned. 'Training, sir.'

'Training?'

'Yes, sir. Close-combat fighting. We're trying out new tactics.' He said it so convincingly that even Oliver was close to believing him.

'Right. Well, very good. Carry on.' The officer marched away.

Laughing uproariously, Gabe jumped on top of Oliver again.

'Get off me, you bloody fool!' Oliver chuckled, pushing him away. He laid back on the grass. Taking a deep breath, he closed his eyes to the weak sun. 'It's over.'

★   ★   ★

'If the war has finished, then why are we patrolling?' Freddie grumbled the next day.

351

'We're making sure the Germans get the message and go home,' Gabe said, yawning.

'Be quiet, the pair of you!' Oliver snapped. His head banged from a hangover that threatened to split his skull. After a night of drinking and celebrating, the order this morning to go on patrol along the roads leading from the village had been unwelcome. Getting the men up and ready proved testing to his patience when he felt as rough as he did.

'We're still in the army,' Big Max murmured.

'When is demobilisation happening?' Freddie asked.

'Sweet Jesus, Freddie, shut up!' Oliver gave him a filthy look. 'I don't know the answer to any of your questions just yet.'

A young private suddenly vomited into the bushes beside the road. It started a chain reaction, and before long, Oliver was joining his men in bringing up the contents of his stomach.

After ten minutes of groaning and gulping mouthfuls of water, the men continued walking along the dirt road. A biplane flew overhead and they stared at it.

'Ours?' Gabe asked.

'Yes.' Oliver watched in awe. He was determined to go up in one of those as soon as he returned to Australia, and if possible, even buy one. They fascinated him and he wanted to learn all about them.

A truck drove past them, full of soldiers. 'They're going the wrong way,' Freddie said, lighting a cigarette.

'They're probably headed for the border.

They're the unlucky ones. One of those divisions that have been selected to go on into Germany itself.'

Freddie stared at him in horror. 'Will we be picked?'

'I doubt it. It'll be the main British and French divisions. We colonials will be sent home with a 'thanks for coming' and a ticket on a ship bound for Sydney.'

'Hallelujah for that!' Gabe grinned. 'It's all I want.'

A private with a shock of red hair who they called Bluey stopped to tie his boot lace. 'When I get home, the first thing I'm going to do is eat my ma's roast chicken dinner until I'm stuffed.'

Gabe grinned. 'The first thing I'm going to do when I get home is ride my horse to the river and swim all day. Then I'm going to eat Mrs Chalmers's delicious food, and then I'm going to go into Grafton and ask Ellen McDougall out on a date.'

Oliver stared at him. 'What? Ellen McDougall? Tom McDougall, the butcher? His daughter?'

'Yep.' Gabe smiled smugly. 'I had my eye on her for a good while before we enlisted.'

'You never said a word about her all this time,' Oliver accused, trying to picture her face and failing.

'Like you, brother, I too can have my little secrets and dreams.'

Oliver chuckled. 'It's been four years. She's probably married with a kid by now.'

Gabe snorted and told Oliver where to go in very unflattering terms.

Freddie threw away the end of his cigarette. 'I want to sleep completely naked in a clean bed for at least two days. Do you know how long it's been since I was fully naked?'

The men laughed.

Big Max stopped abruptly and dropped to one knee. 'What's that?'

Instinct made the others do the same.

'I thought there was a ceasefire order?' a voice said from behind Oliver.

Peering through his field glasses, Oliver focused on the small group of men walking across the uneven field towards them. They had no hats, and he couldn't identify them by the shabby clothing they wore.

'Lost Germans or returning locals?' Gabe asked, kneeling next to Oliver.

'I can't tell.' Oliver glanced around at their position. A shallow drainage ditch ran along the road. 'Stand ready!' he called, jumping into the ditch.

The men all followed and leant against the side of the ditch, their rifles pointing at the distant figures. In painful slow minutes, they waited for the group to walk closer until they were a mere twenty yards from the ditch.

Oliver gave the signal and they all reared up out of the ditch, rifles at the ready. 'Halt!'

'Don't shoot!'

'We're British!'

'We're unarmed!'

The wretched group stuck their hands up, except one who was being helped along by his buddies.

'British?' Oliver cautiously stepped out of the ditch. The soldiers wore filthy ragged uniforms and were terribly thin and unshaven.

'Aye, we've been prisoners for ten months. We've not had any food or water for days. The Germans let us go yesterday afternoon. We've been walking ever since.' The tallest man indicated to the other men with him. 'We're from the King's Own Yorkshire Light Infantry.'

The man who was being held up by his friends collapsed. The group closed in around him.

The tall one spoke to Oliver. 'I'm Lieutenant Wilkins. Our friend here is very sick. Do you have any water?'

Oliver nodded, and with a signal to the others, the rifles were lowered and the men all joined together to hand over water and the food rations they always carried.

'The Germans said it was all over?' one of the prisoners asked in disbelief.

'Yes, mate.' Gabe handed him his water canteen. 'We've won.'

Another of the prisoners fell to his knees and cried brokenheartedly.

'Come on, fellas. Let's get you back to camp.' Oliver holstered his pistol and helped the crying man to his feet.

Big Max pulled the ill soldier onto his back and carried him, while the others leant on Oliver's men to give them the strength to make it back to the village.

Gabe, his arm around one of the Yorkshire men, walked beside Oliver. 'You never said what you'll do first when you get home.'

A warm feeling came over him. 'When I get home, I'm going to kiss my wife and hold my son.' Oliver smiled and let his mind finally think of the wonder of being home again, something he'd dared not dream of in the last four years.

Epilogue

Blue Water Station, March 1919.

Tilly stood by her father's grave. A soft warm breeze lifted the hair from her neck, cooling her slightly. Summer still held its grip on the land, and the brown grass crackled under her feet. The sun blazed from a clear blue sky. A crow called from the gumtree branches above her head while cicadas droned their endless high-pitched song.

She bent and placed her wedding bouquet against her father's headstone. 'I'm married, Papa. I married Luke yesterday,' she said quietly. 'Everyone is here for the wedding. You would have enjoyed it. Grandpapa gave me away in your stead. He cried.' She smiled, remembering the moment when he'd walked her down the rose petal covered path between the rows of white wooden chairs filled with family and friends.

'You would have liked Luke, Papa. He loves me very much, and I adore him.' Emotion swelled in her chest when she thought of Luke and the way her body had responded to his lovemaking last night. He'd touched her as though she were the most precious person in the world, and her love for him at that moment had grown boundlessly.

'Everyone was wondering where you'd got to.' She jumped at the sound of Oliver's voice.

He walked up the slope to join her by the gravestones. 'I had a feeling you'd be here.'

She gazed at him, still not believing that he was back, safe and whole. Three days ago, her brothers had finally returned from France. True, they had changed somewhat. They were older, wiser and much thinner, but they were home, and she found she could relax again.

'My little sister is all grown up and a married woman now.' Oliver smiled, the fine lines at the corners of his eyes crinkling.

'I grew up when Papa died. I had no choice. You just weren't here to see it.' She felt a little distant with him. Since his return, she had been busy with the wedding preparations and he had been spending all his time with Jessica and Alfie. Family and friends had arrived en masse the day after the boys had returned, and with a full house, Tilly and Oliver had had no time to talk properly.

'You've managed everything so very well, Til. I'm proud of you.'

'It's my home. After Papa died, I had to learn how to runs things. Grandpapa is too old, and he took Papa's death very badly.'

Oliver touched the headstone. 'I can't take it in that he's not here. When I walked through the front door, I expected him to be there with everyone else.'

She took a deep breath. 'It's difficult to get used to.'

'And now you're to move away from us all, off down south to Kangaroo Valley to start a new life with your husband.'

'Yes. It's my turn to leave Blue Water.' The excitement of a new adventure and sadness at leaving her home fought for control.

'Luke is a good man. He idolises you. I know you'll be happy with him.'

Silence stretched between them for a moment.

'I'm sorry,' Oliver finally said.

Tears welled in Tilly's eyes and she couldn't speak.

He touched her back gently. 'I should have written.' His voice broke on the last word.

'Yet you didn't,' she whispered, hardly able to speak.

'I couldn't. I'm sorry.'

'Sorry isn't good enough!' The anger she felt at his betrayal reared up, needing to be released. 'You were my big brother, my closest friend. The one I looked up to, aspired to be like. I always wanted your approval. We were like twins, born only a year apart. I'd never known a moment when you weren't there. Then suddenly you left and you took the others with you. Gabe who was our shadow, the Jessup boys, Big Max and Drew, Patrick and Freddie. You took them all away from me!'

'I'm sorry!'

'I could have coped with all that better if only you'd written to me! I went from having you all with me, like I had done since I could walk, to suddenly having *no one*!'

'I know.'

'Then why didn't you write?' She wanted to slap him hard.

'Because very soon after landing in Gallipoli, I

359

realised the hell that we were in, and I wanted to come home. But I couldn't. I was also responsible for making the others enter that hell too. At any moment any one of them could be dead. I felt I'd caused that with my bold talk of wanting to go on an adventure! I couldn't face what I'd done. I couldn't face writing to you, because I missed you and home so much it was like a physical ache in my chest for four years!' Tears ran down Oliver's face and Tilly's heart broke for him.

He walked away a little. 'To survive, I had to pretend that home didn't exist. I had to focus only on being a soldier and getting everyone home.'

Her anger lessened. 'And I hear you were one of the best.'

'It was all or nothing.' He heaved a shuddering sigh. 'I thought I wouldn't make it through; that in every battle I'd feel the bullet which would end it for me. And when Patrick and Samuel died, I believed none of us would ever return home; that we'd all be killed. And I was the cause of it.'

'How were you the cause? You didn't make the others go with you.'

'In the beginning, I made it all out to be the right thing to do, to defend our country. What did I know? How could I have been so presumptuous to think I knew better? Aunt Connie accused me of enticing the others to enlist with me. I denied it. They could make their own choices, but in all honesty I made it all out to be such a great thing to do that they'd be mad not to come with me.'

Pity filled Tilly's chest. He'd carried demons on his back for four years. 'No one blames you.'

His shoulders slumped. 'They don't have to. I blame myself.'

'The boys would've enlisted after you'd gone anyway. None of them would've stayed behind.'

'Maybe so.' He shrugged. 'Gallipoli showed me that I'd led them into a war which would likely kill us, and I couldn't live with myself. None of it was an adventure, not as I imagined. So I made it my mission to look after them all. But I failed. Only five of the eight of us returned home. Most would consider that good odds, but I don't.'

'It wasn't your responsibility to bring them all home safe.'

'I felt it was.' Oliver squatted down beside their mother's grave and touched her etched name. 'She was beautiful, our mother.'

'I barely remember her.'

'People say you're like Grandmama, another Kitty McKenzie; and in many ways you are. But sometimes you have our mother's look. I missed seeing that while I was away. It was another thing to miss.'

She looked out over the surrounding fields that led down to the river. 'In the morning I'm leaving to travel to my new home with Luke. You must promise me that you'll come with Jessica and Alfie to visit us as often as you can.'

'I promise.' He came to stand beside her and gazed at the same view. 'Jessica loves you and will give me no peace if we don't see you often.'

361

'She's the sister I never had.'

'I'm a lucky man.'

'We've both been lucky to find the spouses we have.'

'That's true. Luke's a good man.' Oliver looked at her. 'Do you forgive me?'

She tucked her hand through his arm and felt the breeze on her face. 'I forgive you.'

He squashed her against him, hugging her tight.

'Hey! You two!'

They turned and watched Gabe run up the slope.

'What do you want?' Tilly smiled at him with love.

'Come on!' Gabe pushed Oliver forward and grabbed Tilly's hand.

'What are you doing?' She shook her head at him in confusion.

'We're off for a swim!'

Oliver balked. 'We're not kids anymore, Gabe.'

'Stuff and nonsense!' he laughed, and taking both their hands pulled them along before letting go and sprinting ahead.

Laughing, Tilly gathered up her skirts and looked at Oliver. 'Race you!'

Hollering like the children they once were, the three of them ran towards the blue water.